Feel the Heat

Books by Lorie O'Clare

PLEASURE ISLAND

SEDUCTION ISLAND

UNDER THE COVERS
(with Crystal Jordan and P.J. Mellor)

Books by P.J. Mellor

PLEASURE BEACH

GIVE ME MORE

MAKE ME SCREAM

DRIVE ME WILD

THE COWBOY
(with Vonna Harper, Nelissa Donovan, and Nikki Alton)

THE FIREFIGHTER
(with Susan Lyons and Alyssa Brooks)

NAUGHTY, NAUGHTY
(with Melissa MacNeal and Valerie Martinez)

ONLY WITH A COWBOY
(with Melissa MacNeal and Vonna Harper)

Books by Lydia Parks

ADDICTED

DEVOUR ME

SEXY BEAST VI
(with Kate Douglas and Anya Howard)

Published by Kensington Publishing Corporation

Feel the Heat

LORIE O'CLARE
P.J. MELLOR
LYDIA PARKS

APHRODISIA

KENSINGTON PUBLISHING CORP.
www.kensingtonbooks.com

APHRODISIA BOOKS are published by

Kensington Publishing Corp.
119 West 40th Street
New York, NY 10018

All Kensington titles, imprints, and distributed lines are available at special quantity discounts for bulk purchases for sales promotion, premiums, fund-raising, and educational, or institutional use.

Special book excerpts or customized printings can also be created to fit specific needs. For details, write or phone the office of the Kensington Special Sales Manager: Kensington Publishing Corp., 119 West 40th Street, New York, NY 10018. Attn. Special Sales Department. Phone: 1-800-221-2647.

Aphrodisia and the A logo Reg. U.S. Pat. & TM Off.

ISBN-13: 978-0-7582-3814-6
ISBN-10: 0-7582-3814-2

First Kensington Trade Paperback Printing: June 2011

10 9 8 7 6 5 4 3 2 1

Printed in the United States of America

CONTENTS

Fight Fire with Fire

Lorie O'Clare

Acknowledgments

Getting to know the life of a firefighter is always exciting, whether in real life or romantic fiction. The men and women who risk their lives, walk through burning flames, know heat hotter than any of us could imagine are men and women cut from a certain cloth. It isn't the life for everyone. But for the firefighters I've met while doing research on their line of work it's definitely the life for them. It is amazing how many firefighters are generational, again proof that certain driven, aggressive personalities come direct from the gene pool.

I would like to personally thank Chuck Ozonoff with Fire Station Number Two in Olathe, Kansas. He gave my son and me a tour, showed us where they live and how they work. Also, thank you to his sweet daughter for communicating with my son on Facebook and helping put me in touch with her father. For the time we were with him, we walked in the firefighter's shoes. It was amazing! Thank you, Chuck, for giving us your tour, and for all you do. We definitely live in a better world because of you!

May God bless!

1

Nate Armstrong squinted, keeping his breathing steady as he stepped gingerly onto the next stair. The floorboards wouldn't hold out long.

"Are you sure there's another kid in here?" he demanded, speaking through the small microphone attached to his helmet. It was getting harder to see. The smoke was like a fog against the special clear eye protection attached to his helmet. As with the rest of his uniform, it was designed to withstand ungodly amounts of heat. Unfortunately, it didn't prevent him from sweating his balls off.

"That's an affirmative." Fire Chief Joseph Campbell spoke clearly, his voice only a bit tinny through the earpiece.

Nate reached the top of the stairs. He counted three bedrooms, two on one side of the hall and a third on the other. Two doors were open. The smoke danced in circles above the floor, curling around his legs as he continued down the hall. Each bedroom appeared unoccupied. Nate made quick work of checking under beds, around dressers, and in closets. No kid.

So far the new equipment they were all using was working

well. It was far less bulky than their previous uniforms and supposedly a lot more fire retardant, which in Nate's line of work was always a good thing. The uniform was made of lighter material, making it a lot easier to move around, but no one thought to install a thermostat in the damn thing. Nate might not die of smoke inhalation or by burning alive, but he would go nuts in the next few minutes from all the sweat dripping down his body and causing every inch of him to itch worse than anything he'd ever experienced. This was one hell of a hot fire, almost too hot to have occurred from something burning on the stove.

"I'm entering the last bedroom on the right at the back of the house."

"Nate! Hurry up!" Campbell suddenly sounded alarmed. "The entire first floor just exploded in flames!"

"Roger that." He didn't need the update. In a matter of minutes he'd be on the first floor, without taking stairs to get there.

Already smoke billowed around him in the hallway, turning darker and closing in around him. Nate didn't have a problem with claustrophobia, but it really sucked when he lost his sense of direction in a small area from thick smoke. Nate knew his training though. And this wasn't his first real fire. Meredith Curve, Missouri, was a far cry from a big city, or even a big town. They were just now receiving uniforms that firefighters in larger cities had been wearing for up to a year now. Accidents happened in small towns, too. As long as he got the entire family out alive, that was all that mattered. He wasn't in this for the glory.

He reached the only bedroom with its door closed. Nate found the handle and tested it. He felt the heat through his glove. If someone touched that doorknob without gloves, their skin would melt clear to the bone.

"What's the kid's name?" Nate asked, feeling a need to keep the conversation going. The heat was getting to him, making it hard to breathe. He kept a close eye on the wood floor, step-ping gingerly in his boots. Smoke crept through cracks in the boards, like serpents taunting him and just waiting for him to fuck up.

"Johnny," the chief told him. "But he goes by Buddy."

"John will get a kick out of that," Nate said, forcing a laugh as he thought of his best friend since grade school, who also had responded to this call. Last he saw John he'd been on the first floor. Nate stared at the floorboards. "Is everyone else out?"

"That's an affirmative. You need to move, Armstrong," the chief warned.

Nate didn't answer but turned the handle and opened the bedroom door. Black smoke rolled over him, forcing him to step back automatically before plowing forward. The heat was too intense and his stomach rolled.

"How old is this kid?"

"Not sure." Campbell hesitated. "His mom is hysterical. Armstrong, you've got less than five minutes. We're position-ing the trampoline below the south upstairs window. Head that way. I need you out of there." His tone grew more urgent. "The structure is going. Find that kid and jump, and you've got under a minute."

Nate didn't need to hear how serious this was. He swore his clothes were melting into his skin. His helmet weighed three times as much as it did when he'd entered the burning house. Sweat dripped down his forehead, chest, and back. But if there was a kid in here, jumping to safety without him would kill Nate as much as burning alive would. He'd never lost a life in the ten years he'd been a firefighter, and that wouldn't change today.

"Johnny?" Nate called out, moving his arms as he hesitated in all of the smoke. "Buddy, are you in here? Buddy?" he yelled. "I know I look funny, but I'm a firefighter. If your eyes are closed, keep them closed and just make a sound so I can grab you. Once we're outside I'll show you how cool this uniform is."

If the kid obeyed and made a sound it would be hard to hear between the crackling boards around Nate, the repeated explosions downstairs as the structure began collapsing, and the buzzing apprehension growing in his ears. Nate knelt on the floor, moving on hands and knees as he pushed toys away and crawled toward a child-sized bed.

He squatted lower, pressing the side of his head to the floor, and stared underneath the bed at the small figure curled into a ball. Nate had no idea if the child was alive or not but grabbed an arm and pulled him out.

"Got him!" Nate announced, lifting the boy into his arms. A rush of relief roared in his gut when the kid curled up against him. "He's alive!" Nate announced.

"Ten four. The south window, now!" Campbell ordered, and started barking orders to those on the ground around him before turning off his microphone.

It seemed like an hour or two later, but only fifteen minutes passed from the time Nate entered the burning house until he jumped from the window with the kid in his arms.

"Excellent timing!" Campbell slapped Nate on the back, although he wasn't smiling.

The other guys surrounding Nate were as smeared with soot and dirt as he was. Campbell was the only one who wasn't filthy. Not that Nate cared. He looked for the little boy he'd just rescued but didn't see him. Nate did see an ambulance pull away from the curb.

"The kid okay?" Nate asked. "Buddy? I promised to show him my uniform."

"They're taking him in for observation. He breathed in a lot of smoke in there." Campbell's expression sobered. "Corelli went with him."

Nate nodded, gripping his helmet in his hand as he ran fingers through his sweaty hair. He needed a shower. "Come on, probie," he said, slapping Gil Harper on the back. "I'll let you shower after me."

Nate might let Harper know how good a job he did today. Harper was barely grown at nineteen and had joined their house six months ago. Nate decided he'd wait until the fear of God left the probie's eyes before giving him any praise. If the kid wanted to be a firefighter, this was what it was all about.

"Feel better?" Chief Campbell sat alone in the kitchen, his hands clasped on the table. He took his time looking up from his coffee and staring at Nate.

"Feel half-human again." Nate rolled his shoulders. "I must be getting old, though. I'm sore as hell. Might have to force myself to pull double time on the weights later. Where is everyone?"

"Have a seat, Nate."

Campbell didn't use first names unless there was a problem. Nate eyed the chief as he pulled a chair out from under the table, flipped it around backward, and straddled it.

"What's up, Chief?" Nate was pretty sure he'd gone by the book today, but hell, the chief was a stickler to policy. "Did I take the stairs with my left foot instead of my right?"

Campbell grunted, lowering his gaze. "I wish you had."

"This is serious," Nate noted, tilting his head and studying Campbell's sober, if not weary, expression. "Looks like it might call for a drink."

He stood, headed over to the refrigerator, and pulled out a bottled water. "Want one?" he asked the chief.

Campbell shook his head. "John didn't make it, Nate."

Nate unscrewed his water bottle. "Didn't make it where?"

"Nate."

He brought the bottle to his lips and paused, staring past it at the chief. Silence grew between them until Campbell sighed loudly and shifted to face Nate.

"John took the first floor. I had four of you in there." Campbell stood and gripped the back of the chair, looking unstable for a moment.

"What are you talking about?" Nate said, his voice cracking. He didn't like the way Campbell was acting or what it sounded like he was implying. "Cut the crap, Chief. You're making it sound as if John really didn't make it." He laughed but stopped with a sharp breath when the chief stared at the floor and didn't say a word.

The water Nate had just swallowed turned to acid in his gut when Campbell finally looked at him. Nate shook his head, positive he wasn't following whatever it was the chief was trying to say to him.

"Where the hell is John?" he demanded.

"He's dead."

"No. He's not." Nate shook his head adamantly. He'd just seen John. They drove to the fire together. He was outside talking with the rest of them afterward, wasn't he? "I just saw him," he argued, gesturing with his water bottle in the direction of the truck.

"Nate, don't make this harder than it already is."

"What?" Nate snapped, turning on his chief. "You're telling me John is dead! My best friend since fucking forever is no longer alive. Then you suggest I don't make this hard on us. Let me tell you something. This is as hard as it gets." Nate slammed his fist into the table, causing a portion of Chief Campbell's coffee to spill around the cup.

The reality of it sank in with a swift kick, nearly taking Nate down. John was dead. His best friend since the third grade. They'd become firefighters together, dreamed of glorious flames and saving damsels in distress. They didn't dream of dying.

The chief didn't say anything but watched Nate. The silence in the room grew unbearable. Nate couldn't stand it, any more than he could get his brain to wrap around this. John wouldn't just die.

"He's dead?" Nate whispered. Acid churned in his gut, growing and spreading until it itched under his skin. With a roar, Nate hurled the water bottle and didn't feel a damn bit better when it exploded against the far wall and water splattered everywhere. "How the hell did he die?" He was yelling. "Why did he die?"

"Sit down," Campbell said.

"I'm not sitting down. I don't want to sit down. Tell me what the fuck happened!"

Campbell had been around the station long enough to know it wasn't wise to tell a man raging with a temper to calm down. The quiet stance he always took when any of them locked horns or fought over a girl or argued about sports seemed grossly inappropriate at the moment.

"The structure collapsed on him," Campbell explained.

If he kept it simple because Nate was too outraged to hear details, there was no way of knowing. But Campbell didn't elaborate.

Nate swallowed the lump in his throat. His eyes suddenly burned as if there were smoke in them again. John deserved a poolful of tears, but he wouldn't get them now, not in front of the chief, not at the firehouse.

"Where is he now?" Nate asked, his voice sounding foreign and oddly quiet and resolved. "I'm going to go see him."

"County General." Campbell looked away first, focusing on his large hands gripping the back of his chair. "He was taken there with the kid you rescued. I just got the call ten minutes ago. The kid is fine."

* * *

Mary Hamilton adjusted her headpiece over her blonde hair then brought the mouthpiece closer to her mouth. "Police," she said for the fiftieth time that day.

"Mary?" a man asked.

"This is Mary." She glanced at the clock. Two more hours to go. She swore the air-conditioning wasn't working right today. Either that or Captain Odgers had the thermostat set at eighty.

"Mary, it's Robert Corelli."

"Mr. Corelli," she said, fighting to sound cheerful. The Corellis still kept in touch with her parents even though her folks had moved to St. Louis over two years ago. "How is Mrs. Corelli? Is everything okay?" she asked, tugging on her uniform shirt as she switched back to her professional mode. She was the primary dispatcher for the Meredith Curve Police Department, which meant a lot of callers were people she'd known most of her life. As she'd been reminded more than once, being born and raised there didn't mean it was social hour when she answered the phones. "There isn't a problem, is there?"

Mr. Corelli cleared his throat and there was a shuffling sound through the phone.

"Mary, hi, it's Elizabeth." Elizabeth Corelli was a year older than Mary. They hadn't hung around much growing up, but Mary knew her well enough to say hi if she saw her in the grocery store.

Elizabeth's younger brother, John, and Nate Armstrong were best friends and Mary had hopelessly followed the two of them around wherever they went while growing up. From grade school through high school, wherever Nate went, Mary followed, and John was always at his side. She might have followed Nate into adulthood, but having grown up with her father being a firefighter, she knew it wasn't a career choice she would like. She'd entered the police academy when Nate and John became firefighters.

"Hi, Elizabeth," Mary said, holding on to her work voice as she played with the cord to her headset. "What's the problem?"

"My parents thought we should call you." Elizabeth hesitated. She cleared her throat just as her father had. "Mary, there's been an accident. Something terrible has happened." Suddenly she was talking very fast. "John was brought in after one of the houses burned down over on Maple Street. I don't know the family, but I guess there were young kids."

Mary tried keeping up. Her mind stumbled over the words "accident" and "terrible." She shot a glance at her logbook, then at the computer screen where she documented all calls when they came in. All 911 calls came to her. She'd dispatched a call to the fire department a couple hours ago when a neighbor called in complaining of smoke. What terrible accident?

And if John was hurt in a house fire, Nate would have been with him. Mary's heart swelled into her chest so fast she wasn't able to catch her breath. She opened her mouth to ask about Nate, but Elizabeth continued talking.

"They transported John to the hospital in an ambulance, but he didn't make it."

"John is dead?" Mary whispered, dropping the cord as her eyes started burning. "Are you sure?"

When Elizabeth laughed it sounded anything but humorous. "Unfortunately, we're sure. He suffered from severe burns and I guess part of the house collapsed on him, or something. I don't have all the details yet. We wanted to reach Nate Armstrong, too."

They wanted to tell Nate that John was dead? Nate wasn't hurt. He wasn't at the hospital. The relief rushing through Mary was so incredibly overwhelming it took her a minute before guilt set in. John was dead.

"I'll contact him." She was numb. "And I'm terribly sorry."

"So am I." Elizabeth mumbled her good-byes and hung up the phone.

Mary stared at the switchboard in front of her. The computer screen had a glare to it and made her eyes burn worse. As terrible as this was, and it definitely was the worst thing that had happened in town in years, Nate was alive, but would be devastated.

Nate and John had been attached at the hip since third grade. Around that same time, Mary had fallen head over heels hopelessly in love with Nate. She'd followed Nate around shamelessly, refusing to be left behind no matter where he went. The three of them were really tight during grade school and into high school.

Nate taught her how to climb trees. He and John were the first to show her how to throw a baseball, shoot a hoop, and they learned to ride bikes together. They didn't teach her any of these things willingly. Whenever they told her she was a girl and to go home, she grew even more stubborn and refused to budge. Mary couldn't remember when she hadn't loved Nate.

And she'd just volunteered to break his heart.

"Crap." Mary stood, stretched, and pulled her headset off. She flipped the switch on her switchboard so she'd hear the phone ring if she walked away, and turned to the back break room.

"The coffee is fresh," Jeremy Meyers said. He had been on the force forever and possibly was old enough to be Mary's father. Jeremy was a confirmed bachelor, though, swearing to all he was too devoted to the badge to settle down and play house. That didn't stop his roaming eyes. He checked Mary out, taking his time, when she paused in the doorway. "How are you today, Miss Mary?"

The numbness was spreading over her entire body. She didn't have a clue how to break this to Nate. The few officers in the break room mumbled about her acting weird when she turned without a word and went back to her desk for her coffee cup.

When she returned, all eyes looked at her expectantly. They

would think something was wrong with her if she didn't tell
them about John. She might as well break it to all of them at
once. It would give her practice for when she told Nate.

"There was a fire over on Maple Street," she began, looking
at each of them when they stared back at her blankly.

"Those are all old houses over that way," Jeremy said, shaking his head. "Faulty wiring will do it every time."

"John Corelli is dead."

"What?" Jeremy gawked at her.

"You're kidding."

"Are you serious?"

Mary went through the process of getting coffee as the men
behind her began all talking at once. She sipped and burned her
mouth as she turned around.

"Captain," she mumbled, coughing and clutching her mug
as the steam and thick aroma rose to her face. "Captain?" she
repeated.

Captain Steve Odgers just turned forty-two the month before. His wife had helped Mary decorate the station and
brought in cupcakes for everyone. Mrs. Odgers was a cheerful
lady, overworked and with several obnoxious kids who took
advantage of their dad being captain of the police department.
Captain Odgers, on the other hand, was a tough man to read.
Mary was pretty sure he'd never thanked his wife, or Mary, for
their work in preparing the office party for him. He seldom
smiled or showed any emotion.

Now wasn't any different. He raised his gray eyes to her, ac-
knowledging her with only a look.

"I need to go to the hospital." She wasn't at all sure that
would be the first place she went. The phone rang at her
switchboard and she took a step backward, still watching the
captain.

He nodded once. "Meyers, take over on the switchboard.
Hamilton, make sure you clock out."

Always a stickler over money and their budget. Captain Odgers didn't offer a word of sympathy. He did give her the last two hours of her shift off, though. Mary accepted that as his form of offering condolences.

The air-conditioning in her brand-new Volkswagen worked perfectly. Mary barely noticed the cold air giving her skin goose bumps, though. She stared ahead of her blankly at the street. She needed to call Nate.

How long had it been since she'd actually talked to him? Mary knew it wouldn't be a matter of him forgetting her. They were adults now. They were both wrapped up in their jobs and neither had much time to socialize. At least that was what Mary heard, since she seldom went out. Whenever anyone went to the local bar or to some event in town, she listened to who was present. No one ever mentioned Nate's name. Just like her, he was married to his job.

When she swallowed, her mouth was too dry.

"Get it over with," she scolded herself, her hands damp when she dug her cell phone out of her purse. The first thing she did was take the ringer off silent, as she did every day when she got off work. Then scrolling down to Nate's name in her address book, she put the call through.

It only rang once before going to voice mail. Mary hung up the phone. She couldn't leave Nate a message telling him his best friend was dead. It was going to be weird enough after not talking to him or seeing him in a couple months to call and destroy him with the news about John. Maybe he already knew. There was a copy of the fire department's rotation schedule inside. At the moment, though, she didn't remember what it said.

Mary left the police station, not giving much thought to her direction as she headed to the old neighborhood. She turned off the main street and took side roads, her surroundings pulling her out of her brooding. The park where they had spent so much time growing up looked small and boring. She spotted the tree they used to climb, but it seemed so insignificant compared to what she'd pictured in her imagination all these years. How long had it been since she'd driven over to this part of town? There hadn't been a reason to come out this way after her parents moved.

As she reached the four-way stop, which had marked the edge of their block growing up, Mary looked to the right before she turned. The first car she spotted parked on the street in front of his parents' house was Nate's Gran Torino. God! He'd looked mouthwatering hot when he used to cruise around in that car.

Right now wasn't the time to lust over a man she would never have. Not only was it a waste of time; it was also incredibly inappropriate considering what had just happened.

"Oh my God," she whispered, terror gripping her when a thought hit her. "What if Nate was with John at the fire when he died?" That would be the worst experience anyone could ever live through, seeing someone so close to them die. Nate would be a mess, unable to handle it.

She parked her car in front of the house she'd grown up in, hoping she wasn't stealing the parking place of whoever lived there now. When she opened her car door, suffocating heat immediately closed in around her. Mary took in the old neighborhood for a minute as perspiration beaded between her breasts and down her spine.

"It doesn't look the same, does it?" Nate hadn't been behind her a moment before.

Mary spun around, slapping her hand on the hood of her car, and stared at the man she adored and who'd been the star act in her fantasies since childhood. Had it been a couple of months since she'd seen him? She didn't remember him looking this good the last time she saw him. And he'd always looked good, but now, this man would put a Greek god to shame.

Nate had sure as hell filled out. He wore his black work pants and T-shirt with the fire department logo on it, and suspenders that managed to add to the broadness of his shoulders. There wasn't possibly a man in Meredith Curve, let alone all of Missouri, who could possibly look as good as Nate did right now.

"It's changed," she muttered, her mouth so dry she would do anything for a cold glass of water.

Staring at Nate didn't help much. Roped muscle pressed against his shirt. The material stretched over his chest, and his arms were just as ripped. She shifted her attention to where his shirtsleeve ended and bulging biceps began.

"I take it you've heard." Nate was staring at her. His eyes still reminded her of melting milk chocolate. His voice lowered to a rumbly growl. "It shouldn't have happened like this."

Nate had an impenetrable aura around him. It was an invisible barrier she'd never been able to crack her way through. But Mary saw the pain lining the creases in his forehead, and the way he pressed his lips together. It was hot as hell and her uniform itched, but she didn't give that, or the way he always seemed so hard to reach, any thought when she walked into his arms.

"I'm so sorry, Nate," she murmured, and her eyes started burning again.

Nate wasn't ready for the hug. He told himself it was a perfectly natural thing to do and he should probably be prepared for a lot more of them once he headed down the street to the Corelli house. This wasn't the Mary who damn near stalked him when they were kids, though. She wasn't tangled pigtails and scuffed knees anymore. He'd noticed the small spray of freckles across her nose, but instead of looking like dots he wanted to connect with a pen, they now looked good enough to place soft kisses on.

And her hair wasn't tangled and in crooked pigtails, but instead she'd pulled it back with hairpieces and her soft curls reflected the sunlight and looked like melting gold. When she was a kid he remembered making fun of the color of her eyes. They were so noticeable they'd stuck out of her head. Now her dark blue, almost violet eyes were so sultry and appealing it was hard to keep his mind focused on the fact that this was just Mary Hamilton.

She looked more like a seductive goddess who would be a perfect distraction from the nightmare that had happened today.

Nate wrapped his arms around her waist, feeling how slender it was. She draped her arms over his shoulders and rested her head against him, letting out a sigh that made his insides tighten.

"I told his family I would tell you. Since they mentioned it, I worried you were off work today. I couldn't figure out what to say, though. And I didn't want to break your heart. How did you find out?" she whispered, but didn't move.

Nate didn't have a problem holding her against him for another minute. Her breasts were large, round, and soft. She was the best thing he'd felt against him in ages. Hell, when did Mary start looking so damn good? He'd known her since they were little kids, but he'd never had thoughts about her the way he was now.

"I found out down at the station and went over to the hospital. My shift is on right now. Then I stopped in at the folks' house before heading down to the Corellis'. Honestly, I really don't want to go down there." He wasn't sure why he was telling Mary this. Like she cared. Obviously she was here to do the same thing. And their embrace was simply her consoling him.

"I haven't been to this neighborhood in ages."

Nate spotted another car approaching from the other end of the block and straightened. Mary must have sensed it because she pulled back, lifting her gaze to his. Damn if she didn't have the most beautiful eyes. They were rare jewels and incredibly dynamic. They still stuck out noticeably, but now the captivating shade simply added to her beauty. They were too dark to be blue. Then he remembered her mother telling Mary her eyes were violet, like the flowers in the yard. They might be violet, but they were a hell of a lot more captivating than the small flowers he remembered that used to grow around Mary's house.

"I think it's been at least three years or so," she added, and shifted her weight.

Nate blinked, realizing he probably was making her uncomfortable by gawking at her stunning good looks. He pulled his attention from Mary and watched a family park across the street. The wife in the car got out with a casserole dish in her hands. Hell, he didn't have anything to take down there.

"That's right," he said absently. "Your folks moved away, didn't they?"

"Yes, a few years ago, to St. Louis." She was still watching him, probably wondering why he was standing on the sidewalk, not moving, like some lame idiot. "Would you like to walk me down there?"

Her question didn't register right away. After he watched the family cross the street and walk up the Corellis' sidewalk, the gnarled tree in their front yard grabbed his attention. How many times had he and John climbed that tree, then made fun of Mary when she repeatedly tried climbing up after them?

"What? Oh, sure." He started walking but looked down at her blonde, soft-looking hair when she wrapped her arm around his. "We picked on you a lot growing up, didn't we?"

"You did?" She sounded surprised, but when she glanced up at him the corner of her mouth twitched upward. "You were ruthless and cruel, Nate Armstrong. What will you do to make up for it?"

He could think of a few things he wouldn't mind doing.

"Sorry," he mumbled, then focused ahead when they neared the Corellis' front porch. God, it used to be ten times larger than this.

"Now would you look there!" Mrs. Peabody, who still looked as old as she did when they were kids, stood just inside the front door and announced Nate and Mary when they walked into the Corellis' house. "If it isn't thing one and thing two," she said, then laughed until she started coughing.

Everyone in the living room, and it seemed half the town was already there, stopped talking, or doing whatever it was they'd been doing, and stared at Nate and Mary.

"If I said it once, I said it a hundred times," Mrs. Peabody continued when she'd finally quit coughing, "I always knew these two would grow up and fall in love. Aren't they the perfect couple?"

2

Mary was ready to leave half an hour after arriving. The moment that old hag made a spectacle of her and Nate when they walked in the door, Nate had stiffened worse than he did when she hugged him, then separated himself from her. He'd managed to keep his distance, and keep at least a few people between them, ever since. She was starting to feel they were playing a game of cat and mouse. Whenever Mary made a move in his direction, Nate would excuse himself from whomever he was talking to and walk away from her.

After standing in the kitchen and staring at more food than the Corellis would be able to eat in a week, Mary started toward the back door. She had made an appearance, would make a point of being at the funeral, but for now getting the hell out of there sounded more appealing than anything. It was bad enough reliving so many childhood memories, some good, some bad, but with Nate so close yet so incredibly distant to her, she'd be better off leaving and having a good cry, mourning two men, once she got home.

More people entered through the front door and for a few

minutes the conversation grew louder as greetings were exchanged and more casserole dishes were accepted. Mary used the moment to sneak out the back door and hurry around the side of the house to her car. As hot as a day as it had been, the evening was equally as muggy. It couldn't rain soon enough to make her happy. The humidity could be cut with a knife.

After sliding into her car, cranking it on, then adjusting her AC and fastening her seat belt, Mary sat for a minute, absorbing the atmosphere of her childhood neighborhood. There were so many good memories around her, and a few bad ones, too. That life seemed a thousand years ago. The fact that everything seemed so much smaller now as she looked at it through an adult's eyes proved how long ago it was. They weren't children anymore.

Nate was anything but a child. Although, she mused, shifting her attention to his Gran Torino parked across the street, he was still as stubborn now as he was when they were in school. He dodged her at least as well now as he did back then.

"Maybe it's time to quit chasing a fantasy," she said out loud, leaning back in her driver's seat as her car cooled down and the radio station she had on buzzed on about the local news and events in the area.

She didn't pay attention to what the newscaster said and instead stared at Nate's car. Why had he always been such an obsession for her? They'd been out of high school for over ten years now. It wasn't as if she saw him every day. Granted, with dispatching all emergency vehicles in Meredith Curve, she always knew where he was in town when she checked the shifts for the fire station. Not that it mattered. Mary was always at the police station tethered to her switchboard. Maybe that's what kept Nate alive in her imagination.

Obviously in real life she didn't appeal to him now any more than she had when they were kids.

"He never settled down, though." The side of her who liked

her fantasy was quick with the arguments. "And he doesn't have a girlfriend." Everyone knew firefighters were hot commodities in every woman's eyes. "But I would make the perfect lady for him." Her mother had been the perfect wife to a firefighter—Mary's father. "Lord," she muttered, and scrubbed her face with her hands.

Mary yelped at the sound of someone tapping on her window. She jumped and her seat belt tightened around her. Nate's hand was next to her driver's side window, his knuckles ready to rap again. He dropped his hand when she pushed the button to lower her window.

"I didn't mean to startle you." He looked tired. "You okay to drive home?"

He thought she was sitting here crying. Well, better that than knowing what she'd really been doing as she zoned off in her driver's seat.

"I'm fine. Thanks for asking."

Nate nodded once and stuffed his hands into his pant pockets. The act forced his T-shirt to stretch down and show off more of his rippled chest. Corded muscle bulged under the material, giving her a mouthwatering view from where she sat.

"It was kind of rough in there," she blurted, not wanting him to walk away just yet.

He didn't move, just stared down at her, almost scowling. "Yup."

She fought for something else to say. "I'm sorry, Nate."

Again he nodded. "It shouldn't have been John," he grumbled, his brows narrowing, giving him an angry, dangerous look. "I was in that house, too. If I'd done my job better..."

"You can't blame yourself," she cried out, then gulped in a breath when he pierced her with eyes that seemed to have turned black. "Nate," she said, forcing her heart to slow down. He already didn't like her, but if she said the wrong thing right now, he'd hate her forever. They were talking about his best friend here. "You're in a very dangerous line of work. John knew that as well as you and I do."

He kept staring at her, not even blinking. Well, at least he hadn't stormed off on her yet.

"It was a terrible, terrible accident. And I know you knew John better than I did, but I think I knew him pretty well. He would rather have gone out in a victorious explosion than wither away as an old man. Yes, he went in his prime. But I heard all the children were saved. All of you, including John, did an amazing job of getting a family with young kids out of a burning house. John wouldn't want you moping around thinking all of this is your fault."

His expression still hadn't changed.

She took a breath and went for broke. It was killing her having Nate look at her like that. "John is going to be pissed, and he'll haunt you, if you keep thinking he didn't do the best job he could have done. And your thinking that you should have done better sort of implies John wasn't holding it up on his end."

Nate blinked. He tilted his head. Then slowly licking his lips, he lowered his attention to the outside of her car door. "That's an interesting twist on things," he muttered.

She exhaled and watched him, praying he wouldn't blow her off—for the thousandth time—and storm away to his car.

"John was an amazing firefighter. Just because I wear a different uniform doesn't mean I don't know the way of things."

Nate's eyes were the color of melting milk chocolate when he lifted his attention to her face. "He was the best," he said sullenly.

"Remember him that way," she whispered.

Nate turned as if to leave. Mary brainstormed, frantically trying to think of something else to say. She didn't want him leaving. The last thing she wanted to do was go home, where she'd inevitably end up masturbating as she allowed every image of him from today to flash through her head, then Photoshop him so his body was next to hers, with both of them naked.

"Would you like—" He hesitated, breaking off before he finished what he was going to say, and stared at the ground, then gave her a side-glance. "You want to go for a drink?" he asked. "I'm not in the mood to go home yet."

Say yes! Say yes! And don't do the happy dance where he can see you!

"That sounds good." She smiled.

Nate didn't smile. "Follow me. We'll go over to Milton's." He didn't wait to hear her response but crossed the street in front of her to his car.

Mary simply watched him, positive she was drooling. Nate Armstrong had just asked her to go for a drink. It might be because he didn't want to be alone and they both knew John really well. Mary wished more than anything John hadn't been ripped out of the prime of his life. It wasn't fair. She'd meant the words she said to Nate, though. And if his mourning would bring them closer to each other, Mary was shameless enough to take advantage of that. They would mourn together. Somehow, she'd show Nate Armstrong she was a good lady to have around.

Milton's was one of three family restaurants in town, and the only one with a liquor license. The establishment was divided in two, half of it being a restaurant with tables where people could sit and eat. The other half was a bar with a few pool tables. They sat at the bar, and after they'd barely finished their first beer Mary saw it was a mistake choosing this spot, and possibly a mistake being at the bar and grill.

Every person entering the bar spotted the two of them and came over to offer condolences. They had heard either on the news, from a friend, or through work that John had died earlier that day in a terrible house fire.

Even Captain Odgers strolled in, no longer in uniform, and approached both of them as if he already knew Mary and Nate were out together. Which he might have if he'd recognized both of their cars outside. He gave her a curious look with her beer in her hand and still in uniform. Mary was off the clock and hadn't had time to go home yet. She gave him the same look back, daring him to say anything or she'd point out he should be home with his wife and kids after being at work all day and not at the local bar.

Odgers looked away first and took the bar stool on the opposite side of Nate, the one where several other people had already sat while offering their condolences and sad stories, which for some reason people seemed to think would cheer him up.

"I was just thinking on the way over here how I used to chase you two off out at the lake when you were teenagers and causing trouble." Odgers waved to the bartender for a beer.

Nate snorted and nodded, lifting his beer and downing a good portion of it. Mary decided she would nurse hers. If Nate needed to tie one on tonight, he had every right, but he would also need a ride home.

"You two would always try to sneak off and not get caught, thinking I wouldn't see you." Odgers slapped Nate on the back and grunted, or possibly for him it was a laugh. "I swear more than once I thought the two of you would grow up to be no good."

Nate laughed, although it sounded forced and his smile faded quickly. Odgers went on longer than the others had, and although Nate finished his beer, he declined a second when the captain offered to buy it for him. Mary remained quiet, listening and watching Nate as he managed professional politeness and courtesy. Finally, Odgers got up to leave, again patting Nate on the back, then giving her a nod before walking away to join others he knew at the bar.

"Do you want to get out of here?" She had to lean into Nate, since someone had turned on the jukebox. "I think I've heard enough about how you and John were when you were kids."

Nate's expression was etched in stone when he shifted, their knees bumping, and looked at her. This time his focus dropped lower than her eyes, to her mouth, her chin. She fought off a shiver when she swore he glanced lower. Was he checking her out? Her breasts swelled in eager anticipation and she knew her nipples were suddenly hard enough that they probably pressed against her uniform shirt.

"We could pick up a twelve-pack, go back to my place," she offered, and refused to look away from him. No way would she back down or appear embarrassed after inviting him over.

"That sounds good." Nate stood and tossed a few bills next to his empty beer before turning to leave. He didn't wait for her to get off the bar stool, nor did he make any effort to hold the door for her.

Which was probably a really good thing. Mary was still in shock. Nate had just agreed to return to her place. No way would she have appreciated the chivalry. Dear God! Nate was coming over to her house. It was all she could do not to skip after him. Now all she had to do was not make a complete fool out of herself once they were alone.

"Where do you live?" Nate stopped in the middle of the parking lot, his keys in his hand when he turned around to face her.

"Over on Walnut Street," she said, praying he wasn't about to come to his senses and realize who he'd just agreed to go home with.

Worry lines still creased his forehead as he took another moment studying her. She didn't have to wonder where his eyes traveled on her body. Everywhere he looked, charges of energy zapped to life just underneath her skin. And as if it weren't muggy enough outside, heat radiated between her legs, creating a pressure that swelled and spread until she feared she would burn to life inside. And this was definitely a fire only one firefighter would be able to put out.

"That isn't too far from here."

She wouldn't say the overused line that nothing in this town was too far from here.

"I'll go back inside and buy a twelve-pack. Want to give me the address?"

When she hesitated for the briefest of moments, panic threatening to take over as it hit her he might still back out, Nate stepped closer, lowering his voice. "Do you really want everyone in town talking about the two of us leaving here together and both of us heading toward your place?"

Hell yes! She'd walk around with that reputation holding her head high.

"Regardless of how you think of me, I have more respect for you than that." Nate popped her on the nose. "Give me your address."

"Four hundred Walnut."

Nate backed up, then headed back inside. All she could do was stare at his buns of steel until he'd cleared the spread of parking lot and disappeared inside Milton's. She'd forgotten how he used to pop her on the nose when they were in high school. Except back then it was to laugh at her when she wanted to go wherever he was going. He would tap her nose with his finger and inform her whatever girl he was going out with that week wouldn't appreciate Mary hanging around him.

"What did he mean, regardless of what I think of him?" She headed to her car, climbed in, and stewed on that as she drove home.

Mary changed clothes, three different times, and was debating on makeup when there was a knock on her door. She almost ran to answer, damn near flying over her ottoman in front of the upright chair her parents had given her before moving to St. Louis.

"It's been one hell of a day." Nate didn't wait for an invitation but entered the moment she opened the door.

Mary watched him enter her home as if he'd been over hundreds of times. It wasn't fair he was so relaxed and she was acting worse than if this were her first date.

"For the life of me I couldn't remember what kind of beer you ordered. I hope this is okay," he said, holding up a twelve-pack of longneck bottles of Budweiser.

"Perfect. Make yourself at home." She closed her door and locked it, then followed him as he managed to find her kitchen.

"Nice place." Nate opened her refrigerator, bent over to place the twelve-pack inside, and pulled free two beers.

"I like it." She was sure she had to look proud as she glanced around her kitchen. She was thirty and had recently bought her first house. Every night when she came home she'd walk through the rooms, glorifying in how every inch belonged to her. Well, her and the bank.

Nate popped the lids off both bottles, searched and found her trash can under her sink, then handed her one of the opened bottles. This time he was more obvious when he took his time looking her over.

"You clean up good, Mary." He tilted his bottle in a silent toast, clinking his against hers, then took a long sip, watching her as he did.

"Thank you." She wanted to say something similar, but Nate hadn't changed clothes—not that he didn't look sexy as hell in his uniform. "I'd like to say the same," she mumbled, and smiled as she sipped her beer.

"Sorry," he said, sounding as if he meant it. "I don't think I had it in me to go home and change clothes. For some reason, it seems as if going home would mean the day would end and

John will really be dead." He shook his head, waving his hand when she would have commented. "I know. That sounds stupid. And I'm not delusional. John is dead. I know that. It's just how I feel."

"I understand, I think. And I'm glad you can say how you feel."

"Well, it's just you and me. Hell, Mary. We've been friends as long as John and I were friends." He took another drink of his beer, saying what he did as if it were common knowledge.

"I never knew you considered me a friend."

A bit of the Nate she remembered surfaced when he looked at her as if she'd just grown a second head. "Oh, I'm sorry. I must have the wrong house. I thought I was coming over to hang out with that pigtailed girl who took forever to learn how to climb a tree." Nate gripped the top of her head, tousling her hair, and walked past her. "Where is your TV?"

"In my bedroom." She followed him into her living room, her head still tingling from where he'd just touched her.

"Oh. Well, give me a few more beers before I try taking you to bed just so I can watch TV."

She could barely swallow, let alone think of a thing to say. Was he actually considering trying to sleep with her tonight?

Nate regretted his words when he saw Mary's look of shock. He told himself she didn't think of him as a man she might consider having sex with. To Mary, Nate was just the boy across the street she grew up with. They were old friends, and he would be smart to remember that. Making himself comfortable on a long couch with its back to her front windows, he stretched out his legs and relaxed his free arm across the back of it.

"Relax, Mary," he said, laughing and making light of his not so subtle comment. "I only sleep with cheap tramps after just a few beers."

"Umm, thanks, I think." She wrinkled her nose, and he got a wonderful view of that light spread of freckles across her nose. She took the other end of the couch, tucked her legs up next to her, and stared at him. "And I probably would have learned to climb trees faster if you hadn't been above me each time making fun of me so I would get all flustered and lose my balance."

"You get all flustered?" He wasn't buying into that one at all. "You're a rock, my dear. Push that line off on some other poor sucker. You forget, I've known you for most of your life."

"Then your memory is rather jaded, *my dear*," she said, emphasizing the term of endearment as her eyes flashed violet. "You were both ruthless and cruel as can be no matter how hard I tried to do anything."

He'd forgotten how much of a rock she could be. No one pulled a thing over on Mary. Even when he had tried bullying her or teasing and taunting her, she always dished it back to him better than any boy he'd ever known. Even now as she got ready to hand him a piece of her mind, she looked hot as hell. Nate let his gaze drop again to the cleavage at the top of her tank top. The shorts she'd put on weren't too short, but with her legs pulled up and her feet bare he saw enough skin he'd be smart not to stare too long or he'd be explaining why he was suddenly hard as a rock.

"I guess I forgot you were a girl," he said, knowing he wouldn't be able to handle her quick mind tonight. Although already he felt coming here was a good idea. Mary was perceptive as always, sensing how much he hated everyone coming up to him at Milton's. But that was Mary. He'd forgotten how much she used to take care of them, always suggesting a way to make him more comfortable or a better way to play a game or do some activity. "Not that I would forget that today," he added, giving her a side-glance as he downed more beer.

"What does that mean?" She didn't sound bent out of shape but more curious. In fact, she leaned forward, crossing her legs so her thighs were spread and only the small bit of denim covered her pussy.

Nate forced himself not to stare and wonder how smooth and soft her inner thighs might be. "It means I was a stupid kid, a boy. You ran around with us so much I guess I quit thinking of you as a girl and just treated you like one of us."

"Is that why you never asked me out?" She asked the question so quietly and immediately drank her beer after she spoke; it was almost as if she hadn't said anything.

Nate didn't drink often, but he didn't think he was feeling the alcohol that much after just starting his second beer. "Is that why I didn't ask you out?" he repeated, staring at her to make sure there wasn't something he'd just missed in her question.

Mary stared at him over the rim of her bottle, those captivating eyes of hers open wide and waiting as if his answer meant something to her.

"Why in the world would I have asked you out?"

Mary's expression fell and she hopped off the couch, hurrying to the kitchen so fast she disappeared before he managed to get around her coffee table.

"What the hell?" he demanded, entering her kitchen behind her, then stopping in his tracks as he stared at her perfectly round ass bent over as she dug around in her refrigerator.

"I wanted another beer," she explained, twisting the cap off and making a face as she did.

"I would have opened that for you." He wasn't sure if he should get closer to her or not. Mary wasn't a goofy girl with funny eyes and crooked pigtails anymore. And she had to know that. "Did I just say something wrong in there?" he asked, thumbing over his shoulder toward the living room.

"Actually, Nate, yes, you did." She bent over again, offering him another incredible ass shot. He could grab that ass, hold on tight, and position her just where he wanted her before he slid his cock—

Hell!

"Why wouldn't you have asked me out? What was so terribly wrong with me?" She put her beer on the counter next to her and crossed her arms, which forced her breasts to push together and show off even more cleavage.

"Wrong with you?" He wouldn't insult her when she was obviously serious by looking anywhere other than her face. "Damn, Mary. There was never a thing wrong with you. But you were my friend."

"You can't be friends with a girl you're dating?"

"No! Well, yes." Nate scrubbed his hair, eyeing her as she narrowed her gaze on him. "Why are we talking about this?" he demanded, deciding it would be safer to bail than try to hold up his end of this argument. Being friends, being best friends, with a lady he was dating would be an incredible yet very rare treat.

"I never thought of you as shallow," she said quietly, as if she was almost disappointed.

Nate decided he'd take the bait. She was challenging him, and in spite of her suddenly sober expression and the way she dropped her attention to her floor, he still knew what she was up to. Nate knew a thing or two about women. He wasn't a kid anymore, either.

"All right, darling, you've asked for it." He took a drink of his beer, then walked up to her and set it on the counter next to hers. "First, a direct answer to your first question. I never asked you out because I thought of you as one of the guys, as my running-around buddy. I was in high school and chased girls who would put out, as most guys did. If I'd ever thought you would be close to gaining a reputation like that I would have kicked your ass."

Mary didn't back up or create space between them. She shifted her hands to her hips, fisting them there, and stared up at him, her lips relaxed and slightly parted, making her look a hell of a lot more kissable than she probably realized at the moment.

"And second," he said, on a roll now and damned if he would let her get a word in before he made his point. "It would be the ideal to date someone who is your best friend, but we don't live in an ideal world. And I'm not one to rose-color everything when it just isn't that way." Today was a damn good example of that, although he decided talking to Mary about anything but John was probably the best way to end the day. "The simple fact is most men and women don't share the same interests. They can date, fall in love, and even marry, but they will always prefer to do things the other one doesn't care for. Like shopping, or fishing, or bowling, or baking pies."

"Nate Armstrong," she whispered, reminding him of the pigtailed girl who used to berate him more than he ever did her. "You're a chauvinist. Who would have thought that behind all that sex appeal you would be so narrow-minded?"

"Sex appeal?" This time he did let his attention drop to her breasts, and standing this close to her he had a damn good view.

Mary threw her hands up in the air and walked away from him. "I dog you twice in one sentence and that is all you hear?"

"Primarily because your insults weren't accurate."

"I like to shop, fish, bowl, and make pies. What the hell does that make me?"

"A good friend."

"But not a good girlfriend?"

There was no way he would let her win this argument. "I guess I'll have to chase down all your old boyfriends and ask their opinion on the matter," he said, clearing the distance between them again.

"Do you do that with every girl you go out with?"

"Nope." Not that he dated all that much. Work kept him

busy and most of the women in town he'd already gone out with, or they were married. "How else would I be able to accurately answer your question?"

Then because he wanted to, Nate lifted one of the soft curls off her shoulder. She hadn't taken her hair down since coming home, and he wondered what it would look like if it weren't pulled back and confined behind her head. Mary snapped her mouth shut and didn't move as he fondled her hair.

"Who all have you gone out with?" he asked, curious. He couldn't remember anyone saying anything about dating her.

"Not many." Her voice had changed, grown softer, huskier. "I dated a guy a while back who lived north of here in Mountain Grove."

"Dated? As in past tense?" Her hair looked like spun gold and was as soft as he imagined it would be.

"Yes. It ended over a year ago or so."

"Must not have been all that if you don't remember exactly when you two split up."

"It wasn't."

Nate shifted his attention to her face and caught her watching him play with her hair. He wasn't quite sure why it pleased him she wasn't dating anyone and referred to her previous boyfriend with casual indifference. It took some effort to stay on track with his argument, though. He would much rather simply learn more about her. Years had passed since they used to hang out all the time, and this woman standing in front of him really intrigued him. Hell, since arriving here he'd given little thought to John. All of his attention was on Mary.

"Doesn't sound as if he were a best friend."

That grabbed her attention. She looked up at Nate, her lips parting and her eyes dark and enticingly beautiful. "We weren't best friends, which is why it didn't work out."

"Now seriously, Mary. You don't believe a couple only

makes it if they are best friends. I know for a fact my mom and dad each have their best friends and they aren't each other. And last I checked they're still married after all these years."

"Good grief! Your parents fought as much as mine did."

"Married couples fight sometimes," he said soothingly. "Best friends fight sometimes, too."

"True." She didn't attack with a vicious comeback.

Had little Mary Hamilton mellowed out with age? The fire in her eyes belied that statement. Nate stared at her lips, wondering what it would be like to kiss them. There was passion inside her, unbridled and fiery. Not only did he see it in the way her cheeks flushed but also in the radiance in her eyes. Mary was damn near the sexiest woman he'd seen in ages, but body language spoke volumes in spite of the perfect curves and bare skin. She could have chosen a more modest outfit, although it was incredibly muggy outside. Mary moved with the confidence of a woman who knew what she had and knew how to use it. Suddenly he was dying to know what she'd learned over the years since they'd been best buds and he'd given little thought to her sexuality.

"Best friends can do other things, as well."

Nate lowered his head, watched her eyes open wider, and captured her mouth. He pulled her against him, feeling those large breasts against his chest. This time, unlike when she hugged him earlier, Mary didn't have a bra on and her nipples poked into his flesh, torturing him with feverish desire, which instantly turned into a raging fire he wanted her to put out.

She groaned, tilting her head back, and opened for him. Her fingers crawled up his arms to his shoulders, holding on tight as she leaned into him. His fingers trailed through her hair, tangling it and grabbing a handful. Then tugging, he forced her head back farther and impaled her mouth.

My God! Mary was the sweet nectar he never knew he

craved. He couldn't flaw her anywhere. And this submissive side of her, buried underneath a bold, brassy, and confident woman, turned him on even more than he thought it would.

Nate wasn't a chauvinist. He had no problem with women doing anything men did. But he wouldn't deny the turn-on when a strong woman capable of doing anything he could do relaxed and let him take charge when they were alone. Especially during sex. Maybe it was some part of his brain, still stuck in the dark ages, that made him want to dominate, take charge and control her actions, force her to yield to him and surrender completely. It was that level of trust that truly turned him on.

Keeping her head angled just how he wanted, Nate began a sultry dance in her mouth, drowning in her heat. She explored as much as he did, circling her tongue around his, neither hindering his progress nor trying to control it. Just kissing Mary got him harder than he'd been in ages. If there was a drop of blood in any part of his body other than his cock, he'd be damned surprised.

With his free hand, he traced the length of her spine, then enjoyed the soft curve of her ass. She was firm where she was supposed to be and mouthwatering soft where a woman should be soft.

"Nate," she gasped, turning her head and dragging in several quick breaths.

He squeezed his eyes shut, rational thought returning and kicking him in the ass at the same time. The blood in his cock flooded through his body as fast as it had drained and gotten him hard.

"God, Mary." He took a step backward, ready for her to kick his ass right out of her home. "I am so sorry."

When he looked at her she blinked, her lips still wet and swollen from his kiss. But as he watched, the brilliance in her eyes faded and she hugged herself, pulling her attention from his face at the same time.

"It's okay," she mumbled.

"Like hell it is. I'd tear into another man without a second thought for doing something like that. I took advantage of you. I shouldn't have done that. I'm so incredibly sorry that I did."

"You said that already."

"You're right." He turned, deciding leaving now before making a bigger ass out of himself would be smart. "Don't hate me, Mary. I swear. Sometime soon I'll take you to lunch. We'll laugh and joke about the old days and have a good time."

He paused after opening her front door, needing to look at her one last time. She'd followed him into the living room but still hugged herself. Her violet eyes were flat, closed off, when she simply nodded.

He knew he still wasn't thinking clearly. As he walked out of her house and pulled her door closed behind him, he swore he heard her say, "I could never hate you, Nate."

3

Mary stared out the window as a soft rain pattered against the panes. A month had passed since John Corelli died, and with all funeral and mourning time passing, the town had fallen back into its normal routine. Life went on. If only Mary could put that day out of her mind. She seemed permanently stuck on the day John died and the day Nate kissed her for the first time.

Only a few calls had come in so far that morning and the station was quiet. Odgers kept a small crew on the clock during the first half of the day over the summer. The town turned lazy, few people doing anything out of their daily routine. Without much to do, her mind had plenty of time to fantasize about Nate.

She hadn't seen Nate since and couldn't decide if that was good or not. Now she had the memory of what it felt like to be kissed by him. And it left her wanting more.

One would think a month after a kiss the fire would finally go out. Mary stood and stretched, feeling the yearning swell inside her as she lived through that perfect moment in time once again. The way Nate had held her, grabbed her hair, tilted her head just right, then impaled her with a fierceness she never knew she craved got her horny as hell every time she thought of it.

The light on her switchboard began blinking. She hadn't switched off her headphones when she'd stood.

"Damn, girl, do your job right and quit daydreaming about something that will never be finished." She plopped down in her seat and took the call. "Police," she said, staring, once again, at the raindrops as they smeared their way down the window.

Instant screaming and crying snapped her attention to the now solid red light in front of her.

"My stove is on fire! I can't put it out!" an older-sounding woman wailed into the phone.

"Okay, ma'am, calm down, please. Give me your address and we'll send help right away."

"I was just cooking my supper. But my show came on. I guess I lost track of time."

"Ma'am, what is your street address?" Mary knew how to remain calm, get the necessary information, and dispatch emergency assistance. Once she had all imperative information, she would stay on the line and calm down the person who had called.

"Three-fifty Ash."

That was in Mary's old neighborhood. "Are you in the house right now?"

As she spoke to the woman, Mary opened another line, already putting the call through to the fire station.

"Oh my God!" the woman screamed in Mary's ear.

"If you're in the house I need you to go outside." Mary muted the elderly woman but continued to listen as she connected with the fire station. "Are you the only one in the house?" she asked, after returning to the woman. "What is your name?"

"Yes. I live here alone. But . . . I need to get my supper."

"Firehouse Number Three," a deep male voice said into Mary's ear.

Mary's insides quickened as she immediately recognized Nate's voice. "I have a call on Three-fifty Ash," she said, then returned her attention to the older woman who was now babbling about curtains her mother had made. Mary stressed again that it was imperative the woman go outside. Then muting the lady on the phone again, she adjusted the other mic to her mouth.

"It sounds like she's elderly and growing confused," Mary stressed.

"Ten four. We're en route now."

Mary hesitated for only a moment before lowering her voice and almost whispering, "Be careful."

She was already returning her attention to the older woman, prepared to try to calm her until emergency vehicles showed up.

"I will be," Nate said, matching Mary's whisper with a deadly-sounding rumble that did a mean and twisted number to her entire equilibrium before he hung up.

"Ma'am, can you tell me your name?" Mary would be damned if she gave Nate the power to utter a few words into her ear and turn her brain into mush.

"Deloris Rose. Are you the fire department? I think a fireman should take care of this fire. I just can't let my mother's curtains get ruined."

"A fire truck will be there in a few minutes, Mrs. Rose. It would be helpful if you went outside so they know which house is yours." Mary lowered her head against her hand and closed her eyes, listening closely as she focused on working with the older woman. "Mrs. Rose, if the fire has spread to the curtains, it will move to the cabinets next. The smoke alone could hurt you bad enough you won't be able to get outside."

"But this is my kitchen."

"Mrs. Rose, go outside now. Can you leave through the front door?"

Deloris Rose started coughing and it took a few tries before Mary convinced her to get out of the house and only another minute before emergency vehicles were on the scene.

Mary didn't often hear the outcome of calls that came in through her switchboard. Usually that didn't bother her. But knowing Nate was putting out a fire and how deadly his job could be twisted her stomach in knots. She would be smart to find a man with a safe job, one where his life wasn't threatened daily. Before she'd given that thought enough time to develop in her head Mary knew she'd go nuts with a man like that and dub him boring as hell, just like his job, before the first date was over.

She'd never considered herself an adrenaline junkie. It didn't bother her being at the station all day. The other cops fought for the few high-profile cases that came into town. Mary was content with her switchboard and had been for almost ten years now. There were plenty of ways she could probably analyze this, but in the end it came down to one simple truth. Mary enjoyed life the best when things didn't change. Keeping it simple worked just fine in her book. That definitely disqualified her as an adrenaline junkie.

It also explained why she continued tormenting herself with wild fantasies of savage kisses in her kitchen. Although in her fantasies it went way beyond a heart-stopping kiss. She loved Nate and had since she was a child. That wasn't going to change, because Mary didn't do change.

"Who needs a counselor when you can analyze yourself so well?" Mary finished entering information on her calls into the computer. She always wrote everything on her notepad, then at the end of her shift entered the information in the program the station used. More than likely she did it this way since she'd been working at the station longer than they'd had the computer program. And again, it added up to her not accepting any unnecessary change.

So if she wasn't into changing how things were, it meant she would always love Nate and she'd never have him. "Are you going to endure this torture for the rest of your life? Remain single and alone?" she asked herself as she logged out of the program.

"What was that?" Lieutenant Jim Maddox asked.

Mary spun around. "I didn't hear you come in, Jim. And sorry," she muttered. "I was just grumbling to myself."

"It's not healthy to talk to yourself, Hamilton." Jim had a contagious grin, which he used a lot more lately since his baby daughter had been born a few months ago. "The best remedy is some of my wife's chocolate-chip cookies." He held out an aluminum pan wrapped in foil. "They're the best in the state," he promised.

"Sounds like a cure for all ailments." She wouldn't refuse him when he rocked up on his heels and held out the tray as if he were showing off rare diamonds he'd just found.

"So how'd the day go?" He leaned against the edge of her desk where the switchboard was and unwrapped the pan, revealing some delicious-looking cookies.

Mary politely took one, although she didn't have an appetite. After grabbing her purse off the floor, then placing the cookie next to it, Mary hurried into the break room, grabbed a couple of napkins, and returned. "This morning we had more calls than this afternoon. It's been quiet for the past hour or so."

She heard the door open to the station this time and turned when Patty Engel, her nighttime replacement, sauntered in chewing gum. The captain had warned Patty more than once about chewing gum while dispatching. Patty's father was mayor of Meredith Curve, and Patty seemed to think the world answered to her and not the other way around. Although in high school she'd been just as big of a bitch and her father had worked at the factory like most everyone else in town.

"Are those cookies?" she said, her squeal as annoying as her broad grin and the bright pink lip gloss she'd painted on way too thick.

Mary didn't get why Patty worked so hard to look good when no one would see her until after midnight when her shift ended. She let Patty swoon around Jim, who didn't appear to mind the flattery any more than he did another opportunity to brag about his wife. Mary wrapped her cookie in the napkins, grabbed her purse, and slipped out the door, mumbling good-bye as she left.

She'd spent a good part of her day figuring out why she seemed to enjoy putting herself through hell over one damn kiss. After determining it was due to love, she now needed to figure out the best way to handle things from here. There were two solutions as she saw it. One, forget about Nate and move on. Or two, find the man and make him hers. The first one meant changing the way she thought. The second one would mean changing the way she lived. Both of them meant changing, something she'd readily accepted she didn't like to do.

"Fine," she grumbled, scratching her hair loose from her head-band as she stepped around puddles in the asphalt to her car. "Just fantasize about him for the rest of your life."

But she'd lived through change over and over again in her life. It was a change when she left grade school and started high school. It was a change when she graduated and found a job. It was tough moving out of her parents' house and into her first apartment. But she hadn't minded a bit when she bought her house and moved again. So there were changes in her life she'd lived through just fine. Now it was time for one more change, and this was the big one.

"It's time to go get my man." She sounded a lot more confident than she felt.

The rain left the early evening noticeably cooler than it had been in ages. There were still a few good weeks left to summer, but she'd take the nice cool night when it was offered. Mary jumped into her car and headed out of the parking lot, determined to see through her plan before she chickened out. One drive by the fire station, though, and she confirmed Nate wasn't there. His Gran Torino wasn't parked out back. If his shift had ended, he would be home for the next two days. All the firefighters worked in shifts of two days on and two days off.

So he might be home.

"Which means you better hurry up before he falls asleep and doesn't hear someone at his door," she ordered herself, and followed the directions she'd memorized off MapQuest after doing a bit of snooping and learning where he lived. She hadn't been the only one who'd finally moved out of their parents' house, although Nate's parents still lived in the house Nate grew up in.

Nate lived just a few blocks from the fire station on a cul-de-sac that was lined with square brick fourplexes. Two apartments downstairs and two upstairs and each building with a parking lot in front of it instead of a yard. The tenants appeared to each have two stalls. Mary drove to the end of the cul-de-sac and turned around, coming back toward the main street and staring at Nate's apartment. His car wasn't there, either.

Where would he have gone after work?

Or maybe he wasn't through with his shift and had done a grocery store run or something. Mary knew the firefighters took turns running errands to keep their house stocked with supplies they needed to live there during their shifts.

There was only one way to end the torment she'd endured since Nate had kissed her, then sauntered out of her house apologizing. For some reason, the poor guy was grossly disillusioned into thinking she wasn't interested in him. And it was way past time to fix that. Mary was going to find him. When she did, she didn't plan on leaving until Nate Armstrong understood without a shred of doubt just how interested she was. If she had to tear off his clothes and throw him down, straddle him, and fuck him, she would do it, by God! Whatever it took. Her personal torture session was going to end.

She wanted Nate Armstrong and had all of her life. Mary knew how to get what she wanted. She worked hard, was honest and up-front. She didn't cheat and she didn't cut corners. Nate was available and she wanted him—no, needed him. It was time to take what should be hers and make it rightfully so.

Nate wasn't at the IGA. She did another run by the fire station house but still no Gran Torino. There was still a couple hours before dark and going home meant admitting defeat. She was on a mission, a mission to change her life for the better. If the way Nate kissed her meant anything, and she had to believe it did, he was interested in her, too. And he'd said he liked her. He'd told her they were friends when he was at her house. If Nate was one of those men who believed he couldn't date his friend, it was time for him to be reeducated.

"Enough already," she ordered herself, slapping her hand against the steering wheel. Mary ignored the teenagers in the car next to her when they gave her curious looks. "Where would you be, sweetheart?" she whispered, glancing up and down the cross street when she slowed for a red light.

There were several other places Nate could have gone to pick up supplies for the station house if he was still working. He could have gone to the hardware store or possibly done a late run to the post office, although it was closed by now. There was also the chance she'd missed him while he was en route to his house or the store. She could camp out in front of his apartment or at the station house. Both would draw attention to her, though.

Mary was already heading toward her old neighborhood before she decided consciously to do so. She would kill a bit of time, then run by his work and home again. Maple Street, where she grew up, ran almost from one end of town to the other. It broke off a couple times but picked up again and Mary turned on Tenth Street, then slowed and cruised the length of the road until she passed the Corelli house. Her old house was several doors down; then Nate's parents' house was across the street.

Everything looked the same, other than her parents' chairs were no longer on the front porch and her dad's pickup wasn't parked in the long, narrow driveway that curved around to the back of the house and the large detached garage. Her parents had been so excited about moving to the big city, Mary never let them know how sad it made her when they left. She cruised on, turning at the corner.

The next street was Ash. "Mrs. Rose," she muttered, glancing down the street, curious how badly the old woman's house had burned.

Mary almost jerked forward when she hit the brake too hard. At the end of the block, parked on the street, was Nate's Gran Torino.

"Gotcha!" she said, grinning, and the next moment wondered what he was doing over here.

She was already heading down the street when a frantic thought that maybe he had a girl over here he was seeing turned her stomach into a ball of nerves. That was an obstacle she hadn't considered. Mary pulled her car up behind Nate's when she saw the address of the house he was parked in front of.

Three-fifty Ash. This was Mrs. Rose's house.

Nate came bounding out of the house, whistling loud enough for Mary to hear inside her car, and came to a halt when he spotted her. There was an odd look on his face when he approached her warily.

"What's wrong?" he demanded, coming around the front of her car when Mary got out.

"Nothing."

Nate's expression immediately relaxed and he exhaled. "Christ, woman. I saw you there and immediately bristled thinking you were bringing me more bad news."

"You associate me with bad news?"

"No." He frowned at her, but those milk chocolate eyes showed no hostility. "Hell no, Mary." He exhaled and wiped sweat from his forehead, causing his brown hair to stand up and for a moment reminding her of the boy she used to know.

The man standing in front of her was anything but a boy, though. "What are you doing here?" she asked.

"I was about to ask you the same thing." He pointed with his thumb toward his car and turned as he did, pulling keys from his pocket and opening his trunk. "But if you really want to know, I was hanging new curtains."

Something swelled inside Mary. Mrs. Rose had been frantic about curtains over the phone. "You're replacing her curtains?" she whispered, worried her voice might crack with emotion. She never would have believed this side of Nate if she weren't seeing it for herself. Nate wasn't soft and compassionate. He was rough and tough and hard as nails.

"Mrs. Rose always tipped well when she was on my paper route back when I was a kid." He bent over the back of his car and dug around in his trunk.

Mary fought the urge to take a step back to better enjoy the view of all that tight muscle pressing against soft-looking faded jeans. His ass was definitely hard as nails. And rippled muscle across his back finished off the perfect picture and one hell of a mouthwatering view.

"I forgot about your paper route," she said under her breath, forcing her gaze up when he turned around with a hammer held in his hand.

"This should work." He looked at the hammer, then gave her his attention. "What are you doing here, Mary?"

This was where she told him the truth. There was no reason to hide her intentions. Her plan was to do exactly the opposite and make her thoughts perfectly clear to Nate.

"Sometimes I drive by my old house," she lied, and shrugged. "I saw your car parked here and grew curious. Plus, I admit I was worried about Mrs. Rose."

Nate didn't blink an eye at her explanation. He did surprise her, though, when he put his hand on her back and turned her toward the house.

"Come inside," he decided, guiding her along as he headed to the front door. "She isn't as with it as she was when we were kids, but Mrs. Rose is okay."

The house had an unbearable smoke smell and was hot and stuffy. Every window had been propped open but the breeze outside didn't cut it when it came to cooling down the inside of the dark, old home. Mary didn't notice any fire damage until she followed Nate into the kitchen.

"Mrs. Rose, this is Mary Hamilton," Nate announced, gesturing with his hammer as he stepped onto a chair that was pushed up against the kitchen sink. "She grew up across the street from me."

"Are you a cop?" Mrs. Rose stood from the other side of her small, round kitchen table and gathered her house robe together at her chest with small blue-veined hands that appeared to have a permanent shake to them. "It's good to hear we have a cop in the neighborhood."

Mary didn't bother correcting Mrs. Rose but instead extended her hand. "I'm so sorry about your fire but glad to see you're okay."

"I am not okay." The harshness in her tone suggested just the opposite. She gestured with her hand at Nate's butt. "Would you just look?"

Mary didn't mind at all getting another eyeful. "I see," she commented.

Nate looked down at her over his shoulder. There was no way he would know she meant his ass, so she simply looked up at him, keeping her expression neutral.

"Put yourself to good use, Hamilton." There was a glow in those milk chocolate eyes, as if he found Mrs. Rose incredibly amusing. "Grab that box of nails there and help me hang this new curtain rod."

"The fireman here knows I can't cook without my curtains." Mrs. Rose looked proudly at Nate's butt.

Mary leaned against the counter, picking up the box of nails and holding a couple up to Nate. She wondered if Mrs. Rose had any sexual interest still alive in her. The woman had to be in her eighties at least. She seemed perfectly content having a conversation with Nate's hard-as-steel rear end, though.

"And I have to have my dinner ready when my show comes on. Heaven sakes, if I don't fix it in time again, I'm likely to burn down my entire house."

"That isn't going to happen, right, Mrs. Rose?" Nate said while holding a nail between his lips. "You're going to stick to the new routine, right?"

"That's right." Mrs. Rose smiled and her face creased into hundreds of wrinkles. "I start my dinner at three thirty and have it ready by four thirty so I can relax before my show starts at five."

Mary was impressed the old woman remembered all that if Nate had just instructed her to abide by this new schedule. Apparently, though, watching Nate's rear end wore her out. By the time he finished hanging brand-new flowery curtains over her kitchen sink, Mrs. Rose announced she needed a nap.

"That was very nice of you." Mary walked alongside Nate to their cars, noticing it was quickly getting dark. "I honestly think I've seen a side of you just now I didn't know existed."

"What side is that?" He stepped in front of her to his trunk and unlocked it to put his tools away.

"You're a big softy." Mary grinned when he gave her a quick, hostile glare. "I just saw it with my own eyes."

Nate waved the hammer at her. "Tell anyone and you'll regret it."

"What are you going to do? Kiss me again?" She didn't mean to say it, but the words slipped out and there wasn't any taking them back.

Nate didn't look at her but replaced his tools and closed his trunk. Then stepping up onto the sidewalk, he moved into her space faster than she anticipated. In the next second, Nate yanked her against his virile body and grabbed both sides of her head.

She only had a moment to focus on the smoldering lust that ignited in his eyes before he closed his mouth over hers.

If his first kiss knocked her off her feet, this one would render her useless for the rest of the night. She might just have to call 911 to get home. Wouldn't Patty have a field day with that one?

Thoughts of anyone else faded out of Mary's mind when Nate tilted her head to the side and deepened the kiss. He growled into her mouth and Mary swore she damn near came right there on the sidewalk.

A heavy, large raindrop splashed on her nose and Mary jumped. Nate straightened, still holding the sides of her head, and kissed her nose right where the raindrop had hit her.

"Another thing you need to learn," he said, his voice low and grumbly.

"What's that?" she whispered, not wanting the moment to end, especially not the way it did last time. Her clever idea to snare him, and all the pointers she'd given herself while driving around town to find him, had disappeared out of her brain.

"I'm always up for a challenge." He gave her a crooked grin as his eyes danced with mischief and something a hell of a lot darker.

He wanted her. Damn it. Nate Armstrong wanted her as badly as she wanted him.

Another raindrop splashed down, this time landing at the top of Nate's forehead. "We better get the hell out of here before we're caught in a storm." He glanced at the sky as he let go of her. "It sure did get dark fast."

Mary just now noticed the black low-hanging clouds above them. She quit looking at the clouds when Nate left her standing there and hurried around to his driver's side door. A panic attack almost caused her to stumble when she flew off the curb.

"Don't you dare walk away from me a second time after kissing me like that." It was all she could do not to slap her hand over her mouth after she snapped at him.

Nate reached for his car door handle and froze, lifting his gaze to hers as more raindrops started splattering around them. Mary made it to the driver's side of her car and stopped. She'd said it and now it was time to follow through. Maybe Nate was just thickheaded enough that she needed to spell it out to him.

It was now or never. "Come home with me," she blurted out, then hurried to open her car door, one to get out of the rain before she was soaked and two so he wouldn't see how red and blotched her face suddenly was.

"I told my parents I would stop by," he said slowly, still frozen with his hand almost touching his door handle and his expression locked on hers.

"Oh." Mary didn't have a clue what to say next. Her experience picking up men was limited at best. She opened her car and put one foot inside, then met his hard look as she gripped the top of her car door. "Fine," she said, deciding she couldn't have been clearer than she was. She might have lost round one, but she had no intention of giving up.

Nate wanted her and he didn't seem the type to play hard to get. Not with the way the man kissed her. But if he had to see his parents, what the hell could she say to that? Nate was dedicated to his family, which was one of about a hundred traits in him that appealed to her.

He continued watching her when she slipped behind her steering wheel and closed her door. Mary gunned her car to life and kicked it into reverse; backing up, then shifting to drive, she pulled out around him, leaving him standing in the rain. He remained there, watching her, when she caught him in her rearview mirror. He was getting soaked as hell.

Nate begged off supper, then made his mother's disappointed expression fade when he told her he was simply exhausted.

"Let the boy go home and crash," Bruce Armstrong insisted, pulling his wife against him when he wrapped his arm around her waist. "Hell, Moni, he can eat with us anytime."

"You're right." Monica Armstrong smiled at her husband, then blessed Nate with the same loving look. "Did you help out Mrs. Rose?"

"Yup." He moved around his parents, scanning the counter until he found the cookie jar. It was full of oatmeal raisin, his father's favorite. Nate pulled out several and popped one into his mouth.

"At least let me send you home with a plate." His mom bustled around him, humming under her breath as she quickly put together a plate with pork chops and potatoes. "God knows you probably aren't eating right."

"Cookies all the way." He caught his father's smirk as his mother scowled at him.

"You're hopeless." Monica grinned at him, holding the wrapped plate in one hand and going up on her tiptoes and kissing him on the cheek. "And too good-looking for your own good. When are you bringing home a bride so your father and I can start harassing you about grandchildren?"

"Moni," his dad complained, saving Nate the trouble.

Mary Hamilton appeared in his mind, standing there next to her car as it started raining and waiting for him to accept her proposal—a proposal that could mean only one thing. The woman wanted him as desperately as he wanted her. He'd be insane to turn down an offer like that from someone as hot as Mary Hamilton. Yet he stood here instead of learning every inch of her sensual body. He had to be losing it.

"That won't happen if I'm walking around exhausted all the time," he informed his mother, taking the plate from her, then bending down and returning the kiss.

"Uh-huh." His mother had the same brown eyes he had and stared at him as if she read his thoughts easily. "Go get your beauty sleep then. Not that you need it."

"Come by this weekend and mow the yard for me." His father patted him on the back as Nate headed to the door. "This rain will stop later tonight."

"Will do," he said, stepping outside and preparing for a mad dash to his car. It was coming down in buckets outside. His father always had been a self-confirmed meteorologist, and most of the time he was right.

"I swear he smelled like perfume," Nate's mother said at the door loud enough for him to hear.

He bounded down the porch stairs and ran to his car, knowing she'd said it so he would hear her. His mother was always good when it came to reminding him there wasn't a thing he could pull over on her.

A few minutes later Nate pulled into Mary's driveway and parked. He stared at her house, and when a curtain moved in her front living room window he knew he'd been spotted. There wasn't any turning around now. He knew she'd felt rejected when he told her he needed to go to his parents'. If he'd been thinking straight he would have suggested coming over after he had dinner with them. Inviting her to his parents' house would have been too awkward. It wasn't as if his parents didn't know Mary really well. She grew up across the street and their parents had been good friends. But explaining why he'd brought her home with him when he didn't quite understand what he was doing here now would have been too painful. Especially when his mother probably would have figured out the truth of the matter before Nate did.

Mary dropped the curtain and turned her back to the window, tapping her fingers against her lips as her heart began pounding painfully. She would have a panic attack if she didn't get a grip, and Nate would be at her front door any minute.

She'd already changed into her long nightshirt, ready for an evening-long pity party and possibly a hot bath. Once her nerves calmed she planned on making herself a nice meal. It was imperative she not give up or start reading Nate's refusal as meaning anything other than what he'd said. He was going to his parents' for dinner.

But now he was here. Maybe if she'd hung around longer instead of peeling out of there Nate might have said he only planned on being over at his folks' for a bit. She'd humiliated herself, twice.

"Don't do it a third time." Mary bounded for her stairs, needing to change clothes before he came to the door.

She was halfway up the flight when there was a firm knock on her door.

"Crap," she said, skidding to a stop and looking over her shoulder at her front door.

There was nothing to do. He had shown up unexpectedly and was going to catch her looking anything other than her best.

Mary retraced her steps, reminding herself how she managed to keep her cool when victims calling in at the station were hysterical, hurt, or terrified. She had training. More than once she'd witnessed a crime that tore at her heart. Over the years she'd learned to wear her mask, keep her emotions under wrap, and maintain a clear head. If she didn't do that now she might risk her best opportunity to show Nate how they belonged together.

"Do this for your heart," she whispered when she reached the bottom of the stairs.

Mary sucked in a deep breath, ordered herself to relax and be cool, then unlocked her front door and opened it. "Change your mind?" she asked, breathing in the moisture in the air as a steady rain fell behind Nate.

His hair was wet and, although short, still managed to form small curls around his face. His clothes clung to him like a second skin, showing off enough bulging muscle for Mary to forget all orders to be cool. It was damn near all she could do not to gawk at the strong, dark, incredibly sexy man standing in her doorway.

"I wanted to apologize." Nate entered her home without invitation, forcing her to step to the side as he moved past her and into the middle of her living room. "I know I hurt your feelings and it took courage to extend your invitation."

"Not really." She was proud of how cool she sounded as she closed and locked her front door. The lock clicked and the thought that she'd just secured the two of them in her home sent a rush of confidence, along with something a lot needier, coursing through her body. "Two people don't kiss each other the way we do without something stronger brewing between them."

When he faced her, those dark eyes of his smoldered. He took his time letting his attention drag down her body, taking in every inch of her, and leaving sparks igniting her flesh until she sizzled with raw, damn-near-uncontrollable need.

"Were you headed to bed?"

She shrugged. "It wasn't as if I had a backup plan when you declined my offer." She walked past him into her kitchen, knowing he'd follow, which he did. "I figured I'd make supper and take a hot bath before bed."

"Do you want me to leave?"

"No," she said before she had time to think about it. It was the truth, though. Now that he was here, if he walked back out she wouldn't be able to approach him again. "I want you to stay," she said firmly.

Nate dragged his fingers through his short, wet hair, making it stand on end. He moved in on her slowly, his raw confidence a powerful mix with the turmoil burning in his eyes. It amazed her how well she read him. When he stopped, close enough their bodies almost touched, the fire burning inside her exploded as need surged inside her. Standing this close and not touching was worse than not having him here. Mary needed him inside her now, immediately, before she attacked him from cravings that had built over the years and ate her alive.

"What am I doing here?" His voice was raspy, rough, and tortured her as much as his nearness did.

"I think you know." She leaned her head back and drowned in his milk chocolate eyes.

Nate touched her face and her eyes fluttered shut. His fingertips raked over her skin, igniting charges of electricity that zapped her repeatedly as he moved his hands until he cupped her head.

"Look at me."

She opened her eyes.

"What do you want, Mary?"

"You." It was all she'd ever wanted. There was her work, this home, normal goals everyone worked toward. She'd accomplished those. But none of them had filled the gap inside her. And nothing would, until she secured her childhood love.

He searched her face for only a moment before lowering his mouth over hers.

4

Nate had stared into Mary's eyes so many times throughout his life. That didn't explain why suddenly he felt he was coming home. Her open submission, the way she looked up at him, her eyes glowing with passion and desire, drew him to her as if she were a magnet. A part of his mind argued this was Mary, the girl who had followed him around growing up, determined to do anything he did. Another part of him pointed all of this out but also reminded him how he had always looked out for her, made sure no one hurt her, that she didn't hurt herself. He'd protected her all his life. Why wouldn't they eventually come together?

He pressed his lips against hers, hardening to stone when she opened for him, and wrapped her arms around his neck. Mary leaned against him, letting him feel her body heat, how her heart pattered in her chest, and her full, round breasts with nipples hard enough to make his flesh tingle where they poked him.

The T-shirt she wore was a simple oversized shirt that fell to her thighs. It was a community service shirt, one they'd given out over a year ago to volunteers who assisted with cleaning up their city parks. He had one just like it. Obviously Mary's was a few sizes too large for her. Had she asked for that size on purpose, knowing she would use it to sleep in? It looked hot as hell on her.

Nate ran his hands down her back to her ass and found skin. When she groaned he fought for control. If she wanted this, he sure as hell wanted to give it to her. But if he did, it wouldn't be a one-night deal.

"I want to fuck you," he growled into her mouth.

She either laughed or choked. His eyes blurred when he raised his head to see her face. Violet eyes glistened under her hooded gaze. Her cheeks were flushed and her lips parted and moist.

"It's about time," she whispered.

"Oh yeah?" He needed her in a bed before he took her right here in the kitchen. She definitely giggled when he scooped her into his arms and headed toward her stairs. "Where's your bedroom?" he demanded, deciding he would understand what she meant by her comment later. Right now any discussion would be mute with the intense ringing in his ears and his body so hard and rigid it was all he could do to climb stairs.

"First door on the left."

Mary was surprisingly light considering how toned and firm her body was. He'd expected more muscle on her but reminded himself she spent most of her time answering phones. He knew she'd been required to undergo the same training all police officers go through during training. She might not be on the streets, but Mary's role was important. Anyone in town knew if they needed the police Mary would answer the phone, and although the mayor's daughter handled the night shift, no one reacted to her the way they did to Mary. She had a confident, relaxed tone that aided anyone in a crisis situation.

That wasn't the only part of her nature that really appealed to Nate. Her confidence didn't make her cocky or overbearing. There was her beauty, her body that drove him mad with desire, but what was inside her added to that physical beauty. Suddenly Nate understood Mary's comment about it being about time.

She'd been by his side for years, right there next to him. He remembered watching any boy like a hawk who asked her out. Nate always knew when she came home from a date. Any girl he'd taken out in high school would put out or get out of his car. He'd been an asshole about that. Which was why he'd never considered asking Mary out. Just the thought of anyone touching her the way he craved touching girls back then would make him mad with rage. He'd been too young to understand why during high school.

After school both of them had jumped into their careers, making the best of themselves. Nate went out with ladies from time to time. Now that he thought about it, he'd always compared them to Mary. Why hadn't he seen that before?

He'd been in love with her for years.

Crap!

Was she in love with him, too?

"This isn't a one-night deal." He laid her on her bed and straightened, stripping out of his clothes as he watched her face for her reaction.

When the corner of her mouth curved into a grin, his heart swelled until he was barely able to breathe.

"Nate," she began, coming up to her knees.

"Not now." He dropped his shirt to her floor, then kicked off his boots. "Later. When we can actually think straight."

Mary smiled as if he'd read her mind. Her eyes glowed in her dimly lit room and her shirt hung over her breasts, creasing and draping those wonderfully curved mounds. Her legs were slim and her thighs curved into hips he couldn't wait to grip as he drove deep inside her.

"What do you mean about this not being a one-night deal?" she asked when he was naked. Apparently she wasn't going to wait until his head was clear.

Nate didn't answer at first but instead took her shirt and pulled it over her head. He sucked in a hard, fast breath, ignoring her when her attention shot to his face. There couldn't possibly be any way she was insecure about her body or concerned he wouldn't love what he saw. Easing her down next to him, he began running kisses along the side of her neck. She smelled like fresh strawberries and tasted sweet and warm.

"How long have you wanted this?" he asked instead of answering. He found her pulse beating rapidly at the base of her neck and pressed his lips against the steady throbbing.

"A while," she whispered, her voice rough with need.

Nate lifted himself onto one arm, staring down at the sly grin on her face. She looked at him, showing him clearly with her expression that she didn't intend to clarify.

"A while, huh?" he asked, lowering his head and brushing her lips with his. "A day, a week, a month, all your life?" he whispered into her mouth.

"Does it matter?" she whispered back at him, her lashes fluttering until she decided to close her eyes and stretch like a cat against him. "Will it make any difference in how we proceed from here?"

"I've been a fool, Mary." He dragged his fingers from her belly button up her middle, watching her jerk under his touch as her breath caught. Her eyes flew open and she stared up at him, her mouth forming a small circle. "You've always been right here. Where the hell was I?"

"You've always been right here, too." She reached for him, taking his arm and pulling him on top of her.

Their bodies pressed together, flesh against flesh. As he began exploring, letting his hands move over skin softer than silk, his need to understand the intensity of his feelings and the emotions he read off Mary wouldn't leave him alone. The need to have her wrapped around him, her heat suffocating him as he worked to make up for lost time, possessed his body.

Mary explored every inch of Nate, running her fingers over bulging muscle and feeling it twitch under her touch. Everything about him was perfect, not that she didn't already know that. But there were things she didn't know about Nate, although she was learning quickly.

His cock stretched between them, pulsing against her thigh. It was long, thick, and incredibly hard. Her pussy swelled, moistened, anticipation creating pressure inside her she could barely sustain. She ached for that first release more than she did for her next breath. Apparently Nate seemed intent on prolonging her agony.

"Why didn't you ask me to do this sooner?" His eyes were so dark as he watched his fingers toy with her nipples. Charges of electrified cravings bolted down her insides every time he pinched or twisted the puckered flesh.

"I didn't know it was my job to point out the obvious." Mary gasped when he pinched a bit harder than he had before. Every inch of her jerked, then melted when he covered the tortured nipple with his scalding mouth and soothed it deliciously with moist, wet heat and his skilled tongue.

"It might be in certain areas from this point forward," he said, moving from one breast to the other.

From this point forward? And he'd been rather insistent about this not being a one-night thing. Did he think they would start dating? Had it really been that simple to snag Nate?

Mary barely managed the simple act of breathing as he fondled, kissed, stroked, and tugged her breasts. Her insides were swollen with turmoil and need, a crashing mixture if they both exploded at the same time. Nate went from barely giving her the time of day to staring at her as if she were his world. She'd never considered herself insensible. Fantasies had their place, but living in the real world proved a lot healthier. There was less disappointment that way. Nate was saying all the right things, treating her better than she ever imagined.

Maybe it was because imagining being with him hadn't been fantasies but simply a peek into how her life would become.

"I will guide you if you want me to," she whispered, and ran her fingertips over his soft, short hair.

Nate looked up at her, moving over her body as he did. "I don't have a problem with that, but I will always protect you."

Nate slid off her before she could stop him, and she tried. Mary grasped at air for her efforts. "Nate, what?" she began.

"Lie down," he instructed.

Mary watched him fish through his pant pocket. When he produced a small foil package, then crawled over her, Mary lay back on her bed and stretched her legs until they were around him.

"I've always protected you, Mary."

Before she could respond, his mouth found hers. Nate made love to her with his tongue as he moved over her, sheathed his cock, then positioned himself so his cock danced with excitement at the entrance of her pussy. She brought her legs up, stroking his sides as she arched off the bed and eagerly tried bringing her pussy closer to his cock. The tip of him was right there, stroking her entrance. Need enveloped her with so much force she damn near dragged her nails over his shoulders before he lifted himself off her and took her hands in his.

His fingers were long and strong. He wrapped them around hers, their hands clasped as he stared down at her. When he slid into her, his expression hardened, his lips pressing into a thin line as his eyes narrowed into slits and finally closed. A low groan built in him and finally escaped. She was positive she'd never seen a man happier.

Whatever emotions flushed inside him, they ignited in her, too. Heat tore at her flesh, sizzling and exploding like hundreds of tiny firecrackers one after the other as he filled and stretched her.

"Mary," he grunted, his voice raw and gravelly. "My God, darling!"

"Yes," she breathed, saying what came out without being able to give it much thought. "More, Nate. All of it. Now."

He obliged with one fluid thrust. Everything erupted when he filled her completely. Her world ignited, light suddenly shimmering around her and growing darker, warmer, until she was engulfed with a sensual heat that swept her out of her life as she knew it. With that first orgasm, Mary experienced sudden clarity. Her body pulsed and tingled, and her mind knew she'd just melded with her soul mate.

It took a moment to focus, but Mary didn't want to miss a moment of their lovemaking. She curled into him, allowing him to go deeper. It mattered so much to feel every inch of him, watch his expressions change from hard concentration to desperate efforts for control.

"You're so tight. So perfect," Nate gasped, letting go of her hands and lowering himself over her as he began a hard, steady rhythm.

It was perfect. Nate's chest hair brushed over the tips of her nipples, electrifying her as he plummeted again and again, deep into her womb. Pressure built and released. Her world climaxed and crashed blissfully. Bright colors turned warm and sultry. The highs and the lows of their lovemaking made for an ideal combination, which sent her floating. It were as if she eased out of her body, riding so hard on the perfection coursing through her body, she experienced sensations she'd never known before.

Mary wasn't a virgin. Neither of them were. Nate's roguish

behavior when he was younger had torn at her heart. But what they shared now, the emotional and physical climaxes he rode right along with her, were sensations she'd never known before.

The moment Nate's body hardened, Mary focused and opened her eyes, suddenly seeing him and everything around her with incredible clarity. He swelled inside her as muscles bulged under his skin. His chest rippled and the cloud of chest hair before her was irresistible to her touch.

When she placed her fingers on him, Nate's eyes opened and he stared at her. "I can't hold on anymore," he grunted.

If she could have told him she hadn't been able to hold on for quite a while now, she would have. Instead she drowned in his perfect milk chocolate eyes, praying he'd meant what he said. This couldn't be the only time they ever made love. She would die if it were. As Nate came, filling her, draining all he had inside her, he also claimed her heart.

Nate stared at Mary's ceiling. She'd cuddled up next to him and her breathing had slowly calmed. They were a perfect fit together. Taking any relationship beyond something sexual was new territory for him. Thinking about doing that after having fucked a woman only once was even newer territory. His insides had curled into a ball. When he should be sated, he felt tense. It would be wonderful drifting off to sleep with Mary, yet his brain spun around with nauseating turmoil.

As her breathing deepened, he thought of crawling out of bed, sliding into his clothes, and leaving. It was the coward's way out and he knew many men might do just that. He'd been the one who'd told her this wouldn't be a one-night stand. Nor did he want it to be. That was what scared the hell out of him.

He wanted Mary. Wanted her as his woman. There was a thick, warm sensation wrapped around his heart and it had drifted into his brain. He worried it might be love and didn't for the life of him know what to do about it.

Were they compatible?

Nate couldn't say he didn't know Mary. They'd been close to each other since early grade school. There were years after high school when they hadn't seen each other every day. But when she was around, he'd always known it. At city functions, when he answered the dispatch phone, when he'd gone out with friends, if Mary was around he knew it.

He thought about a time just over a month ago when he'd seen her at one of the local bars. She'd been out with a few girlfriends, but Mary hadn't looked as if she'd really been with them. She'd sat at the bar, nursing her beer, smiled, laughed, and watched her friends dance or flirt with other men. More than once she'd looked his way, her smile changing, growing more sensual, needy. She'd known they were meant to be together long before he'd figured it out. Now that he had, why the hell was it scaring him to death?

He remembered how pretty she'd looked with her blonde hair down and her figure-hugging short dress showing off her large breasts and perfectly shaped legs. More than one man had approached her, a few of them blocking his view. Once he'd actually considered talking to her himself, deciding it might be a good idea if he played official chaperone, especially when he knew the creeps who tried coming on to her.

Mary had held on to her smile when each guy walked away and every time had eventually shifted her attention back to Nate. Now that he thought about it, possibly she kept looking at him because he was watching her. He'd given her signals and he hadn't realized it.

Nate stared down at Mary and casually brushed a loose strand of blonde hair away from her face. Her thick, dark lashes fluttered over her eyes and slowly they opened. He loved how she stretched like a cat, arching her back as she raised her arms and straightened her legs, pressing every inch of her warm, sultry body against his.

"You're so much better than I ever imagined you would be," she told him, her eyes pure violet as she stared up at him.

Nate swore she looked so open, so trusting and devoted. Men would kill to have a woman adore them as Mary appeared to do him at that moment. And the feeling rushing over his flesh, leaving him feeling more alive, and sizzling with intense male satisfaction was an incredibly good feeling.

"You've got a few skills of your own." He tapped her nose, grinning when she wrinkled it.

"Are you hungry?"

He hadn't given food a thought, but as she mentioned it his stomach growled his answer for him. Mary's smile broadened and she started to push herself out of the bed. Nate grabbed her, flattening her on her bed and trapping her there with his body.

"I'm starving," he muttered. "The food can wait, though."

He fucked her again, this time flipping her over on all fours and taking her from behind. Feeling her from different angles, drowning in her heat as she pulled him deep inside her, taking all he had and holding on to it as if she never planned on letting go, pushed him over the edge faster the second time.

It didn't stop them from making love again. He wanted her off the bed, against the wall, leaning over the bed, then over the kitchen table. By the time it was late into the evening, Nate wasn't sure he'd be able to stand, let alone drive home.

They were in her living room, after having sex on the stairs and ending up with Mary bent over her coffee table. Nate loved the shape of her ass, the way his sheathed cock disappeared inside her and reappeared coated with her thick, white cream. No matter how many times he took her, no matter the positions, she didn't slow down or beg him off. Instead Mary devoured all he gave her as if she'd been starving, parched, and her body drank from him greedily.

"Good Lord," she cried out, collapsing over her coffee table, still on her knees with her arms stretched out over her head. She turned her face to the side, her cheek flushed a deep rose as her blonde hair fell to her shoulders, damp and in thick strands that clung to her neck. "I give; you win," she said, managing a laugh.

Nate knelt behind her, his entire body sore and so damned sated he doubted he would be able to take her again that evening if he tried, not to mention, he was pretty sure they'd just used the last condom. He ran his hand up her back and she made a purring sound, arching against his touch and offering a mouthwatering view of her round, soft ass and her soaked pussy.

"I'm just glad you said it first."

Mary laughed and attempted rolling over. Her legs tangled with his and he pulled her to the living room floor. Both of their bodies were damp and the smell of sex hung heavily in the air. Parts of him were numb as other parts of him felt more alive than he'd felt in ages.

"Have we made up for lost time yet?" she asked.

He shifted so he could see her face. She searched his expression and her smile faded, although not from her eyes. There wasn't any way she'd be able to hide her happiness if she tried. It was another thing Nate had learned throughout the evening. Each time they made love it became clearer to him. He read Mary like an open book. When she hesitated, she pursed her lips as if she might blow a kiss. When she wasn't sure about something, her violet eyes turned more blue. And when she was floating in bliss, Mary's eyes were the most perfect shade of violet and her cheeks rosy with life and contentment.

He'd never thought of her before as so easy to understand. Women usually were confusing as hell. Nate understood now it was because none of them had been his woman. He brushed her damp hair from her face, enjoying how her lashes fluttered, but her body remained completely relaxed. A trust and unspoken commitment already existed between them. Nate couldn't say how long it had been there. But it wasn't bridged this evening.

Now he knew how he'd ended up over here. It made perfect sense why Mary had so boldly suggested he come over. There wasn't any doubt why he'd so greedily kissed her before tonight. She was his soul mate, his other half—his better half.

"I'm not sure we'll ever make up for lost time," he told her, feeling himself sober as he continued stroking the rosy shade covering her cheek. "But I don't regret the past any more than I will the future."

"Why is that?" Her face grew serious, too, as she studied him.

"Because you've always been mine, Mary."

Her expression didn't change. She watched him, looking as if she waited for him to say more. There was more to say. He felt it. But words weren't falling out of him. All he could tell her was what had been on his mind. Although speaking it out loud made it sound ridiculous instead of being the incredible revelation he'd felt when the realizations had first surfaced in his brain.

"I've watched you all my life." He forced himself to say what he thought she wanted to hear. "I've always been there, making sure you were safe, making sure no men harassed you."

"If I'd chased the girls away from you, you would have been pissed."

Nate decided he really liked the way her freckles came forward when she wrinkled her nose at him. He moved his fingers over them, stroking her nose until she shook her head. The damp strands of hair fanned over her face.

"It ate me alive every time you drove off with one of those

bimbos." She tried lifting her hand from between them and brushing her hair away.

Nate did the job for her, wanting her to remain cuddled next to him. He wasn't ready to stand and discover how much they'd overdone it that evening. Right now he felt good, perfect even. Soon enough he would endure sore muscles, but he doubted it would come with any regret.

"You make it sound as if there were so many."

"There were too many," she stressed, answering immediately. "Granted it was the worst during high school."

"And every time any girl climbed into my car you were right there, too, my dear," he reminded her. There were a few girls he regretted trying to seduce. More than one of them had an agenda.

Mary's face turned stubborn and she straightened against him. In spite of knowing he wouldn't be making love to her again right away, his cock still reacted to her moving her body against him, brushing her hip into his cock as she tried rolling so she was on top of him. It was a position he could live with and he lifted her, rolling flat on his back and allowing her to straddle him.

She stared down at him, her hair falling forward around her face. "That was because I didn't want them to be with you. I wanted you to notice me."

"Trust me, sweetheart. I noticed you."

"You didn't treat me the way you did all those other girls."

"I didn't like them."

"You were out fucking girls you didn't like?"

It was on the tip of his tongue to tell her he hadn't fucked any of them other than two at the end of his senior year. He wouldn't put himself on the defensive and wasn't sure she'd believe him, anyway. This wouldn't be about him trying to convince her he'd always loved her. Up until earlier this evening, he hadn't realized how strongly the emotion had been bubbling inside him, simmering and waiting for the right moment to explode and consume him. When it had, it had felt better than any of the times he'd come this evening. Loving Mary made his life complete.

"I seem to remember more than a few jocks stepping over their clumsy feet to get next to you."

"There were a few." She bent her arms and rested her weight on her forearms as she crossed them over his chest. "None of them were you, Nate. You were the only man I've ever wanted."

"God, Mary." He wrapped his arms around her, pulling her closer and kissing her.

Mary cupped his face, her legs stretched and the heat from her pussy scorched his flesh as she moaned into his mouth. He managed to lift both of them into a sitting position, keeping her facing him with her legs stretched out behind him. Even as they continued kissing, the ringing sound in his fogged brain seemed to grow louder. More than likely a really good meal was in order. They would shower and cuddle in bed. He knew Mary had to work in the morning, but he had the next two days off. Although he'd promised to mow his dad's yard, he wanted to spend every minute he could with Mary.

"Nate." Mary broke off the kiss and pushed against him, trying to stand up.

It was instinct at play now. He tightened his grip, needing her next to him.

"Nate," she repeated. "I think it's your phone. It's not my ringtone."

The fog snapped out of his brain and he turned his head, finally hearing his phone ringing while his brain still stumbled over all of his newfound knowledge of Mary.

"Crap," he moaned, moving to stand and pulling Mary up with him.

He didn't say anything when she clung to him for a moment. It wouldn't surprise him a bit if he'd fucked her enough she wouldn't be able to stand without wobbling for a bit. She managed to hold her own, though, when he headed up her stairs to her bedroom.

His ringtone was intentionally louder than most phones' because of his line of work. Although the firefighters used headpieces and two-way radios to communicate with each other, there were times when he didn't want to miss a phone call, especially if it was from his parents, while he was in the truck or in the fire station with all the noise from the other guys echoing off the high ceilings.

By the time he'd found his phone on the floor, it had stopped ringing. Apparently it had fallen out of his pant pocket when he'd anxiously stripped earlier. It was lying faceup and the screen was still lit up in the dark room when he picked it up.

Mary stood in the doorway naked, with her hair delightfully tousled, as she flipped on her bedroom light. "Is it important?" she asked.

Nate stared at the number, his stomach twisting in knots all over again, although this time they weren't as life changing as they'd been with Mary.

"It was the firehouse number." Work didn't call on his days off. None of the firefighters did that to each other. Although he'd gotten some sleep at the firehouse during his last shift, he'd also worked one of the worst fires he'd worked in a long time and it had killed his lifelong friend.

John! What would John think about him and Mary? Nate stared at the phone, knowing Mary had said something but for a moment not hearing her. John would be proud. If anything, he'd probably tell both of them it was about time they pulled their heads out of their asses and saw the light. A crushing amount of sadness threatened to knock the wind out of Nate.

John would need to be his best man. There wasn't anyone else. Any man who stood with him at the altar would know he was simply a stand-in for the man who should be there.

It was wrong, not fair, fucking unreasonable as hell. John shouldn't have died. He was supposed to remain alive. A memory hit Nate that he'd forgotten about. Back in high school when they were juniors, possibly seniors, he and John had a serious heart-to-heart. Nate seemed to remember it had occurred right after they'd had one terrible fight. He and John had fought more times than Nate cared to count, each time ending up with both of them nursing bloody noses and a few bruises and enough grass stains to get yelled at by their mothers.

John had told him he knew who Nate would marry. In fact, he'd laughed in Nate's face, telling him it was so obvious only a numbskull wouldn't see it. Nate continued staring at his phone as he remembered his best friend's words.

Even our mothers already know who your wife will be. Everyone knows. You're the only one too dense to see the obvious.

They'd fought again after that. Nate had bulldozed John, demanding to be told what the entire goddamn town was saying about him. He'd never had a serious girlfriend. There were girls. There were always girls. But he never cared about any of them or gave them as much as a thought when they weren't around.

"I'd completely forgotten about that," he muttered under his breath.

"Forgot about what?" Mary came up around him, looking at his face, then his phone he still held in his hand. "Was there something you were supposed to do?"

She'd misunderstood what he'd said and thought he'd just received a phone call from someone reminding him he was supposed to be somewhere else. It was his perfect out, if he'd wanted to take one. Nate looked at her, letting John drift from his thoughts and gazing into her pretty eyes that were suddenly filled with concern and slowly masking all those radiant emotions that had made her glow all evening. She was waiting for Nate to hurt her.

And apparently he'd been a blind son of a bitch for enough years she was ready for it to happen. There was no doubt in his mind now who John had been talking about.

"I'm not going anywhere." The words were worth it just to watch the shadow of doubt and concern fade from her face and her eyes and once again the happy glow return.

"Who called?" she asked, nodding at his phone.

"Work."

Mary nodded, understanding. And she would. They were both in lines of work where emergencies didn't mean unplanned meetings in the morning with bigwigs that all of them suddenly needed to prepare for. In their lines of work, an emergency meant someone's life was in danger.

"Go ahead and call them back. I'll grab clean towels and we can shower before eating. Does that sound good?" Already she'd walked out of her room, that perfect ass of hers shifting from side to side as she disappeared around the doorway and down her hall.

Nate followed her, watching her reach into a narrow closet and pull out two thick towels, then flip a light on in her bathroom. When she bent over her bath to turn on the water, his dick danced in appreciation and awe. He could get used to following her around her house while she was naked.

Somehow he managed to return the call and put the phone to his ear as it rang.

"Firehouse Number Three." It was Mike Holden, who was two years older than Nate and had been a firefighter longer than Nate. They never worked the same shift. Mike and his crew came on when Nate and the others took their two days off.

"Mike, it's Nate. Did you just call me?"

"Yeah, buddy. Sorry to wake you up. We're calling in everyone, man. I'm really sorry, but dress out. There was an explosion out at the grade school and several of the houses to the east of the school have already burst into flames."

5

Mary stood at her open front door, watching Nate back out of her driveway. The urge to run after him, beg him to let her go with him, made it impossible to stand still. This wasn't high school. Nate wasn't taking off to go run around with his buddies or cruise the main strip in town or chase girls. He was going to work.

Her cell phone chirped from her kitchen and she backed up, closing her door and flipping the lock before heading to her phone. A mixture of satisfaction and trepidation made for a bad combination in the pit of her gut. She grabbed her phone, tugging on her nightshirt Nate had lifted off her only hours before. Now he was gone.

"Hello?" she asked, not recognizing the number.

"Lock your door." Nate's deep baritone curled around her like a warm, comfortable blanket.

"I already did."

"You don't know how good you looked standing in the doorway watching me leave."

Mary laughed in spite of the sickening feeling growing inside her. Her hair was a tangled, damp mess and her oversized nightshirt clung to the perspiration drying on her body. "I look like shit, but thanks."

"No, you don't." He sounded amused. "You look very well fucked. And I made you look that way. I'm rather proud of my work."

"I'm rather proud of your work, too." She leaned on the counter, resting her chin on her hand, and drew invisible circles with her finger as she listened to him breathing on the other end of the line. "It was wonderful, Nate," she admitted.

"Do you want me to come back tonight?"

His question lifted the churning in her gut, although the trepidation still hung heavily inside her. "I would love that."

"I don't know how long I'll be out."

"I know." It crossed her mind to call Patty. She would have taken the initial call before dispatching it and might know more details than what Mary already knew. "I'm sorry you didn't get a shower before you left."

Nate snorted. "I'll be ten times as dirty when I'm done."

"It sounds like one hell of a fire."

"I can see the smoke already and it's dark."

The trepidation grew to fear. "Please be careful."

"This is what I do, Mary." Something changed in his tone.

Mary understood. Firefighters needed women by their side who were as strong as they were. Their work was incredibly dangerous, possibly the most dangerous of all emergency jobs. They walked into the blaze, confronted the flames, and were very well trained to do so. Her thoughts lingered to John and a sick feeling rose to her throat.

"Even the best-trained firefighters risk danger," she whispered.

"Yes, we do."

She sighed. "I know you'll be careful."

"I always am. It can be a very dangerous job, sweetheart."

Something in his tone lingered between them. He was pulling back, unsure. Mary was, too. Entering into a relationship with Nate was what she'd always wanted. Why had she never given thought to the worry and panic she would endure every time there was a fire. Her life was good, busy, and fulfilling. She had her own home. She did well at her job. Her place in the town was secure and she was well liked.

But then, so was Nate, on all the same aspects. No one would cringe or bat an eye if they suddenly announced they were a couple. The fear existed only between Nate and her. As they'd made love she'd seen into his eyes. They had never been darker or deeper. And while he and Mary had fucked, taking each other in so many different positions, learning every intimate detail about each other, she hadn't doubted the feelings between them.

It was normal to have doubt afterward, right?

"I know how dangerous your job is. I dispatch the calls to you, remember?" She hoped her tone sounded light. Then deciding changing the subject might be a good idea, she added, "I'm trying to remember if I know anyone who lives alongside the grade school."

Meredith Curve had one grade school and one high school. Their town was small but strong in community. It wouldn't surprise her if quite a few volunteers showed up to help put out the fire.

The sound of Nate's car engine faded in the background as a car door opened and closed. He sounded winded, as if he was sprinting to his apartment, then hurrying around inside gathering his clothes.

"They're all families with kids." Nate didn't elaborate or comment on whether he knew anyone over there by the school.

Maybe he didn't focus on whose house it was or who might be in serious danger but simply focused on the fire. "I wonder how the school exploded. That doesn't sound right."

"I don't know."

"If it was a bomb, or intentionally started by someone, it could be a fire burning with chemicals." She knew a bit about the different types of fires and different methods used to put them out.

"I'll find out when I get there." He grunted, mumbled something about her holding on a second; then there were background sounds, probably as he changed into uniform. "I'm heading back out now," he informed her a minute later.

Mary continued leaning against her counter, tapping her finger against her lips. "Would you know if there was going to be another explosion?"

"I'm backup on this. I won't know anything until Holden briefs me."

Mike Holden had always been a creep. He thought he was God's gift to all women and more than once had asked Mary out, refusing to accept she wouldn't be interested in dating a man like him. Just the thought of Nate's life being in that jerk's hands turned her stomach even more.

"Is he a good firefighter?" she asked.

"Seems to be." Nate didn't elaborate, and once again she heard his car engine gun to life.

Mary was bothering him. Nate couldn't think about her right now and focus on his work. It was imperative he do his job perfectly, not just for his safety but also to protect all others in danger from the fire.

"I guess I should let you go. Please be safe."

"Mary, this is what I do."

"I know that, Nate. Just promise you won't try and be a hero."

"Yup."

She'd lost him, for now. Nate was in firefighter mode. Her father and grandfather were firemen and Mary understood when they put everything out of their heads other than dealing with the crisis at hand.

There wasn't any way she could soak in a long, hot bath and she didn't have an appetite at all. Mary opted for a quick, steamy shower, then got dressed afterward and pulled her hair back into a ponytail at her nape. Pacing the house all night wouldn't do her any good. Mary knew her town and she knew her people. In a crisis situation everyone got out and helped. Granted, they would have to stay back while the firefighters did their job. But as soon as people were rendered homeless, someone in town was right there to take them in, make sure they had clothes and food, and see to all their needs.

Her man was fighting this fire. Mary didn't want to stay home and wait for him to return. Mary's mother hadn't paced a path into the living room floor. When Mary's dad was called out on a really bad fire, Mary stayed home alone, safe and sound, while her mother went out with her man, standing by if he needed her and there the moment he was out of danger. Mary would do the same.

Nate parked his car two blocks away. Heading down the street toward the fire, he breathed in thick black smoke that grew eye-watering dangerous before he'd neared the scene. Holden held a two-way as he stood beside the larger of their firehouse's two trucks. Already Nate saw the fire had damn near surpassed their equipment's ability to put it out. With the right skills and a bit of luck, they possibly would be able to control it so it wouldn't spread farther. Nate scanned the two houses next to the school. The house closer to the school yard was already on fire. Smoke billowed out of windows of the second house. They needed to drench that house to prevent spreading.

Campbell was on the other truck, bellowing orders as he

gestured wildly and held a cell phone to one ear and a two-way to his other. Nate bypassed Holden and headed over to Campbell.

"We've got one hell of a goddamn mess. That's what we got!" Campbell yelled into his phone. "Hell yes, I'm running this show. We've got backup here." Campbell turned his head when Nate approached. "Armstrong is here now. You hold out a bit longer and we'll send in reinforcements. Keep your head straight."

Nate glanced over his shoulder at Mike Holden and understood. Holden ran the night shift. Nate had guessed he'd show up and take orders from Holden, which didn't appeal to him. The guy was a prick. But Nate knew how to follow the chain of command. His personal feelings didn't get in the way with dealing with a fire. All the way here he'd lectured himself about following Holden's command and to not think about Mary.

But Holden wasn't running this show. Campbell had shown up, which forced Holden to step down. So how was Holden handling it? He was standing over by his truck and sulking, instead of jumping into the pits of hell and bringing the fire under control. Nate shook his head and returned his attention to Campbell as he moved closer to hear what the older man wanted him to do.

Campbell looked at Nate as he moved closer but didn't hang up his cell phone until Nate stood in front of him.

"You look worn-out," Campbell snapped, giving Nate a quick once-over before returning his attention to the fire.

"I'm good. Where do you want me?"

Campbell glanced at Nate again but pulled out his two-way when it began chirping, and listened to the broken comments in between bouts of eruptive static.

"I think we've got the school stable for now." Campbell spoke to Nate but kept his attention on the two houses.

Nate had known Fire Chief Campbell since his father and

Mary's father were volunteer firemen on this force. The man was better at paying attention to two or more situations than anyone else Nate had ever known.

"Who is in the first house?" Nate asked, stepping closer to Campbell.

"Rivers and Montgomery."

"You've got two probies bringing that fire under control?" Nate complained, ignoring the tilt of Campbell's eyebrow as he shot Nate a side-glance. "I'm going in, make sure they've got everything under control."

"You'll stand by." Campbell didn't bark his order. He spoke calmly and with the cool authority of someone who already knew he was respected and that no one would dare challenge his decision.

Nate stared at the dark, ominous windowpanes on the first floor of the house. They reminded him of black eyes, of a soulless creature who was burned alive inside. A creature all too capable of taking human life without blinking an eye, and contemplating whether or not to do just that. It suddenly looked just like the old house on Maple, which was now an empty lot. It was gone and so was John.

They wouldn't lose another firefighter tonight.

"Chief, I'm fine," Nate stressed, moving closer to the older man. He could ignore Campbell's order to stand by and march into the house and take over. Rivers and Montgomery were both in their early twenties, and although Nate had never worked with them before since they worked the opposite shift, both men would respect his rank and follow his instruction. Nate respected the chief too much, though, to go against his orders. "I've got this one. I promise. Let me go in."

"Armstrong," Campbell said, giving Nate his full attention. "You've just come off shift. Two reliable witnesses reported your car has been parked at Mary Hamilton's house. I'm guessing you haven't slept in a good twenty-four hours."

Nate looked at Campbell. Word was already around town that he'd been at Mary's?

"I'm fine," he stressed.

Campbell didn't say anything but looked past Nate. He followed the chief's gaze and squinted at the two vehicles coming down the street, their bright paint jobs visible even through the smoke as they drove along the school yard and parked on the street a block away when they couldn't get any closer.

"Well hell," Campbell muttered.

It was no secret the chief hated dealing with the press. Something collapsed inside the house and Nate jumped. Campbell cursed and started yelling into his two-way radio. Nate studied the structure, ignoring the reporters who were probably running around the school, anxious to get the latest story and report it to everyone in Meredith Curve who wasn't already there.

Nate glanced over his shoulder, staring at all the people lining the edge of the school yard and standing silently in the night, watching and waiting for whatever might break into flames next. His father used to tell him people loved drama. Even something as horrific and deadly as a fire, where people might die and those who lived scarred forever, sometimes homeless, and too often robbed or irreplaceable personal items that meant so much only to them. There were those who would stand around and gawk, utter their words of sympathy, while others returned to their safe and comfortable homes to make a casserole. All these people had one thing in common: They all believed the firefighters on the scene would soon have the fire out.

Nate thought of John and wondered if he might be nearby, waiting, watching to make sure everyone would be okay. There wasn't any doubt in Nate's mind John wouldn't want any deaths.

"I'm going in," Nate decided, turning to the truck to pull off necessary supplies.

Campbell was barking into his two-way, but Nate knew the chief heard him. Nate could have whispered his intention to disobey a direct order and Campbell would hear it.

Nate pulled out a helmet, tested the radio inside, then strapped it to his head. He flipped on the speaker, fully ready for Campbell to start yelling at him. When Nate was ready, he marched past Campbell, then broke into a run and entered the house.

"Rivers is in the far back bedroom on the left side of the hall." Campbell wasn't yelling. He quietly explained to Nate where the other men were. "Montgomery should be visible."

"Negative," Nate said, squinting and flipping the switch to the large flashlight he'd carried in with him. "Montgomery!" he yelled through the thick, rolling smoke. "Chief!" he continued yelling. "That sound we heard was the ceiling falling in on the right front corner of the living room."

A spew of profanity filled Nate's head. Campbell was known for his colorful words. Nate let the man rant without trying to communicate; instead he searched the living room, scanning it with the beam of his flashlight.

"Montgomery!" he yelled again, running the circular beam over the ceiling.

Drywall hung in torn clumps and long wooden beams had split, their splintered black ends looking like bones protruding out of a deadly wound. The house was going to collapse, just as the one he'd been in last month had done. Montgomery wouldn't go with it, though.

"Don't worry, John," Nate whispered.

His thoughts went to Mary as he repeated his scan over the fallen ceiling, this time training the beam on the floor and squatting, his breathing coming hard and rough in his mask.

He'd heard the tension in her voice over the phone. Her father and grandfather had both worked for the volunteer fire department. Mary knew the dangers involved in his line of work. Knowing and living with it firsthand were two very different things, though. She wanted him. Their feelings had evolved way past those of casual friends during the first couple of times they'd made love. That didn't mean Mary would be able to carry through with her emotions knowing Nate's life would be put in danger occasionally, when fires like this broke out.

An incredibly loud crackling sound split through the air. Nate ducked to the ground, rolling to his side as his hands went to protect his head. Another beam split through the ceiling, this time in the hallway.

"Campbell!" he yelled into his mouthpiece. "Get Rivers out of here, now! Secure the other house. I'll find Montgomery."

"Armstrong!" Campbell bellowed.

"Do it!" Nate yelled, staring hard at the new beam, which was now on the floor.

The smoke around him was damn near black as coal. Seeing through it was hard to do. As he rolled again, tender muscles in his legs from an evening that had started out so perfectly screamed in protest when he sprang to his feet. In the next moment, he broke out the front window, giving the smoke an outlet.

"Montgomery? Can you hear me? It's Armstrong. I'm getting you out of here, so hang tight." He should be able to see the man if he was in the living room. Smoke rolled out of the window, but it was still damn hard to see.

"Nate, I'm giving you five minutes; then we're pulling you out of there." Campbell sounded oddly calm. "God might be on your side, though. It's pouring again."

Nate glanced at the broken window. Through slow rolling black smoke, he couldn't tell if it was raining outside or not. "Thanks, John," he whispered.

"What was that?" Campbell asked.

"Someone's on our side," Nate said, returning his attention to the room as he started crawling through the fallen beams and Sheetrock. Nate reached inside his helmet, breathing in a gulpful of nauseating smoke. He coughed until his eyes burned and watered, but managed to flip off his microphone. "Okay, John," he whispered, adjusting his helmet after his coughing fit subsided. "Where's Montgomery? Do you see him?"

Nate grabbed one of the beams and pulled it off another beam. More smoke wrapped around him, and the temperature in the room reached dangerous levels. He swore his uniform started melting to his skin. His muscles burned throughout his entire body, which kept Mary on his mind. Had she gone to bed? Was she waiting up for him? Or had she decided falling in love with a firefighter wasn't what she'd thought it would be? It sucked they hadn't been able to spend more time together, bond, and establish a relationship with roots deep enough that a fire like this wouldn't destroy them. He planned on building that foundation right away.

One night of lovemaking, followed by one of the worst fires he'd ever endured, for the second time in just over a month, wasn't enough time to secure him in her heart. Mary might easily decide he wasn't worth the pain and fear of losing him. He would return to her house when this was over. He made that decision and it encouraged him to dig deeper, tossing drywall and broken beams out of the way as he searched for Montgomery.

"A boot!" he yelled. "John! We found him!"

Nate started laughing, which spurred on another coughing fit. Frantically scraping debris off the downed firefighter, he finally had everything cleared off Montgomery and yanked off his glove to search for a pulse.

"He's alive!" Nate hurried to turn on his mic and got an earful immediately from Campbell, who'd apparently been screaming at him ever since he'd turned it off.

"He's alive!" Nate repeated, collapsing to the ground next to Montgomery as exhaustion suddenly hit him so hard he worried he might not be able to stand.

"How far are you from the front door?" Odgers's voice came through clearly. The police had obviously stepped in to help.

Nate tried turning to see the door. "Not far." He couldn't see shit through the thick smoke.

"Can you bring him out? How hurt is he?"

"He's got a pulse, but he's not responding. He was buried under a few fallen beams, but I think it was the falling drywall that knocked him out. There's no way to determine if anything is broken." Nate could barely see his hand. Heat engulfed him, making it hard to breathe even with the helmet and mask on his face and head. "John helped me find him."

Campbell started barking orders. They weren't directed at Nate. He crawled to the downed man, touching the man's face and searching for blood. He didn't see any. His equilibrium seemed to be off kilter. Nate swore the floor was starting to slant. He braced his feet so he wouldn't slide into Montgomery.

"Hold on, buddy," he said, for a moment seeing John and not Montgomery. "You won't die again on me. I won't allow it."

Nate ran his hand down the back of Montgomery's head, still not finding blood but feeling a decent-sized lump.

"It's just a knock to the head, old boy. You're thickheaded enough it won't hurt you any. I've never known a man more stubborn than you, Johnny boy."

Apparently Montgomery felt the need to bring Nate back down to earth. He coughed and blinked, staring blankly at Nate through his dirty mask. His mouth moved, but Nate didn't hear what he said. Nate stared and his brain shifted as he stared at Shawn Montgomery and not John Corelli.

"Can you stand?" Nate asked, raising his voice as he realized the crackling from burning wood exploded around them so loudly it was impossible to hear anything, including his own voice. Another minute in this house with his brain seeing and talking to people who weren't there and both of them would be dead.

Nate reached for Montgomery and the younger man held out his hand, gripping Nate's. A few minutes later the man stood, willingly wrapping his arm around Nate's shoulder. It just took a few steps toward the door for the rest of Nate's rational thinking to kick in. At this rate, they'd never make it to the door in time.

"I sure as hell hope nothing is broken inside you," Nate grumbled, turning to Montgomery and lifting the man, then tossing him over his shoulder as if he were a very large and incredibly heavy bag of potatoes.

Nate damn near fell on his face when Montgomery relaxed, almost crushing Nate with his weight. Nate put one foot in front of the other, focusing his thoughts on Mary and carrying her up her stairs. That had been nothing, and he'd moved up a flight with a hard-on that had raged with enough fierceness it almost threw him off balance. He would get out of this house and he would carry her up that flight of stairs again. It wasn't his time to go. He hadn't thought it was John's time, either, but Nate's lifelong friend was dead. Nate wasn't; Mary wasn't. And he wanted a future with her.

Nate saw the door. The damn thing had shut. Nate didn't remember when it had shut. He'd left it open when he entered the house. How in the hell was he supposed to open it with a two-hundred-pound man draped over his shoulder?

"Campbell!" he yelled into his mic. "Open the goddamn door."

"What? Repeat, Armstrong. Open the door?"

He hadn't stuttered. "Open the fucking door. My hands are full."

"Armstrong, the front door is wide open. Hold your position. We're coming in."

The door was open? Nate spun around and crashed into a wall. Montgomery howled and stiffened, his uniform belt grinding into Nate's shoulder. Nate swore the asshole had ripped his uniform to shreds and filleted his flesh while he was at it.

"Christ almighty!" Nate wailed, fighting to hold on to his balance and not let Montgomery slide to the ground. "Relax, damn it, or I swear I'll leave your ass in here to melt."

That would be the last thing he would ever do and Nate didn't doubt for a moment Montgomery already knew that. The man relaxed, though, once again turning into a boneless mass of incredibly too much weight as his arms draped over one side of Nate and his heavy legs, with his heavy steel boots, barely missed kicking him in the balls.

An explosion shook the house as the staircase crashed. Wood split and shattered, falling into black holes. Other fragments of burning wood floated upward as flames whipped around them. The heat in the room reached dangerous levels. Nate's lungs burned so badly the ventilation in his helmet wasn't cutting it against the fire quickly closing in around them.

The clothes both he and Montgomery wore were completely fire retardant, according to multiple tests they had endured in order to pass safety codes required for firefighters to wear them. Nate wasn't convinced he wouldn't melt inside them, leaving his body no longer identifiable but clothed in the intact uniform.

"Cut it out," he grunted to himself, wheezing against the thick smoke that was now successfully burning his eyes in spite of the protective helmet he wore. Which at the moment felt as if it weighed a good hundred pounds.

There would be no morbid thoughts. "Sorry, John," he said under his breath, searching the growing flames as they taunted him and maneuvered themselves as if they plotted to trap him in the house. Smoke shifted and grew, taking on different shapes and making it damn hard to tell what around him was real and what wasn't. He might have to let Campbell know he had been right. Nate was exhausted. His eyes were playing tricks on him. Already he'd lost the front door, which supposedly was wide open. "Damn it, buddy," he complained, squinting to see in front of his face. "You'd be a good friend right now to get me to the goddamned front door."

Something tall and rectangular appeared through the waves of smoke. Nate forced one foot in front of the other. There was the front door. He was sure of it. He grinned, thanking his lifelong best friend in his head at the same time as Holden and Randy Smith stormed into the burning house.

Nate had never been happier to see either man.

Nate stumbled outside as rain pounded the ground. He ripped off his headgear and shook his head, feeling his world teeter but no longer caring. Holden and Smith took Montgomery from him as paramedics rushed to them. Raindrops splashed on his face, in his eyes and his mouth. Nate stumbled away from all of them, enjoying every fresh breath of air he inhaled.

"It's going to be damn hard to give you an award when you're being reprimanded." Campbell gave Nate a look that was as close to a grin as the chief ever came. "You're definitely going to give me a detailed report," he continued. "Talking to dead people," he grumbled, turning away.

Nate was about to ask why he would be reprimanded, or awarded, for that matter, when the structure of the house collapsed and men around him shouted as hard sprays of water continued dousing it from the long hoses extending from the trucks. As if trying to compete, immediately following the explosion thunder roared from the sky and lightning lit up the night.

The quick light showed Nate a small group of reporters, hovering under umbrellas and snapping pictures. Jennifer Wilson, one of the reporters and someone he'd seen a few times over the years for a quick fuck, grinned and waved. She said something to her cameraman and he shot a picture of Nate. Jennifer's smile turned toothy. She expected him to come talk to her, possibly give her an exclusive. It wouldn't surprise him if she wanted more than news for her article. Neither was going to happen, though. There was only one woman he wanted to see.

He didn't give Jennifer more than a moment's attention when he spotted Mary. She looked like a drowned rat as she hurried forward, her concerned expression changing into a wide, happy smile as she started running.

If the reporters weren't sure a burning house would grab everyone's attention, they sure as hell would shift their focus to Mary Hamilton when she leapt into Nate's arms, wrapping hers around his neck and laughing.

"Thank God you're okay," she whispered into his ear as she clung to him.

She jumped back, letting go of him just as quickly when he staggered, suddenly feeling as if he'd just tied one on.

"Oh hell, Nate." Mary slipped her arm around his waist and searched the crowd around them. "I wonder if I can take you home yet."

She was here. Better than that, she was here at his side, already thinking for him, making sure he was taken care of, and ready to step up to bat for him when she'd decided he'd had enough fun. This was what it felt like to have a woman by his side, what some men so callously referred to as their ball and chain. Nate felt anything but trapped. His heart swelled over her concern. At the same time, though, exhausted or not, he couldn't leave if there was still work to be done.

"I'll let you know when I can leave." Nate started to move and caught the chief giving the two of them a rather curious stare. Campbell wasn't the only one watching them. The firefighters and paramedics glanced their way repeatedly as they walked along with Montgomery, who was now secured in a gurney.

"You can barely stand," Mary complained, moving so she stood facing Nate. Her soft violet eyes were loaded with concern. "Nate," she said, speaking quietly so they weren't overheard. "You've been awake over twenty-four hours, haven't you? And with everything that we did," she added, then let her voice trail off.

A hell of a lot had happened just this evening. Finally seeing how Mary had been his all along was overwhelming in itself. Hours of mind-blowing sex and he had to admit he was lucky to still be standing.

"I'm fine," he told her stubbornly, and absently shoved a wet strand of hair that had escaped her ponytail behind her ear.

"You forget," she said, her tone still calm but her eyes focused and staring up at him. "I grew up in a firefighter's home and I don't know how often I heard my mom tell my father if he didn't keep up on his sleep he would make a situation dangerous by not thinking straight. So please, let's see if we can't get you home to bed."

He watched her cheeks flush and her eyes darken to their pure, raw natural color as she suggested taking him to bed. Nate doubted he would be able to do much else other than crash on his pillow at this point. But give him a bit of sleep and, with Mary cuddled next to him, he didn't doubt for a moment he would wake up eager to consummate their new relationship all over again.

"Now if this is going to mean you aren't going to dispatch any of the good fires to us anymore, I might have something to say about all of this." Campbell actually grinned as he rocked up on his toes and smiled approvingly at Mary as she leaned into Nate. "And I am sorry, Miss Mary, but I'm not sure you're going to be able to hold this stubborn brute up much longer."

"I think you might be right about that. I told him he needed sleep."

"Mary," Nate warned under his breath.

She pressed her lips together, but her eyes glowed with satisfaction as she beamed up at him.

"You think you can drive him home?" Campbell turned serious and focused on Mary, ignoring Nate.

"No one is driving me anywhere," Nate informed the chief. "I drove myself here and I can drive home."

"From what I hear you can't even find a front door."

"I drove here as well," Mary said softly, chewing her lower lip.

"I doubt anyone would ticket your car, Mary. Take the man home. He's already a hero. Let's keep him that way."

"A hero?" Mary's grin seemed to make the night a bit brighter.

6

Mary sipped coffee and stared at the morning paper. The front page was plastered with several impressive pictures of the house fire next to the school, as well as a rather large shot of her leaping into Nate's arms.

She stared at the picture, which showed her backside, her hair pulled into a ponytail, and her arms wrapped around Nate's neck. His arms were possessively pinning her against him. She glared at the caption underneath the picture of the two of them, knowing Jennifer Wilson, the bimbo who'd stalked Nate during high school and flirted with him like a brazen hussy throughout their adult life, had written the article about the fire and the captions underneath each picture.

The caption under Nate's picture rudely and boldly stated: *Hero of the day, firefighter Nate Armstrong, Who will be in his arms next week?*

Jennifer was jealous, having tried over the years repeatedly to snag Nate and now having learned she'd finally failed. Mary had Nate now and didn't plan on ever letting him go.

The phone rang at the same time the light lit up on her

switchboard. Mary lowered her mic in front of her mouth and answered the call. "Police," she said, holding on to her professional voice in spite of how that front-page picture pissed her off.

A cruel whisper hissed into her ear, "Have you figured out who started the fires yet?"

Mary instinctively checked to make sure the call was being recorded. "What fires?" she asked, her heart suddenly pounding in her chest.

"Those two house fires. I almost got rid of both of them."

Mary stared at her switchboard, not blinking once. No one else was in the station right now. The new kid, Lawrence Pearson, was on crossing guard duty, Meyers was in the patrol car cruising the town, and Odgers was down at city hall visiting with the mayor.

She straightened, knowing she could handle this. If everyone on duty were at the station they'd be huddling around her making her nervous. This way she could think clearly, and the first thing she heard from her caller was that he claimed responsibility for two fires, one of which had killed a firefighter.

"Who else were you trying to get rid of?" she asked, locking her fingers together tightly and staring at the small light that showed the call was recording.

"Oh, come on, Mary," the man said, his voice dropping a notch. He chuckled. "I bet even you could figure that out."

He was speaking to her as if she knew him. Mary would worry later about who he could be. Right now, she needed as much information out of this man as she could get.

"That's why I answer the phones; I'm not an investigator," she said, also laughing, and at the same time reaching for her second phone to contact the captain. Being alone while talking to this creep might have its advantages, but it was her job to alert Odgers or report a possible crime as soon as possible.

"You're one of the lucky ones, though. Your good looks will

get you far in life. Those who aren't as blessed spend their entire life struggling and being ignored. But I'm smarter than the most gorgeous person in this piss-ass town," he informed her, his tone turning sinister. "I figured out how to get everyone's attention. And this call has confirmed what I already guessed. You stupid cops don't have a clue about those fires. Pretty people spend their time fornicating and ignore obvious clues until they disappear and fade away."

"It sounds like I'm not one of the pretty people." She didn't want to chide him, but at the same time, anything and everything he said would be used against him. Already he'd given her some valuable information. "If you and I are the same, maybe you could give me a hint about one of those clues you mentioned."

His laughter turned her stomach, bringing bile to her throat as she activated her backup phone, then clipped it to the recorder that would send out an automatic message once the captain picked up. He would be told there was an emergency at the station and to return ASAP.

"Every single clue is already in your pretty little head," the caller whispered.

Mary watched the light on the recorder begin flashing, telling her Captain Odgers was hearing the emergency message right now. She returned her attention to the switchboard, then closed her eyes, trying to concentrate.

"Your voice sounds familiar to me. Do we know each other?"

"It does?"

She panicked when his voice suddenly sounded rushed, frantic. "Please don't hang up."

"So now you want to talk to me, when before all you had time to do was run after fire-chasing assholes."

What? Mary's jaw dropped. Her caller was talking about Nate and John, who were also the two men he wanted dead.

This guy had killed John and wanted Nate dead. But why? And if he knew she'd chased after Nate and John that meant he grew up with her. Who the hell was he?

"I have plenty of time now." She fought to keep her voice calm. "And I don't chase assholes anymore."

"I knew you'd see how they really were. Good looks don't make a person, Mary. Do you know that? You have to see what is inside."

He paused for a moment, but Mary couldn't think of a thing to say. Her mind raced, trying to remember every kid in her grade while growing up. For the most part, other than a few students coming and going, she went to school with the same kids from kindergarten through her senior year in high school. If she could just keep this guy talking maybe she'd figure out who he was.

"What did you think of my fires?" he asked, whispering again.

Mary snapped her attention to the doorway leading to the main entrance and exhaled, grabbing her heart, when Odgers damn near slid into her cubicle area.

"What?" he began.

Mary waved her hand, using her other hand to cover her lips with her fingers, indicating the captain should be quiet. She flipped the switch to put her caller on speaker while Odgers continued looking at her wide-eyed, his gray hairs standing up, windblown, over his brown hair.

"I thought they were quite beautiful, didn't you?" the caller asked. "Wait a minute. Why do I sound different?" he demanded, his tone turning harsh.

Mary stood, continuing to gesture to her captain, whose expression still looked bewildered.

"It's okay. I put you on speaker. I needed more coffee."

"No! I'm not talking to anyone but you, Mary."

"Don't worry," she said, laughing and ignoring the strange

look Odgers gave her. "I'm here all alone. Everyone else is out on their beat for the day."

"Really?"

"Sure. That's how it always is." She tried sounding relaxed and cheerful as she scribbled on the notepad in front of her.

She wrote: *He started the two house fires.* Then added: *Killed John Corelli.*

Captain Odgers's eyes grew wide as he moved closer to her switchboard.

"Now if that doesn't just prove to me how much all those cops are assholes."

"Why do you say that?" Mary asked, glancing at her captain when he pulled his cell out of his pocket.

"Because a beautiful woman is alone at the police station all day long while those jerks skip around town in their fancy uniforms thinking they are all that. But they aren't. No one is protecting you."

"Maybe you should protect me," Mary said, lowering her voice.

"Mary," he said, suddenly sounding exasperated. "I'm a very, very intelligent person. If guys with brains got all the pussy instead of guys with brawn, every lady in this town would be tripping over the others to get to me. I know if I came down there, you would arrest me."

"I can't arrest anyone, silly," Mary said. She thought she lied pretty well and almost grinned at the odd look the captain gave her. "All I do is answer the phones."

"You're proving to me more and more what idiots our cops are. No wonder they didn't guess those two fires were started on purpose. And I hate that there has to be a third, but it will be necessary. Then you'll open your eyes and realize good looks don't matter as much as brains."

"Why is a third fire necessary?" Mary asked, turning in her chair when Odgers jumped up with his cell pressed to his ear.

He moved into the hallway, probably so he could speak and not be heard, but continually glanced at her and the switchboard.

"Because, sweet Mary, you're fucking Nate Armstrong."

Mary spun back around, gawking at her switchboard. "What? Why do you say that?" she stammered. Had the entire town come to that conclusion after seeing her leap into Nate's arms plastered across the front page of the paper?

"You're too damn smart for him, Mary. I know you haven't forgotten. Think! Think!" the caller began yelling. "Think and remember. You always were the smartest," he said, his voice a cool, chilling rumble through the phone. "Next to me, of course."

There was a click and Mary leapt out of her chair. "Are you there?" she said. "Hello, are you there?" Then she slapped her desk in front of the switchboard. "Damn it!" she hissed, yanking off her earpiece when the light that was lit up showing the caller was on the line went dead.

An hour later, Campbell, the fire chief, and Odgers talked quietly in the break room. Mary flipped her switchboard to speaker and paced, desperately wanting to be part of their conversation yet knowing she had to man the phones. There hadn't been a call the entire time Campbell had been here, as if the entire town were hushed in quiet anticipation, already aware of the caller who had claimed responsibility for killing a fire-fighter, threatened to kill another, and said he did all of it because of Mary.

"Campbell told Odgers they already suspected arson on the fire that killed Corelli." Jeremy had returned in the cruiser shortly after Campbell showed up and had dubbed himself official eavesdropper. He'd made himself at home in the doorway of the break room, commenting from time to time on something the chief or captain said, as if he were supposed to be part of their conversation. Then just as easily, he'd slip away from the break room and come to her to give her an update. "Now Mary, you need to think," he said, narrowing his brows as he gave her a firm look. "This fruit loop is starting fires and killing firefighters for you. Who do you think he is?"

She hadn't thought about anything else and was pretty sure she told Jeremy as much with a look. "I don't know." And it was bugging her to death. "There's something familiar about his voice."

"Mary?" Odgers yelled from the break room.

Mary stepped around Jeremy and entered the break room. "Yes?"

"Meyers, man the phones!" Odgers yelled, then, without waiting for a response, gestured to the chair in between him and Campbell. "Have a seat, Mary."

Mary did and stared at the tape recorder in the middle of the table, noticing it wasn't on. The two men had been listening to the phone call.

"There are a few things this guy says that I want to ask you about."

"Okay."

"First of all, he is claiming responsibility for two house fires in the past month. Campbell tells me his men have already determined a small handmade bomb was ignited in the furnace of the first house fire," Odgers said, letting his words fade off. He didn't have to add that it was the fire that had killed John. The knowledge hung heavily in the air around them. "His men are over at the house that burned last night by the school. If they determine a bomb was ignited in the furnace, then our caller is more than likely definitely for real."

It hadn't crossed her mind that they didn't believe the caller at first. Mary had had a few prank calls over the years but none that sounded as twisted and weird as this call. He was too crazy not to be for real.

"We've got commonalities in the two houses." Campbell

took over the conversation. "Both homes were old, made out of wood, had outdoor entrances to cellars that weren't used as part of the family dwelling, and would go up in flame quickly if a fire was intentionally started."

"So our guy is either familiar with fires or simply observant and made good guesses on which houses would easily ignite into flame."

Campbell nodded. "It isn't rocket science with some of these old homes. And the guy made a point of saying how smart he was."

"Which leads me to a question," Odgers said.

Mary pulled her attention from Campbell and switched it to Odgers. Her captain was watching her with those watery eyes and his bushy eyebrows pulled tightly together. "I want you to think hard, Mary. He says you already have all the answers."

"I know." Mary relaxed her face in her hands for a moment. "I keep hearing him say that in my head and wish to God I knew what he meant by it."

"He also said you were the smartest in your class other than him."

"Anyone who went to school with me would know I often made honor roll." She wasn't bragging. "There were several of us who usually got the award at the end of each semester."

"Were there different levels?" Odgers asked.

Mary wondered if he knew whether his kids ever made honors or not. He didn't sound familiar with the award for grades, and Mary was pretty sure the schools still gave out the small ribbons for students who pulled all A's.

"Actually, there were. There were high honors, honors, and second honors. If you got all A's, you got high honors. I think one B was honors and two B's were second honors."

"Which one did you usually get? And was there someone who always did better than you?"

"Lord, Captain. That was a long time ago." She lowered her

head again, dragged her fingers through her hair, and barely noticed when they tangled where her hair was tied back. She tried remembering grade school, then high school. Memories of being in the gym: her name being called, and standing and facing everyone when she was handed a ribbon for her hard efforts. Everyone would applaud and she'd always searched the kids' faces on the bleachers until she found Nate. Usually he had made a face at her. "I remember the award ceremonies, but they all seem to run together. That was a long time ago."

"I understand," Campbell said, reaching out and patting her hands, which she hadn't realized until that moment she'd clasped together until her knuckles were white. "I'm happy if I can remember last week sometimes. But we still have a firefighter in danger," he added, his tone clipped and concerned.

His words grabbed Mary's attention. And she was sure that was his intention. He studied her, understanding crossing his face. "We're going to make sure nothing happens to Nate," he added, and cleared his throat. "I've already sent one of my guys over to his place to check on him and he isn't there."

Campbell didn't say anything else but stared at her. Mary dropped her gaze but wouldn't put her privacy over Nate's safety. "He is asleep at my house," she said under her breath.

Thankfully neither man reacted to her admission. Campbell did pull out his phone, though, and placed a call. "Armstrong is over at Mary Hamilton's house sleeping. You know where she lives? ... Okay, good. Go wake him up. I want someone with him until we have this cleared up."

Mary glanced from her captain to the fire chief, more than anything wanting to race out of the break room and over to her house. She wanted to be with Nate. He would be safe and at the same time he would protect her. No crazy person would hurt either of them if they were together.

"What's that?" Campbell asked, still on the phone and looking at her and Odgers for the first time since his conversation began. "Positive confirmation? You're sure?" He paused and nodded. "Excellent. Very good.... Yes. Go check on Armstrong. Have him give me a call."

He hung up his phone and stared at Odgers. "Both houses burned as a result of a homemade bomb being tossed into the furnace."

"Interesting." Odgers scratched his nose, focusing on the tape recorder. "Mary, I need you to try really hard to remember the names of the other students who made honors while you were in school."

Nate grumbled as he headed down the stairs, ready to give whoever it was pounding on Mary's front door a piece of his mind. They were hitting it hard enough to break it down and they were about to learn the hard way she wasn't unprotected anymore.

Nate flipped the lock and yanked the door open, then glared at a runt of a man standing in front of him, his fist raised to knock again. "Did I wake you?" he asked, shifting his weight from one foot to the other.

"What do you want?" Nate growled, and tried hard not to stare at the scars all over the puny man's face.

"Captain Odgers sent me over here, sir."

Nate stiffened, the fog lifting from his brain in the next second as he stared at the strange small man. "What's wrong? Who are you?"

The small man laughed, "It doesn't surprise me you don't remember me, Nate. But we went to school together. I'm Dudley Milestone. I started down at the station about a month ago, helping with reports and filing. I work with Mary."

The strange little man's face lit up as he mentioned Mary. There was something vaguely familiar around the guy's eyes, but Nate was pretty sure he'd remember a guy who looked like this.

"Is there something wrong with her?"

Again Dudley shifted his weight. "There is," he said almost inaudibly.

"What?" Nate didn't mean to yell and scowled when the little guy winced. "What's wrong with Mary?"

"They sent me over to get you." Dudley began wringing his hands. "Someone called into the station this morning and claimed responsibility for the two house fires in the past month, including the one that killed John Corelli," the guy added, dropping his voice to a dramatic whisper.

"Wait right there." Nate raced up the stairs, taking them two at a time, and damn near dove into his clothes. He was coming back down the stairs with his shoes and socks in hand, still barefoot. His shirt wasn't tucked in and he wasn't going to think about what his hair looked like. It was his day off and Mary was upset. He would take care of her first and worry about him later. "Let's go."

He frowned when his car wasn't in the driveway. Then remembering Mary had driven his car to her house last night, he figured she must have used it to get to work this morning. She wouldn't have had a way to get back to her car until she got off work and he drove her to it.

"You're driving," he told Dudley, and glanced across the street when an older woman stood at her front door staring at him. Let the neighbors talk. They would just have to get accustomed to seeing him with Mary. "And gun it, little man," Nate ordered, managing to squeeze his tall frame into the small car before adjusting the seat to give himself enough legroom so he could put on his shoes.

The grotesque little man looked incredibly proud of himself.

Mary paced the hallway between the break room and her dispatch cubicle. The captain was in the front hallway, talking quietly on his phone as he stared out the large window facing the street. It was after three. Two more hours and she was out of here. Once she was alone with Nate it would be easier to put all of this into perspective. The fire chief had headed back to his station, his morose look mirroring her own expression. She tapped her finger against her lips as she repeated the call in her head.

There wasn't any reason to play it back again. Since this morning she'd heard the recorded call a handful of times and it played in her head repeatedly, the man's voice taunting her.

"I've already got all the answers," she mumbled, wishing she could make sense of it. All she could figure was the man meant she already knew him. Hell, she knew everyone in Meredith Curve. There weren't many in town her age she hadn't gone to school with. She couldn't think of anyone she knew who would intentionally start a fire.

Although today someone had proved they weren't as right as she'd thought. Mary never would believe one of their own would hurt anyone in town. Meredith Curve had its bad guys, crooks and vandals. But as long as she'd been on the force, there had not been one single murder. She'd witnessed a few accidental deaths. Tragedies happened. They were awful. And up until this morning she had thought that was what John's death was, a terrible tragedy.

Now she knew he'd been murdered.

"Mary, we need to talk." Odgers stopped her pacing when he appeared in the hallway.

The door to the police station opened and a wave of thick perfume floated toward her. She peeked around the doorway as Odgers turned and groaned.

"Is it true you received a threatening phone call this morning, Miss Hamilton?" Jennifer Wilson was a splash of pink with too much makeup on her face and perfume applied heavily enough to be nauseating.

"Where did you hear that?" Mary didn't see what Nate had ever seen in this bitch.

"Jennifer, you need to hold on for a few minutes." Odgers took Mary by the arm and started escorting her away from the reporter.

"I heard the caller holds you responsible for John Corelli's death?" Jennifer called out, ignoring Captain Odgers's comment about waiting a few minutes. Her singsong voice rang off the walls of the station. "Is it true there is an insane man in town so infatuated with you that he is trying to kill another of our honored firefighters?"

Mary tripped over her own feet, Jennifer's words slicing through her like a sharp knife.

"Mary." Odgers almost pulled her into the break room and turned her, holding both of her arms now. "Ignore her and listen to me."

Mary blinked, staring at Odgers's watery eyes and thick, bushy eyebrows as they closed in on each other. "What's wrong now?" she asked, not wanting to hear any more bad news.

"I sent Pearson over to your house to meet the firefighters Campbell sent over there when Armstrong didn't answer the door."

"I'll go unlock it." She tried turning from Odgers, but he held his grip on her.

"Mary," he stressed, sounding almost apologetic.

"What?" She stared at him. "What's wrong? Where is Nate?"

"We don't know," he said on a sigh, and finally let go of her. "They managed to get into your place and searched the entire house. I'm told it looks as if he was asleep and dressed quickly, then left. A few of his things are still there, but, Mary, Nate isn't there."

"He doesn't have a car and I can't imagine he would wake up this early in the day and start walking somewhere." She shook her head, her brain already on overload, and this new bit of information simply wouldn't sink in. "He's got to be there, Captain."

Odgers shook his head. "Your neighbor across the street, Mrs. Rush, reported Nate Armstrong left your house about half an hour ago with a very small man, who appeared to be somewhat disfigured. He was driving a new, bright orange Volkswagen."

"What?" She almost stumbled backward but grabbed the counter and shifted her attention around the room before settling it on the doorway. There was a mean reporter out there who would have a field day with Mary's frazzled brain. "You don't think the man who called me went over to get Nate?" It didn't make sense. "Nate wouldn't take off with someone he didn't know."

"We're guessing the man probably told him something convincing enough to make Armstrong leave willingly with him. According to Mrs. Rush, this man was almost a foot shorter than Nate, possibly half his weight, with scars all over his face. He had brown hair, was dressed in slacks and a tie, and had a huge grin on his face when he got into his car and backed out of your driveway."

"And I'm supposed to know someone who meets that description?" She'd never actually lived through a nightmare before. It was definitely the most unpleasant experience she'd ever endured. "God, Captain, I need more clues."

"Okay. You went to school with him. He was smarter than you are. Apparently most would refer to him as very ugly. He obviously resents good-looking people. And he knows how to build a simple bomb and start a fire deadly enough to bring down a house."

Mary stared at him, listing his sentences in outline format in her brain and reviewing them as she willed a face from her past to appear. Smart and ugly.

"Oh my God," she whispered, covering her mouth with her hand. "There was a boy." She hurried past the captain and down the hallway to Jennifer.

Immediately Jennifer thrust her microphone in Mary's face. Mary grabbed the thing and tossed it over her shoulder. "I need your help," she began.

"What the fuck?" Jennifer screeched, leaning over the counter and staring at her microphone when it clamored to the floor and rolled under a chair. "Get that right now, you snide little bitch," she hissed, pointing her dagger-like fingernail at Mary.

"Listen to me!" Mary grabbed Jennifer's hand.

Jennifer yanked it out of Mary's hand and glared at her, hatred rimming in her dark eyes.

"I need your help. I need to remember someone we went to school with."

"Like I'm going to fucking help you do shit." The classy reporter was suddenly showing her true low-class colors—and her intense hatred and jealousy of Mary.

"Jennifer," Odgers said from behind Mary. His calm voice had Jennifer snapping her attention to him. "You can interview Mary later. Right now, listen to her. Maybe you can be responsible for cracking this case wide open."

Jennifer closed her mouth slowly, shifting her attention from Odgers to Mary.

Mary didn't wait for her to say anything. She just wanted her memory, not her friendship. "Back when we were in school, there was this boy who had scars all over his face. I think it was from a bad case of chicken pox or something. He always made honor roll and he dressed funny. Do you remember him?"

Jennifer wrinkled her nose and stared at Mary with hard, cold eyes. "He doesn't sound like someone I hung around with."

"I don't think any of us hung out with him." Which might have something to do with why the man was completely insane today. He was bitter from a life with no friends and his ugly appearance. "But we believe he might be the man who called into the station this morning and claimed responsibility for two house fires. The description matches, but I just can't remember his name."

"I wouldn't know." Jennifer didn't seem concerned about helping Mary and racking her brain to try.

Mary sighed. "Jennifer, this man has just abducted Nate. We need to find him. Will you please try to remember?"

"Nate?" Jennifer whispered, her entire expression transforming as she stared past Mary and moistened her lips. "Is he okay?"

"We won't know until we can figure out the name of the man who took him so we can determine where he lives." Mary was running out of patience. The urge to lean over the counter and grab the little bitch, then shake her until she told Mary whether she remembered the name of the boy from their childhood or not.

"It sounds like you're describing Ugly Dud." Jennifer shrugged.

"Ugly Dud?" Mary frowned, tapping her lips and glancing over her shoulder at Odgers. "I don't remember anyone called that."

"Of course not. You only had eyes for Nate."

Mary ignored the comment. "What was his real name?"

"How would I know? He wasn't exactly someone I associated with. May I have my microphone back, *please?*" She stressed the word "please" with too much sweetness.

"Ugly Dud." Mary repeated the name as she squatted and picked up the microphone. "Dud. Maybe his name was Dudley, or something like that."

"Maybe." Jennifer snatched the microphone out of Mary's

hand as soon as she stood, then inspected it meticulously for damage.

Mary looked at Odgers. "A yearbook might help."

"There are some across the street at the library."

An hour later, Mary scoured over the yearbook from her graduating class with Odgers next to her flipping pages from the class that had graduated a year later. Jennifer and her cameraman paced behind Mary. Patty had agreed to come in early and dispatch, which freed Mary from the station. She'd practically run across the street and through the library. The librarian asked more questions than Jennifer had as she found the yearbook for the police.

"There aren't any pictures anywhere of anyone named Dudley." Mary leaned back and sighed, a headache throbbing at her temples. She'd overheard Odgers's phone calls when reports came in announcing no one had spotted Nate or an orange Volkswagen yet. If he was hurt, or worse, because of her, she'd never forgive herself.

Why had she decided suddenly, after all these years, that she couldn't live another minute without Nate? If she'd left him alone, some creep from her past, a person she had absolutely no memory of, wouldn't have lured Nate away from her home.

The creep had to be good. Nate wasn't gullible. He wouldn't have gone with the guy if he'd suspected him in any way. And if this jerk was that good at bluffing, he would be just as good at killing.

A mean shudder attacked her, and Mary hugged herself, fighting the urge not to hit the desk with her fist. Somehow she'd figure this out. Nate would be okay. She would find him.

There weren't any other options.

"Look here." Odgers leaned into her and pointed at the yearbook she'd just looked at. There was small print under the second page of pictures of her senior class.

Mary stared at the words next to Odgers's stubby finger. They were the names of the classmates whose pictures weren't in the yearbook.

"Dudley Milestone," she muttered, a flutter of hope squeezing her chest. "I swear I don't remember him."

"That would fit the profile he painted for us." Odgers patted her shoulder as he stood and stretched. "If there is a Dudley Milestone living in this town, we'll find him."

Mary had no intention of sitting around and waiting. "I'm riding with you," she announced, sticking to Odgers's side.

He was a smart man not to refuse.

According to the post office, there was only one Milestone in Meredith Curve. Mary sat in the passenger seat of Odgers's personal car, his new Jeep that smelled faintly of cigars. Her stomach already had twisted in a knot so tight and painful, the dull stench of smoke didn't really bother her. She glanced several times at her side mirror and Meyers and Pearson, who were in the squad car behind them.

"Here's the street," Odgers said when he slowed and signaled to turn right. "Meyers, I want you two to stay back. Park here by the curb where you've got a good eye on us but aren't visible from the house. We'll stay on the phone with each other."

Mary noticed how white his knuckles were as he gripped his cell to his ear and laid out their game plan to his cops in the car behind them. Odgers pulled up in front of the house next to the Milestone home.

"There's a garage behind the house." He pointed.

Mary followed the narrow gravel drive that curved and disappeared behind the house. "If there is an orange Volkswagen in there, we've got him."

"Stay here." Odgers jumped out of the Jeep before she could protest.

Her heart exploded when he shut the door. She couldn't just

sit there and wait to find out if Nate were alive or dead, injured or not. After twisting in her seat and seeing Meyers and Pearson sitting in the squad car at the end of the block, she told herself to calm down. Maybe she'd never done a stakeout before, but Mary had the same training the rest of these guys did. Sometimes that meant being patient and waiting for the right moment. It also meant following orders, even when it made her nuts to do so.

Another car turned onto the street, this one not stopping and parking as Meyers had. It approached slowly, looking vaguely familiar.

"Crap," Mary hissed the moment she recognized Jennifer and her cameraman.

As she drove by Jennifer gave Mary a smug look. They slowed at the end of the block, pulled a U-turn, then parked halfway down the block from where Mary sat.

She told herself Jennifer wouldn't disturb a police situation just to get her story. More than likely, Jennifer had sat through more stakeouts than Mary knew. As if to prove her right, Jennifer put the car in park, then pulled out a small compact and began powdering her nose.

Mary's cell buzzed in her pocket, making her jump. She banged her elbow on the door handle and noticed Odgers standing at the edge of the driveway toward the back of the house.

"God," she whispered, rubbing her elbow, then pulling out her phone. It was Odgers calling her. "Is the car in there?" she demanded, still whispering.

"Yes, ma'am."

She watched him rock up on his feet as if he were proud of himself for finding the house. They had moved quickly on the location, now that she thought about it. She gave thanks for small blessings and sent up a silent prayer Nate was all right.

"Here's what we're going to do. My boys and I are going to

surround this place. I want you to go to the front door. Say whatever you want when he answers. It won't matter. You'll only be with him a minute before we enter. If Nate is with him we arrest him; if he isn't we drag Milestone in on suspicion of arson and kidnapping."

"And murder," Mary added. "He killed John."

"Yup. If we nail the arson charge we'll add murder."

Mary watched Meyers and Pearson get out of the car and start hurrying down the street. Pearson already had his gun pulled.

Damn! This was for real. She was in the middle of a bust, which was somewhere she'd always dreamed of being. But not at the risk of Nate's life. Refusing to give too much thought as to what she'd say when Milestone answered the door, she pushed her way out of the Jeep and headed across the lawn.

Her knees trembled as she neared the man's house and her heart was lodged in her throat, causing her to wonder if she'd be able to say anything at all. She rapped solidly on the door, not wanting to look around and see where everyone had positioned themselves. All she needed to know was if Nate was all right.

"Who is it?" a voice demanded harshly from the other side of the closed door.

"Dudley?" she asked, her voice meeker than she'd wanted it to be.

No one said anything and no one opened the door. She stared at the painted wood, fidgeting with the bottom of her shirt and rubbing her damp fingertips along her uniform belt. When the lock on the door clicked, she jumped and fought off a shriek. Instead, when a very grotesque-looking small man, probably a couple inches shorter than her, opened the door, she actually managed a smile.

"Dudley," she repeated. "I knew it was you."

Something shifted in his pale blue eyes. A mask of worry

seemed to disappear as his lips went from frowning rigidly to being fuller, relaxed.

"You know me?" He sounded like a child, bewildered and amazed.

"We went to high school together, silly." She prayed he wouldn't notice how she shook with fear. "I know you never gave me a lot of attention, but I knew who you were," she said, dropping her voice to a sultry whisper.

It might have been cruel preying on this man's vulnerability. Obviously he'd craved attention so desperately that he went to the extreme to assure he got it. Murder and abduction weren't excusable, though, regardless of how painful his life might have been.

"Why are you here and not at work?" he asked, frowning although he couldn't hide his delight at her being at his front door.

"They let me off early when we couldn't find Nate. He was at my house, but I guess he took off." Mary shrugged, trying to make it look as if it weren't something she was concerned about. "I knew it was you who called me earlier," she added, whispering. "So I thought I'd come over and we could talk. May I come in?"

He considered her request for a moment, apparently weighing the likelihood that she brought backup. "Sure, why not? The more the merrier." His laugh sounded bitter, if not deranged. It was the same laugh that had given her the chills over the phone.

When he stepped back to allow her into his home, Mary spotted the large figure crumpled on the floor. "Oh my God!" she yelled, darting past Dudley Milestone and sliding to the floor next to Nate. "What have you done to him?" She couldn't hold up her charade any longer as she screamed at Dudley, "If he's dead—"

"You think I'm an idiot," Dudley snarled, his delighted expression fading as well. "I was smarter than you!" he said in an accusatory tone, pointing his finger at her. "Everyone noticed you and him," he complained, curling his lip as he glared at Nate. "But I'm even more intelligent now than I was in high school. He isn't dead. Not yet. I wouldn't let him die without truly knowing deep, mortal pain."

"Dudley Milestone!" Captain Odgers appeared from behind the corner of a hallway. He leapt into the room, his gun pointed at Dudley. "You're under arrest!" Odgers yelled.

Everything became a mass of confusion in Mary's eyes. There were people all around her, talking at once. Dudley protested loudly of his rights being violated, but she didn't pay attention. Instead she leaned over Nate, pressing her body to his, and pulled him into her arms.

"You're going to be fine, sweetheart, just fine."

Several days later, Mary entered her house, laughing as she pulled the key from the lock and juggled two grocery bags in her arms. "I think we bought way too much food."

Nate was right behind her, his arms also full of groceries. He managed to close the front door before following her. "There's no such thing." He was laughing, too.

"I'm going to have to put some of these away before we start cooking."

Nate plopped his bags on her counter and grabbed her before she could pull the contents out of any of the bags. "They can wait," he said, pulling her into his arms. "It's been one week since you helped me come to my senses and realize how much I love you."

"One hell of a week," she muttered, but couldn't help smiling.

John's funeral had been tragic and sad, but Mary knew if he was there, and a big part of her believed he was, he would be so proud of the two of them for finally seeing the light.

"I have a feeling life with you will always be an adventure," Nate growled, and nipped at her lower lip. "But we'll coast through just fine. We love each other, and that is what matters."

She blinked, staring up at him. He'd been using that little four-letter word quite a bit since he'd first spent the night, and it amazed her how much power it held. Her heart fluttered at the same time something swelled in her gut, moving lower and growing until the throbbing between her legs wouldn't be ignored.

"Yes, we do love each other," she murmured, her voice cracking.

"I was going to wait until dinner, but I've never been good at keeping quiet about a surprise." His milk chocolate eyes pulled her into them as he gazed down at her. "Here." He thrust something against her chest.

Mary looked down, not noticing that he must have pulled something from his pocket. But as she stared at the small, square box her mouth went dry. She didn't want to know what expression was on her face, but however she looked, it brought a large smile to Nate's face.

"Open it," he encouraged.

She did, her fingers damp and trembling, and stared at the narrow silver band with one small sapphire set in the middle of it in a beautiful setting. "Nate, oh my God."

He did her the favor of taking it out of the box, then slipped it on her ring finger. "It really fits. Mom promised me it would."

"Your mom?" He'd actually planned this. "I thought you weren't any good at secrets." She stared at her finger with the gem glistening on the silver band and admired its beauty.

"It was my mom's first engagement ring and her mom's before her. When each couple had more money, they bought nicer rings."

"There would be a ring nicer than this?" Her senses finally came to her and she looked up suddenly, grabbing his shirt when the room seemed to teeter. "Are you asking me? I mean, are you?"

"Asking you to marry me?" He wrapped his arms around her and lowered his mouth to hers. His kiss was hungry, on fire, and full of promises of a wonderful night ahead. "Mary Hamilton, yes. I want you to marry me."

"Yes!" She jumped so hard they banged into each other, but she didn't care. Nate lifted her into his arms, heading for the stairs. "What about the food?"

"What I want to eat I'll do in the bedroom, my dear."

She cuddled into him, feeling the ring against her fingers. Her dreams had come true. And now her fireman would take her upstairs and show her that the best way to put out a fire was by adding more heat to it.

Heat Wave

P.J. Mellor

Special thanks to Karen Hankins

1

_____

If she didn't have sex soon, she was going to burst into flames, creating her own flash fire.

Summer Wadsworth tried to concentrate on other things as she scrunched her face in an effort to alleviate the itch beneath her facial mask and then resumed applying the last coat of polish to her toenails.

The somewhat sexy-looking meteorologist on the television news droned on about the heat wave currently encompassing most of the Texas Gulf Coast. Red flag warnings for flash fires due to dryness, burn ban in effect, yada yada yada.

Boy, could she relate.

Restless, she glanced out her living room window at the tan sprigs that had once been her grass and sighed.

Kaboom!

Lola, her beagle, flew through the pet door in the kitchen as though someone had thrown her into the house.

The dog made a beeline for the sofa, diving under the throw pillows. Head buried, she whimpered and shook.

"What was that? What happened, Lola-belle?" Walking on

her heels, toes splayed by the foam spreaders, Summer hobbled to the kitchen window.

To prevent smudging, she grabbed a meat fork from the wire basket by the sink and shoved back the edge of her curtains.

Immediately she released the curtain and screamed, the fork clanging into the stainless-steel sink, as a giant ball of fire rolled through her backyard.

Boom.

As she was knocked off her feet, pain shot through her skull a split second before darkness overtook her.

2

Thorne Paxton winced at the sound of the siren filling the air as he tightened the strap holding his long board to the top of his truck. After checking his gear, he jumped into the cab and fired up his engine.

He should have known he wouldn't get a day off. With the burn ban and number of flash fires plaguing the town of Harper's Ferry, virtually every firefighter was on call 24 / 7. Deep within his pocket, his cell phone vibrated against his leg.

"And there is your personal invitation," he said, turning left onto the coastal highway, his truck spitting up gravel from the beach parking area. Chris must be moving slow today, he thought, braking for a family to cross the road. Chris Martinez, the dispatcher, usually sent out the call to cell phones before the siren blasted through the community warning system.

Casting one last disgruntled look in his rearview mirror at the perfect waves breaking against the shore, he turned inland.

The Bay Station was the second to respond. Thorne jumped from his truck as the emergency vehicle rolled to a stop and men began dragging hoses toward a lone duplex. One side of the brown brick structure had flames licking out of its broken windows while black smoke oozed from the adjoining home.

Watkins, the officer on duty, met them. "Looks like an old tank on the vacant lot behind the property was the origination point. There's a trail burnt in the backyard to substantiate."

Thorne wiped a drop of sweat from his eye. "Victims?"

"None that we know of yet." Watkins cocked his head toward a group of three gray-haired ladies clustered together across the road. "They're from the old house yonder. Old-maid sisters. Said no one lives in the side of the duplex that's engulfed. Said a woman lives in the other side, but they don't know if she's home or not. We're trying to keep it contained to the one side, regardless." He wiped the sooty sweat from his face with the back of his arm. "I need you and these men to join me for a body sweep of the attached unit."

Jaw clenched, Thorne pulled on his goggles and respirator as he followed the line of men around the back of the smoke-filled house.

A small dog jumped through the pet door as they approached, skidding to a halt in front of Thorne.

The dog sneezed, then issued a weak bark.

Thorne released his respirator mask and pulled one glove off with his teeth. He dropped to his knee in the grass and held out his hand for the dog to sniff. When the animal came closer, he scratched her ear. As soon as the dog's body relaxed, he scooped her up and yelled, "I have a little survivor out back! Someone come get him." He glanced down at the shivering dog. "Sorry. Her!" he yelled. "Someone come get her!"

Relieved of his burden, he dropped to his knees at the entrance and followed his comrades into the black smoke-filled kitchen. On hands and knees, each man holding an ankle of the man in front of him to prevent disorientation, they made serpentine progress, sweeping out with their free arms. Looking for bodies. It was the part of the job he liked least. Unless you counted actually finding a body.

It was a small duplex. They found no one. On their way back to the rear door, they continued sweeping. The lead was going through the door when Thorne heard a soft cough. He stretched to sweep his arm farther.

"Ow," a voice said through the smoke and the noise from the other firefighters in the next unit.

"Watkins!" Thorne spit out his respirator. "Watkins! We got a live one!"

3

Thorne waved away the EMT heading toward him and stared at the green-faced woman stretched out on the gurney. As he watched the rise and fall of her chest while she breathed in oxygen, he noticed tendrils of smoke wisping out of her wild-looking dark hair.

"Hey." He tapped the EMT attending the woman. "Is her hair on fire?"

The tech's eyes widened and he hurried to tap her head. His shoulders slumped. "No, thank God. Just looks like smoke got trapped in her hair." He grinned, exposing a mouthful of silver braces. "She has a lot of hair."

"She sure does." And, right now, it looked like she'd stuck her finger in an electrical outlet. Thorne wondered if her hair was always that . . . big, for lack of a better word.

While he stood and watched, her eyelids fluttered open. For a moment her eyes looked unfocused; then her eyes widened and she jackknifed to a sitting position, shoving the technician aside. "Lola! Move! I have to find Lola!"

Thorne caught her as she tumbled from the gurney. "Easy. Is

Lola your dog? A beagle, about this tall?" He bent his knees and held his hand about a foot off the burnt grass.

"Yes!" Tears glistened in her unusual eyes. "Where is she? Is she okay?"

"She's fine," he assured the woman, stepping close in case she didn't have her balance yet.

"That's right," the tech chimed in. "They gave her a hit of oxygen, then stashed her in the crate by the back of the truck." He pointed.

"A crate?" The woman sounded horrified. "What kind of crate?"

The tech had returned to the ambulance. Thorne could only blink at her.

She grabbed his arm. "What kind of crate did they put my dog into?"

He blinked again before he found his voice. "Did you know you have a green face?"

Summer's hands flew to her face, tight beyond words thanks to her now extremely hard facial mask. She spun to run back to her house to try to wash the cement-like mess off her face, but the fireman stopped her before she'd moved more than a step.

"You can't go back in there yet."

"But I have to get this stuff off." She clawed at her hard face. "It itches!"

The man looked like he wanted to recoil from her and she couldn't really blame him. She could only imagine how she looked.

He was staring at the top of her head. She rolled her eyes up as far as she could, but, of course, she could see nothing. "What are you looking at?"

"Your hair. It's still smoking a little." Before she could stop him, he reached a long arm out and swiped his hand across the top of her hair a couple of times.

"It's not on fire, is it?" Surely she'd have felt it if it were.

He shook his head. "No. There's just . . . a lot of it."

If she could have felt anything in her stony face, she was sure she'd have felt heat flush her cheeks. Just her luck. The guy before her looked like a tanned centerfold—okay, she couldn't really tell that, because of his firefighting attire, but she had a good imagination. She scanned him from the tips of his spiked sun-streaked hair, down his soot- and sweat-stained face, over his slicker-covered body to his long, black rubber-encased legs and feet. Oh yeah, make that a great imagination.

And here she stood in her late grandmother's muumuu-style housecoat. She didn't even want to guess at what her hair and face looked like. Oh, crap. Her recent pedicure was all messed up. The dry grass adhering to the polish made her feet look like a collection of ten weird Chia Pets someone had neglected to water.

Tears stung her eyes. Some first impression she was making. He was still staring at her, so she felt compelled to explain. "It's my day off. I was giving myself a spa day. Since my creep boss pays poverty wages, I can't afford to go to a real one." She touched her hair and would have winced, if her face could express anything, at the feel of the voluminous hairball sticking out from her scalp. "I did a conditioning treatment on my hair and let it air-dry."

"Must have been a hell of a lot of air."

Biting her lip, she reminded herself this man and his fellow firefighters had saved her and Lola.

A tall, Ichabod Crane–looking man loped up, wiping his face with a towel. He removed his hat and hood, swiping the towel over reddish-looking sweat-soaked hair. "You the home owner?" She nodded. "Anyone beside you and the dog in there?"

"No." She pulled her voluminous robe around her. "The other side has been vacant for as long as I've lived here." Taking a deep breath, she noticed the men packing up. "Is it okay for me to go back inside now? I would really like to wash this stuff off my face."

The man's eyes narrowed. "Does it hurt?"

"No, it's just uncomfortable."

"And ugly," the first man she'd been talking to said with a smile that was blinding white in his tan face.

"Smooth, Pax," the tall man said. "If you're through dazzling her with your charm, it's time to pack up."

"Can I at least go get dressed and grab a few things?" She clutched the arm of the man who seemed to be in charge. When he glared down at her, she released the slicker, shoving her hands in her pockets. "Sorry. But I really do need to go back into my house."

"Not allowed. You just regained consciousness. You have no business going back into all that smoke."

"It wasn't from smoke inhalation! I hit my head when the explosion—"

"What explosion?" Ichabod loomed over her.

"I don't know! All I know is I heard a boom and when I went to look out the window a big fireball was heading my way. Then another boom happened and . . . well, that's all I remember until I woke up by the ambulance."

"You're lucky to be alive. You can't return to the house. I'm sorry," he seemed to add as an afterthought.

The hunky firefighter stepped up beside her. "I can go for her, sir. She'll need some things, her ID, money or credit cards, clothing—"

"Money and credit cards?" Horror filled her. She turned back to the tall man. "Are you charging me?"

Ichabod gave a bark of laughter. "He means for a motel. Don't look so crushed, miss. Everyone knows you can't live in a smoke-damaged house until the arson and reclamation crews do their thing."

"But I have a dog. Hotels don't like dogs. Well, some of

them are okay with it, but do I want to stay in those kinds of places? I mean—"

But the tall man was walking away, motioning with his hand to the firefighter standing next to her. "Handle it, Pax; I'm outta here."

4

Summer trudged behind the broad back of the firefighter the man had called Pax, Lola at her heels, as they made their way to her back door.

"I don't understand why I can't stay here," she grumbled. "Most of the smoke is gone now. I'd be fine. And I— oomph!" Her face slammed into the broad back in front of her. The hard fabric of his coat smelled of smoke.

"Steady," he said, turning and grasping her arms. "Easy," he said in a low, gentle voice as though she were a wild horse.

Attractive image.

She swatted his hands away. "Will you stop! I'm fine." Furiously she blinked back the tears welling in her burning eyes. Okay, maybe she was sort of pathetic, but he didn't need to know that.

His white grin flashed. He reached out to lightly tap on her hardened facial mask. "But you are human, right?"

Summer and Lola growled.

Pax held up his hands. "Easy. Just kidding."

"Not funny." She glanced around his arm at her open back

door. "Is it okay to go in now?" And if it was, why couldn't she stay?

"Just tell me what you need and where it's located. I can get it for you." He pulled his mask back up and waited patiently.

That was the problem. While she'd like to think she was disoriented from the blow to her head or from the smoke and related events, in truth she was—at best—a haphazard nester. In other words, she had no idea where anything was in her home. Okay, those were the exact words, unfortunately.

Organizational skills were one of the few traits her mother had failed to pass down to her. Height? Check. Heck, about half of the men in the seaside town of Harper's Ferry were shorter than her, even when she was barefoot. That was probably why she kept sneaking peeks at the yummy firefighter who stood a good head above her five feet nine and a half inches. Where was she? Oh yeah, traits from dear old Mom. Eye color? Check. Wild, frizzy hair? Check. Although, in all honesty, Summer's mother's mane was coiffed and straightened to within an inch of its life these days, bearing very little resemblance to Summer's out-of-control locks.

The fireman stood, looking down at her expectantly.

"Um." She racked her brain in an effort to remember what she needed and where it might be found. "You know, I hate to bother you. Why don't you just grab my purse? It's hanging on the hook on the back of my bedroom door. I'll just go stay at a motel and buy new stuff to use until I can come home again."

"I got the impression you were strapped for cash. Why would you want to replace everything instead of using whatever was salvageable?" His gaze raked her from the top of her head to her toes before he looked her in the eye. "You really want to go out like that?"

She attempted to narrow her eyes, but the facial mask was now shrink-wrapped to her face. "Do I have a choice?"

He shrugged and pulled his mask down again. "There's bottled water in my truck and clean towels. You can wash most of the stuff on your face off. I can grab some clothes. They will smell a little charbroiled, but if you have stuff in drawers, they won't be as bad."

The relief that washed through her lasted about a second. Did she really want this guy pawing through her panty drawer? Then again, what choice did she have?

Shoulders slumped in defeat, she said, "Fine. There's a tote bag on the floor of my bedroom closet. Underwear is in the top drawer of the chest. Just grab whatever is in the drawer. There are sweats in the bottom drawer." Sweats were a good plan. She could wear them as outerwear and sleep in them. So what if the temp was near one hundred degrees? It was just temporary until she could get out to a store. "I'll replace anything else I need."

He nodded and pulled the mask up again, motioning for her and Lola to stay outside.

Suddenly weak, Summer sank to sit on the cement patio, absently scratching Lola's ear. The dog wiggled in an effort to get closer, not stopping until Summer pulled her into a hug. "What are we going to do, Lola-belle?" The dog's fur was warm and smelled smoky. "We really, really don't want to go back to *Grandma's,* do we?"

Lola whined, bringing a smile to Summer's lips. Or it would have, had the stupid mask not prevented facial movement.

"I don't blame you," she told the dog, "Grandma isn't much fun. And she's not a dog lover, is she?" Despite the smell, Summer planted a kiss on the dog's head, smiling at how her mother would react to being called Grandma to a dog.

Summer sighed and blinked back tears. Now here she was, twenty-six, divorced, back in the little beach community she'd sworn to leave in the dust, working for a lecherous, mean-spirited, miserly man, barely making ends meet. It had taken almost a year to save enough money for the down payment on her little duplex. A year of scrimping and saving, having no social life, in order to buy Lola's dog food.

A year in which Summer's mother never missed an opportunity to remind her of what a mess she'd made of her life by letting a Wadsworth get away. Cory may have been a member of the illustrious Wadsworth family, but he was still a creep.

Closing day for her little duplex had been the happiest day of Summer's life. Finally, she could breathe again.

And now this. Her heart had plummeted when the fireman had told her she couldn't stay in her house. Where would she go? How much would a motel cost? How long would her money last?

5

The firefighter stepped through the back door, her duffel bag and purse gripped in his big hand. "I hate to tell you this, but it looks like a tornado hit your bedroom." He shook his head. "We're usually neater than that, Miss . . . ?"

"Oh!" Summer set Lola on the patio and stood, extending her hand. "Wadsworth. Summer Wadsworth." They shook hands. "But you can call me Summer."

Especially since the Wadsworth portion didn't technically apply anymore.

"Thorne Paxton."

"Hi, Thorne." She smiled. Well, she tried to smile, anyway. "And don't worry about the room." She shrugged. "I'm still in the process of moving in," she fibbed. It was sort of true because she really *was* still in the process—it just happened to be a long process. "The fire trucks are leaving. Don't you need to take off?"

The fireman handed her purse to her and set the duffel on the patio. "I followed them in my pickup. Today was supposed to be my day off."

They stood staring at each other for a few seconds before Thorne cleared his throat. "I didn't see a car when I drove in. Do you need a lift to a motel?"

"My car's in the shop." And it would likely stay there until she scraped up enough money to pay for the new water pump. "Do you know any nearby motels that take pets?" She mentally calculated her available credit. "And do you have any idea how long I will have to stay out of my house?"

He raked a blunt-fingered hand through his hair and shook his head. "I'd guess no more than about two weeks. Basically just as long as it takes the reclamation people to get the smoke out of everything." He shifted from one booted foot to the other. "Um, I don't know much about motels in the area, since I just moved here a few months ago. But I do know of a place that allows dogs."

"Is it expensive?" She picked up her belongings and her squirming dog.

"Nope. I'd say it's pretty reasonable. And the owner is willing to negotiate."

"What motel is it?" Maybe it was the one she'd just seen on the evening news, the one that operated a call girl business on the side. That would be just her rotten luck.

"Well, it's not actually a motel. Not anymore, anyway." He led the way toward a dusty red Tundra pickup truck.

"Wait." She grabbed his arm, tugging him to a stop. "If it's not *actually* a motel anymore, what is it?"

He stared at his feet for a moment, then raised incredibly blue eyes. "My place."

6

"Your place?" Summer's voice squeaked. What kind of woman did he think she was? Her tight face reminded her of her green facial mask. A glance at her less than come-hither attire startled her. What the heck was he thinking? Who in his right mind would be attracted to someone who looked like this?

Hard on that thought came another: no one in their right mind! What if he was some kind of pervert or criminally insane? Then again, how would someone like that pass the test to become a firefighter?

It was all so confusing. Maybe she had inhaled more smoke than she thought.

Thorne watched the woman. Her tight green face didn't give much away, but the way her gaze darted around told him she was having issues with his suggestion. That was okay. Frankly, he was having a little trouble wrapping his brain around what his impulsive mouth had just said.

"It's not much," he felt compelled to tell her. "My grandparents ran a little beach motel. They left it to me. I don't use it

as a motel, so there's plenty of room for you. And your dog."
He shrugged. "It's nothing fancy, but the price is right." Swallowing his misgivings, he flashed what he hoped was a reassuring smile.

Her eyes narrowed. "Why don't you run it as a motel?"

"It's not my thing, for one. For another, it's not in any condition for business. I doubt I could get the permits required to rent to guests." Another shrug. "Not sure I'd want to, anyway."

"How much?" When he didn't respond, she stepped closer. "You said the price was right. How much are you planning to charge me?"

"What? Nothing. I just told you it's not fit for paying customers. You said you would have a problem finding a place that would allow pets. I have more than enough room and don't give a damn if you have a whole zoo as long as you take care of them and pick up any, um, droppings. Now, are you going to take me up on my offer or not?"

When she continued staring, he turned and walked toward his truck. He wasn't going to beg her. Damn it all, he was just trying to be a nice guy.

"Wait!" She caught up to him, her hand on his arm halting his steps. "I'm sorry. I didn't mean to sound ungrateful. But I also can't stay with you without paying. If you won't accept my money, what will you accept? Services?" Her eyes widened at her statement. "I mean, like helping clean up, not, well, you know."

He scanned her slight form. Well, what he could see of it in the hideous garb she wore. He'd have to be pretty damn hard up to lust after that. He wasn't that hard up. Yet. "No, I don't know. You're going to have to spell it out for me."

Her slender throat worked convulsively a few times before she finally said the words. "Sex. I'm willing to offer my services—"

Swallowing a laugh, he decided he didn't want to make things easy for her, for some reason. With exaggerated slowness, he dragged his gaze up her body again. "Thanks, but I'm not interested."

"W-hat? No! I wasn't offering sex! I—"

"Sure sounded like it to me, lady," he said, resuming his trek to his truck.

"Will you stop turning your back on me?" She yanked his arm none too gently. "Let's try this again. I will work for my room, but not on my back."

"I don't recall asking." Jaw clamped, he shook her off and opened his door.

"Crap! I'm sorry! I jumped to the wrong conclusion." Her shoulders slumped beneath the loud print. "Big surprise." Her eyes met his and he realized they were more a deep blue than turquoise. Or maybe the color was enhanced by the green goop on her face. "Can we start over?"

Why didn't he just get in his truck and drive away? The surf would still be up for the next hour or so. He glanced down at the creature with the green face, the wild print pup tent she wore flapping in the Gulf breeze, and felt his resolve slip. What was it about this woman that caused him to throw caution to the wind and want to ride to her rescue?

It was unsettling.

It was stupid and totally uncharacteristic.

It was . . . oh, son of a bitch, no! His gram's words echoed through his memory, telling him how one day he'd meet *the one*. The person who was his destiny. His other half.

Dread curled in his gut. Could his destiny possibly have frizzy, smoke-filled hair and a green face?

Her dog chose that moment to latch onto the leg of his jeans and growl. Just his luck.

Destiny came with a dog.

7

Summer shifted her gaze, horrified to realize Lola had attached herself to the poor man's pant leg. "Lola!" She could not afford to buy new clothes for herself *and* Thorne. "I'm sorry. She's really a very nice dog." Summer bent and tugged at Lola's little vibrating body in a useless attempt to get doggy teeth out of denim. "Lola! Cut it out!"

Thorne glanced at Summer and her dog and bit back a smile.

"Are you all right, honey?" The cluster of three gray-haired ladies he'd seen hovering across the street approached in a knot of bony Bermuda short–covered legs and white walking shoes. Their rotund torsos were clothed in matching Hawaiian print shirts, he noticed, each a different color.

"I'm fine," Summer said, rising to her full height and tapping her green cheek. "Or at least I will be once I get this mess washed off."

He took that as his cue to grab the gallon water jug from behind his seat and a clean beach towel. "Here," he said, handing the towel to her after he'd thoroughly wet it. "Maybe this will help."

"What a nice young man," the geriatric ringleader in the screaming yellow print shirt said, her bright red lips curving into a smile. "Is this your new beau, Summer?"

8

"Miss Laura, you're such a tease!" The combination of the sun beating down on her and the fierce glare of the firefighter made Summer sweat. "This is one of the firemen who helped today. Thorne Paxton. Thorne, this is Laura Davis. And the other two ladies are her sisters, Flora and Cora."

Thorne's lips twitched. "Sisters, huh? Pleased to meet you."

"Triplets, actually," Summer supplied. "Miss Flora," she indicated the woman in the hot pink print shirt, "was my second-grade teacher, and Miss Cora," she pointed to the remaining triplet, dressed in a lime green print, "was my junior high phys ed teacher."

"Were you a teacher, too, Miss Laura?" Thorne asked politely.

"Damn straight," Laura replied, her chest puffed out. "I taught English, mostly accelerated classes, at the high school for almost fifty years." She patted Summer's arm. "This young lady was my star pupil." Laura shook her head, a sad look on her wrinkled face. "We had such high hopes for her. She could have been a Pulitzer Prize winner or at the very least Katie Couric's replacement." Laura's sisters nodded their agreement.

Summer stood, her back stiff, in silence, Thorne noticed. Obviously she didn't agree with her former teachers' high opinions. Why was that?

Summer scrubbed at her face with his wet beach towel. Too bad she couldn't make herself disappear right along with her facial mask, she thought. She continued rubbing long after her raw skin told her the facial mask was gone.

A warm hand on her arm halted her scrubbing. Knowing it was futile to continue hiding under the wet towel, she peeked out at Laura's kind face.

"That's enough," Summer's former teacher told her. "You're apt to rub all your skin off if you keep that up. Now, please tell us what happened. We've been eaten up with curiosity!"

With a sigh, Summer handed the towel back to its owner. "I'm not really sure. I heard a loud bang, like an explosion; then Lola flew through the doggy door. Within seconds, it happened again. I was knocked out and don't really remember much until I woke up next to the ambulance."

"You poor thing," Flora said, her sisters nodding in agreement. "What are your plans? We heard the other gentleman say you couldn't stay in your house for a while."

"Right." Summer nodded and glanced at the fireman leaning against his truck door, arms crossed over his broad chest. The bulky jacket was gone now and the gray fabric of his T-shirt stretched taut across his broad shoulders. Beneath the tight sleeves, his biceps bulged. She swallowed, wishing she had another choice about her accommodations.

"We'd offer to let you stay with us, but we're all staying in one room while the house is being repainted." Laura shrugged. "I'm so sorry, we just haven't any spare room."

"No problem," Thorne said, pushing away from the truck and reaching for Summer's bag. Before she could protest, he tossed it and her purse behind the seat. "Summer's staying with me."

All three older women gasped. Summer could identify. She had almost gasped, too.

"But where will you be, Summer?" Laura cast a critical eye at Thorne. "What if we need to get in touch with you?"

"She'll be at the Sea Breeze Motel, out on Route Three." Thorne gripped Summer's elbow, gently guiding her to the passenger door.

"Bill and Edna's? I thought they retired to Florida."

"Yep. I own it now. They're my grandparents," he explained.

When he'd settled Summer into her seat, she hissed under her breath, "You said your grandparents left the motel to you. I thought they were dead!"

Thorne tsked and shook his head before grinning at her. "That's what you get for thinking. I never said they were dead, just that they left the place to me. It's not my fault you jumped to conclusions."

"You have my cell number," Summer called to the sisters, who all nodded. "If you need to get in touch with me, just call." She gave a finger-wiggle wave as Thorne fired up the powerful engine and dropped the truck in gear.

"Was it really necessary to blab about my lodging arrangements?" She glared at Thorne, who was grinning as he pulled onto the highway.

"You don't strike me as the kind of girl who worries too much about public opinion." He reached across the seat and tugged at her housecoat. "Case in point."

"Give me a break! I wasn't planning to leave my house. How was I to know a stupid fire would happen?"

She had a point, but he found he liked teasing her. The way her cheeks darkened to a becoming shade of pink fascinated him.

Her dog escaped her arms and walked across the seat to

stand on her hind legs, forefeet against his shoulder, while she sniffed his ear.

He swallowed a laugh and hunched his shoulder, but the little dog would not take a hint. "Tell your dog I don't let females stick their tongue in my ear until the second date."

"Lola!" Summer dragged the rigid dog back to her side of the car. "Behave," she warned in a low whisper.

Thorne flipped on his left turn signal and turned into a gravel parking lot. At least she assumed it used to be gravel. The tires crunched, throwing up a plume of gray dust in the truck's wake. They rolled to a stop in front of a little frame building with a steeply sloping faded pink roof. The white paint hung in precarious peeling sheets, the bare wood exposed in more places than paint covered. Above a door with a window criss-crossed with duct tape, a dusty sign flashed.

" 'Off-pen-vac' ?" She really didn't mean to snicker, but the place was even worse than she'd expected.

"Don't laugh. It's paid for. And it hasn't burned down." He turned off the ignition and stared at the flashing sign. "I guess it wouldn't hurt to have the sign fixed." He glanced her way. "It's supposed to say: 'Office, Open, Vacancy.' "

"But it's not an office, you're not open, and there is no vacancy because it's no longer a motel. Right? Why bother fixing the sign?"

"Because it looks stupid flashing partial words."

"Why don't you just turn it off?"

"Can't." He reached for her things, looking distinctly uncomfortable.

"Why can't you?" She gathered Lola in her arms and reached for the door handle.

"It's a long story." He hopped out of the truck and hurried around to help her and Lola down.

"We've got time." She nuzzled her dog's warm head. "Don't we, Lola?"

Thorne heaved a sigh. "Gramps fancied himself a handyman. It may have been true when he was younger, but, well, in later years, he did some weird stuff." Thorne dug in his pocket, then shoved a key into the lock on the office door.

"Oh?" She watched him wiggle the key and jerk on the door. "Do you need help with that?"

"Hmm? Oh, no. It's just a little tricky. Takes a few tries to open." The door swung open on rusty hinges. Thorne flipped on a fan as he headed to a large scuffed front desk. "Anyway, Gramps fixed a lot of stuff around the motel himself. Including the electricity. Somehow he managed to wire it all together. If I want lights or air, I have to have the sign on, too."

"Can't an electrician fix that?" She set Lola down to sniff around the front office, then smiled when the dog sniffed a dusty fake plant and sneezed.

"One would think. Dave, the only electrician in town, has been too busy to do more than look at it and tell me what to do until he can get out here to fix it."

"What did he say?"

" 'Sleep with the lights on.' "

9

The Davis sisters watched the truck turn onto the highway.

"Do you think it was a good idea, allowing that young man to drive off with our Summer?" Cora asked, scratching the bridge of her nose.

"We had no choice," Laura assured her. "Summer is not a child anymore and, alas, we're not her mother."

"I should say not!" Flora made her way to the street. "Good Lord, Laura, we're old enough to be her grandmother." She looked both ways and proceeded to cross the hot asphalt.

"Hah," Laura harrumphed as she followed her sisters. "Speak for yourself."

Flora stopped and turned to glare at her sister. "Laura, we're all the same age. Give it up."

"Well, I just don't think it looks proper for a young man and woman to cohabit without benefit of matrimony. Summer just met him. We know nothing about him," she argued, hurrying behind her sisters as they made their way home.

"I thought he said he was Bill and Edna's grandson," Cora

said, stepping up onto the wrap-around porch of the old Victorian home the sisters shared.

"Exactly my point, Cora! He *said*. We have no idea if what he said is, in fact, true or false, do we?"

They entered the house and paused as they always did in the entry hall.

"Well, damn it, Laura, if you have something to say, say it." Hands on hips, Flora glared.

"I think the Snoop Sisters need to revitalize their business. At least one more time."

"You know we're not really the Snoop Sisters, don't you? You realize it's just our way of referring to ourselves on occasion?"

Laura strode to a round table in the parlor and lifted the side of the embroidered tablecloth to open the minifridge hidden beneath. "Of course I realize that! I'm not senile! I'm going to have a beer. Anyone else want one?" She handed an amber longneck to each sister, then twisted the top off hers and took a long swig. "Okay. Let's sit down and come up with a plan."

"A plan?" her sisters said in unison, their eyes wide.

"Don't look so shocked. Of course we'll need a plan. We need, number one, to make sure Summer and Lola are safe. We need to check out their accommodations."

Flora nodded and took a sip of her beer. "I think we also need to find out more about her young man and what his intentions are toward Summer."

Cora agreed. "It wouldn't hurt to check out the sleeping arrangements, if you get my drift. After all, we all know men are after only one thing."

10

Thorne grabbed a fistful of keys and rounded the desk. "There are eight cabins, not including mine and the one my grandparents used for storage. I don't know which key is which, since they're not labeled. I thought we'd check out the cabins before it gets dark and I'd let you choose the best one."

She paused by the door. "Why does it matter if it gets dark?" She hoped the niggling feeling she had was wrong.

"I'm not exactly sure if they have lights or even electricity."

"I thought you owned the place. How could you not know something like that?"

He braced his fists on his lean hips, a muscle ticking in his jaw. "Because I had no intention of renting it out. It didn't matter. I'm staying in Gram and Gramps's unit. It has air, lights, and water. That's all I needed to know."

"Do the cabins have TVs?" She hurried to keep up with him as he headed across the dusty parking lot toward what she could only assume was the first cabin. It looked more like a garden shed.

"I don't know, I guess. Maybe. I'm not holding anything

back here." He flashed a quick grin. "But without electricity, what does it matter?"

He tried three keys before the door swung open.

They recoiled at the stench, Summer gagging.

"What is that smell?" she asked through the hand shielding her nose and mouth.

"I have no idea, and I'm not sure I want to know." He slammed the door and moved her along the little path to the next cabin.

"Is that the ocean I hear?" She paused, listening intently.

"Yep. Well, the Gulf." He waved his arm. "It's just on the other side of that berm of sea grass."

"Is there a beach?"

"Yeah, not much of one, but I guess you could call it a beach."

She sighed. "I love the beach."

He grinned as he unlocked door number two. She loved the beach. What do you know. Things might just work out.

"Well, at least it doesn't smell." He flipped the light switch, but nothing happened. "Looks like this one has no power."

"It also has no room." She glanced around at the stacks of dusty broken furniture. "There's not even room for Lola in here."

"Let's go see what's behind door number three." He locked the door and continued down the path to the curve. "As I recall, the units on this end have two bedrooms and kind of a little kitchen. Maybe you'd be more comfortable here."

"Is that a fireplace?" She stepped cautiously into the darkened cabin.

"Damn. No, it's a hole in the wall. Something could be living in here. Let's try the next one."

"Define 'something.' " She frowned at Thorne's back, noticing the little sweat marks darkening the light gray fabric. Maybe whatever it was would necessitate Thorne spending the night. In her bed. In her arms. Strictly for the practical purpose of protecting her, of course. Forcing her eyes from his firm backside, she trudged behind him. She needed to concentrate on something other than the possibility of who or what could be living in the last cabin. Whatever it was, she hoped it would be safe to stay in close proximity. In her arms, Lola squirmed. They were both ready to rest.

Relief swept through her as light flooded the room when Thorne flipped the switch inside the door of the fourth cabin.

"Let there be light." He strode to the air conditioner built into the outer wall, beneath the large window, and twisted a knob.

Nothing.

He checked the thick cord that ran to the outlet directly below, then whacked the air conditioner a couple of times.

His shoulders slumped. "Sorry. It just doesn't want to be turned on."

But I do. Closing her eyes, she prayed she hadn't said her lustful thought out loud. How stupid could she get? There were enough things going wrong in her life at the moment; she definitely didn't need the odd attraction she felt when she was near Thorne.

When she opened her eyes, Thorne stood mere inches from her.

Her heart pounded so loudly, she wouldn't have been surprised if he heard it. Slowly, she licked her dry lips.

Thorne swallowed and she watched in fascination as his Adam's apple bobbed with the action.

"Are you hungry or thirsty?" he asked in a low, sexy voice.

Oh yeah, baby. What did you have in mind? Images of her dragging her tongue over his spectacular body flashed behind her closed eyes.

"Summer?" She opened her eyes to find Thorne staring. "Are you okay?"

"Hmm? Yes, I'm fine. Why?"

"Well, it sounded like you moaned when I asked if you were hungry."

"Oh!" She jumped back. "Um, yeah, I guess I am." Her stomach, bless its heart, substantiated obligingly with a loud growl.

"Let's grab something to eat; then we'll keep searching for a cabin for you and your mutt."

Lola bared her teeth and gave a little growl.

"Hey!" Summer cuffed his hard arm. "Tell her you're sorry. You've hurt her little feelings."

Thorne snorted and walked to the door. "I don't talk to animals." He opened the door and motioned Summer out. "Let's eat."

Summer stepped over the threshold when the old air conditioner clanged on, wheezing to asthmatic life.

"Great timing." Thorne bent to check the locked door, then straightened with a laser white smile. "Should be good and cool by the time you come back."

"Wait!" Summer dug in her heels as he propelled her toward the truck. "I can't go out in this! I need to change."

He nodded and switched directions, walking her back toward the little office. Lola trotted along behind them. "I should probably take a quick shower first, anyway."

A shower sounded heavenly. Of course, a shower with her firefighter as her personal bath toy sounded even better, but she knew that wasn't likely. "I'd kill for a shower about now."

Thorne's laugh washed over her, making her want to snuggle up and wait for it to happen again. Which was totally stupid.

"No need to commit murder," he said, guiding her to the left of the office. "I had a new hot-water heater installed when I moved in. There's plenty for both of us." His smoldering gaze met hers. "Unless you'd care to share to conserve water?"

11

"I-I'm good," Summer finally stammered. "And, besides, we hardly know each other."

He flipped on a light and walked across a surprisingly spacious living room to a narrow door. He smiled. "Good point. But lighten up. I was joking."

"Oh." Darn.

"Towels are in the cabinet under the sink and there's shampoo and soap in the shower. My sister left some shower gel when she was here. You can use that if you'd rather have it. It's in the medicine cabinet."

He had a sister. They had something in common. "How many sisters do you have?"

He looked surprised. "One. Trust me, it's more than enough."

"You don't get along?" How sad. She didn't know what she'd do without her meddling sisters, even though they lived close to Dallas. Crap. In all the excitement, she'd forgotten to call them. Or her mother.

"Are you okay?" Thorne's voice brought her back.

"I just realized my family doesn't know where I am or what happened."

"You want to call them before your shower?"

She dug into her hobo-style handbag and finally located her phone. "If you don't mind. I just need to check in or they'll be worried. Especially if they hear about the fire."

"They live around here?" Surely he'd have noticed anyone even slightly resembling the woman standing in his living room. Now that the green goop was gone, she was pretty. In a wholesome, girl-next-door kind of way. Too bad he'd never been attracted to the wholesome types. "How many sisters do you have?" It wasn't any different from the question she'd asked him. Why did he feel like he was intruding?

"Two," she answered with a small smile. "Autumn and Spring."

He blinked. "Get out of here! Your folks actually named their daughters after seasons?"

She grimaced. "I'm afraid so. Growing up, we hated it. But now it's—" She held up her hand, her attention now focused on the person on the phone. "Hey! It's me. I'm good. I—oh, you heard about it already?" She flashed a smile, then turned her attention back to her call, while he made no bones about listening.

Summer smiled at whatever was said. "T.M.I., Sis, T.M.I. . . . Yeah, I'm okay. . . . No, the fire was on the other side; we just had a lot of smoke. . . . I'm not really sure." She sighed. "I don't know who Mom's sources are, but yes, I did leave with a fireman." She glanced at him, then turned her back and said in a lower voice, "Yes, he is. . . . None of your business, okay? . . . Well, yes, we did go to a motel, but he owns it! He's just being nice. . . . I will. Okay. . . . Call Spring and tell her. . . . Thanks. Me too." She ended the call and smiled. "My sister said to tell you thanks for putting up with me."

He'd bet her sister said more than that. He smiled and nodded. "Are you going to call your mom before you take your shower? If you are, I'll take mine first."

"Oh! I'm sorry. Sure. Go ahead. I do need to call my mother, anyway."

Thorne turned on the shower and stripped. It was a good thing he was taking his shower first. That way he could cool off before he was tortured with imagining her standing naked in his shower with nothing separating them except a hollow door with no lock and a shower curtain.

No doubt about it, he needed to hustle through dinner and drop her at her cabin. The longer they were together, the more tempted he'd be to discover what she hid under her pup tent.

He looked down at his erection and bit back a groan.

It was going to be a long night.

12

After she'd hung up from her mother, her cell immediately rang. She squinted at the caller ID and saw it was her sister. Shoulders slumped, she rubbed her temple as she answered. "Hi, Spring, I assume you've heard everything by now, too."

She reclined in the squishy brown leather chair and examined the broom-splatted texture on the ceiling. Thorne really needed to paint.

"All I have to say is can I run away from home and stay with a hunky firefighter, too?" Summer's sister laughed, snorting into the phone. "Details, woman, I want details!" She heaved an exaggerated sigh. "I want to live vicariously."

"I tried to tell you not to rent the garage apartment at Mom and Dad's," Summer felt compelled to point out.

"Yeah, I know."

Summer jumped up to pace the small living room, glancing now and then at the little cabin that would be her temporary home while she talked.

Feeling alone and bizarrely lonely for her family, she picked up her sleeping dog and settled on the sofa with Lola in her lap.

Summer squirmed on the couch and shot a glance at the closed bathroom door. Thoughts of Thorne's sexy mouth on her nipples made them ache. If Thorne made a move on her, would she be able to resist? Did she want to?

Summer groaned and tore her gaze from the bathroom door. She'd never denied her sexuality, but after her divorce the opportunities for sexual gratification had been few and far between. In fact, she couldn't even remember her last time.

But being in such close proximity to easily the sexiest man she'd ever met had her thinking way too graphic thoughts about her host. Thoughts she had no business thinking. But it was difficult to carry on a conversation knowing Thorne was naked in the next room.

"I just called to make sure you're okay. And to tell you I support you in whatever you decide to do." Her sister's voice brought her back to the conversation.

"What? What are you talking about?"

"Mom said you were thinking about reconciling with Cory, that you and he were working things out at the motel."

"Are you freaking kidding me? She said that?" Summer jumped up, dumping Lola on the couch. Furious, she paced from one end of the cramped living room to the other. Passing her reflection in a mahogany-framed mirror, she wouldn't have been surprised to see steam coming from her ears. In a low voice, she half-growled her words. "I am not, repeat not, getting back together with Cory Wadsworth. Ever."

"That's a relief! I—oh, shoot, my ride's here. Gotta run! Love you!"

"I love you, too," Summer whispered as she pushed the disconnect, too distracted by the renewed flash of lust heating her, along with the steam wafting from the bathroom, to remember much of the conversation.

* * *

Thorne quietly closed the bathroom door and took a deep breath. Damn. Why was it whenever he found someone who interested him, she ended up taken? Who had Summer been whispering her love to?

He twisted the bulk of the towel he'd wrapped around his hips to hide the remnants of his erection. No doubt he'd lived alone too long when he didn't even think to bring clothes into the bathroom anymore. He briefly considered dressing in his dirty clothes, but they were beyond merely soggy, thanks to the leaking shower door. Maybe he could make a dash into the bedroom without Summer noticing.

Swinging the door open again, he barely had time to react when Summer fell into his arms.

"Oh!" She did a face plant into his chest, her hands going to his waist in an effort to regain her balance.

The precarious tuck job on his towel gave way, the towel falling into her hands.

They stood, frozen in shock. Her wide-eyed gaze was locked on his penis. As a result, it was rapidly recovering.

Belatedly he covered his jewels with his hands and edged toward the bedroom.

"I-I'm sorry!" She thrust his towel toward him. "I didn't mean to—"

"I know. It was an accident. Let's forget it, okay? I'm going to get dressed while you shower. Do you need anything?"

You, deep inside me. But, of course, she couldn't say that. Heck, she shouldn't even be thinking it. Flushed and clean-smelling after his shower, Thorne looked good enough to lick. All over. She swallowed. "Um, no, I'm fine. Thanks."

"You have clean clothes?"

Unfortunately. She nodded and held up the duffel he'd packed for her.

Holding the towel in front of him, he continued to back out of sight. "I'll just get ready and wait out here for you, then."

Closing the door, she leaned against the steam-warmed wood and sighed. She had to get a grip before she did something stupid.

Like throw Thorne to the floor and have her wicked way with him.

13

Thorne paced the living room and listened to the sexy sound of his shower. Showers had never had the erotic effect on him the current one had—maybe it was because of the person taking it.

He closed his eyes, picturing Summer's nudity as the steamy water slicked over her skin.

With a growl he stomped into the kitchen and pulled open the freezer door. Grabbing an ice cube, he stumbled in his haste to get to his bedroom. Behind the door, he immediately shucked his jeans, letting them and his boxers drop to his ankles.

Ruthless, teeth clenched, he gripped his dick, squeezing the erect shaft hard while he ran the rapidly melting ice up and down it in an effort to deflate his current raging boner.

"What the hell is she doing in there for so long?" he grumbled. Sure, he realized it took women longer to shower, but she was heading into record-breaking shower time.

Meanwhile, his libido was in overdrive and he was desperate to hide his reaction to her.

He mopped at the melted ice with his discarded towel, then pulled up his pants.

The shower was still running when he reentered the living room. On the sofa, her little dog snored softly.

Slow steps reluctantly took him to the closed bathroom door.

Summer rubbed her aching nipples long after the soap was washed off in an effort to stop the needy ache filling her. Instead, her nipples grew impossibly harder.

With a frustrated moan, she squeezed more of the citrusy-smelling shower gel into her hand. Heck, she may as well get it over with so they could go eat.

Unerringly her hand went to her slick folds. She spread her legs, reveling in the feel of hot water sluicing over her as she stroked the satiny gel over her swollen labia.

She moaned, locking her knees to remain upright, when her questing fingers found the hardened nub. Her breath hitched as her arousal zinged into the stratosphere.

Close. She was so close.

Her free hand found her nipple and plucked, twisting almost to the point of pain.

Her other hand rubbed her clitoris. Harder. Faster.

Breath coming in huffing pants now, her hips began bucking with each stroke.

Eyes squeezed tight, she imagined Thorne's hand bringing her such pleasure. Thorne's mouth at her breast. And lower.

Her orgasm slammed into her, the pleasure so intense, it buckled her knees.

She swallowed a reflexive scream of fulfillment, resulting in a keening sound that echoed from the tiled walls.

Weak, she leaned against the cooler tile while she waited for her heart to resume its normal beating, her breathing to regu-

late, before she could even attempt to get out of the shower and
dry off.

Thorne swallowed convulsively, head thrown back against
the closed bathroom door, and took gulping breaths while he
squeezed his newfound erection through the denim. Hard.
Willing it away.

An ironic laugh threatened. How the hell was he supposed
to keep his cock in his pants when his guest was on the other
side of the door, naked, pleasuring herself? Oh yeah, that was
exactly what she was doing in there; he knew it.

And it was killing him.

14

"I'm glad you suggested going to a drive-in for our food." Summer glanced over at Thorne as he navigated the truck into the drive-thru lane of the local hamburger place, Buddy's Burgers. She looked down as her less than casual attire of sweatpants and oversized sweatshirt. "I think I'd be pretty much underdressed for anything else." Especially since she'd forgone panties and a bra in favor of comfort in the hot weather. Her femininity was also a little tender, thanks to her sexy shower, so it was a double relief to be pantyless.

"No problem. I don't know about you, but I'm starving. I wouldn't have had the patience to sit somewhere and be waited on."

She tore her gaze from the bulge in the front of his jeans and swallowed. "Yeah, I'm starving, too." She reached behind the seat for her purse. "Order me a number one with double meat."

"Put your purse away. This one's on me."

Laura burped. " 'Scuse me." She looked at her sisters in the darkness. "Do you see Summer?"

Cora shook her head. "No, it's dark as pitch out here. Why isn't he using the parking lot lights, I wonder?"

"Who knows? Flora, pass me another beer, please."

"Don't you think you've had enough?" Despite her words, Flora fished another bottle from the wheeled cooler and passed the sweating longneck to her sister.

"His truck's gone," Cora pointed out. "Else he's parked it behind the motel somewhere."

"Good. I hope he's gone. That way, we can talk to poor Summer and convince her to go stay in a more reputable place while her home is being cleaned." Laura peeked into the window of the first cabin. "Durned windows are so filthy, it's nigh unto impossible to see anything."

"Let me look." Cora nudged her sister aside and stood on tiptoe, her face pressed against the dirty glass. "Looks like it's filled to the brim with furniture." She dusted her hands on her walking shorts. "Obviously Summer isn't staying in this cabin."

"Onward!" Laura pointed with another fresh longneck, its contents sloshing out onto her hand as the sisters made their unsteady way toward the next little building.

"Wait!" Flora grabbed the back of Laura's shirt, halting her progress. "I thought I heard her dog barking."

They paused, frowning in concentration.

"That way!" Cora grabbed the plastic handle and pulled the cooler in the direction of the sound, her sisters bringing up the rear.

"It sounds like it's coming from there." Laura pointed and hiccupped.

The sisters stared at the door of the little cabin on the curve of the parking lot. A distinctive bark was immediately followed by a howl.

The sisters' gazes met. "Lola," they said in unison.

The sound of toenails scratching the back of the door mingled with the increasingly excited barks as the women neared the door.

Laura marched to the door and knocked, setting off another round of howling. "Summer is obviously not here."

"Try the door," Cora said. Flora nodded her agreement.

Laura's shoulders slumped. "Locked."

Flora sniffed. "Does anyone else smell smoke?"

Laura snorted. "And you accuse me of having too many beers! I just—oh my Lord!"

Her sisters looked toward where her shaking finger pointed. "Fire!"

15

Summer took a sip of her vanilla malt and gave a satisfied sigh. "That was so good. Thanks for dinner, by the way. But I wish you'd let me at least repay you for the hamburger I ordered for Lola."

Thorne's smile flashed in the darkness while he waited for the light to change. "I can afford to buy your dog a burger. Don't worry about it."

The sound of sirens split the night. Within seconds, a fire truck blasted through the intersection in front of them.

Thorne frowned and pulled his cell from the holster. "That's weird."

"What?"

"That was the vehicle from my station." He held up the phone. "And I didn't get a call."

"You told me it was your day off. Maybe that was the reason?"

The light changed. Thorne punched it, the powerful truck laying rubber as he made the turn. "We're about to find out. They're heading in the same direction we're headed."

* * *

Flashing lights bathed the little courtyard of the Sea Breeze Motel.

Summer gasped at the sight. "Oh no! Lola!"

Thorne grabbed her arm, preventing her from jumping from the truck as he pulled into his parking place. "Wait! I'm sure she's fine. But even if she's not, there's nothing to be gained by you charging over there now. You'll just be in the way."

Summer tugged, but he held firm. "Let go! I have to find out if she's hurt or, or—" She broke off on a sob.

"Summer," he murmured, pulling her across the seat to hold her close. "Everything's going to be okay, sweetheart. You just need to give the crew time to do their job. Okay? Can you do that?"

She nodded and sniffed against his shirt.

A tap on the driver's side window startled them.

Thorne buzzed down the window. Chris Martinez stood grinning at him.

"Damn, Pax, you near gave me a stroke when this call came in!" Chris wiped the sweat from his forehead with his forearm. "Where the hell have you been? We were fixin' to do a body sweep for your sorry ass." He grinned. "Lucky for you that you turned up—saved us some work."

"What happened?" Thorne stepped down from the truck and turned to help Summer.

"A fire," Chris supplied.

"No shit. I want to know where and how."

Chris shrugged. "Near as I can tell, it started by the old air conditioner unit under the window."

"My dog—" Summer tried to push past the men, but Thorne held her back.

"Little beagle?" Chris asked. Summer nodded. "Dog's fine. She's with the old ladies over yonder."

"You'd better go see about her and find out what the triplets are doing here," Thorne told her. "Maybe there's a problem at your house."

They watched Summer scurry across the parking lot while the crew packed up the vehicle. Behind the nose of the fire truck, the remains of Summer's temporary home smoldered.

"You gettin' any of that?" Chris turned to stare at Summer. Thorne knew exactly where his friend's eyes were trained because his were ogling the same area.

And he didn't like it one damn bit.

"Shut up, Martinez. Don't you need to get on the vehicle?"

"So that's a negatory?" Chris shook his head in mock resignation. "You're getting old. There was a time you'd have—"

"I said, 'Shut up'!" Without waiting for a response, he stomped across the lot to talk to the sergeant.

Summer held a wiggling Lola close, avoiding most of the sloppy doggy kisses as she observed the guilty looks on the Davis sisters. Her eyes narrowed. "Tell me again why you all came here tonight?"

Laura straightened from the rolling cooler behind them as she uncapped another beer and took a healthy swig. After she swallowed, she looked at her silent sisters, then at Summer. "Ah, hell, looks like the cat's got their tongues." *Burp.* " 'Scuse me. Well, we were worried about you. After all, none of us really know your young man and—"

"Miss Laura, he's not my young man."

Laura waved a wrinkled hand. "Regardless. As we've often told you, we consider you the niece we never had. My goodness, we were only looking out for your welfare, young lady, and now you're acting as though we're intruding!"

Her sisters nodded solemnly.

Immediately chastised, Summer put her hands on the stooped shoulders of Flora and Cora and pulled Laura into the group hug. "And I appreciate it; really I do. I'm sorry if I sounded ungrateful or angry. Gosh, you saved Lola's life! I owe you." Laura burped again and Summer realized she smelled beer on the other two women as well. "How much have y'all had to drink?"

"I dunno." Cora picked up the lid of the cooler and peered inside. "Mercy! There was nigh unto two cases in here when we started."

"How many are left now?" Summer craned her neck to see into the cooler.

"Three!" Flora sounded scandalized . . . and slightly buzzed. "How'd that happen, d'you think?" *Hiccup.*

Worried, Summer glanced around the empty parking lot. "How did you ladies get here?"

Laura straightened, shoulders thrown back. "We are not such old fools that we'd consider drinking and driving, my dear." *Burp.* " 'Scuse me."

"Well?" Summer glanced over and saw Thorne making his way toward them. "How the heck did you get here?" she whispered.

Laura pointed to her dusty white walking shoes. "We walked, of course. We're mall walkers, after all. We've logged many miles since we retired. Why, the trek here was less than half our usual."

"Do you usually carry along a cooler full of beer?"

"Of course not! But today has been, well, an unusual day. Besides the obvious unsettling incident at your house, we're still in a severe drought, you know. Why, we simply brought along our own refreshments to prevent becoming dehydrated on our journey."

"Plus, we weren't entirely sure we remembered the direction of the motel correctly," Cora added.

"Ladies." Thorne walked up and winked at the women. "Were you, by chance, here when the fire started?"

The women were quiet for a moment.

"Well," Laura said, "we may have been. We were trying to find Summer when we heard little Lola barking. I don't recall seeing any flames or smelling smoke at that point, do you?" Her sisters shook their heads. "It was while we were trying to figure out how to retrieve Lola that we first noticed the smoke smell, followed immediately by the flames in the window. Why are you questioning us? We've already talked to that nice young man from the fire department."

"Yes, ma'am, I know. I was just wondering." He looked at Summer and squeezed her shoulder. "Good thing they were here. I had to whack the old air conditioner to get it going earlier, remember? I should have known better. You and Lola can stay in my unit tonight. Until I get someone out here to take a look at all the units, in fact."

"Your unit?" all three women and Summer said.

"It's the only one I know is safe at the moment, so yeah, my unit." He crossed his arms and waited.

"Thorne?" Summer touched his arm while she clutched her dog to her chest. "Could I talk to you, alone, please?"

"You tell him, Summer!" Cora said in a stage whisper.

"You go, girl!" Flora's comment ended on another hiccup.

Summer glanced over her shoulder at the women, then whispered, "I don't think they should be alone tonight. They've had a lot to drink."

His first impulse was to point out the women were on foot, not driving, but one look at her concerned face told him there was no point in beginning an argument he was bound to lose. "I have plenty of room here, but I worry about the safety of the other cabins now."

"Is there enough room for them in your place?"

Maybe it was a better idea to have three senior citizen chaperones than to be alone, all night, with Summer.

But, damn, he'd had high hopes for the evening ending in a much different scenario.

"I guess we could make room," he finally said. "The couch makes a bed and one of them could sleep on my recliner." He grinned. "Of course, that means you and I will have to share a bed."

"In your dreams!" Hers too, she suspected, but she wasn't about to admit it. Horny. She was just horny. It had, after all, been a very long dry spell, sexually speaking.

"We couldn't help but overhear." Laura and her sisters stood right behind them now. "And while we appreciate the offer, I'm afraid we can't stay." *Burp.* " 'Scuse me."

Summer turned panicked eyes to Thorne. "Make. Them. Stay," she enunciated through clenched teeth.

"Now don't go getting your knickers in a wad," Cora chimed in. "Laura means we cannot agree to the sleeping suggestions."

Before Thorne could tell them he'd been kidding about him and Summer sharing a bed, Laura began talking again.

"Yes, I'm afraid I'm something of a restless sleeper. Have been most of my life, I'm told, which makes it a good thing I never married. You see, I can't abide sleeping with anyone. And my back precludes me sleeping on your recliner. I'm afraid none of us can sleep there, since we all have a touch of osteoporosis. And dear Summer is much too tall to comfortably sleep there, as well."

They all looked expectantly up at Thorne, who gave an inward sigh. "Okay. Here's the deal. You ladies bunk in my cabin and Summer and I will take the dog and go to my beach house."

"What beach house?" Summer hefted the dog higher. Lola bared her teeth at Thorne as though she too doubted his motive.

"I have a place out past the highway. I'm fixing it up. That's why I've been staying at the motel. It has a single bed and a couch," he told Summer. "So you can choose to sleep wherever you want. What do you say?"

"I say go for it!" Flora sang out. "It sounds like a hoot. You need more fun in your life, Summer."

"I absolutely agree," Laura said. Cora nodded her agreement.

"Fine. Let me grab some of my stuff."

"Ooh!" Cora said as they all trooped behind Thorne and Summer. "This is going to be an adventure! I just love adventures; don't you?"

Thorne glanced at Summer. He knew she wasn't wearing any underwear. He also knew how easy it would be to rid her of the baggy sweat suit once they were alone.

"Yes, ma'am," he told Cora as he held the door for the women, "I surely do."

16

Thorne unlocked the door of his beach house and looked down at Summer as she lagged behind. Was she planning on making a run for it? And, if so, where the hell did she think she would go? Besides, the dog would slow her down.

"Does she need to do her business before you come in?" Why not give her an excuse, since she was obviously hesitant?

"No, she just went before we left the motel. Thanks, anyway." Summer made slow progress coming up the stairs but eventually stood at his front door, clutching her ornery dog as she visually scanned the weathered house. "How long have you lived here?"

"I bought it when I made the decision to transfer from Houston." He glanced around the crowded living room and knew it looked less than habitable. "I always wanted a place on the beach, and when I saw this was for sale and in my price range I grabbed it." He shrugged. "I figured I could stay at the motel while I fixed it up. Only problem was it had a lot more fixing up than I'd counted on. I figured it would take a month, two tops."

Summer eyed the drywall leaning against the wall. "How long has it been?"

"Counting today? About six months, give or take a week."

Summer returned his smile. Polite conversation was a good thing. It kept things informal but not so much so that she would be tempted to strip him bare and lick him all over.

Not that she was tempted; she was just saying . . .

When Summer released Lola she growled low in her throat and latched onto the lace of Thorne's running shoe, thrashing her head from side to side.

"Lola! Cut it out!" Summer knelt and tried to disengage her dog's sharp little teeth from the shoelace. "I'm so sorry. She doesn't usually act like this, really. I don't know what's gotten into her. Maybe she's stressed from the fire or something." She tugged at her dog again.

"Or maybe she just took an instant dislike to me." He watched the little dog chew furiously on his lace.

"What? Don't be silly. She barely knows you. There, she stopped. I—oh no! Lola, no!"

She watched in horror as her dog squatted on the other side of the crowded living room. A large dark spot immediately spread on the carpet. What was Lola thinking? She never did stuff like that.

"Lola!" Summer lunged for the dog, but Lola was faster, running and hiding behind the stacked drywall. And the way she was acting, it probably wouldn't stay dry for long.

"I'm so sorry! Bad dog, Lola!" Summer finally touched the dog's collar and dragged her into her arms. "If you'll give me a second to lock her in the bathroom, I'll clean this up."

"Don't worry about it; I planned to trash the carpet, anyway. Who puts carpet in a beach house?" He turned her to face a little hallway. "The bathroom is at the end of the hall."

Lola whined when Summer sat her on the shining gray marble-tiled bathroom floor. "Behave! What's gotten into you,

Lola-belle?" She scratched the dog's ears and placed a kiss on the shiny black fur on top of her head. "Thorne is trying to help, and if you keep attacking him and wetting on his floor he will kick us out. So be good, okay?"

"The bathroom looks great," Summer said as she made her way down the hall. "Was it like that or did you redo it?" She stopped and blinked. "Wow, you've been busy!" Thorne had already cleared most of the furniture from the room and was standing by the telltale wet spot. "What can I do to help?"

"If you could grab the other end of the drywall, I'd appreciate it. I'll do most of the lifting; you just need to balance your end and steer."

Obediently squatting and gripping the top and bottom of the wallboard, she said, "No problem. Where are we putting it?"

He inclined his head. "Over on the other side, against the far wall of the kitchen."

It took a few trips, but eventually they moved all of the drywall to the kitchen.

"Now what?" Summer swiped at the sweat trickling down the side of her face. "Whew! Is your air on?"

"Nope. There is no air. Yet. It's next on my list." His laugh boomed in the small space. "Don't look so worried. There's a decent breeze off the Gulf at night and the house has the perfect east-west exposure. It's really not too bad."

"If you say so." She looked at the piles of furniture stacked in the kitchen. "Where am I going to sleep?"

"Since there's only one bedroom, you can have it or the couch. I've slept either place, so I don't mind."

"Um, Thorne? Exactly where is the couch?"

"It's in there . . . somewhere. I want to get the wet carpet out of here before I drag it back in."

"May I help?" She followed him to the far side of the living room.

"I'm planning on it. I'll start ripping it up off the tacks and you hold it as I roll. Then we'll carry it out and toss it down to the beach. I'll cart it off tomorrow."

Ripping out carpeting sounded a lot easier than it was in reality. Balancing the discarded carpet roll, she watched the muscles in Thorne's arms flex and bulge with each section he removed.

Finally, the last of the carpet separated from its tack strip. Grunting, they dragged the now huge roll of stained, smelly carpeting onto the balcony. It took a few tries before they successfully hoisted it above the rail. It fell to the sand below with a muffled thud. The disintegrating pad soon followed.

Remembering Summer's shower earlier, Thorne had no problem accepting when she offered to let him shower first. The big problem was he remembered her sounds during her shower too well and found the stinging cold water did nothing to calm him down.

Throwing on a pair of pajama pants for modesty, he returned to the living room. Maybe he could work off his major boner by moving heavy furniture while Summer showered. He swallowed a groan at the thought of Summer, naked, again, in his shower.

Baseball. Think of baseball.

"Towels are under the sink," he told her, absently shaking his leg to dislodge her dog from his pajama leg. "Oh, and your dog left her calling card in the corner."

"Lola! Let go." Cheeks heating, Summer glanced at Thorne through her lashes. Lordy, he looked good, all tan and lean, the smooth skin of his bare chest gleaming in the indirect light from the kitchen. Wait. What did he say? "She pottied in there, too?"

He nodded. "I flushed her other gift but figured I'd let you have some of the fun. You can mop the floor. Mop and bucket are in the broom closet just inside the kitchen. Pine-Sol is under the sink." He turned his broad back to her and began pulling at the stack of boxes.

Mortified, she grabbed the mop and bucket and made her way to the bathroom, Lola trotting at her heels. "Lola, you're lucky you're so cute. It's the only thing keeping you safe right now."

Thorne finished rinsing his face and torso in the kitchen sink and unrolled a wad of paper towels. While he dried off, he surveyed his handiwork. With most of the furniture still stacked in the kitchen, along with the boxes, the living room didn't look too shabby.

The tile revealed by the carpet had cleaned up decently. It would have to be replaced, but at least it was moderately clean and much better than the ratty old carpet.

The old sofa bed held a prominent place in the room, its faded dark red upholstery looking almost inviting. He'd agonized over whether he should open it and make the bed up for Summer or leave it folded for a while. It would be less obvious if he left it folded.

He glanced at his impromptu wine bucket—okay, it was actually a galvanized bucket filled with two trays of ice cubes, but it was doing a decent job of chilling the bottle of wine he had *borrowed* from his grandmother six months ago. And both wineglasses were chip free.

The water turned off.

Thorne jumped onto the couch, casually draping an arm over the back, and propped his bare feet on the box he'd covered with a pillowcase so he could use it as a coffee table.

A few seconds later, he heard the bathroom door open and the distinctive clickity-clack of the demon dog's toenails on the tiled hallway.

Dog and owner entered the living room and stopped.

Summer surveyed the room, complete with the lit candles sputtering in the empty beer bottles, and smiled.

The dog bared her teeth and growled.

"Okay, that's it, Lola." Summer scooped up the dog and marched back to lock her in the bathroom.

Taking a deep breath, Summer closed her eyes, remembering the seductive scene in the living room. At least she hoped it was set for seduction.

She certainly was.

But did she have the guts to follow through with the lusty plan she'd formulated in the heat of the shower? She didn't have much experience as the aggressor. Okay, she didn't have any experience.

Miss Laura's voice echoed in her mind: *You'll never get the experience if you fail to take a chance.*

17

"Hi," Summer said in a breathless voice when she reentered the room.

Thorne was still semi-reclined on the end of the couch, but she noticed he'd poured two glasses of wine. As she approached, he stood and handed her a cool glass.

"Thanks." She took a sip and sat on the couch. Thorne followed her. "Um. This is good. I like sweet white wine."

His smile seemed even whiter by candlelight. "My grandmother does, too. It's from her wine rack."

Summer laughed, relaxing into the cushions. "My gram always liked sweet wine, too." She took another sip and tried to tamp down the emotion choking her at the thought of her late grandmother. "She'd have loved this," Summer said in an emotion-clogged voice. Her hand did a small, encompassing wave. "All of this. She loved the beach, beach houses, sweet things like wine and chocolate." Their gazes met. "And handsome men," she finished in a whisper.

"Oh yeah? You think she'd think I was hot?" He scooted

closer to Summer, his body heat causing a bead of sweat to trickle down her back, under the sweat suit.

"Stop hinting. You know you are."

"Aren't you hot?"

Setting her glass on the makeshift table, she decided not to play coy. "Well, I'd never really thought about it, but I guess I'm okay looking—"

His laugh made her stomach quiver.

"You're more than okay looking and you know it. But that's not what I meant. I mean literally. Aren't you hot with no air conditioning and wearing sweats?"

"Oh!" Inhaling her sip of wine, she choked at the burning sensation filling her throat. Relieved when Thorne took her glass, she covered her fiercely blushing cheeks with her hands. How stupid could one girl be? Of course he was talking about wearing sweats in the heat. He must think she was an idiot.

"Hey. You okay?" His voice was close when she nodded. Very close. So close she could smell the wine on his breath. Still sweet. "I think you're overheated from wearing so much garb."

"You do?" She relaxed a little, allowing him to push her hands down while he trailed light kisses along her hairline.

"Mm-hmm." He nuzzled her neck, then kissed his way to her jaw. "Short-circuits the thought waves," he murmured, nibbling the edge of her lips. He brushed a kiss across her suddenly starving mouth. "Don't worry; I know exactly what to do."

"Oh?" She sank into the deliciousness of his kiss as he lowered her deeper into the cushions of the old couch.

"First," he said against her lips as he broke the kiss, "we need to get you out of some of this before you get heatstroke."

"If you say so. After all, you're the professional."

Cooler air swept up her rib cage when he pulled up the hem of her sweatshirt. She breathed a sigh of contentment.

"Better?" His hands found their way beneath the remaining portion of the shirt to cup her breasts.

"Oh...yes." Arching her back to better fill his hands, she strained for his lips.

"It's going to be hard to kiss you with all these clothes between us." He pulled the sweatshirt over her head, throwing it away from the couch.

They groaned at the feel of skin on skin.

"Better?" he asked, again kissing the side of her throat as he made his way downward.

She nodded, breath lodged firmly in her lungs, but didn't know if he saw her, since he was cupping her breast in his hand, alternately licking and blowing on the puckered nipple. She had problems regulating her breathing.

"We should probably get you out of these, too." He shoved at the elastic waistband.

Her heart tripped. She'd never been a particularly sexual person. Did she dare let go of her inhibitions with Thorne? She knew she could trust him with her body. But could she trust him with her heart?

The thought stunned her. Her heart? Her heart had been securely protected for over a year now. She'd just met Thorne, but she sensed he had the potential to make whatever heartache she thought she'd had with Cory look like a junior high emotion. Was she willing to risk it?

Yes.

Thorne clenched his hands in a fist as he dragged the thick sweats from Summer's delectable body. He'd suspected she went commando beneath the bulky outfit, but now he knew.

He wasn't sure he could handle it. Handle her. Ah, damn, why did she have to look at him like that? Why were his hands shaking at the thought of touching all that smooth skin?

Why was he talking to himself?

Thorne had always been too busy, too self-centered, too

whatever, to have a serious girlfriend. He only dated women who had the same attitude.

And now here he was, allowing three old ladies to stay in his cabin while he all but dragged the woman beneath him to his less than habitable beach house. Was she screaming, running for the door? Hell no. She was lying there, naked like some sex goddess, looking at him like . . . like he was something special.

What the hell was he going to do now?

18

He's going to bolt. Summer could see it in his face. One second he was huffing and puffing, trying to devour her, his hands everywhere, and the next he had a definite deer in the headlights look.

Damage control. She needed damage control. Big-time.

But what?

Of course, she did what she had to do—she grabbed the waistband of his pajama bottoms, scarcely noticing the softness of the well-washed plaid fabric, and tugged.

The rippled muscles of his abs contracted, bowing into his abdomen, and the bottoms slid lower over jutting hip bones to snag on something else that was jutting.

His warm hand seized her wrist, halting her progress.

If she'd thought she'd experienced heat before, it was nothing compared to what she saw in his eyes. Holding her breath, she glanced down at the obvious bulge and licked her suddenly dry lips.

"Don't." His breath hissed through his teeth.

Swallowing around the lump of fear and excitement, she

dragged her gaze up, ever so slowly up to meet his. What she saw made her want to squirm on the rough fabric of the sofa. Instead, she steadied her nerves and took a deep breath. She wanted him. Really, really wanted him. If she stopped now, she just knew she wouldn't have him. Possibly never would have him.

That wouldn't do.

Praying she'd interpreted his expression correctly, she boldly toyed with her nipple in what she hoped was a provocative manner.

It surprised the heck out of her to find it felt pretty dang good.

Resuming the all-important eye contact, she half-whispered, "Don't what?"

"Don't look at me like that." Pinning her with his weight, he grasped and held their joined hands above her head, his clothed erection pressing intimately against her nudity. "You don't know what you're doing."

"Oh?" In extreme slow motion, she tugged her left hand free, then dragged it down his damp shoulder, over his ribs, not stopping until she reached his waistband, low on his hip. It only took a slight movement to raise her head and trace the small cleft in his chin with the tip of her tongue.

Against her breast, his heart pounded out a message telling her he was not immune to her actions.

Emboldened, she slid her hand between their stomachs, not stopping until she closed her fingers around the outline of his impressive erection. A slight squeeze had his breath catching and Summer biting back a smile.

Score one for the good girl.

As she thought about her next move, he surprised her by sliding down until his hot lips covered her nipple, drawing it deep into his mouth. Now it was her turn to have a catch in her breathing.

Glorying in the sensations rushing through her, she lay there, scarcely breathing, in awe at the sheer beauty of the man doing such delightful things to her willing body.

Catching a moan of disappointment when the cool air bathed her newly released breast, she didn't have time to protest before Thorne kissed his way down and situated his broad shoulders between her now widespread legs.

"Pretty," he said in a low voice, his breath on her wetness sending shivers to every nerve ending, puckering her nipples.

Her hips bucked when he trailed a fingertip along her desire-swollen folds. Would it show a total lack of control to beg him for more?

Instead of closing his mouth over her weeping flesh, as she'd assumed he would do, he surprised her by plunging his fingers deep.

She clamped her legs tightly together.

This would not do. She was the sexual instigator this time and here she was just lying on the couch like a sacrificial virgin.

Not gonna happen.

Shoving on his firm, tanned chest, she finally got a little space and didn't stop until she had neatly flipped their positions. It meant losing the sexy feel of his fingers, at least for a while, but it couldn't be helped.

She was woman; hear her roar.

It wasn't as easy as it seemed in the movies, but she finally managed to get up onto her knees on the narrow couch and knee-walked backward, taking his pajama bottoms with her.

For a few world-stopping seconds, she rocked back on her heels, glorying in the moment, thrilled with her sexual aggression.

But when she realized Thorne was rallying, attempting to move, she knew she had to act. Fast.

Licking her lips again, she meant to let her body slowly lower in a gentle sexy glide until they were breast to chest. In her mind, she saw her slink lower and lower still until her mouth closed over the part of him eagerly straining toward her.

Unfortunately, her mind saw a totally different view than was reality.

Mid-glide, she lost some of her balance and most of her momentum, causing her to do what some might consider a belly flop.

It left Thorne breathless, all right, but not in a good way.

19

"Your elbow," Thorne wheezed. "Move your elbow!"

Realizing the hard ridge was definitely not his hip, Summer gasped and struggled to get off the sofa with what little dignity she had left.

And promptly fell on her backside onto the cold tile.

Thorne jumped up, tangling his feet with hers in his pajama pants, and fell with a muffled curse, knocking the breath out of her.

Down the hall, Lola barked wildly, her toenails sounding loud as she clawed at the bathroom door.

A buzzing sound had Summer shrieking as she hopped back on the couch.

"What's that? A snake? A bug? If it's a bug, it has to be huge! I—"

"It's my cell," Thorne said with a laugh, scooping the phone up off the tile. "Damn."

Their eyes met.

"I have to go." He stood, shoving his legs into his pajama

pants. "It's the station." He strode toward the back of the house, presumably to the bedroom to get dressed.

Thorne was a firefighter. Firefighters fought fires. And with the drought the little coastal town was experiencing, it only made sense he would be on call more than he was home.

She pulled her sweatshirt back over her head, not really caring when she noticed it was inside out, and reached for her discarded pants.

Down the hall, Lola howled louder.

Thorne came down the hallway, almost running into Summer as she made her way to get her dog.

"Sorry." He steadied Summer, his hot hands practically burning holes in the sleeves of her sweatshirt. Warm lips brushed her forehead. "I'll be back as soon as I can."

She stood for a while after the screen door banged shut, after she heard his truck fire up and the sound of his engine fade away. Slowly, she brought her hand up to touch her fingers to the damp spot where Thorne's lips had touched.

Slow steps took her down the hall to get her dog.

She opened the door and groaned. "Lola! Bad dog!"

Lola had found the toilet paper and redecorated the bathroom. It looked like a blizzard had struck.

No sirens split the air. Thorne frowned at the readout on his cell, then connected. "Hey, Martinez, what's up?"

"Where the hell are you, man? You need to get to your motel, pronto!"

Thorne pressed harder on the accelerator as his truck flew low down the asphalt coastal highway. "Shit! Another fire?" No doubt about it, he had to have the whole place rewired.

"Worse, dude." Martinez sounded suspiciously like he was smothering laughter.

"Okay, I'm pulling into the lot. Where are you?"

Martinez stepped into the courtyard and waved his arm.

Thorne slid his truck in the dirt to come to a stop a few feet away from his friend and hopped out of the cab.

"Where's the fire?" His gaze darted around the courtyard, past the lone fire truck. "Is it already under control? Was it just one unit?"

Martinez gripped Thorne's shoulder and pointed. "Oh, there was a fire, all right, but it was just a harmless bonfire in the middle of the motor court."

"I don't understand. Why the call? What is the vehicle doing here?"

"Oh, you will, bro; you will." Still holding Thorne's shoulder, Martinez guided him around the truck. "Got a nine-one-one reporting flames coming from the old motel. Knowing it was your place, we lit out like a bat out of hell." His hand on Thorne's shoulder tightened, turning Thorne. "And that's what we found."

Thorne followed the direction Martinez indicated and saw Laura, Flora, and Cora wrapped in blankets beside a bonfire.

He strode to the women. "What happened? Are you all right?"

Laura straightened, casting him an imperious glare. "Of course we're all right! We were just checking off yet another thing from our to-do list, but these—these *men* don't seem to understand."

"They're not the only ones," Martinez muttered.

"What, exactly, don't they understand, Miss Laura?"

"This!" Laura dropped her blanket, revealing more pale, wrinkled skin than Thorne ever wanted to see.

Her sisters followed suit, which led the attending firemen to act quickly to reinstate the blankets.

Thorne clamped his palm over his eyes. "My eyes! Miss Laura! Why on earth would you and your sisters want to parade around . . . like that?"

Laura released a pent-up sigh. At least, he thought it was Laura—he wasn't about to look.

"You can turn around now," she said in a reasonable-sounding voice. Of course, she'd sounded reasonable before—right before she and her sisters had flashed him.

He peeked through his fingers, relieved to see the old ladies were once again covered from shoulder to bare feet in gray blankets. "What were you thinking?"

"Have you ever heard of the bucket list?" she countered.

"You mean the movie?"

"Not really. I mean a list of things you want to see or do before you die."

He nodded, not at all sure he liked where this seemed to be heading.

"Well, we made ours a few years ago. Oh, don't look so shocked; we're in our eighties, you know. Where was I?"

"Our list," Flora, or maybe it was Cora, reminded her.

"Right. Our list. One of the things on it was to dance naked in the moonlight." *Burp.* " 'Scuse me. Since we were alone for the night," she paused, glaring at the firemen as they climbed aboard their vehicle, "and the courtyard was vacant, shielded from view of the street, we decided to check it off our list."

Her sisters nodded like it was a perfectly rational thing to do at—he glanced at his watch—two o'clock in the morning.

Thorne raked his hand through his hair. For this he'd left a warm, willing female.

"You're okay?" The three women nodded, pulling their blankets closer around their nudity. He turned to his friend. "And there was no damage? No problems? Paperwork?"

"Not unless you want to press charges for reckless intoxication."

Thorne bit back a smile when he heard the women gasp. "I know I probably should, but I know they didn't mean any harm. Let's all just go to sleep and forget it." He turned to the women, who were now huddled against the door of the manager's cabin, and pointed his finger. "No more drinking tonight, got it?" They nodded. "And no more fires or dancing naked. Is that clear?"

"Young man." Cora stepped forward. "We know our rights. There is no law against adults over twenty-one drinking or being naked on private property."

Narrowing his eyes, he leaned forward. "There is when it's *my* private property."

After getting the sisters settled again, he wasted no time in driving back to the beach. Would Summer be willing to continue what they'd started? Was he willing?

He pulled his truck beneath the stilted house and ran up the steps.

The house was quiet and dark. A glance at the sofa confirmed Summer wasn't waiting to finish what they'd started.

With slow steps, he brushed his teeth and changed back into his pajama pants.

The door to the bedroom stood ajar, proving too much temptation to resist.

His forefinger gently pushed the door open.

Summer lay sprawled on top of the covers of his bed. She'd shoved the legs and sleeves up on her sweat suit, but the moonlight cast a definite glow to her sweating face.

Stubborn woman. Did she think he was going to attack her if she dared take off the sweats?

Maybe.

Out of nowhere, a growling ball of black and tan fur leapt at him.

20

Hot. Summer was so hot. She turned on the bed, wishing she were naked. Wishing Thorne was there, naked with her, while she was making wishes. Hey, why not? After all, things had progressed pretty fast earlier. Had Thorne not been called away, they could very likely have been sharing a bed.

A scream split the air, jolting her from her semi-orgasmic dream state.

Amid the yelling, Lola's distinctive growl rose.

This could not be a good thing.

By the feeble light of the hall, Summer saw a man stood locked in battle with Lola. Thorne.

He did not appear to be winning.

Summer shook the remnants of her luscious dream from her head and rolled to her feet. Obviously her dog was intent on ruining any possibility of her wishes coming true. Heck, with the way her dog was mauling him, he'd probably run screaming into the night.

"Lola!" Squatting, Summer tugged at the growling, vibrating animal. "Lola! Be nice! Let. Go."

Finally Lola released Thorne's pant leg, allowing Summer to pick her up.

"I'm so sorry! I'll lock her in the bathroom again so you can get some sleep without fear of dog attacks."

When Summer returned, Thorne was in the bed. Her bed. Well, okay, technically not her bed, but still . . .

Swallowing in an effort to alleviate her dry mouth, she could only stare. Dang, he made one hot picture, moonlight reflecting off his broad, bare shoulder.

He smiled, his teeth flashing white in the dimness.

"Um, I can take the couch," she finally said around the lust constricting her throat. Yes, she was horny. Yes, she'd been lusting after the firefighter spread before her like a smorgasbord before a lifetime member of Weight Watchers. But the fact was she was just too much of a chicken to do anything about it.

Still smiling, Thorne flipped back the corner of the sheet and patted the mattress.

Did she dare take what she so desperately wanted, what she needed?

She took a hesitant step closer. Then another.

"Summer?" The sound of his hushed voice caused her nipples to pucker beneath her sweatshirt.

Their gazes locked.

Even in the limited light, she could see the heat in his eyes.

His hand stopped her from crawling into bed.

"I'm tired, Summer. It's been a hell of a day and night."

Obviously she'd misread him. Before she could recoil, his warm hand gripped her knee, holding her in place.

"Stay," he said, his thumb rubbing fiery circles on her knee through the cumbersome material. "I just meant I want to save my energy for more interesting activities." He walked his fingers up to the juncture of her legs, causing her to squirm against his inflaming touch. He pulled her farther onto the mattress by cupping her sex with his palm and pulling.

When they were nose to nose, he whispered, "Lose the sweats. Please."

21

Summer had never in her life been so uncoordinated. At one point, she suspected she may have elbowed Thorne in the jaw in her hasty effort to strip.

Breathing hard from the exertion—okay, maybe she was more than a little turned on as well—she finally slid beneath the covers. "Your turn," she huffed out with a smile.

In response, he flipped back the cover to reveal all he wore was a smile.

It was her new favorite outfit.

Sliding eagerly into his arms, she couldn't stifle the little shimmy of eagerness she did when his heated skin touched her. Full body contact. She loved it.

She wanted more.

His lips brushed light kisses across the end of her nose, her cheekbones, her forehead, avoiding her starving mouth and the deeper kiss she craved.

The strains of an old song—"Set Me Free"—filled the bedroom.

Crap! Her whole body tensed within Thorne's embrace. Did Cory have spies who tipped him off as to the most inopportune time to call?

Mood instantly lessened, she eased from the heated promise of Thorne's arms. If she didn't answer, who knew what Cory would do in an effort to locate her? "I'm sorry," she whispered. "I should probably get that."

In answer, Thorne's hot hands continued to stroke her as she leaned over the side of the bed and felt for her cell.

Pressing the button to quiet the obnoxious ringtone, she snapped into the hand piece, "What?"

"About damn time you answered your phone," the nasal tone of her ex-husband echoed in her ear, setting her teeth on edge. "Where the hell are you?"

"None of your business, Cory. What I do and where I go no longer concern you. We're divorced, remember?"

He responded, but it was difficult to pay attention with the delicious things Thorne's hands were doing to her legs and breasts.

He tweaked her nipple, causing her breath to hitch.

"What's wrong?" Cory demanded.

"Nothing; I—ah!" Thorne's talented fingers stopped playing with her slick folds and slid deep. Her hips bucked, grinding against his erection.

"Are you with someone?"

"Again, Cory, none of your business." Her hips wiggled in a little happy dance against the mattress when Thorne began kissing his way over the swell of her buttocks, occasionally taking little nips along the way.

"Is someone with you?" her ex persisted in a strident voice.

Thorne reached for the phone, his brow raised questioningly.

Nodding her permission, she relinquished the phone.

"Yes." Thorne smiled and spoke directly into the receiver, then disconnected. He pulled her back against his heat. "Now, where were we?"

Much as she wanted nothing more than to lose herself in his arms, she felt compelled to explain. "He's just going to keep on until he finds where I'm staying. You know that, don't you?"

Leaning back, he looked down at her, his gaze so hot she wanted to tell him to forget she'd said anything. Forget her stupid ex-husband who had control issues. Forget everything except how it felt when they were together.

Finally he spoke. "Is that what you want?"

"Of course not! But this is Cory we're talking about. His entire life, whatever Cory wanted Cory got."

"Even you." It wasn't a question and it made her feel small and exposed. Maybe even a little stupid.

She didn't like feeling stupid.

"Not anymore." She yanked the sheet to cover her nudity, clutching it around her shoulders. "If it bothers you so much, you're free to leave."

"It's my bed. My house, in fact."

Staring at the sheet, she muttered, "I know. But at the moment, I have nowhere else to go. I can sleep on the couch if you—oh!"

His chest plastered against the sheet covering her, he gave a quick squeeze to pull her closer. "You're not going anywhere." His hot breath at her ear caused a little shiver of excitement to race through her. His teeth nibbled on her earlobe a second before his mouth began trailing a string of kisses down her vulnerable neck. "Unless you want to, of course."

It took considerable effort, but she finally managed a tiny shake of her head as she dragged enough air into her lungs to whisper, "No, I'm fine just where I am."

"Just fine?" He growled against her neck, his hands slipping beneath the sheet to toy with her nipples and lower until his palm cupped her sex. "I can make you feel a lot better than just fine."

No kidding.

But after her divorce, she'd sworn to never be the compliant partner again. While she was perfectly content to just lie there and relish all the delicious things Thorne was doing to her, a part of her screamed to be more proactive.

Hooking her heel around his calf for leverage, she flexed her thigh and pushed off the mattress, neatly flipping him to his back.

Now what? If she didn't do something soon, he would resume control. It wouldn't necessarily be a bad thing, but it just wasn't what she wanted. Not right now, anyway.

Pinning his hips to the mattress with her inner thighs, she leaned closer, allowing the tips of her nipples to graze his upper abs and chest as she made slow progress up his body until her lips brushed his.

"Ah-ah-ah," she whispered against his mouth, wrestling his hands from her rib cage. Palms together, she stretched until her hands held his above his head. "You've done so much for me, let me do something for you for a change, okay?"

His Adam's apple bobbed. "What did you have in mind?"

In reply, she dragged the tip of her tongue along the roughened edge of his jaw. Raspy and slightly salty. Onward, down his neck, then she nipped at his throat. "Mmm," she purred, alternately kissing and nibbling across his shoulder. Heading south, she trailed kisses diagonally until she came to an erect nipple.

She paused, worrying the nub with the edge of her teeth, smiling against his skin at the harsh intake of his breath. Swirling her tongue around and around the nipple, she finally drew it into her mouth, swallowing a chuckle at the way the muscles in Thorne's abdomen contracted against her with the action. Heat radiated from his erection where it nestled against her thigh.

His penis twitched, brushing her sensitized skin as she continued her trek, his powerful body vibrating beneath her questing hands and lips.

She was excruciatingly aware of his straining control. His muscles jerked and contracted beneath her lips and tongue. The powerful, musky scent of sexual excitement and testosterone wafted around her.

It would be so easy to give in, to do what they both yearned for her to do, to slide down and take him into her equally eager body.

But if she did that, she would be giving up control. She wanted to be the one doing the controlling, even if it was only for a little while.

Rolling to the right, she slid from his body and the temptation to let nature take its course.

Mind made up, she grabbed his erection in a less than tender, loving way, judging by the way he gasped.

"Oh!" He was pulling back. She tightened her grip. If she let him get away she'd never be in control.

"S-stop!" His back bowed off the mattress, his hands blindly grasping her arm where she held him in a death grip.

"What? Oh! I'm so sorry!" Could she be a bigger klutz? She'd planned to take him in her mouth, so she needed to get on with it before he decided she really wasn't worth the trouble. Forcing a smile, she kept her eye on the target. "Let me make it up to you."

Thorne clutched the sheet in his fist, panting. Had any other woman practically ripped his dick out by the root, he would want nothing to do with her. Ever. It had to be the undeniable fact that Summer was *the one* that made him react differently. Way differently. In fact, it sort of turned him on.

Maybe he was a latent masochist?

The drag of the sharp edge of her teeth against the tender skin on the head of his cock slapped that notion out of his mind.

Not wanting to make any sudden moves, he grasped the sides of her head, gently pulling until he disengaged her mouth.

Gaze locked with his, she absently stroked his fainting penis back to life.

"I-I thought you would like for me to do that," she said in a sad-sounding little voice.

"I do, baby; I do. Just not right now." Even in the dimness, he could see the hurt on her face. Damn it, what was it about the woman that made him want to tell her it was okay, even if it meant mutilation? "I also like it when you do this." To demonstrate, he pulled her higher until he could stroke the head of his cock with the tip of her nipple.

His cock liked it, too.

"And this?" she asked in a breathy voice, rising to her knees. Leaning down, she sandwiched him between her breasts, then rocked gently, gliding his erection in and out of her cleavage.

His hips bucked off the bed. "Oh yeah," he finally managed to say, gripping her and pulling her to straddle his hips.

Crunching his abs, he took her sweet-smelling nipple into his mouth, rolling the pebbled tip with his tongue before sucking it deep into his mouth.

They both groaned.

Her wet folds slid up and down his abdomen, grinding her pussy into him.

There was so much he wanted to do with this woman, so much he wanted to do to her, to have her do to him. . . .

But right now, he was heading fast into sexual overload.

He needed release and he needed it now. He groped between the mattress and springs for a condom.

With one last pull on her breast, he released her and looked up into her glazed eyes.

"But there's one thing I'd like even better," he said in a strained whisper as he made a new land speed record for rolling on a condom.

He wondered if she had any idea how much it turned him on when she sat rubbing her nipples like she was doing.

Grasping her hips, he positioned her, watching her smooth-skinned sex align with his sheathed and ready for action cock.

"Hmm?" She regarded him with a heavy-lidded gaze.

"Fucking you," he grunted out as he flexed his hips.

22

Her eyes widened at Thorne's graphic words, then widened more at the feel of his hardness probing her wetness a second before filling her.

Her breath caught. Her nipples puckered painfully. Her back arched. Yes! Her long dry streak was coming to an end.

Thorne thrust higher, his hands biting into the flesh, where he clutched her hip bones.

Against her swollen clitoris, his muscles contracted in an incendiary way, giving her the urge to rub against him as hard and fast as she could in an effort to reach the orgasm lurking just out of reach.

His abs bunched tighter as he came up off the mattress to suck on her aching nipple.

It made her impossibly wetter.

She clutched his head tightly to her breast, her hips bucking wildly of their own volition. Her increased wetness made it difficult to maintain her intimate contact.

Thorne sat fully up, holding her tightly against his heaving chest as he pumped into her receptive body.

Despite her wishing it would last forever, all too soon she felt *it*. The big O. And from the way her heart raced, her lungs seized, it promised to be a biggie. The orgasm to end all orgasms, the stuff legends were made of, the proverbial earth-shattering climax.

Poised on the brink, she held what little breath she had left, wanting to prolong the experience. To savor the thrill of it all. To... what the heck did he think he was doing?

Oblivious, Thorne pounded into her with single-minded determination. And from the way his eyes were scrunched shut, from the way his thrusts were increasing with the rate of his breathing, it was a safe bet the orgasm he was racing toward was not hers.

That would not do.

She finally drew enough air into her starving lungs to speak. "W-wait!" Hands spanning his corded neck, she squeezed and gave a little shake to get his attention. "Stop."

It took a few more thrusts, but his lean hips finally stopped their furious pumping. His iron grip eased a tad.

Breathing hard, he opened his eyes, looking slightly dazed. "What? Why?" As if to change her mind, he ground against her, still buried deep. "C'mon, baby. We're so close—"

"That's the problem! We aren't that close. At least not now." At his widened gaze, she shrugged and hurried on. "Thorne, it's been a long time since I've, well, been with anyone." She tilted his head until they were eye to eye. "There was a time when I thought I'd never be with anyone like this again."

Her fingers stopped whatever he was about to say.

"Sex with you is great. It's fun. But I need more. I need an earth-shattering, mind-blowing orgasm." Allowing her eyes to plead, she wiggled to close what little distance remained between them. Their gazes met. "And I don't care if it takes all night, I intend to get it."

With a grimace, he eased from her body, ignoring her protesting gasp.

"Wait right here."

23

Slipping on the tile, Thorne ran, buck naked, to the stack of boxes in the kitchen. Ripping open the tops like the madman he had become, he searched and tossed aside two boxes before he found the stash of sex toys junk his cousin's fiancée had left.

If Summer wanted an earth-shattering orgasm, he damn well was determined to see that she got one. Or more.

Hell, if she was that horny, he had no problems with their copulating like bunnies all night long. Tomorrow was his day off.

The thought stopped him in his tracks.

If Summer was *the one,* and with each breath he was more sure she was, what lengths was he willing to go to in order to keep her?

He glanced in the bag of sexual goodies in his hand. Did he even know how to use some of that stuff?

A slow smile curved his mouth. Maybe, maybe not. But they could have one hell of a good time figuring it out.

He stopped after the next step.

Maybe he should check out the stuff first, familiarize himself so he didn't look like a fool.

"Thorne?" Summer's voice had slipped from huskily sexy to somewhat confused.

"On my way." Gripping the bag, he strode toward the bedroom door.

It wasn't rocket science; he could bluff his way through if necessary.

Summer knelt in the middle of his bed, the sheet pulled just high enough to cover her nipples. While Thorne had been out of the room, she'd practiced several alluring positions, finally settling on sex kitten / pinup girl. The cooler air from the open window tickled her bare bottom, then whispered up her spine, causing her nipples to pucker and ache beneath the edge of the sheet.

In the partial light, her gaze traced his handsome features before sliding down his strong neck to broad shoulders. The bag he clutched scarcely registered, so intent was she on checking out all of his assets. Turned out, her imagination hadn't done him justice when she was contemplating what he'd look like without his firefighter garb. A fresh wave of excitement washed over her. From his smooth, tanned chest, to his lean narrow, paler hips, to his colorfully sheathed and still-impressive erection, he was all hers.

Well, for tonight, anyway.

"Let's see if we can't get earth-shaking orgasm number one going." He sat on the edge of the mattress and pulled a small bottle out of the bag in which he'd been rummaging.

"What is it?" Clutching the sheet, she edged closer.

He angled the bottle toward the light. "It says it's a stimulating oil to enhance female pleasure."

"Sounds good." She brushed the edge of her breast against his arm. "Do we put it on me ... or you?"

In response, he waggled his eyebrows. "How about both?"

Nodding, she held out her hand.

After he'd poured a small puddle into her palm, he dispensed with his condom and liberally oiled his fingers before reaching for her.

Their mouths met.

Her hand closed around his erection at the same time his questing fingers found her already-excited flesh.

The first touch of his warm hand on her aching folds felt so fabulous, so right, she almost wept. Within a few seconds of oiled fondling, however, things began to heat up. A lot.

Beneath her hand, Thorne's penis wasn't the only thing stiff. His whole body was rigid.

Fire streaked from his hand to her clitoris as flames licked straight up her vagina. To say it burned was a gross understatement.

"Shit!" Thorne yelped, and pulled away from her grip. He grabbed his shaft, waving it through the air. "I'm on fire! What the hell is in that stuff?"

It took a second to respond since she was intent on gripping her crotch and rocking back and forth against the sheet. "How should I know? You're the one who had the bright idea to use it!" Dang, it stung.

Gathering the sheet around her, she lunged from the bed. "Get out of my way! I have to wash it off!"

"I'm coming with you! I have to get this shit off before I become a eunuch!"

Lola yelped for joy and ran out when they opened the bathroom door.

Summer made a beeline for the big tub, twisting the handles on full blast as she flipped the drain plug shut.

"Are you nuts?" Thorne jerked open the clear glass shower

door and slammed down the control lever. "I don't have time for the tub to fill!" he yelled over the roar of water.

A glance at the scant inch of water in the bottom of the deep tub convinced her. Dropping her sheet, she followed Thorne into the steaming shower.

"Move over!" Her elbow connected with firm abs. Doggone it, she had to get the fire sauce off before she burned off her labia. There was no way Thorne could be feeling the burn as much, since all of his parts were on the outside.

Hard hands gripped her shoulders, setting her firmly on the opposite side of the big enclosure. "It's a double shower. You use those controls."

Ordinarily, she would have thanked him. After all, she had been raised to be polite. However, with her nether region threatening to go up in flames at any moment, she kept her mouth shut and reached for the handheld shower.

Twisting the dial, she aimed the needle-like spray directly at the part screaming for relief.

Within seconds, the fire between her legs dissipated to a less than pleasant intense heat. Did she dare try to use soap?

Behind her, Thorne heaved a sigh.

"What was in that stuff?" She accepted the bottle of shower gel and took a hesitant sniff. "Thanks." It had a clean fragrance.

"No problem. It helps the sting on burns, so I figured it couldn't hurt to try." He sighed again, the sound echoing from the glass walls. "I don't know what was in the oil. I don't know about you, but I have no desire to try that crap again."

"Hah! Considering my, um, parts are so sore and swollen, that won't be happening." They turned off their respective faucets.

The shower enclosure plunged into quiet, enclosing them in a misty cocoon. Gradually, the muffled sound of water running in the tub drifted in.

"Maybe I should sit in the tub a little while," she said, accepting a towel from him as she stepped out of the shower.

He nodded and finished drying. "I'm going to get a beer. Would you like something? I have beer, a little white wine, and some orange juice, if it's not expired. Oh, and water."

"No, thanks."

Gingerly lowering into the warm water, she winced. Through her eyelashes, she saw him watching her as he pulled on a robe. "Water stings a little."

He nodded and left the room.

The stinging subsided a bit, allowing her to comfortably slide lower until the water covered her shoulders.

Behind her closed eyes, images of her new sexy roommate flashed by, an embarrassing reminder of her lack of a successful orgasm.

The question was, what was she going to do about it?

24

Thorne tossed his empty bottle in the trash and popped open another beer while he waited for Lola to do her business.

A gentle breeze off the Gulf cooled the sheen of perspiration that broke out over his body every few minutes.

"For her pleasure, my ass." He chugged his beer, then wiped his mouth with the back of his hand, glaring at the innocent-looking bottle of oil perched on the railing. During his first beer, he'd read the label just to make sure he wasn't really going to burst into flames. It was basically cinnamon oil. Go figure.

"Lola?" he called in a low voice. "Aren't you done yet?"

"Thanks for letting her out." Summer's quiet voice came from behind him.

Squinting into the darkness, he pretended to look for the beagle. "No problem. Figured it was either that or clean up. Have you had your dog's bladder checked?" He turned with a smile, letting her know he was teasing. "Did you find the gel I left by the bathroom door? Aloe works great on burns."

She nodded, looking out at the waves. "I'm much better.

Thanks. Again." Her gaze met his as she stepped closer, dropping the robe he'd loaned her. "Want to try again?"

The slight rub of her breasts against his arm had him instantly hard. Hell yes, he wanted to try again. And again. And
again. But the fact was his cock, while definitely interested, still
burned more than a little.

And it was a sure bet her tender parts were worse off than
his; she just didn't know it yet.

His grandfather's sage advice echoed in Thorne's mind:
When in doubt, leave it out. His grandfather always maintained
it applied to many situations, although Thorne doubted Gramps
had ever thought of Thorne's current dilemma.

Damn, she was gorgeous, standing in the moonlight. Easily
the sexiest thing he'd ever seen.

Maybe if they were careful . . .

He took a small step toward her but stopped when the raw
skin of his erection brushed painfully against the loops of the
robe.

Unable to resist, he cupped her breasts, brushing the pads of
his thumbs lightly over the distended nipples. Summoning all
of his resolve, he touched his lips to one puckered tip, then another, before he straightened up.

Summer made a little sound in her throat and arched, thrusting her nipples higher. "More," she finally managed to say. Despite her earlier discomfort, she knew she wanted Thorne.
Now. The discomfort of the ointment from hell was nothing
compared to the deep ache of unfulfillment.

To her utter disappointment, he pulled her robe back up.
Stunned, she allowed him to pull the sleeves over her arms. He
snuggled the collar up around her neck before tying the belt.

"How's that?" His hushed voice would have been soothing
had they been snuggling, naked, after hot sex. As it was, it was
irritating, not to mention a little condescending. Did he hon-

estly think being dressed and warm would take her mind off the fact that she'd missed out on quite possibly the best sex of her life?

Jerking away, she took a deep breath and counted to ten. "How is that? How do you *think* that is? I'm horny and aching. I assumed you were, too. Dang it, Thorne, we were so close! How can you just turn it off and walk away as though we weren't within seconds of, of—"

"Fucking? Don't look so shocked, Summer. That's exactly where we were headed. You know it; I know it." He turned and tossed his empty bottle in the recyle can on the deck before turning back to look at her. "But the fact is we hardly know each other. I'm too old for that. And you strike me as the type of woman who would develop a strong case of morning-after remorse. Together, not a good mix."

She whirled on him. "What are you saying, Thorne? Are you trying to tell me you're not interested in whatever we might do?" Summoning her courage, she flicked her fingers against his robed but still obvious erection. Fueled by anger now, she ignored his intake of breath. So she'd shocked him. Good.

She was tired of being the good girl. Tired of having sex on other people's timetables.

She wanted sex.

She wanted it now.

And she wanted it with Thorne.

Pushing aside her usual shyness, she stalked him to the edge of the deck, not stopping until she'd backed him against the railing.

None too gently, she shoved his robe aside, baring his lean hips and impressive erection. With a hard shrug of her shoulders, her robe fell around her bare feet.

At another time, she might have paused to enjoy the sexy caress of the ocean breeze on her skin as it swirled around her body, tugging her nipples to sensitized peaks. But, for now, she was too focused, too eager for the naked man in front of her.

Closing the distance, she didn't stop until her breasts were pressed to his firm pecs, heartbeat to heartbeat.

He opened his mouth, but she didn't want to hear anything he might have to say. Not now. She'd waited far too long.

Grasping his ears, she pulled him down to her hungry mouth, nipping his lower lip before plundering his mouth with a kiss so carnal it took her breath away.

Thorne didn't hesitate for long.

Hot, hard arms crushed her against his body while each of them fought for control of the kiss.

Hooking her right leg around his thigh, she inched her way upward until his hardness probed her still-tender opening.

Bracing her forearms on his shoulders, she rose a little more until they were aligned.

She broke the kiss, breathing hard against his mouth. "Now," she urged. "Do it now! Fuck me!"

Thorne's sweat-slicked chest slid against hers. His hands cupped her buttocks. His knees flexed, powerful thighs rubbing erotically against the backs of her legs.

With a guttural grunt, he impaled her.

Heat. Everywhere was heated. Inside and out. Good Lord, she was burning up.

Clutching her knees against Thorne's waist, she rose up, then dropped back down onto his erection, causing them both to groan.

Soreness was forgotten as she increased the tempo, angling for just the right amount of friction. Close, she was so close.

"Faster! Harder!" She bit his ear, her hands grasping at the short strands of his hair. It wasn't enough. She wanted to pull him totally into her body. Absorb him. Then do it all over again.

The thought gave her pause, and in that instant her orgasm snuck up on her. It pounded into her as surely as the waves pounded the shore, drowning her in delicious pleasure, dragging her under into sheer bliss.

Thorne's back stiffened, his arms threatening to cut off her oxygen supply as he smashed her face into his shoulder.

Thorne and Lola howled at the same time.

25

Gradually, Summer regained her hearing. The cool breeze caressed her naked back while Thorne's heated flesh warmed her front. It took a moment, but she finally recognized Lola's soft, snuffling sounds. As soon as Summer's muscles would obey her command, she would check on her dog.

"Summer?" Thorne's low voice was a sexy growl in her ear.

She smiled against his chest. "Hmm?"

"Your dog is chewing on my ankle."

Reality intruded. Okay, it slapped her in the face. Back stiff, she paused. They were still . . . joined, for lack of a better word. What was the protocol for, well, *unjoining*? Did one just climb off, redress, and go on?

Maybe she should say something clever, like *Thanks, that was fun. Here's your penis back.* The thought had her swallowing a giggle.

At their feet, Lola continued her assault on Thorne's ankle. Summer had to do something before her dog drew blood. Assuming she wasn't too late.

With as much aplomb as she could muster, she peeled her abdomen away from the rock-hard abs of . . . what was Thorne to her now? Her lover? Her boyfriend? Her boy toy? She swallowed another hysterical giggle.

Sex had never been so much fun.

Thorne shifted, obviously uncomfortable with either their after-coitus body alignment or her dog. Or both.

Lola's growls elevated in pitch, which meant she was beginning to enjoy what she was doing a little too much.

Summer used the movement to finish the separation, gingerly touching her toes to the sun-warmed deck, and stepped back.

She tugged her robe from beneath her pooch and quickly slipped it on.

"Lola, cut it out!" She scooped Lola into her arms, nearly toppling Thorne in the process. "I'm so sorry! She's usually a people person—I mean, dog."

As if to disprove Summer's statement, Lola bared her sharp little doggy teeth and growled low in her throat.

Thorne winced as he glanced down at the redness on his ankle and tied his robe. "No offense, but that's kind of hard to believe."

"No, really, she is." Summer's arms ached from struggling to hold the squirming dog.

He ran a hand through his hair and looked out at the waves for a moment before looking back at Summer and Lola. "I think maybe it would be best for everyone if I went back to the motel. At least for tonight," he hurried on when Summer started to protest. "I really should be checking on things there, anyway. You know, Miss Laura and her sisters." He chuckled, the sound scratchy in the night air, and shrugged. "This way, you and your dog can have some privacy."

He already regrets having sex. The thought caused a lump in

Summer's throat. Did he think she went around stripping and throwing herself at every man who came along? The thought gave her pause. Of course he did. Why wouldn't he?

He stepped around her, causing Lola to renew her escape efforts, and disappeared into the house.

"Oh, Lola-belle," she said into the warm fur head, "what have I done?"

Paused inside the door, Thorne heard Summer's soft words and wanted to bang his head against something. Hard. What the hell had he been thinking? They were practically strangers.

So what if he knew, deep down, she was *the one*? She didn't know it. Yet. As far as she was concerned, she'd been taken to a secluded beach house and fucked on the damn balcony. She may or may not remember it was consensual. Hell, he could be facing charges. He could lose his job.

In his bedroom, he made quick work of throwing a few things into his duffel bag. Damage control was definitely called for, but what could he say? Leaving was about his only option.

But he had to say something. Something besides *wham-bam-thank-you-ma'am*.

Back on the balcony, his tentative touch on her shoulder caused her to jump. Remorse turned his stomach. Poor thing probably thought he was ready for round two.

"You don't have to go," she said, her words fast and low. "I can leave. It's your house, after all."

"You don't have a car, remember? I don't mind. I have stuff I need to do back at the motel. I—what are you doing?"

"Putting my number into your phone," she said, her fingers clicking on the keys of his cell phone. "Call me if you change your mind." Their eyes met, hers crinkling with her smile. "Or if you need help with the triplets."

Chuckling, the tenseness in his chest easing, he reclipped his phone on his belt. "That just might happen." His lips brushed the tip of her nose, eliciting another growl from her dog.

"Pleasant dreams. I have a few things I need to take care of tomorrow, but I'll be back in time to take you to the mall so you
can pick up some clothes."

Nodding, she watched him walk to the railing. Within seconds his footfall on the wooden stairs quieted. His truck engine
roared, then faded away, leaving nothing but the sound of the
surf.

"C'mon, Lola, let's try to get some sleep. But I warn you,"
Summer said as they entered the house and locked the door, "if
you try hogging the covers again, you're sleeping in the bathroom. Got that?"

The trill of her cell caused her heart to stumble. Was it
Thorne calling already?

Almost afraid to hope, she looked at the screen. Dang.

"Hi, Miss Laura." It was difficult to sound upbeat and
pleased to hear from anyone other than Thorne.

The thought gave her pause. She'd have to think about that
later.

"Hello, dear. Did you have a lovers' spat?" Miss Laura
asked, then hiccupped. " 'Scuse me. We don't mean to pry—"

"Like hell!" someone yelled from the background.

"Shut up, Cora; I'm on the telephone." Laura's sharp tone
caused Summer to feel sorry for Cora. "Now, where was I? Oh
yes. We don't mean to pry, but we couldn't help but notice
your young man had returned to the motel."

He's not my young man. Darn it. Could he be, someday?
The thought caused a tickle of excitement in the pit of her stomach. Did she want him to be hers? Crazy as it sounded, she did.

"Oh no, he just felt he needed to do some things at the Sea
Breeze. And he wanted to give me some privacy."

"Privacy! That's the last thing you need, young lady. In fact,
we've been discussing just that while we enjoyed our cocktails
this evening. And we have come up with a plan. Be ready bright
and early tomorrow morning."

26

Late the following morning, Summer exited Miss Laura's car on wobbly legs. She leaned down to peer into the interior through the open driver's side window. "Are you sure you don't want me to drive you home? It's no trouble at all." Plus, she vaguely remembered Laura had lost her driver's license several years ago.

After riding to and from the downtown shopping district with the women, Summer understood why the octogenarian was forbidden to drive. Summer's life had flashed before her eyes a couple of times during her morning trip. But the old ladies meant well. They'd bought her breakfast and taken her for a makeover at the local department store.

"Oh, we're not going that far, dear." Miss Laura's voice brought Summer back to the present. From the backseat, the sisters nodded. "We offered our services to your young man."

"Excuse me? What did you say?" The mental picture was enough to shock anyone.

"I said we're going to help Thorne refurbish the motel. We'll be staying there for at least the next week."

How the eighty-plus-year-olds planned to help was a mystery, but Summer smiled and nodded politely.

"I still wish you'd let me drive you to the motel. Thorne can give me a ride back."

"Oh, Thorne's not there at the moment, dear. He went surfing today."

Surfing. The thought clutched her heart. Sure, she'd seen his board on the roof of his truck. It didn't take a rocket scientist to deduce he surfed. Yet, in typical head-in-the-sand fashion, she'd toppled right into his arms. Despite her previous experience with a husband who'd rather surf than work. Who would rather surf than do just about anything else. Including being with her. Didn't she learn anything from her time with Cory Wadsworth?

"I see." And she did. Now if she could just convince her foolish heart to stop fluttering at the thought of the hunky firefighter. Stupid. It was just stupid.

They'd just met.

They'd just had incredibly hot sex.

Conflicted, she returned Miss Laura's wave and watched the big fins of the old Cadillac Coupe de Ville as it made its way to the beach access road, throwing up plumes of sand in its wake.

A squeal of tires on asphalt announced the car's successful trek through the sand. Horns blared as Miss Laura navigated the big car up the hill, bobbing and weaving across the lane markers.

"Try not to think about it," Summer murmured as she made her way up the steps to Thorne's beach house. She would let Lola out, then play with the new cosmetics. The saleslady had promised a newer, sexier look while Miss Laura and her sisters urged Summer on.

"It's worth a shot, I guess."

* * *

Summer applied the quick-drying top coat onto her new pedicure and wiggled her numb lips. The stinging had abated about half an hour after she applied her new, lip-plumping gloss, thank goodness. Now, her lips just felt slightly swollen and numb. She couldn't wait to see how she looked. The rest of the new makeup looked pretty good, in her opinion.

Lola snored softly from the other end of the couch and didn't so much as twitch when someone pounded on the door.

Was it Thorne, already? Maybe she'd misjudged him. Gingerly walking on her heels, she threw open the door.

"Cory. What are you doing here?" While she'd love nothing better than to shut the door on his smiling face, she was brought up better.

Shirtless, he stood smiling at her, unmindful or uncaring of the picture he made with his broad tanned chest, low-slung board shorts, and rubber flip-flops that had seen better days. His teeth shone white, his baby blue eyes hidden behind wrap-style sunglasses. Bright green goop covered his nose.

"Babe, that's not much of a greeting after all the time and effort I put out to find you."

"So sue me." Hand on her chest, she feigned surprise. "Oh, wait, you already did. Go away. We're divorced. We have nothing to say to each other."

"Babe, don't be like that! I was your husband—"

"Don't remind me!"

His hand prevented her from slamming the door. "At least let me come in for a drink of water. Then I'll leave. Promise. Please?"

Shoulders slumped, she stepped back to allow him entrance. "Fine. But then you're out of here."

He planted a smacking kiss on her forehead as he walked past her. "Babe, careful, you're apt to hurt my feelings."

"I'd like to hurt more than that," she grumbled, shutting the door.

"Whoa!" Cory stopped a few feet into the living room and looked around. "Babe, you've outdone yourself this time. This is a mess, even by your standards." He removed his sunglasses and narrowed his eyes at her. "What the hell happened to your mouth?"

"What?" Racing down the hall, she skidded to a stop on the marble bathroom floor, grabbing the edge of the sink to halt her progress. The image staring back from the mirror looked hideous. Lips swollen to purple-pink bubbles of flesh that looked ready to burst, she looked as though she were one step from a severe allergic reaction.

"Oh no!" Cool water did nothing for her condition. In fact, she soon realized she couldn't feel the water on her swollen lips.

"Babe." Cory leaned against the door of the bathroom. "You okay?"

Tears stung her eyes. Blinking furiously to avoid smearing her new eye makeup, she glared at him. "No, I'm not okay! Look at my lips!"

"No offense, babe, but I can't help looking at your lips. I mean, dude, they're all over your face." White teeth pulled on his lower lip.

"Do not laugh at me! I mean it, Cory. If you ever had any feelings for me, you wouldn't laugh. You'd help me!"

With a sigh he stepped into the bathroom. "What can I do? Did you eat something you were allergic to, maybe?"

"No," she whined. "It has to be the new lip-plumping gloss I just bought this morning."

"Well, it sure did its job. Ouch! No need to hit."

"You're not helping!"

"Okay, how about antihistamines? Do you have any?" He opened the medicine cabinet and took down a small white bottle. "Here. Take a couple of these. Drink a whole glass of water with them. That's my girl."

Summer paused from drinking to shoot him what she hoped was a *drop-dead* look. "I'm not your girl. I haven't been for a long time now."

He trailed the tip of his finger down her arm, brushing the side of her breast. "That could change, babe. Your mother would like that."

Water sloshed when she jerked away from his touch. "Well, I wouldn't. And my vote is the only one that counts."

Obviously ignoring her body language as well as her actual language, Cory closed the gap between them, sliding his arms around her waist to pull her closer. His hips swayed suggestively, his hardness rubbing against her abdomen. "We were good together, babe. Remember our honeymoon? We set the sheets on fire."

"So what? You did that with everyone. Too bad I didn't discover it until after we were married." Hands on his chest, she shoved until he stepped back.

"Aw, come on, babe," he said, following her back to the living room. "I've changed."

She whirled, hands on hips, wishing Lola would wake up and attack. "Really? What were you doing today?"

"You mean besides looking for you?" She nodded. "Surfing. Why?"

"Exactly my point."

"Oh, come on!" Yelling now, he paced the open area in the living room. "What do you have against me surfing? I surfed when we were dating. It's not like you didn't know I loved surfing."

"That's the problem, Cory. I was always second." She gave a watery laugh. "Or even less, if you count your girlfriends."

"I told you, I changed."

An accidental glance at the noticeable bulge in his shorts caused her to recoil. After being with Thorne, she was nauseated to think she'd ever had sex with Cory. And that's all it had been. Was that all it had been with Thorne? Truthfully, probably. But she sensed something else with Thorne. Something she'd never had with anyone else. A possibility of sex turning into something more. She was tired of playing it safe. She wanted to explore whatever might happen with Thorne. Or anyone else, for that matter, if things didn't work out with Thorne. Anyone except her ex-husband. "It's time for you to leave."

"Let me take you to dinner. We both have to eat. I could zip home and be back in less than an hour."

"I have plans. And even if I didn't, I don't want to go out with you, Cory. Not tonight, not ever. I don't know how much clearer I can make it."

"But Victoria said you'd had second thoughts—"

"Yeah, well, that's wishful thinking on my mother's part."

"She's still hoping for Wadsworth babies."

"She's going to have to get over it." Long strides took Summer to the kitchen. "All I have is tap water. Warm tap water because I can't get to the freezer for ice. Take it or leave it."

"I'm not all that thirsty now," he said as he opened the door.

She walked back to make sure she locked the door when he left.

He was still standing on the deck, just over the threshold.

"It's really over between us, isn't it, Sum?" The pathetic look on his face gave her pause. "I guess," he continued, "I always thought we were just on a break and everything would work out. What a headbanger, right?"

Summer sighed and stepped onto the deck. "If I led you to believe there was ever a chance of us reconciling, I'm sorry."

"Was I that bad for you?"

"We were bad for each other. Now we need to get on with our lives. Separately. Good-bye, Cory."

"Bye, Sum." He pulled her into his arms for a quick hug. "Have a good life."

* * *

Thorne shook water droplets from his head and face as he walked up the beach toward his house. Toward Summer.

It had been a stupid thing to do, leaving her after making love, but in some way he was glad it happened. Having last night to think about things and clear his head without the red haze of lust had been helpful. Now he could pursue her without sex getting in the way. Not that he didn't intend to get horizontal with her at each and every opportunity. Now he had at least a semi–game plan. A plan that included being a part of her life from here on out.

The couple embracing on his deck stopped him in his tracks.

"What the fuck?" Thorne increased his pace, bare toes digging into the warm sand with each angry stride.

As he rounded the corner, the shiny black Lincoln Navigator with the boards strapped to its top snagged his attention.

Know your enemies. It could work.

27

Summer stopped splashing her mouth with cold water and listened. The rumbling continued.

A quick dab with the towel and glance in the mirror confirmed she still looked like someone had hit her in the mouth, but it couldn't be helped.

If Thorne was outside, why hadn't he come in or at least knocked? And if it was Thorne's voice she heard, who was he talking to?

She stepped out onto the deck just in time to see Thorne help her ex-husband secure his surfboard to his truck, give Cory an *attaboy* slap on the back, and head toward the deck.

By the time Thorne reached the top of the stairs, she was practically vibrating with anxiety. Of course, it was anxiousness. Why would she be angry? Wait a minute. He'd obviously been with her ex-husband for the last—she glanced down at her watch—hour and a half. Dang right, she was angry. They had no business having anything to do with each other. Crap! Were they comparing notes about her? It was pretty much common knowledge that Cory was capable of just about anything. What about Thorne? Had she been horribly mistaken about him, too?

He paused at the edge of the deck, the muscles in his throat working, jaw set.

"What have you been doing?" she blurted out.

His eyes narrowed. "I could ask you the same question."

Two long strides brought him in front of her, close enough for her to see the hardness in his eyes, feel the anger radiating from his fit body.

Anger? Why the heck would he be angry? She hadn't done anything.

"What? What are you talking about?"

"This!" He tapped her lips.

A gasp escaped at the needle-sharp pain his action caused on her swollen lips. "Cut it out! That hurt!"

"Maybe lover boy Cory will kiss it and make it all better. Then again, we both know that's how it happened in the first place."

"What are you talking about?" She grabbed the back of his waistband as he started into the house. "I haven't kissed Cory in over a year, not that it's any of your business."

He spun on her. "I'm not stupid, Summer. I know kiss-swollen lips when I see them."

She released his shorts, letting the elastic snap. "Well, you're wrong, bucko. You absolutely are stupid if you think that's what happened." Shoving him aside, she walked into the house, willing away the impending tears, and plopped down on the couch beside a still-sleeping Lola.

Thorne towered over her, hands on his hips.

Their gazes locked.

"I bought new makeup today," she finally said. "The lip gloss was supposed to plump up my lips."

"It worked." Thorne's lips quivered.

"They looked worse earlier."

"Have you looked in the mirror?"

"Thorne, you're not helping."

"What was wrong with your lips before you bought that goop?"

One shoulder lifted. "I guess I wanted to be more attractive. Since I didn't have any makeup with me, I decided to try a new look."

"Well, it's definitely different. Whatever look you were shooting for, you missed." He scooped her off the couch and sat down with her on his lap. "Don't cry. I was just teasing. I think you look pretty." He ran his fingertip along the edge of her strapless sundress, tickling her exposed cleavage. "I like your new dress." He frowned. "You aren't planning on wearing it to work, are you? I mean, it's nice, but kind of revealing. I guess what I'm saying," he stammered on, "is I would rather be the only one seeing you in something this sexy."

"Oh?" She did an experimental wiggle and was immediately rewarded by a returning thrust of his cloth-clad erection.

"Mm-hmm," he said against her neck, trailing nibbling kisses up to her ear. "But I'd rather see you out of it."

Heat from his hand streaked up her leg as his fingers stroked higher and higher until they reached her weeping flesh.

Pausing, his breath coming faster, he whispered gruffly in her ear, "You entertained your ex without any panties on?"

"Keep feeling," she said on a giggle, then gasped when his fingers tugged at the strap of her thong and slipped beneath the strip of fabric.

His left hand, which had been kneading her breast, shoved her bodice down to her waist.

He lowered his head, his breath hot against her erect nipple. "No bra. I'm liking this dress more by the second. Easy access."

All talk stopped when his mouth covered her nipple, tugging and sucking it deep into his wet heat.

Beneath her skirt, his fingers were busy, stroking up and down her slick folds.

Just as she thought she could take no more teasing and was about to grab his hand to show him what she needed, his finger found its mark, sliding deep, causing her to arch in his embrace, a guttural groan sounding deep in her throat.

Frantic for release, she bucked against his hand, squirming to gain access to his shorts. Shaking, she pushed her hand beneath the wide elastic until she found the hot hardness she craved. Awkwardly, due to her position, she squeezed and stroked his length, smiling when his hips rose to follow her hand.

It wasn't difficult to expose his penis. A little more effort was required to pull up her skirt enough to turn and straddle his lap. All the while, his fingers worked their magic, plunging into her receptive body, flicking and tugging on her clitoris until her climax threatened.

She paused, watching in fascination, the contrast of his tanned hand against her pale exfoliated lips ratcheting up her excitement. The need to feel his erect flesh deep inside her had her breath coming in shallow huffs while her pulse pounded in her ears. Yet she couldn't force herself to stop his hand or move from the exquisite torture.

Her muscles tightened. Every nerve ending began to tingle.

In voyeuristic fascination, she watched as her climax rushed from her body, soaking Thorne's hand and shorts. A full body shiver washed over her. Still he continued to stroke her, smoothing her wetness over her heated skin, exciting her all over again.

"No," she managed to whisper, the sound rasping through her dry throat. "Not without you. I want you." Her thighs flexed, pushing her to her knees. Deep inside, his fingers fluttered, causing her to gasp in pleasure.

Thorne took advantage of her stillness to suck her breast

deep into his mouth again, rolling the turgid nipple with his tongue. Fluttering its tip while he fluttered her labia with his fingers, he sent her into sensory overload. At that moment, she knew he could do anything and everything to her and she would welcome it. Revel in it, even.

But she'd meant what she'd said.

Before another orgasm could take her breath, she pushed his hand away and mounted him, rocking her hips against his until he was deeply seated, the head of his penis kissing the opening to her womb, tickling her deep in her core.

Thanks to her height, he was able to continue pleasuring her breast while he moved his hips in leisurely thrusts.

It was beyond pleasurable, beyond nice. But she wanted more. Much more.

Locking her knees to his lean hips, she rose on her knees until his erection almost slipped out, then plunged downward until their pelvic bones bumped with a satisfying slap of skin against skin.

So far gone, she could only repeat her bold move a few times before her orgasm washed over her, pulling her in with its powerful undertow, drowning her in sensation.

Thorne's back arched; the muscles holding her clamped tightly to him became rock hard. A guttural sound erupted from his throat.

Summer collapsed on him, her cheek resting on his sweat-slicked shoulder, as she gasped for breath. At her bare breast, his heart beat a thunderous tattoo against her own.

His panting breaths heated her cheek and ear. "Summer?"

"Hmm?" She kissed his shoulder, then covertly licked. Deep within, his penis jerked, bringing a smile to her swollen lips.

"That's nice," he gasped, "but could you tell your dog to stop gnawing on my ankle?"

28

"Lola! Stop that!" Awkwardly Summer tugged her bodice up and her skirt down. There was no graceful way to get off his lap. With a silent prayer she wasn't flashing him, she settled for falling sideways, then scooting until she sat beside him.

Lola's soft growling filled the silence as she continued to nip and chew on Thorne's poor ankle.

With a sigh, Summer grabbed Lola and strode to the door, not stopping until she'd locked the little dog out on the deck.

Thorne had covered himself and was checking for damage when Summer returned.

"I'm so sorry," she said, sinking to the couch as she wondered if she should stay on her end or plaster herself to his side, hoping for an instant replay.

His cell began to vibrate across the floor. Immediately a siren split the quiet comfort of the waves breaking on the beach.

Thorne scooped his phone into his hand and pressed a button. "I've got to go."

"Are you coming back?" Say yes.

He shrugged but still didn't move toward the door. "I don't know. It's a brush fire, but I won't know if it's been contained until I get on-site."

She nodded.

He stepped forward. She thought for sure he was going to kiss her.

Instead, he tapped her lips with his index finger and grinned. "Maybe I should stay away awhile, to give your lips a chance to deflate." At the door, he looked back. "I need to tell you I'm going surfing tomorrow with your ex. Wait, before you get upset, I'm just going surfing with him to see if he's any good."

"Why?" Arms crossed, she concentrated on not clenching her fists. "I mean, why are you telling me? It's a free country and I could care less about what Cory does."

"I just didn't want you opening a can of whoopass on me. Let me finish. I had my reasons for spending time with him. First of all, I like to surf. But mostly, if he's any good, I have a buddy who could help him get a sponsor to go on the pro circuit." His teeth flashed white with his grin. "I figured anyone who surfed as much as you said he did had to be pretty good. Plus, you said he won't leave you alone. If he goes on tour, problem solved."

"I didn't ask you to solve any of my problems."

"You're welcome." He spun on his heel and stomped through the door.

After a beat of hesitation, she hurried to the deck in time to see him reach his truck.

"Wait!" She leaned as far over the deck as she could without risking a fall. When he looked up, she swallowed and said, "I'm sorry. I shouldn't have said that. Thank you. Really."

In the blink of an eye, he stood before her, grinning down at her. He pushed her against the rail as he shoved her bodice to her waist. For the next few seconds he suckled and squeezed her breasts voraciously. Then he stepped back and tugged her bodice back into place.

"Thank you," he said with a smile and a wink. "Really." He reached into the pocket of his shorts and pulled out the thong he'd removed in the heat of their passion and handed it to her. "Your decision whether or not you put it back on." He winked again. "I'm planning on taking it off you as soon as I walk back in the door later."

Before she could respond, he'd disappeared. The roar of his truck engine soon followed, then slowly faded away.

The sappy smile on her face refused to dissipate long after the glow of Thorne's taillights disappeared. Lola tugged on Summer's hand, but she ignored her, reliving the best sex of her life and anticipating more to come.

Lola's hacking cough brought Summer back to reality with a thud. It took less than a second to realize what was happening. She ran into the house and grabbed her phone.

Thank goodness the vet was still in.

"Dena!" she said, scanning the room for her purse. "Don't leave! I'm bringing Lola in." Without waiting for her friend to reply, she disconnected and hit the next number, pacing and checking on her dog every few seconds. "Miss Laura? . . . I'm sorry to ask you, but could you drive me into town? . . . Now. Lola's swallowed another pair of panties."

Thorne paused outside the door of his beach house. Maybe he should go back to the motel again tonight. But he was tired.

And horny.

On the drive back to the beach, all he could think about was sliding into bed, into Summer's welcoming body.

But first, he needed a quick shower to wash the smoke off.

The house was dark and quiet. Was Summer asleep? No

demon dog snarled from the darkened bedroom, so he considered it a good omen.

Despite his shower, he still sported a monster erection by the time he padded into the bedroom.

The bed was empty.

Had she left a note somewhere? Or had she gotten tired of waiting for him and gone home? Martinez had told him the arson and reclamation people were finished with her duplex. The furniture was still out for cleaning, but she could go home if she wanted.

And what about him? Was that what he wanted? They could still date. But after making love with her, he was loathe to let her out of his bed.

A yawn crept up on him. Her stuff was still strewn around his bathroom. That had to mean something.

Meanwhile, the bed beckoned. Suddenly bone tired, he crawled naked between the sheets and stretched out, enjoying the tactile pleasure of the crisp cotton against his skin. His eyelids drifted shut.

As soon as Miss Laura and her sisters drove away, Summer scampered up the stairs. Just the sight of Thorne's truck parked under the deck had made her wet. Thank goodness the old ladies were out past their bedtime and not inclined to socialize.

Dena, the vet, had wasted no time in retrieving Summer's panties and Lola was now resting comfortably in the kennel overnight for observation.

Which meant Summer and Thorne had the house to themselves.

And the bed.

Almost giddy with anticipation, she quietly locked the door behind her.

Thorne's wallet and phone lay on the makeshift table by the

couch. She put her purse next to them and stepped out of her sandals.

"Thorne?" she whispered at the bedroom door as she wiggled out of her dress. His deep breathing told her he slept, so she opted for a quick shower.

A few minutes later, she dried off and applied the new perfumed lotion she'd purchased during her shopping trip. The sultry scent filled the steamy bathroom.

Turned on and feeling more than a little naughty, she impulsively dabbed a drop of the coordinating perfume on the tip of each puckered nipple.

Beside the bed, she tugged on the sheet, revealing in inch by agonizing inch the magnificent body of her new lover.

Thorne slept on.

She crawled up on the mattress and slid across the sheet until her nakedness was pressed along the length of his, then pulled the covers up over them.

A shiver skittered up her spine at the seductive friction of the sheet on her bare skin. And at the breathtaking rightness of her skin against Thorne's.

She made her way up his neck to his earlobe in slow, deliberate, wet kisses.

Thorne slept on.

Her fingertips danced up the smoothness of his firm thigh, through the warm nest of curls to the silken length of him. Opening and closing her hand, she manipulated his sex from his testicles to the tip and back again until he grew long and hard, his weight heavy in her hand.

Thorne slept on.

A wicked smile curved her lips as she shimmied down. With slow, breath-catching movements, she circled each of her nipples with the tip of his penis as she grew wetter and more excited.

Unable to resist, she took him into her mouth, circling his

bulbous head with the tip of her tongue, licking his hard length, then sucking him deep into her eager mouth. His hips twitched, driving him deeper, but he slept on.

Frustrated, she climbed to straddle him, sliding her needy length against his heat until they were aligned, mouth to mouth, heart to heart.

It wasn't enough.

Inching higher, she paused to enjoy the feel of his breath against her aching nipple.

"Thorne?" she whispered, then manipulated his jaw until she could get her breast into his mouth.

Immediately he began to suck, his hips moving suggestively, his erection bumping her bottom.

Stretching out along his glorious nudity, she once again thanked fate for her long torso when with her downward push and his thrust he pushed into her aching folds. She ground her hips against his, pushing him higher, deeper, and began her ride.

29

Thorne sighed. It was the hottest sex dream he'd had in years. Maybe ever. Of course, it would be better if it were real and he were making love with Summer. But, damn, it was definitely the next best thing.

He ran his hands over her silky skin and greedily inhaled her seductive scent as he suckled her virtual breast.

When she took him into her, damned if it didn't feel real. Hell, he was alone and naked in his bed. So what if he masturbated? He was going for it.

His hips pistoned into her wet heat while he sucked harder on her breast, worrying the taut nipple with the edge of his teeth. His tentative nip only fueled his dream lover's passion, making her impossibly wetter.

She rode him hard, her imaginary breath fanning his face while her breast gently slapped his cheek.

Even the sensation of her nails digging into his shoulders felt real. She said something hot and dirty against his ear, but his sex-crazed brain couldn't decipher the words. Then she bit his ear. Hard.

Thorne's eyelids flew open.

Summer reared back, her luscious breasts bobbing with each energetic thrust and grind of her hips on his.

For a second he could only watch in awe that such a goddess was attempting to fuck his brains out.

He could live with that.

Around his eager cock, her slick muscles began contracting, pulling and sucking on his sex until he had no choice but to follow her into a tsunami of orgasmic sensation.

Throughout the rest of the night, they reached for each other in an attempt to sate the insatiable lust flaring between them.

Sunrise bathed the room in a soft glow while they waited for their breathing to regulate again.

Thorne couldn't stop smiling as he lay there, holding her sweat-slicked body close. He knew he should be tired. He'd surfed, put out a fire, and set a new personal best for the most consecutive coitus in a twenty-four-hour period. And he couldn't wait to break his record.

Summer placed a kiss over his heart and smiled up at him in the early morning light. "Good morning." She stretched, dragging her breast upward.

It took very little effort or encouragement on her part for Thorne to take her into his mouth and suck until he felt her growing wet against his leg.

Rolling, he grabbed a condom from the open drawer. As soon as he'd rolled it on, he pulled her until she straddled him. It was a position they'd discovered to be the most effective in pushing them both to the edge in record time. It would do, for now. But he had four days off coming up and he planned to spend them deeply embedded in his current bed partner.

And she wasn't only his current bed partner but his future, if he had any say in the matter.

They climaxed within seconds of each other.

She rolled to his side, her hands still busy stroking his chest, his hip, his thigh. "I love the way you say good morning."

There it was, his opening.

"Maybe that's because you love me." He held his breath when her hand stopped moving, tightening his grasp on her shoulders when she tried to put distance between them. "Stay here. We both know we have something special. I want you to move in with me."

"We just met!" She made a halfhearted attempt to move away from him, then wilted, her breasts snuggling up against his side, where they were meant to be. "How can we possibly be falling in love?"

"We're not possibly anything." He planted a hard kiss on her swollen lips and waited.

"I was going to tell you I'm moving back into my house today or tomorrow. Miss Laura and her sisters are loaning me some furniture until mine has been fumigated or whatever they're doing to get rid of the smoke."

"Wouldn't it just be easier to stay here? We're going to be sleeping together every night, anyway. Why not let me take care of you?"

This time, she broke his embrace and slid to the edge of the bed. "Because I have a home of my own. A life of my own. And a job I have to go back to in two days."

"So quit. You said you hated the job anyway." He sat up and pulled a T-shirt over his head, then reached for a pair of shorts from the floor.

"No." Her voice was muffled from the dress she was slipping over her head. Her head popped through the top of the dress and she wiggled as she tugged it down to cover her nudity. "I said I hated my boss. Besides being cheap, he says inappropriate things and can't keep his hands to himself."

"All the more reason to quit," Thorne persisted, trying to

tamp down the rage he felt at the thought of a boss being a sexual predator, especially a boss of the woman he loved.

Sighing, she rounded on him, hands on her hips. "If I quit, I'd have to give up the luxuries I've become accustomed to, like eating and living indoors. Plus, I have a dog to support."

"Yeah, where is she?" His ankle was still sore and he didn't want to be ambushed.

"She ate a pair of my panties and spent the night at the vet's office."

"Is she okay?" Lord knew, he wasn't overly fond of the dog, but he knew Summer loved her, which meant he had to learn to love her, too.

"Yes. She does dumb stuff like that occasionally. By the way, how's your ankle?"

"It's fine. Summer," he said, pulling her into his arms, "I'm sorry about telling you to quit your job. I had no right. It'd be like you telling me to quit the fire department."

"True. Although you did say you went part-time so you could surf more."

"No." He massaged the sudden tension stiffening her spine. "I said I went part-time after I moved from Houston and I like having the extra time to surf. Big difference. I'm part-time because they only have part-time firefighters in Harper's Ferry. So I have more time to surf." He leaned close and nipped her earlobe. "Or make love to you."

"Would you quit surfing if I asked?"

Would he? "Yeah, if it was that important to you, sure."

Suddenly, it wasn't all that important to her.

Smoldering Lust

LYDIA PARKS

Prologue

Fourteen years ago

"You can't just leave me here." Hannah hated the note of desperation in her voice, but she couldn't help it.

"Watch me." Sterling sneered as he put his arm around Juli Tucker and walked away. Juli grinned in triumph over his shoulder.

Hannah stood gaping for a full minute before she thought to follow them. She stumbled into a hallway choked with couples making out and people drinking and smoking. Everyone yelled over deafening music, and some guy shoved her against a wall as he passed.

Her ears rang, her stomach tightened, and tears burned her eyes. Pushing her way through the throng, she made it to the door in time to see Sterling Mason's Audi turn out of the driveway and the taillights disappear into the total darkness of surrounding pastureland.

"Jerk!"

Tears started down her cheeks as she stood in the doorway. How could he do this to her? And how on earth was she going to get home?

If he'd abandoned her at a party in town, she could have walked. But this place had to be at least thirty miles from Tillman. And the generator she'd noticed as they were walking in meant the place was abandoned. There wouldn't be a phone.

Hannah discreetly wiped her eyes as she turned to search the crowd. Most people looked to be in their twenties at least, not much chance of finding anyone she really knew. Her only option was to ask a stranger for a ride back to town and hope he or she wasn't a psycho.

How could she have been so naive? She'd thought Sterling was sincere when he apologized and asked her out. She had no idea he was still angry and only wanted to get even.

A guy stepped in front of her. She tried to back out of his way, but he followed. "Hey. Want to do a line?"

She looked up into the bloodshot eyes of a man nearly twice her age.

He placed his hand on her shoulder and breathed his putrid breath in her face. "We could fool around. Nice young thing like you needs someone—"

Hannah shoved his hand away and hurried in the opposite direction, not caring where she went as long as it was away from the creep at the door. Weaving around more couples, she climbed stairs to the second floor of the ancient house, hoping for a quiet place to hide long enough to pull herself together. Or at least long enough to quit crying.

She followed a hallway and slipped into the first dark room with an open door. Pressing her back to the wall, she wiped her eyes.

How could Sterling have done this to her? She'd never speak to him again, except maybe to tell him off. What an absolute jerk!

The tears wouldn't stop. She used her sleeve to mop them from her face.

Although she could still hear music, the room was quieter than downstairs. If she could just figure out—

Footsteps and voices in the hall helped dry her tears. Please don't let it be the creep. She held her breath and listened.

The door squeaked open and Hannah backed into the corner, wishing she were invisible.

The couple who walked in probably wouldn't have noticed her if she'd stood in a spotlight. They kissed and shed clothes as they stumbled across the room, and were down to their underwear when they fell together onto a bare mattress that had either been left behind long ago or brought in just for the party.

Hannah wondered if she could get out without them seeing her.

"We don't have much time."

The guy's voice, deep and lusty, sounded familiar, and there was something about his blond hair and build. He was tall and slender but athletic looking, like Lee Evans.

Lee had always been one of the best-looking boys in town, in a scruffy sort of way. Hannah had known him all her life, but she'd only discovered how great he looked when she'd stumbled across him playing basketball shirtless last year. He'd been the star of her erotic daydreams ever since.

Over the past few years, she'd seen Lee with more than half the girls in school at some point, as well as a few who looked older than high school age. The redhead in his arms at the moment had probably left college behind.

It was Lee, wasn't it? Hannah couldn't be certain since their faces were hidden by shadows, but she was fairly sure. The hall light illuminated their bodies from the shoulders to the knees. Muscles in his back and arms flexed as he reached down and pushed the woman's panties to her thighs, then removed his shorts. She kicked off her panties and wrapped her legs around him. His hands slid up to her breasts and hers ran over his back.

Oh my God, they're about to do it.

Hannah had never actually seen a couple have sex. She knew she shouldn't watch but was drawn to the sight. She could almost feel his hands on her flesh and taste the kisses she'd fantasized about for a year.

The woman raised her knees on each side of Lee, and he reached between them.

Hannah swallowed hard, her mouth suddenly dry. She *should* leave.

The woman murmured and rose up to meet his force as he entered in one long stroke. They froze, joined, for a moment, and then started into a steady rhythm.

Hannah's crotch grew heavy. She imagined what it would feel like to have Lee thrusting into her as she watched him thrusting into the redhead.

The couple grunted and moaned together as their movements quickened with thrusts wet and deep.

"Harder," the woman said, her voice thick. "I'm coming."

Hannah bit her bottom lip to quiet her breathing and fondled her own breast, squeezing the hard nipple.

"Oh, fuck, yes," the woman whispered.

Lee pumped harder, faster, and then both cried out in ecstasy.

Their movements slowed and then stopped, and they lay together breathing hard.

Lee rose up on his elbows. "Shit. Who's in here?"

Hannah gasped and charged through the doorway, praying he wouldn't see her as more than a blur. Once clear of the room, she glanced back as she ran and then stopped with a grunt when she hit something.

Or someone.

"Oh, I'm sorry. I—" She stared up at . . . Lee?

"You okay?" he asked, grabbing her arms to keep her from falling.

She nodded as a storm of emotions washed over her, leaving her in tears again. Her embarrassment at getting caught watching the couple in the room faded to some strange sense of relief at knowing the guy wasn't Lee and then gave way to the helplessness she'd felt when Sterling first ran out on her. "Not really." She wiped her cheeks with the backs of her hands.

Lee released her arms but didn't step away. "Who brought you here? Mason?"

She nodded.

He sighed. "I saw him leave with someone else."

She nodded again.

"Guy's pretty stupid for being so rich."

Hannah laughed and wiped away fresh tears. "Thanks."

"Want a ride back to town?"

"Yes, please."

He followed her down the stairs and through the crowd. She tried not to look at anyone, hoping they wouldn't notice she was crying.

Her tears finally stopped as she walked beside Lee in silence to an old pickup truck parked at the edge of the yard. He opened the passenger's door and leaned in to rearrange things. "Sorry for the mess," he said, backing out.

The truck smelled of motor oil and leather, with a hint of stale French fries. Before he closed her door, she caught a glimpse of jeans and shirts folded and stacked on the seat, as well as a tool belt on the floorboard, nearly hidden by old newspapers, empty fast-food bags, and crushed Coke cans. Hannah buckled her seat belt, then flattened her hands between her knees to ward off the cold night air.

Lee jumped in and pumped the gas pedal. The ancient engine roared to life on the second try.

"She's loud, but the heater works," he said. "It'll warm up in a bit."

He had a soothing, deep voice that was nothing like the one

she'd mistaken for his. How could she have been so wrong? Maybe it was because in all the years they'd known each other she couldn't remember him ever saying more than a dozen words to her.

The truck bounced through a ditch and onto the road, and trash tumbled over her feet.

"Sorry," he said.

"Looks like you live in your truck." She pushed the mess to one side and glanced over to gauge his reaction.

His face, glowing green in the dash lights, gave nothing away. He wore a crooked smile she'd always found more than a little attractive. "Sometimes."

They followed the gravel road until it tied into pavement. He looked at her once or twice, probably to see if she was still crying, but didn't say anything.

"I'm sorry you had to leave the party for me," she said.

"No big deal. I was just looking for someone."

Hard to believe they could live all their lives in a town the size of Tillman and know so little about each other. She was fairly sure Lee lived somewhere on the outskirts of town with his father. Had his mother died, or were his parents divorced? She didn't know. And he didn't show up at school every day, but when he did he sat quietly through classes. She had no idea if he'd ever been in any real trouble. In spite of her fantasizing about him almost daily, they may as well have lived on different planets.

"Do you mind dropping me off at my house? I live at Two-ten Elm."

"No, I don't mind." He smiled again. "And I know where you live."

"You do?"

"Sure. It's the nicest place in town."

He obviously knew more about her than she did about him.

Twenty minutes later, he pulled to the curb across the street from her house and turned off the engine. "Sure your dad's home?"

She gazed out at the dark house. "Yes, I'm sure. He goes to bed early." Her stomach knotted at the thought of telling her father she hadn't really planned to stay at Crystal's house. He would be so disappointed in her.

"Want me to walk you to the door?"

She met Lee's concerned gaze and shook her head. "No, thanks. I'll be fine."

"He won't hurt you, will he?"

"No, of course not."

"Good."

She frowned at the realization that his question might be grounded in personal experience. Was that why he spent so much time in his truck?

Hannah slipped out the passenger side and walked quietly around the front of the vehicle, the crunching of gravel under her shoes the only sound in the night.

Lee waited, leaning against the driver's door.

"Thank you, Lee. I really appreciate your help." With her hand on his arm, she stood on tiptoe and kissed him.

He sucked in a quick breath.

His lips were incredibly soft and warm, and he tasted a little of mint.

Unable to move, she stood looking up at him, feeling his breath whisper across her face, enjoying his masculine scent. His eyes glistened in the soft lights from porches and windows as they studied hers. Then he dipped his head and returned the kiss.

His mouth opened, parting her lips, and he cupped her face with one hand as his tongue swirled around hers.

She felt suddenly dizzy and fell against him.

He wrapped an arm around her and drew her up hard as he reached deeper, tasting, inviting her closer.

She'd never been kissed like this, only dreamed of contact so sensual and perfect, and grabbed his shirt to hold on. The world around her faded to nothing but his touch and scent, and his amazing mouth.

He pulled her into his embrace.

He was hard beneath his jeans, and awareness flared in her belly, drawing her closer. She remembered the sounds of the couple and the way their bodies met in urgent need.

Then suddenly his hands were on her shoulders and his mouth was inches away.

Gasping for breath, she stared up at him.

The skin around his eyes crinkled with a smile. "You better go in," he said softly, "before it's too late."

Heat clawed up her neck as she realized what she'd just done. He must think her an immature idiot for throwing herself at him. Girls probably did that all the time.

Then his warm palm cupped her cheek again and he tenderly kissed her lips. "Good night, Hannah," he whispered against them.

She stumbled when he released her.

Turning, she hurried across the deserted street. At her front porch, she retrieved the key from under the flowerpot and glanced back.

Lee leaned against his truck watching her, one boot crossed over the other, arms folded across his chest, wearing his crooked grin. She'd never seen a sexier guy in her life.

1

"Chief?"

Lee smiled as he turned to answer. After only three days, he wasn't quite used to being chief of his own fire department. "Yeah?"

Tommy pointed toward the front door. "You got company."

Lee dropped the sponge into the bucket, splashing suds on his boots. He nodded toward the half-washed engine. "Can you finish this by yourself?"

"Yes, sir."

"Good." Wiping his hands on his pants, he walked around the engine to find his guest wearing a suit and waiting outside his office. "Well, Mayor Richards. What an honor it is to have you visit." Lee stuck out his hand. "*Sir.*"

Charlie Richards laughed and accepted the handshake. "Cut the crap, Lee. Do you have anything resembling coffee around here?"

Lee led the way to the kitchen. "I can scrape something out of a pot." He filled two cups, placed one in front of Charlie, and sat across the table with his own.

They sipped, and Charlie winced. "This is pretty bad."

"Yep. Keeps me awake when nothing's burning down."

Charlie sipped again. "You know, I really want to thank you for taking this job."

Lee shrugged. "It was an offer I couldn't pass up."

"Oh? Too many women chasing you around in Seattle?"

He laughed. It was good to sit with someone he'd known all his life—something he hadn't done in twelve years. He wasn't sure Charlie would understand.

"Things have changed a bit around Tillman since you left, huh?" His friend studied him from across the table.

"I suppose. Having you as mayor is a major change."

Charlie nodded. "Yeah, I guess it is. Lisa really turned my life around, you know?"

Lee had met Charlie's wife and their two girls, Katie and Amy, but still had problems coming to grips with him settling down. Charlie had been the biggest partier he'd known in high school.

"I have to tell you, Lee, how much I appreciate you covering my ass all those years. If you hadn't pulled me out of the ditch now and then... well, I guess I wouldn't be here talking to you."

"Hey, let's don't get too mushy, huh?"

Charlie nodded. "Check."

They drank more coffee.

"Oh," Charlie said, "our city manager's back from her conference. You probably want to go over your budget request with her before the council meeting Monday. The council listens to Hannah, so you definitely want her on your side."

"Okay, thanks."

Charlie grinned. "How long has it been since you've seen Hannah Hayward?"

Lee worked at keeping the effect of just hearing her name off his face. "Fourteen years."

"Ah." Charlie drained his cup and rose. "I think you'll be pleasantly surprised." He placed the cup in the sink and stopped at the kitchen door. "And don't forget the barbeque on Sunday. It's the last one of the season, so it'll be a pretty big deal. I'll need you there to make sure we don't burn down anything."

Lee raised his cup. "You got it."

"Thanks for the coffee." Charlie waved as he hurried away.

"Chief Evans is here."

Hannah glanced up from the spreadsheets. "Send him in, Mattie."

The young woman, looking strangely flushed, nodded and disappeared.

When Hannah looked up again, she sucked in a breath of surprise.

Holy cow!

The man who stood in the middle of her office was tall and broad shouldered, with sandy blond hair just long enough to be sexy. A dark blue T-shirt stretched across muscles that rippled when he moved, and it bunched over what were no doubt washboard abs. He filled his faded blue jeans nicely enough to be a model.

Hannah swallowed hard as she rose and extended her hand. "Lee. How nice to see you again."

He took her hand firmly in his and flashed the crooked grin she'd admired so long ago. "Pleasure's all mine."

Excitement tingled up her arm as he held her hand longer than necessary and studied her with eyes the color of warm chocolate.

When he finally released her hand, she cleared her throat and motioned toward the guest chair.

Lee sat, taking her in as if sizing up a meal.

Hannah resisted the urge to squirm in her chair. What was

the matter with her? It was just Lee Evans, a guy she'd known forever, not some international film star.

Well, that wasn't exactly true. She'd never really known him, had she? The night their senior year that he'd rescued her, she'd realized he knew a lot more about her than she did about him. When she'd thought about it later, that realization had embarrassed her, made her feel like a snob.

Now she felt more like a starstruck groupie than a snob.

Get a grip.

She straightened a stack of papers. "So, what brings you to my office?"

"The budget."

"Ah, yes." She thumbed through the stack she'd just straightened until she found the page she wanted. "Your budget request is much larger than a town this size can afford. We're not Seattle."

"That's true. Fortunately."

"Oh? Didn't you like Seattle?"

He leaned back in the chair. "You know what they say: Bigger isn't always better."

Heat climbed up the back of Hannah's neck and flashed across her cheeks at his suggestive comment. She suddenly remembered feeling him hard against her as he kissed her all those years ago.

"Although," he continued, "it's sometimes more fun."

She hated that she was blushing but could do nothing about it.

"Whatever you say," she said, shooting for nonchalance.

His soft chuckle made her blush even more. She needed to redirect the conversation and his attention.

"Are these items in order of priority?"

He leaned forward to peer at the paper. "Not necessarily."

"Can you prioritize them?" She handed the list to him.

He took the paper and shrugged with one massive shoulder.

"Everything on here's important. Maybe I can give you a tour and you can help me."

Something in his voice sounded like a cross between a proposition and a challenge, and she answered before she could stop herself. "Perhaps."

"This afternoon?"

"Uh, yes, I think I can do that."

"In an hour?"

She checked the clock on her desk, trying desperately to remember what was on her schedule. Her brain wouldn't click into gear. It seemed stuck on the possibility of spending time with the hunk of a man now standing in front of her desk.

"An hour and a half," she managed to get out.

"Good." He leaned over to place the budget request back on her pile and smiled down at her. "See you then."

In spite of her best efforts not to, she watched him walk from her office, his tight jeans showing off the most amazing male butt she'd ever seen. She listened to his footsteps fade down the hall, and then fell forward onto her desk.

"Oh my God," she whispered.

"You need something?" Mattie leaned through the doorway.

Hannah straightened and shook her head. "No, nothing."

The young woman stepped in, lowering her voice. "Isn't he gorgeous?"

"What?"

"The fire chief. Isn't he incredible?"

Hannah opened her planner to write in the appointment and glanced out the window at the firehouse across the street. "I hadn't noticed." She looked up to see Mattie raising her eyebrows in disbelief.

"Whatever you say, boss." The young woman left, shaking her head.

Taking another deep breath, Hannah closed her planner and

turned to gaze back out the window in time to see the front door of the firehouse close.

The thought of Lee just across the street did nothing to slow her heart rate. He'd certainly grown into the promise he'd shown as a teenager of being handsome. She still remembered the excitement of kissing him, of standing in his arms. No doubt she'd blown the whole thing out of proportion over the years. After all, she'd been only seventeen at the time and hadn't had a lot of experience. Still, he'd definitely aroused her.

As he was doing now.

The phone made her jump.

"Yes," she said into the receiver, turning back to her desk.

"Mr. Mason's on the line."

Hannah sighed. "Put him through." Any other time, she would have enjoyed talking to Sterling. Their stormy high school romance had cooled to friendship after college. And in spite of his sometimes-annoying personality, their shared interests in politics and books usually offered entertaining discussions.

Besides, hanging out with Sterling now and then meant she didn't have to waste time fighting off the town's eligible bachelors.

The line clicked as Mattie transferred the call.

"Hi, Sterling."

"Dinner?"

"Not tonight." She gripped the phone tighter, preparing to lie. Or at least stretch the truth. "I have a lot of work to do."

Silence suggested he wasn't happy with her response.

"Tomorrow, then," he said. "I'll pick you up at five."

Sterling tended to leave no room for refusal.

"All right."

"Don't work too hard. You don't want to get bags under your eyes."

Before she could respond, he hung up.

* * *

Lee paced the engine bay, waiting for the clock to cooperate.

Charlie had been right; Hannah Hayward had been a surprise. She'd always been pretty, but she'd grown into a true beauty.

He pictured her looking up at him from behind her desk, her chestnut hair pulled back from her gorgeous face, her silk blouse open low enough to show off a hint of cleavage, her lips full, red, and tempting. Damn! He'd been afraid she would notice just how interested he was.

But what had really knocked him out was the one thing that hadn't changed. She still had incredible green eyes that held the depths of oceans. Those eyes had always both drawn him to her and kept him at arm's length. As a kid, he'd been afraid she could see right into his soul.

Of course, now he knew better. Now he knew he could tease her and make her blush. Damned if that hadn't turned him on even more. He'd been ready to drag her out from behind that desk and see if she tasted as good as she had so long ago.

As he made another turn around the bay, he reminded himself that he needed to keep his hands to himself. He couldn't afford to screw this up. This was his opportunity to do what he really wanted, to run a fire department. And not just any fire department but the fire department of his hometown. This was his chance to show Tillman exactly how much he'd changed, what he'd made of himself. It might also be his one chance to rid himself of his past.

The front door opened and he squinted at the glare of unfiltered Colorado sunshine preceding her into the building. Hannah stepped through the light as an angelic vision producing the most devilish thoughts.

2

Hannah found Lee waiting just inside the door. He looked at home beside the shiny red fire engines filled with equipment she could only guess at the use for.

"Glad you could make it," he said, his voice much too sexy.

"I certainly couldn't turn down a tour." She glanced around, reminding herself that she was here on business. "Looks nice. You've cleaned up the place."

"Yeah, it needed cleaning." He turned and led the way around the older truck, slapping a fender as he passed it. "Unfortunately, cleaning won't help this one."

"Why not?"

He glanced back over his shoulder. "Doesn't run."

"Oh."

Walking alongside the newer vehicle, he pointed. "Hoses are old, and the pumps need overhauls. Doesn't do much good to race to a fire when you can't perform once you get there."

She streaked the newly applied wax on the engine's red exterior with one finger. "I guess it doesn't matter how nice the equipment looks if it doesn't work."

"Oh, how true," he said.

Heat rose to her face.

At the far side of the garage, past two fire engines and a red pickup truck carrying a large tank and metal boxes, he stopped at a door, hand on the doorknob. "I haven't even gotten to the back of this one yet." Pushing open the door, he stepped aside.

Careful not to touch the oily door frame, she peeked in at a disaster area. Rusty axes and other tools lay strewn around the room, along with overturned gas cans and tangled ropes. Only one side looked neat and orderly. "What happened?"

"Except for the wall we've worked on, it was left this way," he said.

"Really?" Why would Chief Black have left everything such a mess?

"Yep. And every firefighter knows taking care of his tool is just as important as knowing how to handle it."

Excitement wormed its way through her stomach. Was he purposely making his comments lewd, or was her mind just stuck in the gutter?

"Let me show you the upstairs."

When he reached around her to turn off the light, heat from his arm warmed her back and her breath caught in her throat. How was she supposed to act professional under these circumstances?

As he led the way across the garage, she found herself studying his backside again.

They climbed a narrow stairway into a large, low-ceilinged room that held an old sofa, two ancient stuffed chairs, a television, several rows of weights beside a weight bench, and a wallful of stacked folding chairs. At the far side of the room, a large brass pole rose through an opening in the floor.

"What's all this?"

He motioned toward the room. "Our first-class training facilities." When he slapped the back of one of the stuffed chairs, a dust cloud rose. "Want to watch a training film?"

The heat from her neck bubbled into her cheeks. "No, thank you. I don't need training."

"Glad to hear that," he said.

She crossed the room under buzzing fluorescent lights, her heels thudding on the wooden floor, and stopped at the brass pole. "You really use this?"

"Yep," he said, from right behind her. "Needs polishing, though. You interested?"

"In polishing your pole? I don't think so."

He walked past her to circle the opening. "I guess I could polish my own pole, but it's more fun when someone else does it."

Hannah shook her head. This was getting ridiculous. She couldn't believe she was not only encouraging but also participating in such juvenile behavior. They had work to do.

She turned to meet his teasing gaze. "Lee, we really need to work on your budget. There's no way the city has the money you're asking for."

His smile faded. "I know. Let me show you the rest of it."

She followed him back downstairs.

"Building's in pathetic shape," he said, suddenly all business. "We need a new roof."

Glancing up, she was surprised to find brown blobs staining half the ceiling. Obviously, the roof problem wasn't new.

"Kitchen's a hazard. We'll make the news when the station blows up because of a leaking gas line." He pushed open a door and stepped into a small, dimly lit office. "You can see here where the foundation's giving way."

When he pulled a trash can away from the wall, she stared at a hole where the concrete floor had cracked and caved in. Wiping back her hair from her forehead, she studied the crack that continued halfway up the wall.

"Great." How could she have let Chief Black convince her that everything was all right? And how could the town possibly come up with enough money to address even half of these problems?

She pictured the faces of the city council members as she explained the severity of the situation. They would think her incompetent, at best.

Turning, she found Lee standing in front of her, watching. His dark eyes sparkled in the soft light from a single desk lamp. He swallowed hard as his gaze dropped to her mouth, and the bottom fell out of her belly.

All her concerns, all the thoughts of budget shortfalls and the city council, faded away. She was suddenly a seventeen-year-old girl standing in front of the best-looking boy in town on a dark street.

He stepped forward and she leaned toward him.

"Hell," he whispered, reaching for her. He drew her up and kissed her.

His mouth covered hers, devouring her, and she gripped the front of his shirt in her fists as she surrendered to undeniable desire. She met his tongue with her own, stroking, drawing, inviting him in.

Her head bumped the wall as he pinned her against it.

His hands slid across her shoulders, over her breasts, and down her sides. He gripped her butt and lifted her. She wrapped her legs around his hips and clung to his shoulders.

He tilted his head to get deeper, and she sucked hard, needing so much more. His musky scent snaked its way through her brain, swallowing what was left of rational thought.

As he pressed her against the cool plaster with his immense, heated body, she felt his erection hardening against her crotch. Oh God, she remembered the thrill of that night, standing in his arms, feeling him hard against her.

He tore his mouth from hers and moved it to her neck, groaning.

Hannah gulped in air. She gripped the back of his neck and his rock-hard shoulders.

He pulled her up the front of his jeans and eased her back down. She opened her legs wider.

As he stroked her with his movements, he sucked a tender spot on her neck. His right hand slid up to her breast and he rubbed his thumb across her hardened nipple as if he knew exactly what she needed.

She gasped.

He groaned again as he rubbed her along the length of his erection. Her clit swelled from the friction and the hunger.

If she could have reached down between them, she would have ripped open his jeans. Her body tightened with need.

His mouth found hers again.

She drew in his breath.

He squeezed her butt, stimulating nerves that arched her back with delight.

"Oh God," she whispered.

Her pussy tightened, wanting more, needing him, and he moved her faster.

Deep waves of pleasure rolled through her body, drawing her hips forward.

Her pussy clenched, probably soaking him through layers of fabric.

And then she came, hard, all at once, crying out into his mouth.

Clutching, holding, grinding—spasms shot through her. Pleasure wracked her torso until it bordered on pain.

And then, just as suddenly, it released her.

She collapsed against him, her head on his chest where she heard his heart pounding to match the speed of her own.

He held her, still swollen and hard against her crotch, and

his quick, shallow breaths fanned the hairs on the back of her neck.

"Chief?"

"Son of a bitch," he whispered. He glanced at the door and stepped away, lowering her quickly to her feet.

If he'd let go of her arms, she might have fallen.

Instead, he eased her into a chair, sat in the one next to her, and rolled it into place at the desk. "You can see why I'm having a hard time prioritizing the work."

"Chief, I—" A young man stopped halfway into the office. "Oh, sorry. I didn't know you were busy."

"It's okay, Tommy. I'll be there in a few minutes. Why don't you make some coffee?"

"Yes, sir."

As soon as Tommy disappeared, Hannah looked up from the budget form to find Lee studying her. His mouth curled into a wicked grin.

She was tempted to slug him and tell him it wasn't funny that they'd almost been caught humping against the wall, but she really wanted to straddle him and comb her fingers through his hair instead.

She rose on shaky legs. "I should go."

"You'll forgive me if I don't follow you out," he said quietly, one eyebrow arched, as he leaned back in his chair and winced.

"I'll, uh, get back to you," she said, straightening her blouse, stumbling, and catching herself on the office door frame.

His voice dropped a notch. "I sure hope so."

She shot a glare back at him and found him laughing quietly.

Lee rearranged the front of his jeans and grunted in relief.

He really hadn't meant to get carried away in his office. It was just that standing so damn close to Hannah, looking down into her beautiful eyes, feeling her leaning toward him had been too much. If Tommy hadn't come in, he might have carried her up to his bed.

Christ. What was he thinking?

He sighed. He was thinking about the woman who had been his fantasy girl since he was twelve, that's what.

The one night he'd gotten close to living that fantasy had caught him off guard. He remembered it like it was yesterday. While searching for Charlie at the old Abrams place he'd run into Hannah upstairs. Actually, she'd run into him, and she was crying. At first he'd thought he was imagining things. No big surprise, since every dark-haired girl he saw was her at first glance. But at second glance, it was still Hannah, and she was clearly terrified. He'd wanted to take her in his arms and comfort her.

He could still remember the smell of fireplaces spicing the cool night air as he stood beside his truck, waiting to watch her cross the street to her house. Instead, she'd stopped to thank him for helping her and kissed him.

She couldn't possibly have known that he'd wanted to kiss her since sixth grade.

He'd wanted so damn bad to ask her out after that night, but he'd never been able to work up the nerve. She was the prettiest girl in town, the daughter of the town doctor, and he was the son of the town drunk. Accepting a ride home after being stranded at a party in the middle of nowhere was one thing; no way would she want to be seen with him in public.

But that was then. They'd been kids. She sure as hell wasn't a kid anymore, and his old man was long gone. Now he was fire chief, and she was city manager. There was no good reason they couldn't share a bed, if she agreed. And, judging by her response, chances were good she'd agree.

Only thing he had to be careful of was letting her close enough to realize just how different their worlds were. Once she knew, she wouldn't want to have anything to do with him.

That thought helped rid him of his hard-on. Lee headed for the smell of fresh coffee.

"Sorry to interrupt, Chief." Tommy poured a cup and handed it to him.

"No problem. Just working on the budget." He watched for a reaction to his statement as he sipped but didn't see one.

"What do you want me to do now?" the young man asked.

"Help me get another load of tools out of the storage room and we'll clean them up. We need enough for training on Saturday."

The boy looked hopeful. "Can I train, too?"

Although he was too young to qualify as a full-fledged firefighter, Tommy had brought in his father, who had given permission for him to volunteer after school. That suited Lee, since the fire department couldn't afford to pay anyone else and he needed help. Besides, Tommy would be a good firefighter when he was old enough to sign up. Too bad Tillman didn't have a junior firefighter program like some departments. Of course, nothing said Lee couldn't start one.

Something about Tommy's old man reminded Lee of his own father. He hoped like hell they weren't too much alike.

"Depends," Lee said.

"Sir?"

"I need an assistant to keep records for some of the training. Think you can do that?"

The young man beamed. "Yes, sir!"

"Good. You can join in for the rest."

Hannah strolled alongside the empty street, enjoying the way twinkling stars and a quarter moon gave the clear night sky a velvety look. Somewhere in the distance, a truck downshifted and a dog barked. The sounds of small-town peace.

Her thoughts, however, were anything but peaceful.

A week ago, she'd been content to play along with Sterling

as he put together his campaign for the state senate. He liked having her on his arm; her father's name helped open doors for him in the rural areas around Tillman.

Now, suddenly, she had no patience for playing along.

More than anything, she wanted to walk downtown to the firehouse, slip inside while the town slept, and continue where she and Lee had left off. Charlie said he was living there. What would he do if she just showed up?

Don't be stupid.

She couldn't throw herself at Lee. She was a mature adult, an important member of the community, not a teenager who could just do whatever she wanted, whenever she wanted.

And what if they got caught together? She'd lose her status as an impartial manager and likely forfeit the town's respect. Tillman was much more conservative than Seattle or even Boston, where she'd spent her college years.

At the high school, she turned a corner and continued on until she reached the football field. Empty bleachers loomed as shadowy monuments to the distant past. Meandering, she ran across a dusty white line glowing in moonlight and followed it along the edge of the field.

"Hey."

Barely biting back a scream, Hannah spun toward the bleachers, where a shadow of a man sat watching her. As he rose, she realized who it was.

"Come here often?" he asked.

She took a deep breath and patted her chest. "You scared me half to death."

Lee stepped toward her. "Sorry, I didn't mean to." He stopped in front of her with moonlight illuminating his smile.

Her first impulse was to leap into his arms.

Fortunately, she'd never been a particularly impulsive person, the one exception being earlier that day.

Excitement rushed through her at the memory.

She swallowed hard and looked away, focusing on swaying trees beyond the empty field. "Why are you here?"

"Couldn't sleep. You?"

She shrugged and dared to look up at his face again. "I thought a walk might help me relax."

"Is it working?"

"Not very well."

He laughed softly, moved closer, and lifted his hand to her face. He pressed his warm palm to her jaw and stroked her cheek with his thumb as his eyes studied hers. "Not helping me relax much, either."

Then he slid his hand around to the back of her head and drew her into a kiss as if it were something they did all the time.

His lips were warmer than hers, and when he opened her mouth with his her knees began to shake. His tongue circled hers as if savoring every last drop of her, and a soft noise rose from his chest.

She raised her hands to his waist.

He wrapped an arm around her and pulled her to him until they met from knees to shoulders. And they fit together perfectly.

She slid her hands up his wide back. Muscles bunched under her fingers, and her body responded with a gush of wet heat.

He leaned in, took more of her, moved one hand to her butt.

She rubbed her abdomen over the ridge of his hidden erection, hard between them again.

He tore his mouth from hers and pressed it to her face. "I'm definitely not relaxed," he whispered.

She laughed at the teasing note of agony in his voice.

He straightened with his arms still around her. "Think this is funny, huh?"

"A little."

Footsteps from the other side of the bleachers drew her attention.

"Hey, is someone there?" a man asked.

Neither of them moved or answered.

The footsteps stopped for a moment, then continued on, accompanied by the jingle of a dog's collar. "Come on, Belle," the man said. "Dang kids ought to be in bed at this hour."

Hannah pressed her face to Lee's shirt to keep from laughing aloud.

He ran one hand slowly down the middle of her back. "Come back to the station with me and I'll *entertain* you some more," he whispered.

She pushed against his chest. "I can't do that."

He took her mouth again and pulled her up closer.

She tried to resist him but couldn't begin to. His mouth was magical over hers, taking just enough, offering his sensuous taste. His tongue stroked hers, starting a rhythm that her hips picked up. He squeezed her butt again and nerves began to sing between her backside and her clit.

His lips curled into a smile against hers.

She pushed against his chest again and managed to draw back enough to look up at him. "What if someone finds us there?"

"No one's at the station this time of night."

Lee Evans in bed. What could be more perfect?

Lee in *her*, that's what.

Her knees buckled, but he didn't seem to notice as he held her weight without effort.

"I know you want to," he said, his voice low and sexy.

"How do you know?"

"I can taste your desire." He kissed her lips. "Feel it in your movements, smell it on your skin." He pressed his mouth to the side of her neck.

Hannah closed her eyes to enjoy the wonderful sensations of Lee seducing her. Even in her wildest fantasies, she hadn't come close to this.

He kissed her neck, then playfully nipped before moving his mouth to her ear. "I could just toss you over my shoulder."

"You wouldn't dare."

"No?"

He leaned down and wrapped an arm around her legs.

She slapped his shoulder. "Lee! Stop it."

He rose and looked down at her. "Come to the station, Hannah."

Could she really do this? They were both adults, but still—

"No one will know," he said, as if reading her thoughts.

Concern that she might be about to injure her career tried to worm its way into her thoughts, but she decided to ignore it for once. She'd sacrificed her personal life for the town. One evening with Lee was all she wanted. How could that be too much to ask?

She glanced around to be sure they were alone again before whispering, "I'll meet you there in half an hour."

He smiled. "I'll be waiting."

Turning, she hurried away without looking back.

Lee snatched the dirty shirt from the floor, opened the closet, and flung it into the clothes basket. Then he returned to the middle of his room and did a slow 360. Not exactly a penthouse suite, but everything seemed to be in order.

He wiped his damp palms on his jeans. Hannah Hayward was about to be all his.

Assuming she showed up.

"Crap."

What if she backed out? He couldn't exactly go storming up to her door and demand she invite him in, as much as he'd like to.

Damn, he hoped she showed up. Being so close to her and not having her just might drive him nuts.

He stepped out into the training room and stopped when he

heard the door downstairs squeak open and the engine bay lights begin to buzz. Trying not to look too anxious, he strode across the room and trotted down the stairs.

She stood just inside the doorway, wearing jeans and an oversized sweater.

He grinned. "Looking for me?"

She shrugged. "I guess."

"Good." He walked past her, squeezing her arm in greeting, and locked the door. Then he turned back to admire her in the bright lights.

Her nose was a little red from the cold and the collar of her sweater had mussed her hair, but her green eyes glistened and her lips still looked plump from their earlier kissing. He groaned in appreciation.

Her eyebrows arched. "What?"

"You're gorgeous."

She laughed and shook her head. "You're just horny."

"Yeah, I am, but only because you're gorgeous."

"I bet you say that to all the girls." She turned and strolled away from him. "Any chance of getting a drink?"

"Sure." He joined her, leading her toward the kitchen. "Hot chocolate, tea, or juice?"

"Really?"

He leaned close as if to share a secret. "I make a wicked hot chocolate."

"Okay."

As he filled the pot with milk and placed it on the burner, he glanced at her. She stood leaning against the counter, watching him. He could tell by her stance she wasn't comfortable.

Good. He didn't want this to end too soon. If they'd picked up where they'd left off at the football field, he'd be toast by now. Besides, he enjoyed spending time near her. He liked the way she looked at him, the way she tucked her hair behind her ear, the way she stood with one foot behind the other. He liked the sound of her voice and the fact that she didn't need to fill the silence with chatter.

He stirred in the chocolate. As soon as it was mixed and steam began to rise, he took out a spoonful and blew on it, then held it out to her.

She reached up and covered his hand with hers, guided the spoon to her lips, and carefully sipped. She smiled as she wiped a stray drop from her chin. "Yum."

Damn.

Barely biting back a whimper, he leaned forward and kissed her lips.

That split second of contact left him hard.

"I couldn't agree more," he said. Burying one hand in her hair, he drew her back to him.

She held his shoulders, and he felt a tremor pass between them. The spoon clattered to the stove as he slipped his arms around her and took her mouth, parting her willing lips. He lifted her to the counter, where he could take his time, and she looped her legs around his thighs.

Her kisses fueled the fire she'd lit years ago. He couldn't get enough. Her tongue met his in a tender duel, offering flavor so sweet and rich, it weakened his legs. He needed to touch and taste every inch of her.

She drew him in deeper, and he reached under her sweater to find bare skin. Soft, warm skin, smoother than satin. She jumped when he touched her, and then moaned softly into his kiss.

He moved his hands up her sides, lifting her sweater, and tore his mouth from hers. With one arm around her hips, he leaned her back and looked down at her full, round breasts. She wore a flimsy tan bra that did little to hide the darkness of her areoles. He covered one with his mouth and felt the nipple bead against his tongue.

She sucked in a quick breath.

He moved to the other side and did the same, and she held his neck and head and tightened her legs around him. He drew air through the fabric and was rewarded with a soft whimper.

But he needed to taste the saltiness of her nipples. He drew down one cup of the bra to reveal the sweet, tender flesh and tight little bud.

"Lee, wait."

Wait?

"The chocolate, it's bubbling over."

He straightened, suddenly aware of the smell of burning milk.

"Oh, shit." He dashed to the stove and turned off the burner, then grabbed the pot and rushed it to the sink, where it hissed and spit as he poured it out and filled the pot with water.

He turned to Hannah and found her standing in front of the counter, her sweater disappointingly in place.

"How about juice instead?"

She laughed. "I'm all right. I don't really need anything."

He grinned, strolled back to her, and wrapped his arms around her. "I do."

She laughed again, and he smiled. Her laugh was wonderfully sexy, just like the rest of her.

"I'm thinking I should focus on one thing at a time," he said.

She nodded.

"Glad you agree." He leaned over and scooped her into his arms.

She squealed and then looped her arms around his neck. "I've never been swept off my feet before."

He kissed her as he started toward the stairs. "I've got a lot more in mind than sweeping."

3

Hannah sat on the edge of the small bed and glanced around the equally small room. Everything was neat and clean, but there were no pictures or decorations—no personal touch.

"Not exactly luxury accommodations." Lee smiled apologetically.

"It's fine." She wanted to point out that the only important part was being in the room together. Her belly sizzled with desire for the man standing in front of her, looking down at her. But she wasn't sure what to say or do. She'd never just jumped into bed with anyone. And her limited sexual experience hadn't left her with an abundance of self-confidence.

She had no doubt about this being purely physical. She'd seen Lee in high school with a different girl every few weeks. None of them ever seemed to complain, although Hannah had noticed a few of the exes casting forlorn looks in his direction. He was the original bad-boy heartbreaker, able to charm the pants off anyone.

Nothing in his actions now suggested he'd changed. He'd charmed her right into his room.

The funny thing was that he looked a little flustered. He took a deep breath, blew it out, and turned his amazing smile on her once again.

"I feel like I should offer you a chance to leave," he said.

"Why?"

He laughed. "I don't know. I just do."

Talk about mixed messages. She could see how aroused he was, and yet he seemed to be backing away. "Do you want me to leave?"

He knelt in front of her and slid his palms up and down her thighs. "Hell no."

When he looked up, she saw something unexpected in his brown eyes, something that looked like honest concern.

And then it was gone, replaced by allure. He leaned forward and slowly, deliciously, slid his warm hands up her sides under her sweater. She raised her arms and he eased the sweater over her head.

His gaze taking in so much of her made her a little uncomfortable, but he seemed to approve of what he saw.

She reached down, pulled his T-shirt off over his head, and tossed it behind her.

It was all she could do to keep from making a ridiculous comment about how amazing he looked. He was more than just toned. Light brown hair dusted tight pecs. Below six-pack abs, a darker line started at his navel and disappeared into his jeans. His skin was tan and smooth, and his arms bulged with muscles that made her mouth water.

She'd always appreciated good-looking men but had never been overly impressed by brawn. Something about tight, hard muscles on Lee, however, did unexpected things to her insides. The fact that he could carry her up a flight of stairs without breathing hard made her giddy.

She ran her hands up his arms to his shoulders and watched gooseflesh follow her touch.

He kissed her neck as he reached around her, and her bra suddenly disappeared.

"Damn," he whispered. "I've waited a long time for this."

She combed her fingers through his soft hair. "What, like half the day?"

He chuckled. "Yeah."

Then he kissed her, and she lost the ability to tell which way was up. He enveloped her in his arms, drew her to his heated body, and filled her mouth with his tongue and his taste.

Hannah clung to him, willing to go wherever he led.

When his mouth left hers, she opened her eyes to find herself looking at the ceiling. Lee covered her without crushing her as he kissed her neck and her face. His body heat warmed her from the inside out.

He trailed kisses down her throat to the middle of her chest and then traced maddeningly slow circles around her left breast with his tongue. Her nipple stiffened as his warm breath caressed it, and it ached for attention.

He drew the hard bud into his mouth, and her back arched up to offer more. She bit her bottom lip to keep quiet.

He sucked and tugged gently from side to side, and spasms of delight shot down her body. She opened her legs wider and felt him center his stomach against her pussy, providing just the right pressure as she raised her hips into him.

Then he eased off, bathing her nipple in warmth with his tongue, and she collapsed back to the bed.

When he started the same treatment on the other side, she wondered if he planned to drive her mad with desire. He sucked her up off the bed again, and she cried out at the intense pleasure.

He groaned against her skin as he licked a line down the middle of her chest and stomach. When he sat up, she frowned and raised her head. "Where are you going?"

He grinned at her with lust burning in his eyes as he flipped off her shoes, dropping them to the floor, then unzipped her jeans and pulled them down over her hips. He backed away, taking her pants and panties with him as if peeling her until she lay in front of him completely nude.

She raised herself to her elbows. "It's a little cold in here."

"Is it?" He drew her left ankle up to his mouth. "Let me see if I can turn up the heat."

He worked his way up her leg, kissing, licking, and nipping her flesh, and she watched him, jumping each time he hit a ticklish spot. The farther up her leg he went, the warmer she felt. By the time he reached her inner thigh, molten heat pooled in her crotch.

Lee backed off the end of the bed, dragging her with him until she reached the edge. He drew her feet up to his shoulders, leaving her open to his warm breath between her legs. His mouth covered her pussy and Hannah gasped.

She gripped the bedspread in her fists, trying to hold back the explosion.

He licked slow and hard, all the way up, ending with a flick to her clit that brought her hips off the bed. Gripping her thighs, he licked again and again, pushing her to the edge until she felt as if her skin blistered with longing.

He groaned and sucked her swollen clit, and the ground dropped out from under her.

She fell into a blazing pool of bliss.

Waves of pleasure pulsed through her, lifting her and dropping her. On and on, until she was lost.

Alone, confused, disoriented, she fought for breath and struggled to find her way back.

As the world returned, she felt the bed rock from side to side.

Over her on his hands and knees, Lee nuzzled her neck. "Warmer?"

She nodded.

"Good." He stretched out on top of her, his bulging jeans centered against her crotch.

Hannah wrapped her arms around his chest, wishing she could purr her contentment. No man had ever brought her to a climax with his mouth. And she'd never experienced such an intense orgasm.

"You taste good," he whispered.

His warm lips on her skin and her own scent mixed with his excited her somehow, in spite of having just come. She held him tighter.

"I want more of you, Hannah." He pushed against her crotch.

She raked her nails up his back and he shuddered. The thrill of having control of such a powerful man excited her even more.

"Then take more," she said.

He groaned as he rolled to one side of her, sat up, and opened a nightstand drawer. With a condom in his hand, he stood and faced her as he brazenly removed his pants.

He had good reason not to be shy, she had to admit. If ever there was a man made to be naked, it was Lee.

The lower half of his body was every bit as gorgeous as the top. His legs were muscular, his hips narrow, and his erection bigger than she'd expected. Watching him roll on the condom made muscles twitch in strange places. She'd never had sex with anyone quite so well endowed.

His expression hinted at primal hunger as he stretched out beside her, his hand caressing her stomach and ribs. She studied his eyes, wondering if he hid any doubts behind his wall of self-confidence. He'd always been a mystery, and was no less so now that she lay beside him.

His erection rested on her thigh, heavy and hard. She reached down and explored, and wrapped her fingers around it, amazed by its girth.

His eyes closed for a moment. Then he grabbed her hand and raised it to his mouth, where he kissed the back of it. "You shouldn't do that right now."

"Why not?"

"Only one of us has come today." He licked his lips as he studied her mouth. "And I want to take you over the top with me."

Hannah started to explain that there was no possible way she'd achieve another orgasm, but he didn't give her a chance. He captured her mouth and kissed her hard and deep as he lifted himself over her, parting her knees with his own. Sensing his urgency, she expected him to work quickly, but he didn't. He settled back on top of her and kissed her, caressing her face, as if it were all he wanted.

Surrounded by his warmth, skin to skin, tasting herself on his lips, she felt desire begin to knot in her belly all over again as if he were kissing her for the first time. She wanted him closer, wanted to feel his hardness filling her, and began to tremble somewhere deep inside.

He moved his mouth to her ear. "You feel amazingly good." His left hand ran down her side to her thigh, and he tugged.

She raised her knees on each side of him, anxious now, and kissed his shoulder.

He groaned and reached between them, gently tracing her pussy with one finger, then sliding in.

The excitement of his touch surprised her.

He stroked her clit with his slick finger.

She gripped him tighter, denting muscles in his back with her fingertips.

He kissed her jaw and the side of her neck as his erection replaced his finger, parting her folds, lubricated coolness against her heated flesh.

She wanted more, and tried to take it, lifting her hips.

He grunted softly and held back.

Heat sizzled through her, searing desire into longing. She locked her lips on his shoulder and opened her legs wider for him.

He started into her slowly, his breath hot on her ear, pushing and drawing back, pushing deeper. He stretched her pussy, filled her, and her muscles thickened around him.

His rhythm eased as he reached her limit. With one long, slow thrust, he buried himself completely and the world stopped.

Her body stiffened.

Every nerve tingled, waiting.

His arms tightened around her.

"Oh yeah," he breathed, his voice low.

His hot breath scorched her skin, a flame to the powder, and her back arched.

His mouth covered hers as long, glorious waves of release rolled through her.

He thrust through each crest, drawing out another and another.

She clung to him, taking more.

Muscles bunched and flattened under her hands as he came.

She held him, meeting his thrusts, sharing his power.

With a low groan, he stilled.

Their hearts pounded against each other's chests as they lay there, panting.

The sound of blood rushing through her ears gave way to a strange buzz. She opened her eyes. "What's that noise?"

Lee raised his head and sighed. "Damn it." He kissed her lips as he lifted himself off of her and hopped to his feet. "It's Dispatch." He snatched his cell phone from the night table as he passed it.

"*What?*" Hannah sat up, grabbing stray pieces of clothing from the bed.

"You look like hell."

Lee glanced up from his coffee to find Dale Pierce, senior

among the volunteers in both age and experience, strolling through the kitchen doorway.

"Thanks."

Dale filled a mug from the coffeepot. "I hear you were up with the State Patrol half the night."

"Yep."

"You should have paged me."

Lee sighed. "Wasn't anything to do except direct traffic. An SUV rolled off the highway at the pass on that narrow section. Took a while to get a wrecker big enough to pull it up and small enough to fit across the road."

"Was anyone hurt?"

"Not seriously. Driver and two passengers were belted in."

"Glad to hear that." Dale straddled the bench and sipped his drink, then placed his mug on the table. "It doesn't look like you've been to sleep yet."

"No, too much to do." He wasn't about to admit that, because of Hannah, he'd been too wound up to sleep. Since getting back around five, he'd scrubbed the kitchen, straightened more of the storage room, gassed up Command One, and gone over the budget again. He'd about spent his last drop of energy, but now it was too late to go to bed. He didn't want to be found sleeping in the middle of the day if anyone came looking for him.

"I can hang around if you want to get some rest," Dale said.

"Yeah?"

The older man nodded.

The offer was too good to resist. "Thanks."

Lee poured the rest of his coffee down the drain, left the cup in the sink, and headed upstairs. He just needed a quick nap.

He stopped inside the doorway to his room, overwhelmed by a feeling of emptiness. It might be the same room he'd been happy with yesterday, but that was before he'd shared it with Hannah.

Sighing and raking his fingers through his hair, he closed the door, sat on the bed, and pulled off his boots. Then he stretched out and closed his eyes.

He could smell her scent, and it made the memory of holding her even more powerful. His arms ached to be around her again.

Shit, this wasn't good. Had he gone off the deep end?

Just because he'd gotten her into bed once didn't mean it would happen again. After all, this was Hannah Hayward, not some woman he'd picked up at a bar. She wouldn't just show up for sex until they got tired of each other.

What the hell was he thinking? She deserved to be treated better.

When he woke an hour later, he knew what he had to do. He showered, shaved, and dressed in his best jeans and shirt. As he trotted down the stairs, he slid his cell phone into its holster, daring it to ring, and he stopped at the office, where he found Dale reading the newspaper.

"Thanks, man," Lee said.

Dale folded the paper, rose, and stretched. "Not a problem. Are you headed out?"

"Just to grab a bite, but I've got my phone."

"Okay." He slapped Lee on the shoulder as he passed him. "I hope it stays quiet tonight."

"Me too."

As soon as Dale left, Lee started toward the door. Should he wait until she walked out and stop her at her car? Or should he just show up at her house and ask her to have dinner with him?

A moment of doubt slowed his step. They obviously had the hots for each other, but could she care about him the way he did about her? It wasn't like they'd been dating the entire time he'd lusted after her. In fact, they'd never dated. They'd never even had a meal together, except in the lunchroom at school, and he doubted she'd known he was there.

Wondering again about his sanity but admitting he had no choice, Lee pushed open the front door and stepped out into the afternoon sunshine.

He definitely wasn't going to her office. If she turned him down, he didn't want her to do it in front of the entire city hall workforce.

No, he'd wait for her to leave.

Leaning against the building, he crossed his feet as if he were standing around to enjoy the sun's warmth. People walking the sidewalk waved, and those driving by stared. The town had changed some, with a few more shops and businesses, but it was still small.

The oversized wooden door to city hall swung open, and Police Chief Tony Bertrand hurried down the steps. He was a little older than Lee and smaller by a few inches. Although hired from out of state a few years back, Bertrand seemed at home in Tillman. When he saw Lee, he waved and crossed the street.

"How's it going today?"

"Good." He shook Bertrand's hand. They'd spent half the night at the accident, but they'd been directing traffic on opposite sides of the wrecker and hadn't had a chance to talk. No doubt they'd have plenty of opportunities to get to know each other in the future. "You get some rest?"

"Yep. Did you?"

Lee nodded, keeping an eye out for movement across the street.

"So, how's the fire department looking?"

"Not great." Lee motioned toward the building behind him. "Hasn't been easy to sort out."

"I can imagine. I think Chief Black was coasting the last few years."

"Looks that way."

Bertrand turned to watch a blue BMW screech to a stop in front of city hall.

The driver looked familiar, although Lee couldn't be sure. "Isn't that—?"

The city hall door swung open again and Hannah stepped out.

"Sterling Mason," the chief said. "He lives over toward Pagosa Springs."

Hannah opened the passenger-side door and disappeared into the vehicle without even glancing across the street.

Lee felt a pit open up below him.

"I hear he's planning to run for state senate," Bertrand continued. "I think he and Ms. Hayward have been an item for a while. Maybe Tillman will have an 'in' if he gets elected."

The rage that flared in Lee's chest was something he hadn't felt in years. Every bit of him wanted to charge across the street, rip open the car door, and drag Mason out onto the pavement. Good thing he'd learned long ago how to hide that rage.

Bertrand glanced back at the car as it sped away. "Yeah, good ol' Sterling Mason, the perfect politician. He'll probably win." He grinned at Lee. "Well, I gotta run. We're helping out with a roadblock tonight, see if we can get some of the drunk drivers off the road."

Lee forced himself to smile. "Good luck."

"Thanks. See you Sunday at the mayor's party?"

Lee nodded.

As soon as Bertrand turned the corner, Lee yanked open the station door. "Son of a bitch," he muttered, marching to the kitchen.

Yeah, Hannah might sneak into his bed, but she went out in public with Sterling Mason.

Things hadn't changed as much as he thought they had.

4

Lee raised the barbell from the hooks and pressed it slowly, enjoying the burn in his chest and arms. He continued the reps in spite of the sound of someone coming in downstairs. It must be Tommy, although he was early.

"Lee?"

He faltered, surprised by Hannah's voice.

Holding the weights on straight arms, he responded, "Up here." Then he finished the set as he listened to her footsteps on the stairs.

He was still trying to figure out what the hell to do. Less than two days ago he'd shared his bed with her, and yesterday he'd found out she was involved with someone else. And not just anyone else but Sterling Mason, the bastard.

Unfortunately, having sex with Hannah hadn't quenched Lee's long-standing desire for her. Truth was he wanted her now more than ever.

Lee placed the bar on the hooks and sat up to find her watching him. He wiped his face and chest with a towel.

"I didn't mean to interrupt," she said.

Damn, but she looked great. She wore gray slacks and a tight black sweater that somehow made her eyes look even greener than usual.

It wasn't fair. What could she possibly see in Mason? Had she forgotten how crappy he'd been to her in high school? Rich or not, the man was scum.

Lee had vowed years ago not to pursue another man's woman. But Hannah wasn't wearing a ring. And she'd let him carry her to bed. She wouldn't do that if she and Mason were serious, would she?

Christ, he was rationalizing.

Maybe being the one she came to for sex wasn't such a bad thing. He knew what he was doing in the sack, and it might be his only chance to get her away from Mason. Lee wasn't sure he'd ever be good enough for Hannah, but he knew Sterling Mason never had been.

He smiled. "You can interrupt anytime."

She returned his smile. "I thought I'd stop by to pick up your latest budget write-up. The meeting's Monday. I should spend some time this weekend preparing."

He nodded, enjoying the graceful sway of her hips as she approached one slow step at a time.

"Maybe we should go over it," she said, standing in front of him.

He reached out and ran his right hand up the outside of her thigh to her hip. "We should definitely go over *something*."

"*Lee*, it's the middle of the day." In spite of her protest, she stepped closer and slid her hand up his arm to his biceps.

"Yes, it is." He drew her closer still and kissed the front of her slacks just at her pubic bone, wishing he could bury his face in her sweet cunt. The memory of her coming in his mouth sent a shiver through him.

She combed her fingers through his hair.

He urged her closer until she straddled him, her arms around his neck. He was hard before she sat, and harder still after. Caressing her ass, he pulled her up against his cock.

Her hands felt wonderful kneading his bare shoulders. He reached up and drew her mouth to his.

Kissing Hannah was intoxicating. As soon as he got a taste, he needed more and tilted his head to reach deeper.

She groaned softly.

When she rolled her hips, he matched her groan.

Forcing himself to end the kiss, he moved his mouth to her tender neck. "My room is ten feet away."

"I remember."

Holding her, he stood and carried her to his room, kicking the door shut behind them. He released her onto his bed and leaned over to steal a kiss.

"I need a shower," he said. "Want to join me?"

Her eyes glistened. "Maybe."

"Good." He pushed off his warm-ups and his cock sprang free.

She stared for a long moment and then drew her sweater off over her head.

Lee watched her undress, enjoying ever bit of her delicious body. Her breasts were full and round and the nipples puckered under his gaze. And her legs were deliciously long and sexy. But even after she stood before him naked and he'd enjoyed a leisurely look that left him rock hard, his gaze settled on her eyes.

Damn. She had the most amazing eyes.

He offered his hand.

She took it and smiled, and he led her to the shower.

As the water warmed, he kissed her and let his hands roam over her body. Smooth skin teased his fingers and he sighed. What would it be like to have her there every time he showered? To make love to her every night?

Dangerous thoughts, under the circumstances. Right now

she was his to hold, but even if he managed to get her away from Mason, it wouldn't last between them. It couldn't.

"I believe the water's hot," she said, her voice breathy.

Lee leaned back and opened his eyes to find the small bathroom thick with steam. "I think you're right." He adjusted the spray, then turned around and lifted her.

She grabbed his shoulders.

Her body felt warm and soft against his, and his cock slid into the cleft between her thighs as he walked her into the shower stall. She squeezed her legs together and he nearly fell to his knees.

Hot water beating against his back and Hannah in his arms had to be as close to heaven as he'd ever get. She drew his head down and kissed him as water splashed into their faces and ran in rivulets between them. Her nipples beaded against his chest.

Christ, she felt good. If he'd thought to grab a rubber, he'd be inside her. But he'd enjoy it more if she was as desperate when he entered her as he felt already.

Besides, that was what she was there for, wasn't it? His sexual skills? His best bet was not to disappoint her.

He sucked her bottom lip between his teeth and tugged on her left nipple, and she made soft noises of need as she pressed her body closer. Then he skated his hand slowly down her side, enjoying the feel of her slick skin. When he reached her lovely ass, he caressed it, stimulating the nerve bundle that made her wriggle.

"Aren't you supposed to be showering or something?" she asked, her voice husky with desire.

"First things first." Holding her waist, he turned her around to face the tile wall, then stood behind her and leaned over to kiss her shoulders.

She flattened her palms to the tile.

He centered his cock between her cheeks and reached around her, working his way to her clit, careful not to get there too soon.

She gasped when he squeezed her swollen nub, and he nearly forgot what he was doing.

Focus.

He nipped her shoulder, drew her back against him, and eased one finger into her cunt.

She reached around and grabbed his ass.

He slid in and out, added another finger as she felt her cunt tighten, and stroked slow and steady.

She leaned back, her head to his shoulder, and he kissed and sucked on her neck. She began to tremble, so he eased up, pulling out.

As soon as her body stilled, he started again.

It was all he could do to keep from sinking his cock in her juicy cunt. Warm water caressed his shoulder and back, and whispered around the base of his cock and over his balls as the scent of her wet skin taunted him.

After the third round, she groaned. "What are you doing?"

"Trying to drive you crazy," he said softly, "like you do me."

"You're succeeding."

"Good." He stepped into the shower's spray to rinse off and then turned off the water. "I know where we can get more comfortable." He kissed her. "Hold on to me."

When she locked her arms around his neck, he lifted her and she hooked her feet together behind him. He kissed her again, and enjoyed her fiery gaze as he carried her to his bed.

He sat, placing her on his lap, and they kissed.

His cock rose against her ass, and he felt her smile. He straightened. "Going for the entertainment factor again, huh?"

She shrugged and glanced down between them. "More or *less.*"

"Hmm. Sounds like a challenge."

She laughed softly, and the sweet sound left goose bumps across his chest.

With one arm around her, he leaned over and fished a condom from the nightstand drawer; then, holding her gaze, he ripped it open with his teeth.

But Hannah surprised him by taking the package from him, withdrawing the condom, and scooting back so that his cock rose between them. He clenched his jaw to hold back a sigh as she rolled the latex slowly over the head and down the shaft, squeezing and stroking as she went. By the time she reached the base, his eyes were nearly crossed.

"Took you long enough," he said, drawing her close and taking her mouth.

She rocked her hips up so that his shielded cock rested against the length of her heat, and she ran the backs of her hands up his stomach and chest, grazing his nipples with her knuckles. He sucked in a breath against her lips and felt her smile again.

Water from her hair dripped onto his arms and shoulders and trickled down the front of her chest. He leaned her back and traced several drops with his tongue, making sure to circle her puckering nipples. When he crossed slowly over one nipple, she tightened her legs around his hips.

Growing desperate to be inside her, he drew her close again and, with his hands under her ass, lifted her until the head of his cock pressed against her folds. She didn't even try to hold herself up, trusting him completely. He raised his mouth to hers, and she welcomed his tongue.

They kissed hard and deep, and he eased her down onto him a little at a time, until she finally had all of him and he was buried so deep he felt as if he'd reached her core. He shook with pleasure.

He turned his head and kissed her shoulder and her throat as he raised her slowly and eased her back down. Soft noises vibrated through her skin. He continued, focusing on her reaction to keep from losing control.

Her cunt swelled, and he felt her clit hard against his cock.

Her ass clenched and released, suggesting a faster rhythm, but he held back, controlling the pace.

She grabbed a handful of his hair and pressed her mouth to his shoulder, and he stopped, buried deep. Her cunt squeezed hard, and he knew he had her on the edge.

He raised his mouth to her ear. "I can't wait to feel you come," he whispered.

She whimpered in response.

As he drew her forward and eased her back, just enough to torture her clit, her whimper deepened into a groan. She tightened her grip on his shoulders and pressed her tits to his chest.

Every square inch of his skin felt alive, longing for her touch. Her fingers dug into his traps, and his muscles twitched. Then she moved from side to side, dragging her tits across his chest, and he shuddered.

He drew her forward again, and again, no longer able to wait. She cried out as she reached the peak.

He'd planned to take her over the top alone, but as soon as her cunt bit down on him he lost it.

He wrapped his arms around her as his cock erupted.

She drew him deeper with each fierce pulse.

Deeper and harder, biting down, emptying him.

When it finally stopped, he held her so close he couldn't tell where his body ended and hers started. Her heart pounded against his ribs, and he felt her breath caressing his neck in short bursts.

"Damn," he whispered.

She nodded.

He held her for a long time, savoring the connection, and then eased his hold.

She sat up and looked at him, her green eyes shining like emeralds.

He tucked a strand of wet hair behind her ear and ran his

fingers down her neck and across her shoulder. Her skin was warm and damp.

"I may need another shower," she said.

He grinned. "Sounds good."

"Alone." She pushed against his chest and eased her legs to the floor, then backed off his lap. With a quick kiss to his lips, she turned and sashayed to the bathroom, smiling back at him before closing the door.

Lee fell back on the bed, arms wide.

It scared him that he had so little control around her, but the risk was sure as hell worth the reward. He'd never found a woman who felt so damn perfect in his arms.

Hannah checked herself once more in the mirror. Except for the nefarious grin she couldn't seem to get rid of, she looked as she had when she'd walked into the firehouse an hour earlier.

She found Lee at his desk. He'd showered downstairs, to her disappointment—she enjoyed seeing him naked, probably a little too much. The man was amazing in many ways.

He sat back and smiled as she stopped in the doorway. His gaze running leisurely down her body made her want to both cover herself and beam with joy at his obvious approval.

He held out a large envelope. "I believe this is what you came for."

"Yes, thank you." She slid the envelope into the side pocket of her shoulder bag. "If I have any questions—"

"Just call. Better yet, stop by. Anytime."

She nodded.

He leaned forward. "Hannah."

"Yes?"

He looked as though he were going to ask her something but seemed to change his mind. "You look seriously fantastic in that sweater." Then he smiled and lowered his voice. "And out of it."

Heat rose in her cheeks and she shook her head. *"Lee."*

The front door opened.

"Thank you," she said in her best business voice.

"You're more than welcome." He winked.

She nodded to Tommy, the young volunteer, as she hurried out into the early dusk.

She really had stopped by for the budget information, hadn't she?

Hannah remembered the way desire had pushed her forward as she walked into the firehouse.

Who was she kidding? She'd stopped by hoping Lee would be alone.

Not only had he been alone, but he'd been shirtless and lifting weights when she'd found him. Dear God, the man was gorgeous. Then she'd had the most amazing sex of her life. Never before had she completely relinquished control as she had with Lee. She'd known he would do nothing but make her feel incredible, and that was exactly what he'd done.

What now? Returning to her "normal" routine was becoming more and more difficult.

Dinner the night before with Sterling had been close to painful. He'd told her that he'd soon be in a position to "step up" their relationship. She'd been trying to decipher the comment when he'd launched into another soliloquy about his campaign. Fortunately, drinks had arrived and she'd been able to tune him out.

She'd spent the whole meal thinking about Lee, trying to decide what to do. Their encounter that had started at the football field had taken her by surprise, more so because it had felt so right. Even the phone call afterward that had terrified her— she'd envisioned volunteer firefighters flocking into the firehouse to find her dressing—hadn't been a problem. Lee had correctly assured her she had plenty of time to get dressed. The memory of him grinning at her before sliding down the brass pole made her smile behind her napkin.

Sterling had accused her of not paying attention to him, and she'd claimed to have a headache. He'd dropped her off and raced away, and she'd spent the night staring at her ceiling, asking herself the same questions over and over. Why, after all these years, had Lee returned to Tillman, and why was he interested in her? More important, how long would he remain interested?

As she tossed her bag into the backseat of her car, she realized she'd left the rest of the budget information in her office.

"Shoot." She slammed the car door and trotted across the street.

City hall was quiet and dark, but she had no trouble traversing the familiar route. At her office, Hannah flipped on the overhead light and began sifting through piles of papers on her desk. In her haste to get to the firehouse, she hadn't even bothered to clean up the day's work.

"Hey, what are you doing here?" Charlie Richards leaned in the doorway. "I thought you left early on Fridays."

Hannah shoved the papers she wanted into a folder. "I do. I mean, I did, but I forgot some of the information I need for the meeting."

"Ah, a little weekend work, huh?"

"I like to be prepared."

Charlie nodded and waited for her with his hands in his pockets. "You are coming to the barbeque, aren't you?"

"I'm planning to."

"I'm happy to hear it. And Lisa will be, too."

She switched off the light and led the way to the front door. As they walked out, she glanced across the street at the firehouse, then looked at Charlie. Perhaps this was her opportunity to find answers to some of her questions. He'd said he and Lee were friends in school.

"Charlie, why did Lee Evans come back to Tillman?"

He shrugged. "I don't know for sure. With his record, he could work anywhere in the country. Hell, he's got more medals than most generals. He was Firefighter of the Year in Seattle last year."

Hannah opened her car door and tossed the folder onto the passenger's seat. She'd seen Lee's résumé. She knew about the medals and honors.

"I kind of think it's a personal thing," Charlie continued. "You know, his dad and all."

"What do you mean?"

He looked at her funny and then nodded. "Yeah, that's right, you were gone when all that happened. When we were twenty, Lee's house burned down. His father died in the fire. Lee tried to rescue him, but a beam fell on him and knocked him out. He ended up in the hospital for nearly a week. After that, he left town." Charlie sighed. "Maybe he's looking for closure."

Stunned, Hannah slid into the driver's seat.

Charlie leaned over. "See you Sunday." Then he straightened and closed her door.

Hannah pulled up across the street from the firehouse and watched as Mr. Walker and his son, Kent, hurried in, followed by a young redheaded woman she recognized but didn't know. Judging from the sounds when Hannah emerged from her car, they weren't the only ones there on Saturday morning.

Two of the three oversized doors were open, but most of the noise seemed to be coming from the back of the building. Curious, she walked around the far side.

Kent, Mr. Walker, and the young redhead rushed out, pulling suspenders over their shoulders and carrying jackets and helmets.

Lee stood in front of a group of twenty or so people, all

dressed alike in brown pants with rings of reflective tape around the legs, and gray T-shirts. Most held orange helmets and brown jackets to match their pants.

The group quieted as Lee spoke. "In order to be of any use to this department, you need some basic skills." He pointed to a fire hose coiled on the ground. "You must be able to move this hose when it's charged, to break through a roof with an ax, and to climb a ladder without hesitating. Most important, you must be able to drag a victim or one of your fellow firefighters to safety." He stepped to what looked like a large dummy without a head. "Jack, here, weighs one hundred and forty pounds. We'll take turns dragging Jack to safety. But first, Tommy's going to lead the group in warm-ups. Ready? Three rows."

The volunteers lined up as ordered and Tommy started them off in a stretching routine.

Lee glanced back at Hannah and smiled. He must have known she was there, but she couldn't imagine how. He walked to her, raking his fingers through his hair. "Here to sign up?"

"Hardly. I just had a few questions, but this obviously isn't a good time."

He glanced back. "I have ten minutes."

She nodded and followed him into the kitchen, where she pulled out the notes she'd made.

Lee stood beside her and they spread the paperwork on the counter where they'd embraced just two days earlier. He went through her questions, explaining terms and dollar figures and smelling much too good. In spite of his steamy glances, he remained all business. The heat from his body warmed her arm and side.

He checked his watch. "I better get back. Feel free to stick around."

She nodded.

He stood in front of her for a long moment as his gaze dropped to her mouth; then he turned and trotted back outside.

Hannah took a deep breath as she gathered her papers together. She turned at the sound of heavy footsteps to find Tommy rushing in.

He nodded. "Hi, Ms. Hayward."

"Hello, Tommy."

The young man grabbed a large container marked: *Water.* "Isn't he great?"

"The chief?"

Tommy beamed. "Yep. We're gonna have the best volunteer fire department in the whole state." He hurried away.

Hannah sighed as she considered the budget problems Tillman faced. The city council would have to decide between replacing a leaking roof on the high school, buying a new police car, and providing one-fifth of the work the fire department needed. *"Great."*

Her own problems felt no less significant as she glanced out the back door at Lee. He held the dummy around the chest and ran backward, dragging it across the yard.

The young redhead watched him intently with what could have been a little too much interest, and unexpected jealousy flooded Hannah's chest.

What on earth was wrong with her? Lee might enjoy sex with her, but he hadn't promised anything. There was no commitment to guard; she understood that. And the thing that had been bothering her since her talk with Charlie the night before was the big question: If Lee was here for some kind of closure, how long would he stay once he found it?

Why did she feel as if a tsunami of heartache was headed her way?

Shaking her head to clear it, Hannah hurried toward her car. She had work to do before Monday night. With or without Lee Evans, her town needed her.

5

"Well done or burned?"

Hannah peered around Charlie at the grill full of charcoal-colored hamburgers and blistered hot dogs. "Um, I think I'll just have coleslaw. But thank you."

He sighed as he flipped a burger. "It's amazing how many vegetarians we have today."

She glanced across the yard full of people to find Lee holding a paper cup, talking to two of the city council members and their spouses. His gaze met hers and his mouth turned up into his crooked smile. He wore well-worn cowboy boots, blue jeans, and a long-sleeved tan sweater that hugged every indentation in his shoulders and chest. He stood out in the crowd like Adonis among the minions.

"Are you ready for tomorrow?"

She returned her attention to Charlie, who stood with a long-handled spatula in one hand and a canned cola in the other, wearing a *Beware of cook* apron.

"Yes, I think so," she said. "I only have a little research left."

"Great. It looks like we'll have a good showing. Everyone I've run into during the past week plans to attend."

"I'm happy to hear it." She looked around. "So, where's Lisa?"

Charlie pointed toward the house with his spatula. "She's putting Amy down for her nap."

Hannah touched his arm. "I'll see if I can help."

She wound her way through the crowd, stopping occasionally to talk, until she reached the side door. As she glanced back, she found Lee watching her again from the far side of the party, this time without the smile.

All she could think about was running across the yard and throwing her arms around him. But now more than ever, she couldn't afford to do that.

She quietly entered the house and followed the sound of Lisa's voice, singing a lullaby. She found her in the girls' room, the closest to the backyard. Hannah stuck her head in and Lisa waved.

Charlie and Lisa had two beautiful girls who were sweet enough to make Hannah sorry she didn't have any of her own. When she'd expressed her regret to Lisa once, the woman pointed out that Hannah was still in the prime of her childbearing years. At the time she had laughed. She couldn't imagine having a man in her life with whom she'd want to have children. But that was before Lee showed up.

Good grief!

What drove her to make the harebrained leap from casual sex to bearing children? Her biological clock must be in overdrive.

That's *all* she needed.

Realizing Lisa would be a while, Hannah snuck back out the door, easing it shut behind her.

"Had me worried."

She jumped and spun around.

Lee studied her with his dark eyes, smiling seductively. "Thought maybe you were trying to avoid me."

She glanced back toward the party.

"It's not that," she said. "I just don't think it's a good idea for us to be seen together right now."

His smile melted.

She studied his face and found his expression suddenly stony, almost as if she'd hurt his feelings.

"Because of the city council meeting," she whispered.

He frowned. "What does that have to do with anything?"

Hannah glanced toward the backyard again and then motioned for him to follow.

She hurried around the house to the garage Charlie had long ago transformed into a shop, knowing the door was usually left open. When the mayor wasn't working or cooking in the backyard, she often found him in the shop, sanding away on his latest piece of furniture.

Inside the windowless room, she searched the wall for a light switch, flipped it on, and then locked the door. The shop had been cleaned—probably for the party—but still held the scent of freshly cut wood. Every tool hung on a hook in its proper place.

Lee stood in the middle of the room, watching her.

"We can't afford for the council to think I'm biased when I make budget recommendations," she said. "Especially not this time. You're asking for most of the money."

"That's why you think we shouldn't be seen together?"

"Yes. Why?"

Lee dropped his gaze and shook his head. "Nothing." He looked at her again and smiled. "I was just hoping you'd come over and talk to me." He stepped toward her as his gaze ran up and down her body.

Anticipating his touch and his kiss made her light-headed. She reached back for the counter to steady herself.

Lee took her face in his hands and kissed her, first tenderly, sweetly, then with more passion. His mouth opened against hers.

She held his sides.

He encircled her in his arms as he reached deeper, offering himself without reservation.

Hannah slid her hands up his back and looped them over his shoulders.

They fit together like puzzle pieces, and her heart raced at the wonder of it.

Lee drew his mouth away and leaned back to look down at her. "I can't seem to get enough of you, Hannah."

"I know what you mean."

"Do you?"

She nodded.

"Good." He drew her back to him, kissing her, and eased one hand slowly down her back. He reached her waistband and slipped his fingers into the back of her pants.

His touch made her tremble.

He released her mouth and trailed kisses down the front of her neck as he unbuttoned her jeans and pushed them down her thighs.

"Lee, what are you doing?"

"You've forgotten already?" he asked, his mouth to her breastbone.

She shoved his shoulder. "You know what I mean."

He stood. "You locked the door, didn't you?"

"Yes, but—"

"We only need a few minutes." He pulled a condom out of his back pocket and held it up. "I came prepared."

"Don't be ridiculous. We can't just—"

"You're wasting time." He leaned close, pressing his forehead to hers so that all she could see was his mouth. "I want you now." His hand sliding over her bare butt made her shudder. "I promise we'll both have fun."

"It's not that." She closed her eyes and raised her head to give his hot mouth access to her neck, her protest already forgotten.

She felt him pushing her pants down as he caressed and nibbled. He must be using the toe of his boot.

Realizing what they were truly about to do caused excitement to puddle between her legs.

"Step out," he whispered, his voice hoarse.

She did so, pushing her shoes off in order to remove her jeans.

He kissed her mouth and then turned her around.

She grabbed the edge of the counter. "*Lee.*"

He wrapped an arm around her waist and leaned over her. "Just enjoy."

Closing her eyes again, she focused on the sensations he produced as he reached under her sweater, caressing her breasts and teasing the nipples. Desire sizzled across her skin. His erection hardened between her thighs, and his abdomen pressed against her butt.

His hands slid down the front of her belly and into the cleft between her thighs, and he closed his teeth on the side of her shoulder.

Her spine stiffened at the jolt of pleasure shooting down to her lower back.

He groaned as if pleased with the result.

His fingers floated across her labia, exploring the surface with a tender touch, and her knees shook. He dipped into her juices and spread them around, stroking and teasing. Then his fingers slid in deeper, capturing her clit between them, and he squeezed.

She bit her bottom lip to silence the scream building deep in her throat.

He let up on her clit and she huffed out a breath.

As he slid in deeper, he squeezed again and she groaned.

He kissed the side of her neck and nuzzled her hair. "Raise that sweet ass for me, Hannah."

Nearly desperate for more, she did as he asked.

He held her around the waist and shoved her engorged clit from side to side. His erection nudged against her pussy.

She couldn't imagine wanting anything more than she wanted to feel him enter her at that moment.

He started in slowly, stretching her, then withdrew and pushed in again and again, each time a little deeper as he tortured her clit. She lost awareness of anything except his powerful body behind her, his hot breath on her neck, and his hard dick filling her.

He moved his hips from one side to the other, touching spots in her pussy she didn't even know existed.

Need pumped through her veins.

Deeper and deeper he went.

Desire clawed at her belly. Muscles swelled and stiffened.

She raised her head and shoved herself back against him, taking all of his cock as release shot through her.

Convulsions started deep in her womb. She gasped as pleasure overtook her in violent waves, jerking her into him and away. And then the waves softened.

He groaned and thrust deeper.

Her climax peaked again and she cried out.

He met each beat with a long, full stroke.

As the orgasm eased, he slowed until he stopped, buried deep, no longer rock hard but still filling her.

His forehead dropped to her back between her shoulder blades, and they both panted.

She'd never realized how amazing sex could be. Undoubtedly due to the fact that she'd never had sex with anyone like Lee.

Her senses returned a little at a time. Fluorescent lights buzzed and the scent of fresh wood filled the air again. Her legs wobbled, but Lee held her on her feet.

He raised his head and withdrew, and she straightened. Her muscles jumped when he gently bit her butt as he helped her back into her jeans. Once he had her dressed, he drew her back around to face him and kissed her, wrapping his arms around her as if afraid she would leave.

She clung to his shoulders, returning his kiss until she finally had to come up for air.

He hugged her to him, breathing hard against her shoulder.

She expected him to make a comment to lighten the intensity of the moment, but he didn't. They stood together in silence.

Lee released her slowly, staring down into her eyes as he stepped away, and then he smiled. "Maybe you should leave first."

She nodded and straightened her hair.

At the door, she glanced back to find Lee with his hands on the counter, his head down, his chest expanding slowly.

It took every bit of willpower she had not to rush back to him.

She stumbled twice as she walked around the house, trying not to question what had just happened. By the time she reached the party she felt steadier but no less confused. Was the sex getting better because she felt more for Lee than just lust?

One of the younger high school teachers, Terri Nowicki, stopped her. "Ms. Hayward, it's great to see you."

"You too," Hannah said.

"I understand the council is voting on the budget tomorrow."

"Yes, they—"

She stopped as she realized who was striding toward her from across the yard.

Sterling frowned. "I looked all over for you. I thought maybe you'd left early."

"No, I, uh—"

He shrugged. "It doesn't matter. You're just in time."

"Holy shit." Lee raked his hair back from his face with both hands.

This was getting dangerous. Every time he held Hannah, had sex with her, it felt closer to making love. His heart pounded from more than just exertion.

Anger had blossomed in his chest when he'd thought she was avoiding him. He understood why she didn't want people to know they were seeing each other, but did she really not want to be seen even talking to him? He'd cursed his father, his life, the whole world before she explained the need to appear neutral. That he understood. Funny thing was he knew she'd recommend what was best for Tillman, no matter what passed between the two of them. Couldn't everyone see that?

Taking a deep breath and blowing it out, Lee straightened. He needed to return to the party before someone started looking for him. At least now he'd be able to watch Hannah without getting noticeably hard.

He turned off the light, let the door close behind him, and followed the trail around the house. As he approached the backyard, he realized conversation had dropped to a single voice. He stopped at the corner when he spotted Sterling Mason standing with Charlie on one side and Hannah on the other, addressing the group.

"I've made it official today," Mason said. "I'm running for a seat in the Colorado state senate."

Nearly everyone applauded.

Mason raised one hand to quite the crowd. "I'd like to make one more thing official today, and announce my engagement to the beautiful woman who has agreed to be my wife, Miss Hannah Hayward."

Lee's heart rose into his throat, blocking his airway.

Mason took Hannah's hand and raised it to his mouth as the crowd applauded again.

Hannah drew her hand away abruptly and scanned the yard. Her gaze stopped on Lee's, and her eyes widened.

Had she thought he wouldn't find out?

Instinct told him to run, leave the scene, escape the next blow, but he couldn't do it. He couldn't let her or anyone else see the wounds she'd just inflicted.

Damn good thing he'd learned how to hide his pain. Gathering it all up and shoving it into a dark corner, he continued into the yard, smiling at the young woman who glanced back at him.

"Hi," she said softly. "Terri Nowicki."

"Lee Evans."

"I know. Welcome to Tillman, Chief Evans."

He tried to focus on her big blue eyes and tight young body. "Call me Lee."

She smiled. "I'm Terri."

"What are you talking about? I never agreed to marry you."

Sterling smiled and nodded at those around them as he spoke to Hannah under his breath. "Of course you did. I told you at dinner that I planned to step up our relationship. You didn't protest. You knew damn well what I meant."

"I didn't. I—"

"Congratulations." Charlie offered his hand to Sterling, and a line of people formed behind him.

This was absurd. She'd never agreed to marry Sterling, no matter what he thought. She should make a public announcement to that effect, but she couldn't do it. She'd look ridiculous to the people of the town she was paid to manage.

And Lee. What could he be thinking? She'd found him watching when Sterling made the announcement, and expected anger or at least some kind of reaction. Instead she saw cool, collected Lee Evans, smiling at Terri and ignoring her.

Had she been wrong about the growing feelings between them? Was it really just sex?

Her stomach turned and she fought a wave of nausea.

"Are you all right?"

Hannah met Lisa's gaze. "Not really."

Lisa took her by the arm and led her across the yard to one of the picnic tables. "What's going on?"

"I don't know. Sterling just told the world we're getting married."

"Didn't you accept his proposal?"

Hannah shook her head. "He never proposed." She searched the yard and spotted Lee again, still talking to Terri. Another wave of nausea washed over her, and she raised her hand to her mouth.

"Let me get you something to drink." Lisa hurried away.

When she returned with a cold drink, Hannah sipped until her stomach settled a little.

Lisa sat beside her. "This isn't just Sterling's announcement, is it? What's up?"

More than anything Hannah wanted a shoulder to cry on, someone to sympathize with her plight, but she couldn't do it. What she and Lee shared was crazy, wonderful, and intensely personal. She couldn't tell anyone.

"I'm just not feeling well," she said.

"You didn't eat a hamburger, did you?" Lisa looked across the yard. "I love Charlie with all my heart, but I wish he'd quit trying to grill burgers."

Charlie waved as he carried a platter of blackened patties to the serving table.

Movement drew Hannah's gaze back to Lee. He and Terri

turned and walked from the yard together. Had he just invited the young teacher back to the firehouse for the same kind of entertainment he'd provided for Hannah?

The possibility caused the threat of tears to burn her eyes. She felt as helpless as she had the night in high school when Lee had come to her rescue after Sterling abandoned her.

Except he wasn't coming to her rescue this time.

6

Lee stood in the field of dried grass, searching for something to take the ache out of his chest. He kicked a clump of dirt, and the smell of charred wood rose with the dust. Amazing that after twelve years the earth still held the scent.

Amazing too that it had been twelve years. In some ways, it felt like yesterday.

He shoved his hands into his pockets and closed his eyes.

Fingers of flame gripped the tops of windowsills, and intense heat scorched his face. Burning wood popped and crackled.

If he hadn't left the house that night, he could have saved his old man. Unlike his father, Lee had been sober; the smell of smoke would have awakened him.

"Dammit." Opening his eyes, he rubbed the top of his right shoulder. Even though it had long since healed, it still throbbed whenever he thought about the fire.

He suddenly felt hopeless. He'd come back to settle things with the old man. Or at least his ghost. Then, after arriving he'd discovered the woman who haunted his waking hours, living in

Tillman and single, and he'd longed to win her over, make her care about him as much as he'd always cared about her. Both goals now seemed out of reach.

How the hell could Hannah have sex with him when she'd already agreed to marry Mason? He'd believed she had more integrity than that.

She had when he'd known her years ago. That was one of the things he's admired about her. Could she really have changed that much?

It had to be Mason, the bastard. He'd changed her. Did she have any idea what she was getting into with that sleazeball?

He sighed.

She couldn't know, and he had to tell her. Even if seeing her was salting an open wound, he had to.

Lee marched to his truck, hopped in, and drove a little too fast to Hannah's house. He pulled to the curb across the street in the same place he'd parked more than a dozen years ago. It wasn't quite dark this time, but it soon would be.

He studied the house, looking for movement. A shadow passed by the front window. It must be Hannah.

Unless she wasn't alone.

"Shit."

Stepping out of the truck, he slammed the door, marched up the sidewalk to her doorstep, and rang the front doorbell before he could talk himself out of it.

The door opened and Hannah stood in the doorway in the same jeans and sweater she'd worn earlier, but she'd replaced her shoes with fuzzy red socks.

He stared down into her green eyes, and the vulnerability he found there knocked the wind right out of him.

She stepped back. "Come in."

He walked into the living room and turned to face her. "Sorry to bother you."

"You're not bothering me." She glanced toward the street. "Isn't Terri with you?"

"Who?"

"Terri Nowicki, the high school teacher, the woman you left with."

He huffed. "You mean, after Mason announced your engagement?"

She closed the door. "Yes, after that."

"You can't marry him, Hannah."

Her gaze jumped to his. "Why not?"

"He's a jerk."

She laughed. "Tell me something I don't know."

"Then why did you agree to marry him?"

Hannah sighed and walked away. "You want some tea?"

"No." Lee glanced around the living room, every bit as classy as he'd expected but somehow cozy, too. He followed Hannah's path to the kitchen.

She stood at the stove, pouring water into a mug. "I didn't agree to marry him."

"But he said—" Lee closed his mouth and frowned at her. It shouldn't surprise him that Mason had lied.

Hannah carried the steaming mug to a table and sat. "One minor detail. He forgot to ask me."

Lee took the chair closest to her. "Son of a bitch."

She nodded. "Yep."

"What are you going to do?" He held his breath as he waited for her to answer.

She stirred her drink, then lifted the tea bag out and dropped it into a saucer. "I don't know."

"You can't marry him."

"I don't intend to."

"Good." It was all he could do not to jump up and whoop for joy.

She frowned at her drink and his excitement waned.

"What's the problem?"

She shrugged. "I don't really want to embarrass him in public. He'd never forgive me, and Tillman could end up suffering if he gets elected."

"How about I just beat the crap out of him?"

She looked up and laughed. "I don't see how that would help."

"Maybe not, but I'd feel a lot better."

"I guess chivalry really isn't dead." Hannah sipped her drink and then looked at him. Discovery sparkled in her emerald eyes. "You've rescued me more than once."

"Have I?" He wondered what she remembered.

"Yes. There was a party in high school when you drove me home; I don't know if you remember that. Sterling had abandoned me and left with his old girlfriend, Juli Tucker. You saved me." Color rose in her cheeks. Was she remembering the kiss they'd shared that night?

"And once in the cafeteria," she continued, "you chased off a kid who was trying to take my lunch money. Who was that? Oh, and then I slipped on the ice one time and really banged my knee, and you helped me up and carried my backpack to the bus for me. Was that in seventh grade?"

He shrugged. "I just wanted to get in your pants."

"*Lee.*" Her rosy cheeks darkened.

He leaned forward. "Still do."

She laughed. "You're relentless."

"Among other things."

With his heart racing, he reached across the table, palm up.

She looked at his hand and then met his gaze. With her eyes still sparkling, she placed her hand in his.

He urged her around the table and into his lap, and she wrapped one arm around his shoulders. He buried his fingers in her soft hair, drew her mouth to his, and kissed her.

It wasn't a white-hot kiss of desire but one of growing passion, deep and sweet. Her taste satisfied some basic need to be close to her but kicked off the constant hunger for the rest of her body that seemed to ride just below the surface.

She tightened her grip and drew him farther into her mouth as she caressed his jaw.

He slid his arm under her legs and stood, and she dropped her head to his shoulder. Nearly desperate, he walked to the living room and stopped.

"Hannah."

She raised her head and looked at him.

"I have no idea where your bedroom is."

She kissed his lips and smiled. "If you put me down, I'll lead you to it."

"Promise?"

She nodded.

He took her mouth again and eased her slowly down the front of his body, groaning at the pleasure. Reluctantly, he ended the kiss as she stepped back and took his hand.

Halfway up the stairs, he drew her back around for another kiss. She met his hunger, opening her mouth to him and holding him. He felt her tits stiffen as she leaned against him.

Lee slid his hands under her sweater to caress her back and waist, savoring her warm, smooth skin. His fingers knew the feel of her already, and touching her was like coming home to a place filled with joy and peace.

She tugged on his shirt and he raised his hands to let her pull it off; then he did the same to her sweater. *God*, she had beautiful tits, and smooth, milky skin.

She backed up the stairs and he followed.

At the top landing, she grabbed the waistband of his jeans and unbuttoned them, and he did the same to hers. They stumbled down the hall stepping out of boots, fuzzy socks, pants, and underwear, touching and kissing. By the time they got to her bedroom, they were both naked and he was way past desperate for her.

She fell across her brass bed with a laugh, and he dropped down on top of her, reclaiming her precious mouth and thrilling to the feel of her heated body under his. She raised her knees on each side of him, and he nearly lost it.

"Wait," he gasped, raising himself off of her.

She looked up, her lips plump and red and her hair spread wildly around her head. "What's wrong?"

"Protection is in the hall."

She laughed and nodded.

"Besides," he said, standing, "I want this to last a little longer than it did at the barbeque."

Lee took the opportunity to calm down a notch as he returned to the hall and fished the condom out of his jeans pocket.

"Damn." Why hadn't he grabbed a few?

Because he'd had no idea he'd end up in Hannah's bed, that's why. The thought made him grin.

"What's wrong?"

He returned to the bedroom to find Hannah lying on her side in the middle of the bed, one leg drawn seductively up over the other, her head propped on one hand.

"Nothing," he said, holding up the foil package, "except we'll have to use this wisely. It's the only one I've got."

Her eyebrows arched.

He tossed the condom onto the nightstand and sat on the edge of the bed, taking in all of her.

She sat up, drew up her knees, and wrapped her arms around her legs. "You're staring."

"You're beautiful."

She grinned and shook her head. "You're crazy."

He swallowed hard. "About you. I'm crazy about you, Hannah. I always have been."

Her eyes widened as she studied his face. "You're serious, aren't you?"

He nodded. His heart raced and his scalp prickled. Never in his life had he opened himself up like this.

She scooted closer and pressed her right palm to his face. "Why didn't you ever tell me?"

He chuckled at the thought. "We lived in different worlds." Amusement left him as he realized this was the time to tell her the truth. He sighed and kissed her hand. "We still do."

Her brow furrowed. "What are you talking about? You're in my bed. We're both here, together."

Was she really so naive?

He grinned at her. "And I can think of better things to do than talk."

"That doesn't surprise me."

He crawled over her, pushing her to her back, then lay beside her and drew her to him. He kissed her throat as she stroked his arms and shoulders.

Her gentleness with his heart touched him more deeply than he'd expected, and he wanted to sink into her, to hold her and watch passion's fire burn in her eyes, but he knew he wouldn't last long enough to do more than embarrass himself.

She wriggled against him, kissing his shoulder.

He eased his right leg between hers and caressed her butt until he'd started her rhythm against his thigh. She wrapped her legs around his.

He took her mouth, matching his tongue to her tempo.

Her juices slicked his skin, and her clit swelled into a hard nub against him.

God, she felt incredible clinging to him, her heated body writhing, small noises of pleasure rising from her throat. If he'd had the rubber on, he'd have given up this torture.

She tore her mouth from his and pressed it to his neck, and her hands curled into fists at his back.

He pulled her up harder.

She came with a cry of surrender, clenching down on his thigh, holding him close.

He kissed her as her movements slowed, enjoying the last of her orgasm. Her uninhibited, honest reactions pierced his heart.

She smiled against his mouth. "Wow."

He nipped her bottom lip and raised himself up on one elbow to enjoy her look of satisfaction. " 'Wow' what?"

"You know what." She slapped his shoulder and laughed. "I think I need a drink of water."

"Sounds good. Need to keep our fluid levels up." He grabbed a glass from the nightstand and headed toward the bathroom.

Hannah lay with her hand over her heart, feeling it slow. Lee had the most amazing ability to turn her on with a simple touch, and his kisses burned through to her soul every time.

Had he really cared about her for so long?

The more she thought about it, the more she remembered him being around to pick up the pieces when things went wrong. Still, he'd never said much to her, until the night of the party. And even then he hadn't been much of a conversationalist.

The man was truly an enigma. Granted, he was a *gorgeous* enigma.

Lee returned carrying the glass of water. She watched him cross the room, surprised again at how incredible he looked. His body was perfect and hinted at wildness—the strength of a bull and the graceful movements of a lion. As her gaze wandered down to his still-engorged erection, the comparison shifted toward the equine arena.

Heat flooded her face at the errant thought.

He was right about the different worlds they'd grown up in,

but things had changed. They were adults now, controlling their own lives.

Her father had always told her small towns had the longest memories. Would Tillman accept them being together?

Did it matter?

Concern knotted in her stomach. The two of them were doing good things for the town she loved. What would she do if she had to choose between Tillman and Lee?

She started at the realization that she'd grown close enough to Lee to even be asking such questions. When had that happened?

She took the glass from him and sipped, watching him study her. He looked completely relaxed and happy, wearing the crooked smile she was beginning to understand might be as much for defense as for charm.

He rested a hand on her knee and slid it slowly up to her thigh. His touch left gooseflesh in its wake. When she reached over to place the glass on the nightstand, he took advantage of the situation and kissed her ribs.

"Hey, that tickles."

"Too bad," he said against her skin.

She squirmed and pushed him back.

He grinned and his gaze dropped to her mouth. Pulling her forward with one arm around her back, he opened his mouth over hers.

His kisses astounded her. Every time his tongue caressed hers, as it did now, she had to close her eyes to the pleasure. He wrapped his arms around her and held her to him with one hand on her butt and the other in the middle of her back. The strength he kept in check thrilled her as she slid her palms over roping muscles and smooth skin.

His erection pressing against her hip reminded her of how

unbelievable it felt when he entered her, and her breath escaped in a rush. He groaned and deepened the kiss, drawing her with him as he rolled onto his back.

Pushing against his chest, Hannah sat up, straddling his hips. His erection rose between them and he looked up at her with hunger glistening in his dark eyes.

She took his hands from her body and raised them to the brass headboard balusters. "Hold on here," she whispered near his ear.

He groaned in protest but did as she ordered. How long would he be able to relinquish control?

Aroused by the power she wielded, Hannah started down his body, tasting, kissing, licking him. She circled his dark nipples, flicking the buds with her tongue, and then moved down his belly. Muscles jerked under her mouth, and he grunted when she hit tender spots, but he didn't let go of the headboard.

When she reached his penis, she found it hard and erect. She stroked the velvety skin with her fingertips as she inhaled his musky scent. Holding the base, she ran her tongue around the head, tasting him, enjoying exploring, marveling at the salty drop of fluid her attention produced.

His buttocks clenched and released, and muscles in his stomach rippled.

Licking her lips, she slid her mouth over the head and as far down the shaft as she could reach. Even with the head nudging at the back of her throat, she didn't get very far.

He groaned deep and long as she slid her mouth up and down.

"Please, Hannah," he breathed, "stop."

She sat up and found him gripping the brass bars with white knuckles, his jaw clenched, his brow furrowed.

"You don't like it?" she teased, licking the flavor of him from her lips.

He opened his eyes and narrowed them at her. "You're about to take me out of the game."

"Oh? So this is a game to you?" She closed her hand around his shaft and pushed down hard.

His head went back and he growled.

She bit her bottom lip to keep from laughing.

But what she really wanted was to watch his face as he came, to see the moment of release. She straddled his legs and reached for the condom.

Before the encounter in his room, she'd never actually put a condom on a man. She'd marveled at Lee's reactions, and planned to do so again.

As she rolled the covering slowly down his erection, she watched concentration tighten his face as he obviously worked on not giving in.

Her own body reacted, too, by tightening with desire. Her nipples hardened and ached, and liquid seeped from between her legs.

Once she'd finished the job, she raised herself up and guided him to her, anxious to take him in.

He released the headboard with his right hand and reached for her.

She froze. "Put that hand back."

He grunted and did as ordered.

Excitement rolled through her like a wave charging up the beach.

She splayed her hands across his chest and eased down onto him, savoring the joy of her flesh surrounding his, of his hardness stretching her soft muscles, of her need devouring his hunger. The farther she went, the more incredible it felt.

He took deep, stuttered breaths as she moved down slowly, and his arms shook. When she'd taken all she could, he groaned.

Her fluids coated them both, providing more lubrication than the condom, and she easily slid up and back down, taking a little more.

He watched her through hooded eyes, his smile gone.

Her body tightened and a spasm shot through her womb.

His expression registered the contraction in pained pleasure, and she felt another rush of power.

She'd never experienced the sensations running through her— the desire to make him tremble, the excitement of controlling their union. She felt the thrill of self-discovery and suddenly realized she could share anything with Lee without fear of ridicule.

Arousal rippled through her entire body.

Unable to hold back, she pushed forward and back, riding his erection to satisfy her own needs, taking him deeper. He grew and hardened.

Pleasure shoved her over a cliff and she lost all the control she'd had.

Her back arched and her eyes closed as release pounded through her muscles.

She rode each burst that clenched her pussy and rolled up her spine.

Such perfect bliss, untamed, irrepressible.

Hot liquid ecstasy.

Perfection.

A measure of awareness finally returned. Lee's hips rose off the bed and she opened her eyes to watch.

His head was back and his entire body shook as release took hold.

"Yes," he breathed.

His rigid prick pulsed inside her as he rose up against her, and she worked to match his thrusts, hard and slow. Her own orgasm continued in gentle waves.

Lee collapsed under her, and she rocked with the last of her need as she watched his face and arms relax. With his eyes closed and a smile of satisfaction curling his lips, he was more handsome than ever.

Drained, she lay on top of him, her head to his chest where his heartbeat thundered in her ear.

"You can let go now," she said, smiling.

His arms came down around her, and he sighed and kissed the top of her head.

Had she ever been this happy? Certainly she'd never been so satisfied, but that was only part of it.

"Hannah."

"Hmm?"

"I—"

They both jumped at the buzzing in the hallway.

Lee raised his head. "Son a bitch, not again." He eased her to his side and rolled off the bed. "It's Dispatch."

The phone continued its buzzing as Lee stumbled through the hall, muttering curses. Hannah sat up, thankful that the phone hadn't started five minutes earlier.

"Evans," he said. He returned to the bedroom, the phone to his ear and carrying their clothes, which he dropped onto the bed. "What's the address?"

Hannah watched him frown. "Repeat that." Then his eyes widened. "Got it." He punched buttons on the phone and snatched his clothes from the pile as he spoke.

"Pierce, get to the station and sound the alarm. We have a house fire at Thirteen Hundred Canyon Road." He nodded. "Yeah, it's the mayor's house. Hurry. I'll meet you at the scene."

Hannah jumped up. "Charlie's house is on fire?"

"Yeah," Lee said over his shoulder as he dashed to the bathroom.

"Oh my God!" She pulled on her panties and blue jeans and drew on her sweater.

Lee ran from the bathroom dressed and swung around the door frame.

Hannah grabbed her shoes from the closet and hurried after him.

He stopped long enough to pull on his boots and then ran outside.

She lifted her coat from the hook at the door. "Wait! I'm coming with you!"

7

Smoke rose from the fire like some kind of monster, swelling to fill up the night. Hannah slammed the truck door and followed Lee up the driveway.

People rushed toward the house from all directions. Lee ran through the crowd, pulling people aside until he found Lisa.

"Where's Charlie?"

Lisa pointed frantically at the house where smoke billowed out from under the eaves. "He went in after the girls!"

Lee motioned to Hannah. "Keep Lisa with you and see if you can get everyone back across the street."

She nodded and took Lisa's arm, then turned to face the crowd. "Listen! Everyone!"

Voices quieted and she realized just how loudly the fire roared. She glanced back to see Lee charging through the side door.

"The fire department's on its way!" she yelled. "We need to wait across the street. Please!"

Lisa sobbed but let herself be led, and Hannah herded the crowd to a safe spot. Then she turned to watch.

In the distance, the siren at the firehouse wailed.

Flames chased smoke from the eaves, filling the yard with a terrifying orange glow. Hannah held her breath, waiting for Lee to emerge.

The fire seemed to spread with exponential speed.

Fear took over and she started back across the street, but before she could reach the yard he stepped through the front doorway, holding Charlie and Katie, and the three of them stumbled into the yard, coughing.

"My babies!" Lisa charged past her and fell to the ground beside her older daughter, then turned to Charlie. "Where's Amy?"

Charlie shook his head but couldn't speak for coughing.

Lee watched, his hands on his knees. "Where's her room?"

"It's the last one in the back," Lisa said. She turned to face the house. "Oh God, it's where the fire's burning! I have to get my baby!"

Lee caught the woman around the waist and drew her back. He pushed her toward Hannah. "Don't let her go in. Understand?"

She nodded and grabbed her friend's arms. Lisa struggled as they watched Lee rush back into the house armed with nothing but a flashlight.

Smoke seeped from the front of the house now, and flames shone in the side windows. Lisa screamed and struggled to get away, but stronger hands grabbed her, and Hannah released her to Chief Bertrand.

Fear gripped Hannah around the throat as she thought of Lee in the burning house. He couldn't possibly see in all that smoke, and the heat was nearly overwhelming where she stood. How could he survive?

Red lights flashed in the yard as the fire engine roared into the driveway. People jumped from it, pulling on coats and helmets.

Dale Pierce ran to Hannah. "Where's the chief?"

"He's inside."

The man turned toward the house. "Shit." Then he dashed off, yelling orders.

Hannah watched through tears as firefighters dragged hoses across the yard. It seemed to take forever to get water flowing, and then it sprayed out in all directions from holes in the ancient fabric.

At the head of one hose, two firefighters started in the front door, crouching behind a wall of water. Then another one in full gear ran in behind them.

The fire monster screamed as water hit it at the back of the house, and things popped and exploded. It sounded like the house was falling apart.

"Lee!" Hannah knew it did no good to yell, but she couldn't help it. "Lee!"

Dark figures emerged from the front door, low and bundled, and fell as a group to the ground. Hannah ran to them and laughed when she realized Lee lay in the middle, holding a blanket, coughing but very much alive.

Dale Pierce raised the face shield on his helmet. "You okay?"

Lee nodded and drew back the blanket. Amy looked up with wide eyes.

Hannah grabbed Lee's arm as he struggled to his feet. "Need to get . . . to the truck," he said between coughs.

They walked together across the street, where Lee handed Amy to Hannah, then pulled a small tank out from behind the seat. He took a deep breath from the mouthpiece and placed it over the child's mouth. "It's okay," he whispered.

Lisa crossed the street, crying, and gathered her child from the arms of Hannah, who then relieved Lee of the oxygen tank. "We've got it," she said.

He nodded and, still coughing, trotted back across the street to take charge of the battle.

Hannah watched in amazement as Lee easily moved people and equipment around, pointing and directing with the precision of an orchestra conductor. In short order, he seemed to have things organized, and they made quick progress. Flames disappeared, and smoke lightened from black to gray.

Medics arrived from Durango and escorted Lisa, Charlie, and the girls to the back of the ambulance to check them out. Hannah joined the throng of spectators and continued to watch. She shivered in spite of the heavy coat she wore.

As things wound down, Lee walked over to her. If she hadn't known who he was, she might not have recognized him with black streaks hiding his face and his hair matted to his head. He wore one of the fire department coats with reflective stripes across the chest and around the arms and held a helmet at his side.

"Hey," he said.

"Are you all right?"

He nodded. "Sure. How about Charlie and his family?"

"They're with the medics. I think everyone's fine, though, thanks to you."

Lee shrugged. "It's what I'm trained to do."

"What happened?"

He glanced back at the house. "Don't know yet, for sure, but it looks like it started in the trash can. Charlie may have dumped out the charcoal too soon."

"How horrible."

"Yeah. Back part of the house is in bad shape, but at least they didn't lose it all."

She nodded, wondering how she'd react if her father's house burned down. Remembering what Charlie had told her, she studied Lee's face. Did he think about his father when he saw a house on fire? Was that what drove him to run into a burning building to save someone?

"I'll ask Chief Bertrand to drive you home," he said. "I'll be here for a few hours yet. And then I want to make sure Charlie's family has someplace to stay."

"I can drop off a sandwich to you later, if you want me to."

His eyebrows rose. "You'd do that?"

"Ham and Swiss?"

"Perfect." He smiled at her for a long time, then turned and strolled back into the action.

Lee walked around the house once more, checking for hot spots. He didn't see anything but knew how tricky smoldering wood could be. He'd check again before he left and swing back by in the morning.

As he started toward his truck, he spotted a sedan parked behind it and recognized the car as Hannah's. The driver's door opened, and she rose from inside.

"Hungry?"

He smiled. "Starved."

"I brought two." She handed him two sandwiches and a bottle of apple juice.

He leaned on the front of her car and unwrapped the first sandwich. "Thank you."

"You're welcome."

In four bites, the sandwich was gone and he felt a little better. He drank down half the juice and then worked on unwrapping the second sandwich.

"Where are Charlie and Lisa?" she asked.

"Staying at her sister's, three streets over."

"And everyone was okay?"

He nodded. "A little smoke inhalation, but they'll get over that."

Hannah sighed and focused on the house. "What happens next?"

"I'll keep an eye on it to make sure we didn't miss any hot spots. The county will send over a fire investigator, and then an insurance adjuster will show up. Hopefully, we'll get all the paperwork processed quickly so they can start working on repairs." He took a bite of the second sandwich.

"I guess this is business as usual for you."

He shrugged. "Fought a lot of house fires in Seattle, but this is the first time I've known the owner. Hadn't really thought about that when I took the job."

"Why did you take the job, Lee?"

He glanced at her, wondering why she was asking. How much of the truth was she looking for?

"Did it have something to do with your father?"

He swallowed hard and stared at the sandwich. "Yeah, in a way."

"What happened that night?"

Lee took a deep breath and blew it out. "My old man was a mean drunk. He used to chase me around with his belt until I learned how to stay out of his way." He looked up at the cloudless sky where stars twinkled as if the world were at peace. "That night, he got plastered and yelled at me about something. When I yelled back, he threw a bottle at me and told me he wished I'd never been born. So I left. I got back a few hours later and the house was on fire. He always smoked in bed. I figured he'd burn the place down one day."

"You tried to rescue him."

He huffed. "Yeah, well, the mean old bastard deserved to die. I don't know why I tried to get him out."

"Because he was your father, Lee."

A lump formed in his throat. He'd never talked about that night with anyone except the police when they'd questioned him. He swallowed hard. "Last thing I said to him was that I wished he'd die and get it over with."

He glanced at Hannah and found her studying him with tears glistening in her eyes.

"You didn't mean it," she said.

He shrugged. "I don't know. Maybe I didn't. Hell of a thing to say, though."

"Only because of the timing." She squeezed his wrist. "It wasn't your fault he died."

"I know." Ashamed of the tears burning behind his eyes, he continued eating.

She stood quietly beside him as he polished off the sandwich and juice.

Restored and in control once again, he stepped in front of her and handed her the bottle and paper wrapping. "Thank you, Hannah."

"You're welcome."

He studied her face, just visible in the dim streetlights. He wanted more than anything to kiss her, tell her how he felt about her, and carry her back to bed for the night.

He drew a dark line down her left cheek with one sooty finger and smiled. Not even dirt could make a dent in her beauty. "Good night." He winked.

"Good night, Lee."

As he watched her drive away, he realized he only had two choices: He had to either tell her how much he cared or leave. There was no middle ground left for him. He couldn't survive waiting in the shadows for her.

Hannah stood at the window of her bedroom, gazing out into the darkness.

The whole day had been extraordinary, starting with having sex with Lee in Charlie's shop and ending with standing in front of Charlie's destroyed house after the crowd had left, listening to Lee admit his worst moment to her. She could tell by the way he spoke that he hadn't told many people about it.

Her heart ached for him. Many kids said hateful things to their parents in the heat of an argument. Most of them didn't have to live with the guilt of that parent's death before they had a chance to take it back.

Watching Lee at the fire had been extraordinary, too. She'd seen exactly what he was made of when he risked his life to get Amy out, and it didn't surprise her. The more she thought about it, the more she realized he'd always been around to help those who needed it, not just her.

That must make it even tougher for him to live with his father's death.

Sighing, she dropped the curtain into place and crossed back to her bed, where she covered her legs and returned the laptop to her lap. The bed seemed amazingly large without Lee in it.

"Back to work." She had almost everything ready for the meeting. One more check of her notes and she'd give up for the night.

The phone ringing made her jump.

"Hello?"

"I didn't wake you, did I?"

She closed her eyes. "No, Sterling, you didn't wake me."

"Sorry about running out on you earlier. I had an appointment I couldn't get out of."

"I'm not marrying you."

Her statement met with a long silence.

"Of course you are," he said. "We've known each other all our lives. We're cut from the same cloth. Who else would you marry?"

"Cut from the same cloth? We're nothing alike, Sterling. I don't even *like* you most of the time."

"You're just angry. Look, I'm sorry I announced it without telling you first. You'll see that I'm right. Just sleep on it, and in the morning—"

"I'm not marrying you, Sterling. Are you listening to me?" More silence.

"Why are you acting like this? Are you seeing someone else?"

"Listen carefully. I've never agreed to be your wife." She huffed. "I went out with you because I thought we were friends. Now I'm not so sure."

"I think you've said quite enough, Hannah. Before you say anything else you'll regret, I'll bid you good night."

He hung up.

Why had she been so nice to him, anyway? True, their fathers had been friends, but that didn't mean she and Sterling had to be. What was it Lee had said so long ago? That Sterling was pretty stupid for being so rich?

She smiled at the memory and returned her attention to the computer screen.

"Hey, Chief. Nice to see you."

"Thank you." Lee shook hands with yet another person he only vaguely recognized.

All seats in the room were full. People lined the walls, and many more listened from the hall. According to some of the older citizens, it was the biggest council meeting they'd ever had.

"Lee, I'm glad you're here." Charlie grabbed his hand and squeezed.

"How are the girls?"

"Fine, thanks to you."

Lee shrugged. "Just doing my job."

"Right." Charlie stood beside him against the side wall and looked out at the crowd. "Quite a turnout, huh?"

The young woman Lee had talked to at the barbeque smiled and waved from across the room, and Lee nodded.

"I see you've met Ms. Nowicki. She's pretty, isn't she?"

Lee glanced at his friend. He wanted to tell him that playing matchmaker was a waste of time, but he wasn't about to admit why.

"Well, I guess I better get this show started." Charlie turned and strolled toward the front.

A long table stretched across the front of the room. Two city council members sat on each side of Charlie, and the treasurer and Chief Bertrand occupied two of the three chairs off to the sides. The empty chair must be for Hannah.

Strangely enough, Lee knew exactly when she entered the building, even before he saw her. Awareness skittered across his chest. He heard her footsteps as she made her way through the back crowd and then hurried up the center aisle.

"Sorry I'm late," she said to Charlie as she placed a pile of papers on the table. She surveyed the room quickly, smiled when she spotted Lee, and then sat.

Those green eyes, focused on him, caused a rush of adrenaline that raised his heart rate as if he were a schoolkid again waiting for her to notice him. She looked fantastic, dressed in a black business suit and gray silk blouse, her hair pulled back.

Lee took a deep breath and blew it out.

Charlie banged a gavel twice. "I call this meeting to order."

The hum of conversation dropped.

Charlie went through the first part of the meeting quickly, introducing the other council members and addressing questions left over from the last meeting. Lee kept losing track of the discussion as he watched Hannah. She made notes, answered questions, and glanced up at him twice.

"The next topic is the annual budget," Charlie said. "I'll turn it over to Ms. Hayward, our city manager, to lead the discussion."

Hannah rose. "Thank you, Mayor." She drew a flip chart out from against the wall. The first page held a bar chart.

"This was our budget last year." As she pointed, she explained the general fund, where income came from, and which expenses had been approved.

Then she flipped to a very different chart with one extra-tall bar at the center. "These are the budget requests for this year. As you can see, the fire department has asked for a three hundred percent increase."

Noise in the room rose again, and Charlie banged his gavel.

"I've reviewed the fire department request," Hannah continued, "and I believe it's not only valid but also necessary for the safety of our town. After speaking to Chief Bertrand and the council members, I believe we can reduce the other areas for this one year to about half of what was requested." She drew lines through the bars. "As you can see, this would still leave us with quite a shortfall, even if we drained a large part of our general fund reserves."

Lee's stomach knotted. How the hell was he supposed to get the fire department into decent shape without funding?

An older woman raised her hand and stood when Charlie called on her. "We could have a bake sale to help raise money."

"And a car wash," a young man added.

The crowd began to offer suggestions without waiting to be recognized.

"How about a fair with races and games?"

"We could auction off the firefighters for a day."

"I'd bid on the chief."

Charlie banged his gavel again. "One at a time."

An older man in the back yelled, "Why don't you ask your fiancé to kick in a few thousand?"

People laughed.

"Okay, that's enough." Charlie raised his hands for quiet.

Hannah glanced at Lee and then squarely faced the crowd.

"I don't have a fiancé, despite rumors to the contrary. And in the spirit of full disclosure, any relationship I have with Lee Evans, the fire chief, has nothing to do with my recommendations."

All heads turned toward Lee and then back to Hannah, and the hum of conversation rose again.

Lee stared at her. Had she just told the town they were seeing each other? She'd certainly announced publicly that she wasn't marrying Sterling Mason.

"I appreciate the suggestions," Hannah continued, "but I'm afraid we need more money than we can raise. The good news is I've started the application process for four different grants to help us out and I think our chances of receiving those grants are good. They would cover the shortfall for the fire department funding and we wouldn't have to touch the reserves."

The knot in his gut faded, and Lee smiled. No wonder Hannah's opinion mattered to the town. She was good at this city manager stuff.

"I recommend we accept the budget currently agreed upon," she said, "and that I continue to pursue the grants."

One of the council members made a motion to follow Hannah's recommendations that was seconded and approved. Hannah slid her chart back to its place against the wall, returned to her chair, and flashed a quick smile at Lee.

Unable to take his eyes off her, he missed the whole discussion on street improvements.

"The last piece of business," Charlie said, "is understandably something I feel pretty strongly about. As most of you know, my house was damaged by fire last night. If it hadn't been for the quick action of our new fire chief, Lee Evans, I probably wouldn't be here tonight. And I know if not for his bravery, my family would not have escaped unharmed. I want to express my personal gratitude, as well as that of the city council of Tillman. Thank you, Chief Evans."

Following Charlie's lead, the city council and the entire audience stood and applauded.

Lee felt a new knot forming—one of raw emotion that swelled in his chest. He hadn't been so touched by any award he'd ever received in Seattle. He looked out at the people of his hometown, then nodded his thanks to Charlie.

When Charlie's gavel came down to end the meeting, the crowd surged forward. Townsfolk filed by to shake Lee's hand and many stopped to find out about volunteering. By the time the crowd began to thin, the fire department had doubled in size.

"You didn't have to do that," Lee said, shaking Charlie's hand again.

"I meant it. Besides, it looks like it was good for business."

"Yeah."

Charlie glanced back at the council table and then stepped closer, dropping his voice. "Full disclosure? When did all this happen?"

Lee grinned.

Charlie shook his head. "I miss out on all the good stuff." He playfully punched Lee's arm. "See you later."

After Charlie left, Lee watched Hannah talk to the remaining city council members for a while. She glanced at him once or twice but continued chatting. Feeling a little foolish just standing there, he slipped out the back door and strolled down the dark sidewalk toward the station.

Hannah had actually told the town about the two of them. He still couldn't believe it. Not only did that suggest she wasn't ashamed to be seen with him; it also implied she considered what was going on between them more than just sex.

He had to be careful not to assume too much. A lot of territory fell between *more than just sex* and *being in love.*

A car pulled up beside him. "Want a ride?"

He leaned down and smiled at Hannah. "Dangerous question."

"Oh?" She smiled back.

"Maybe I should drive over, just in case I get a call."

"All right." She started to pull away from the curb but stopped. "Lee."

"Yeah?"

"You can bring your toothbrush, if you want to."

He laughed and nodded. "Okay."

She drove off.

"Hot damn." Hannah had just invited him to spend the night. Maybe the amount of territory was shrinking.

He watched her car disappear into the darkness as he hurried to the station.

8

"Why did you do it?" Lee pushed the porch swing back to start it moving.

"Do what?" Hannah sat beside him, her shoulder against his.

"You know what. Tell everyone about us."

She laughed softly. "So we could sit out here on the swing together without worrying about getting caught."

"That's it?"

"Sure. What other reason could I have?"

Lee shook one of the chains supporting them. "Nice swing."

"See?"

He looked at her. "This could still backfire on you, Hannah. A lot of people in this town remember my old man. A lot of people hated him, and for good reason."

"So?"

He sighed and pushed the swing again. "You ever heard the saying 'the apple doesn't fall far from the tree'? Some people believe that."

"Do you?"

He shrugged. "I don't know."

"Well, I don't." She slipped her hand into his and lifted it over her head so his arm encircled her shoulders.

He drew her close and kissed the top of her head, enjoying the fruity scent of her shampoo.

"Next issue," she said.

"What?"

"I want to know what you meant when you said we live in different worlds."

He sighed. This wasn't really a conversation he wanted to have, but she was right. They needed to have it. "We're different. You grew up with a father who loved you and took care of you. I looked after myself. You went to college. I did whatever I got paid to do, until I could afford to get out of here. You always stood up for what was right. I did some things I'm not real proud of."

"What did you do that's so horrible?"

"Well, I used people. Had lots of girlfriends I didn't care about."

"Why?"

He shrugged. "Warm place to sleep, food. Acceptance, I suppose. And I stole stuff when I was a kid."

She rested her hand on his leg.

He took a deep breath and blew it out. "I went to jail when I was fifteen. Got caught stealing. I have a juvenile record."

She leaned back against his shoulder and looked up at him. "Lee, none of that matters. Not now. Not when it comes to us."

He swallowed hard. "Hannah—"

"Lee, I watched you run into a burning building to save a child. That's who you are now. That's what's important."

He studied her eyes, amazed by the acceptance he found there.

Maybe she was right; maybe the past really didn't matter.

Maybe the only thing that mattered now was the way his heart sang when she was near.

He kissed her, unable to do anything else. Her lips were what he needed more than anything.

As she opened her mouth, he turned and pulled her closer, running his hand across her ribs and up to the side of her breast. Her hand warmed his leg, and its proximity to his cock resulted in a hard-on that was already uncomfortable.

He wanted her with a new level of desire that surprised even him.

Lee drew his mouth from hers and pressed it to her forehead. "If you don't want to get caught doing more than swinging out here, we better go inside."

She nodded.

He released her and helped her up with a hand on her lovely ass.

"*Lee.*" She halfheartedly swatted his hand away.

Grabbing his coat and the shaving kit underneath it, he followed her into the house.

"Do you want something to eat? I have a leftover pot roast, or—"

He caught her around the waist and drew her close. "I want you," he said in her ear.

She laughed and tried to push his arm away. "Lee, please."

"Please, what?"

"Please let go."

"Really want me to?"

She quit struggling. "Only long enough to go upstairs."

"Hmm." He nuzzled her hair. "I can do that."

She climbed the stairs in front of him, laughing and flashing sexy grins, and staying just out of his reach. When they got to the doorway of her room, he charged forward and grabbed her around the waist again.

She squealed but looped her arms around his neck.

Holding her against him, her feet off the floor, their lips pressed together, he walked her to the bed, where he tossed his things. Still kissing her, he eased her down to her feet, then un-buttoned his shirt and tore it off.

Her warm, soft hands slid over his chest and shoulders, and he sighed against her lips. How could a simple touch feel so good?

He straightened and smiled down at her as he removed her sweater; then he took her mouth again and cupped her breasts, marveling at the way they fit his hands.

She drew him with her as she sat, and he crouched between her knees. Holding her close, he sampled each tit, licking and sucking her taut nipples. She stroked his hair and made sweet sounds of pleasure.

"I hope you brought protection," she said.

He grinned up at her as he reached for his shaving kit, opened it, and turned it over. His toothbrush and razor fell out, followed by three dozen condoms.

She laughed. "Do you think you have enough?"

He shrugged. "You said I could spend the night. I didn't want to run out."

She shook her head. "You're insane."

"Is that a problem?"

She cupped his face. "No." Then she leaned forward and kissed him, drawing him into her precious mouth.

He eased her over to her back and ended the kiss long enough to undress them both. She lay back and watched, smil-ing and licking her lips. As he opened a condom and rolled it on, she sucked her index finger slowly into her mouth.

He grunted as he fell forward. "You're a wicked woman."

"Is that a problem?" she asked, imitating him.

He shook his head. "Hell no." With his feet still on the floor, he lowered himself to her, enjoying the feel of her breasts against his chest and her thighs opening around his hips.

He kissed her neck and her throat and caressed her body until she began to squirm. Then he stood and drew her legs up in front of him.

She watched him with her green eyes wide with trust that squeezed his heart. He kissed her calves as he stroked the length of her smooth thighs. She hooked her feet around the back of his head.

Reaching between them, he circled her warm cunt, pleased to find it already juicy. He slid one finger across her clit and into her slippery heat, and her eyelids drooped with pleasure. She drew in a slow breath, and her tits rose as the nipples puckered.

Needing to be inside her, he withdrew his finger and eased the head of his cock between her swelling labia, holding back to savor the feel of her.

Almost as wonderful as her cunt swallowing him was the sight of her. Arousal arched her back and darkened the rosiness of her cheeks. Her mouth opened, and the tip of her tongue slid across her bottom lip.

He pushed deeper as he traced their union with his fingers and followed her juices down to her ass. He pressed gently and she sucked in a quick breath. Kissing and nipping her calves, he pushed his cock deeper and eased his finger into her tight ass, filling all of her at the same time.

Muscles clenched and he watched as he thrust slowly into her hot cunt.

Her eyes closed, her head went back, and she grabbed fistfuls of the bedcover. Ecstasy furrowed her brow and she cried out.

Christ, she was beautiful. He clenched his jaw to hold back. Her cunt clamped down so hard on his cock, he shook.

Her pulses slowed. Her mouth relaxed and her hands opened. He withdrew from her ass, eased her legs apart, and stretched out on top of her again, kissing her face as he pushed against the last of her orgasm.

"Oh my God," she whispered.

He kissed her lips. "What?" he asked against them.

"How can it keep getting better?"

He smiled.

She slid her hands down his back to his butt and he grunted at the pleasure of her touch. Then she raked her nails up his back and he sucked a long breath through his teeth.

She locked her legs around him and gazed into his eyes as he maintained a slow, easy rhythm. He stroked her temples and her beautiful face. Then he kissed her, pouring into the kiss all the wonder of making love to her. She held him, taking all he offered as if she understood.

As they kissed, her hands slid over his back and sides and shoulders, touching him everywhere at once, leaving electric sparks of excitement. The sparks arced together into a charge that ran like liquid fire down his spine and into his balls. He groaned at the intense pleasure and tore his mouth from hers.

Wrapping himself around her, he focused on the amazing way her cunt held him, fighting against each withdrawal and welcoming each thrust with gripping heat. She undulated under him, mirroring his movements, taking more of him each time, holding him tighter.

Her stuttered breathing near his ear pushed him past the point of return and he gave in, releasing control, plunging head-first into the inferno.

The world vanished, leaving the two of them joined, melted into each other, fused.

Her soul burned white-hot, branded his, claimed him.

His love for her reduced his fears and his past to ashes and they floated away on a breeze.

He trembled with joy.

Did she know? Had she shared the cleansing fire?

With his last thrust, he felt the final pulses of her climax and smiled.

"Hannah," he breathed.

"Yes, Lee?"

What could he say? He had no words to describe what he felt.

He sighed.

She combed her fingers through his hair, stroking the back of his head.

A loud buzz brought him up to his elbows. "That's not my phone."

"It's the doorbell," Hannah said.

"Think you can ignore it?"

A longer buzz rose from downstairs in response, followed by another.

"I guess not," she said.

He kissed the end of her nose, pushed himself up, and then sat on the bed beside her.

After a moment, she sat up and smiled at him. As he watched, she grabbed her pants and sweater, slipped them on, and straightened her hair as she crossed the room.

The doorbell buzzed again.

"All right, I'm on my way," she said.

Halfway down the stairs, she realized who must be at the front door. Only Sterling would be so persistent and impatient.

She considered turning around and heading back upstairs, but she knew it wouldn't help. She'd have to face him eventually. At least maybe he'd listen if they were face-to-face.

When she opened the door, he nearly knocked her down as he barged in.

"What took you so long to answer? And what happened to

your hair?" He draped his scarf over the back of a chair and started to unbutton his jacket.

"Don't get comfortable, Sterling. You're not staying."

He turned and stared at her. "I beg your pardon?"

"I'm busy."

He glanced around the room and stepped closer. "Doing what?"

"That's none of your business."

"Look, I apologize for not being clear at dinner when we were discussing our relationship. I didn't mean to surprise you with my announcement."

"Sterling, we have no relationship. Listen to me. I'm not marrying you." She picked up his scarf and held it out. "I'd appreciate it if you left now."

He grabbed her wrist as his face reddened. "You will not embarrass me like this. You know damn well—"

"Get your hands off her, Mason." Lee took the last few stairs at a trot and strode toward them. He'd put on his jeans and shirt, but his open shirt fluttering behind him revealed muscles large enough to intimidate anyone with half a brain.

Sterling released her and backed away. "What the hell are you doing here?"

Hannah stepped between the two men. "Please, Lee, I can handle this."

Lee stopped with his hands fisted at his sides and a cold glare leveled at Sterling.

She tried again to hand the scarf to Sterling. "I'm sure you'll find someone else. Maybe Juli Tucker's still around."

His eyes widened as if horrified by her words. Did he really think she'd forgotten? It didn't matter that he'd left poor Juli crying at school two days later. Hannah had even felt sorry for the girl.

"And," Hannah said, "if you need to see me for any reason

in the future, you can make an appointment with my office manager."

Sterling snatched the scarf and leaned toward her. "If I'd known your tastes ran toward this kind of trash, I'd never have asked you to marry me, anyway." He pointed at her face. "You'll regret this, Hannah."

"I don't think so." She opened the door and waited.

He glared at Lee, who took a step toward him. Sterling stumbled backward through the doorway, then spun around and marched down the front steps.

Hannah closed the door.

"You should have let me throw him out."

She shook her head and turned toward Lee, who had visibly relaxed. "That wouldn't have been wise."

"Maybe not, but it would have been fun." He took her hand and drew her to him.

She hugged him, sighed, and looked up into his warm gaze. "Thank you for coming to my rescue. *Again.*"

"It's what I live for, sweetheart." He smiled. "Well, that and the sex."

"Of course." She stood on her toes and kissed his lips, then moved out of his embrace and started toward the kitchen. "How about some tea?"

"Depends. Think we'll have time for a quickie while the water's heating?"

She laughed. "You're insatiable." But her face warmed at the thought of sex in the kitchen with Lee. She glanced back. "We could just skip the tea and take our time."

He wrapped his arms around her, groaned, and kissed the side of her head as he walked her forward. "Sounds perfect."

She laughed again. "Good."